Ian Maclaren

Kate Carnegie

Ian Maclaren

Kate Carnegie

ISBN/EAN: 9783337061173

Printed in Europe, USA, Canada, Australia, Japan

Cover: Foto ©Andreas Hilbeck / pixelio.de

More available books at **www.hansebooks.com**

KATE CARNEGIE

BY

IAN MACLAREN

NEW YORK
DODD, MEAD AND COMPANY
1896

TO

A CERTAIN BROTHERHOOD

𝕱aithful in 𝕮riticism

𝕷oyal in 𝕬ffection

𝕿ender in 𝕿rouble

CONTENTS.

CONTENTS.

LIST OF ILLUSTRATIONS.

KATE CARNEGIE.

CHAPTER I.

PANDEMONIUM.

IT was the morning before the Twelfth, years ago, and nothing like unto Muirtown Station could have been found in all the travelling world. For Muirtown, as everybody knows, is the centre which receives the southern immigrants in autumn, and distributes them, with all their belongings of servants, horses, dogs, and luggage, over the north country from Athole to Sutherland. All night, express trains, whose ordinary formation had been reinforced by horse boxes, carriage trucks, saloons and luggage vans, drawn by two engines, and pushed up inclines by a third, had been careering along the three iron trunk roads that run from London to the North. Four hours ago they had forced the border, that used to be more jealously guarded, and had begun to converge on their terminus. Passengers, awakened by the caller air and looking out still half asleep, miss the undisciplined hedgerows and many-shaped patches of pasture, the warm brick homesteads and shaded ponds of the south. Square fields cultivated up to a foot of the stone dykes or wire-fencing, the strong grey-stone farm-houses, the swift-running burns, and the never-distant hills, brace the mind. Local passengers come in with deliberation, whose austere faces condemn the luxurious disorder of night travel, and challenge the defence of Arminian doctrine. A voice shouts "Carstairs Junction," with a command of the letter r, which is the bequest of an unconquerable past, and inspires one with the hope of some day hearing a freeborn Scot say "Auchterarder." The train runs over bleak moorlands with black peat holes, through alluvial straths yielding their last pickle of corn, between iron furnaces blazing strangely in the morning light, at the foot of historical castles built on rocks that rise out of the fertile plains, and then, after a space of sudden darkness, any man with a soul counts the ten hours' dust and heat but a slight price for the sight of the Scottish Rhine flowing deep, clear, and swift by the foot of its wooded hills, and the "Fair City" in the heart of her meadows.

"Do you see the last wreath of mist floating off the summit of the hill, and the silver sheen of the river against the green of the woods? Quick, dad," and the General, accustomed to obey, stood up beside Kate for the brief glimpse between the tunnel and a prison. Yet they had seen the snows of the Himalayas, and the great river that runs through the plains of India. But

it is so with Scottish folk that they may have lived opposite the Jungfrau at Mürren, and walked among the big
trees of the Yosemite Valley, and watched the blood-red
afterglow on the Pyramids, and yet will value a sunset
behind the Cuchullin hills, and the Pass of the Trossachs,
and the mist shot through with light on the sides of Ben
Nevis, and the Tay at Dunkeld — just above the bridge
— better guerdon for their eyes.

"Ay, lassie" — the other people had left at Stirling,
and the General fell back upon the past — "there 's just
one bonnier river, and that 's the Tochty at a bend below
the Lodge, as we shall see it, please God, this evening."

"Tickets," broke in a voice with authority. "This
is no the station, an' ye 'll hae to wait till the first
diveesion o' yir train is emptied. Kildrummie? Ye
change, of coorse, but yir branch 'll hae a lang wait the
day. It 'll be an awfu' fecht wi' the Hielant train. Muirtown platform 'll be worth seein'; it 'll juist be michty,"
and the collector departed, smacking his lips in prospect
of the fray.

"Upon my word," said the General, taken aback for
a moment by the easy manners of his countryman, but
rejoicing in every new assurance of home, "our people.
are no blate."

"Is n't it delicious to be where character has not been
worn smooth by centuries of oppression, but where each
man is himself? Conversation has salt here, and tastes
in the mouth. We 've just heard two men speak this
morning, and each face is bitten into my memory. Now
our turn has come," and the train wound itself in at last.

Porters, averaging six feet and with stentorian voices,
were driving back the mixed multitude in order to afford
foothold for the new arrivals on that marvellous landing

place, which in those days served for all the trains which came in and all that went out, both north and south. One man tears open the door of a first with commanding gesture. " A' change and hurry up. Na, na," rejecting the offer of a private engagement; " we hev nae time for that trade the day. Ye maun cairry yir bags yersels; the dogs and boxes 'll tak us a' oor time." He unlocks an under compartment and drags out a pair of pointers, who fawn upon him obsequiously in gratitude for their release. " Doon wi' ye," as one to whom duty denies the ordinary courtesies of life, and he fastens them to the base of an iron pillar. Deserted immediately by their deliverer, the pointers made overtures to two elderly ladies, standing bewildered in the crush, to be repulsed with umbrellas, and then sit down upon their tails in despair. Their forlorn condition, left friendless amid this babel, gets upon their nerves, and after a slight rehearsal, just to make certain of the tune, they lift up their voices in melodious concert, to the scandal of the two females, who cannot escape the neighbourhood, and regard the pointers with horror. Distant friends, also in bonds and distress of mind, feel comforted and join cheerfully, while a large black retriever, who had foolishly attempted to obstruct a luggage barrow with his tail, breaks in with a high solo. Two collies, their tempers irritated by obstacles as they follow their masters, who had been taking their morning in the second-class refreshment room, fall out by the way, and obtain as by magic a clear space in which to settle details; while a fox-terrier, escaping from his anxious mistress, has mounted a pile of boxes and gives a general challenge.

Porters fling open packed luggage vans with a swing, setting free a cataract of portmanteaus, boxes, hampers, baskets, which pours across the platform for yards, led by a frolicsome black leather valise, whose anxious owner has fought her adventurous way to the van for the purpose of explaining to a phlegmatic Scot that he would know it by a broken strap, and must lift it out gently, for it contained breakables.

"It can gang itsel, that ane," as the afflicted woman followed its reckless progress with a wail. "Sall, if they were a' as clever on their feet as yon box there wud be less tribble," and with two assistants he falls upon the congested mass within. They perform prodigies of strength, handling huge trunks that ought to have filled some woman with repentance as if they were Gladstone bags, and light weights as if they were paper parcels. With unerring scent they detect the latest label among the remains of past history, and the air resounds with "Hielant train," "Aiberdeen fast," "Aiberdeen slow," "Muirtown"—this with indifference—and at a time "Dunleith," and once "Kildrummie," with much contempt. By this time stacks of baggage of varying size have been erected, the largest of which is a pyramid in shape, with a very uncertain apex.

Male passengers—heads of families and new to Muirtown—hover anxiously round the outskirts, and goaded on by female commands, rush into the heart of the fray for the purpose of claiming a piece of luggage, which turns out to be some other person's, and retire hastily after a fair-sized portmanteau descends on their toes, and the sharp edge of a trunk takes them in the small of the back. Footmen with gloves and superior airs make gentlemanly efforts to collect the family luggage, and are rewarded by having some hopelessly vulgar tin boxes, heavily roped, deposited among its initialled glory. One elderly female who had been wise to choose some other day to revisit her native town, discovers her basket flung up against a pillar, like wreckage from a storm, and settles herself down upon it with a sigh of relief. She remains unmoved amid the turmoil, save when a passing gun-case tips her bonnet to one side, giving her a very rakish air, and a good-natured retriever on a neighbouring box is so much taken with her appearance that he offers her a friendly caress. Restless people — who remember that their train ought to have left half an hour ago, and cannot realise that all bonds are loosed on the eleventh — fasten on any man in a uniform, and suffer many rebuffs.

"There 's nae use asking me," answers a guard, coming off duty and pushing his way through the crowd as one accustomed to such spectacles; "a 'm juist in frae Carlisle; get haud o' a porter."

"Cupar Angus?" — this from the porter — "that 's the Aiberdeen slow; it 's no made up yet, and little chance o't till the express an' the Hielant be aff. Whar 'll it start frae?" breaking away; "forrit, a' tell ye, forrit."

Fathers of families, left on guard and misled by a sudden movement "forrit," rush to the waiting-room and bring out, for the third time, the whole expedition, to escort them back again with shame. Barrows with towering piles of luggage are pushed through the human mass by two porters, who allow their engine to make its own way with much confidence, condescending only at a time to shout, "A' say, hey, oot o' there," and treating any testy complaint with the silent contempt of a drayman for a costermonger. Old hands, who have fed at their leisure in callous indifference to all alarms, lounge about in great content, and a group of sheep farmers, having endeavoured in vain, after one tasting, to settle the merits of a new dip, take a glance in the " Hielant " quarter, and adjourn the conference once more to the refreshment-room. Groups of sportsmen discuss the prospects of to-morrow in detail, and tell stories of ancient twelfths, while chieftains from London, in full Highland dress, are painfully conscious of the whiteness of their legs. A handful of preposterous people who persist in going south when the world has its face northwards, threaten to complain to headquarters if they are not sent away, and an official with a loud voice and a subtle gift of humour intimates that a train is about to leave for Dundee.

During this time wonderful manœuvres have been executed on the lines of rail opposite the platform. Trains have left with all the air of a departure and disappeared round the curve outside the station, only to return in fragments. Half a dozen carriages pass without an engine, as if they had started on their own account, break vans that one saw presiding over expresses stand forsaken, a long procession of horse boxes rattle through, and a saloon carriage, with people, is so much in evidence that the name of an English Duke is freely mentioned, and every new passage relieves the tedium of the waiting.

Out of all this confusion trains begin to grow and take shape, and one, with green carriages, looks so complete that a rumour spreads that the Hielant train has been made up and may appear any minute in its place. The sunshine beating through the glass roof, the heat of travel, the dust of the station, the moving carriages with their various colours, the shouts of railway officials, the recurring panics of fussy passengers, begin to affect the nerves. Conversation becomes broken, porters are beset on every side with questions they cannot answer, rushes are made on any empty carriages within reach, a child is knocked down and cries.

Over all this excitement and confusion one man is presiding, untiring, forceful, ubiquitous — a sturdy man, somewhere about five feet ten, whose lungs are brass and nerves fine steel wire. He is dressed, as to his body, in brown corduroy trousers, a blue jacket and waistcoat with shining brass buttons, a grey flannel shirt, and a silver-braided cap, which, as time passes, he thrusts further back on his head till its peak stands at last almost erect, a crest seen high above the conflict. As to the soul of him, this man is clothed with resolution, courage, authority, and an infectious enthusiasm. He is the brain and will of the whole organism, its driving power. Drivers lean out of their engines, one hand on the steam throttle, their eyes fixed on this man; if he waves his hands, trains move; if he holds them up, trains halt. Strings of carriages out in the open are carrying out his plans, and the porters toil like maniacs to meet his commands. Piles of luggage disappear as he directs the attack, and his scouts capture isolated boxes hidden among the people. Every horse box has a place in his memory, and he has calculated how many carriages would clear the north traffic; he carries the destination of families in his head, and has made arrangements for their comfort. " Soon ready now, sir," as he passed swiftly down to receive the last southerner, " and a second compartment reserved for you," till people watched for him, and the sound of his voice, " forrit wi' the Hielant luggage," inspired bewildered tourists with confidence, and became an argument for Providence.

There is a general movement towards the northern end of the station; five barrows, whose luggage swings dangerously and has to be held on, pass in procession; dogs are collected and trailed along in bundles; families pick up their bags and press after their luggage, cheered to recognise a familiar piece peeping out from strange goods; a bell is rung with insistence. The Aberdeen express leaves — its passengers regarding the platform with pity — and the guard of the last van slamming his door in triumph. The great man concentrates his force with a wave of his hand for the *tour de force* of the year, the despatch of the Hielant. train.

The southern end of the platform is now deserted — the London express departed half an hour ago with thirteen passengers, very crestfallen and envious — and across the open centre porters hustle barrows at headlong speed, with neglected pieces of luggage. Along the edge of the Highland platform there stretches a solid mass of life, close-packed, motionless, silent, composed of tourists, dogs, families, lords, dogs, sheep farmers, keepers, clericals, dogs, footmen, commercials, ladies' maids, grooms, dogs, waiting for the empty train that, after deploying hither and thither, picking up some trifle, a horse box or a duke's saloon, at every new raid, is now backing slowly in for its freight. The expectant crowd has ceased from conversation, sporting or otherwise; respectable elderly gentlemen brace themselves for the scramble, and examine their nearest neighbours suspiciously; heads of families gather their belongings round them by signs and explain in a whisper how to act; one female tourist — of a certain age and severe aspect — refreshes her memory as to the best window for the view of Killiecrankie. The luggage has been piled in huge masses at each end of the siding; the porters rest themselves against it, taking off their caps, and wiping their foreheads with handkerchiefs of many colours and uses. It is the stillness before the last charge; beyond the outermost luggage an arm is seen waving, and the long coil of carriages begins to twist into the station.

People who know their ancient Muirtown well, and have taken part in this day of days, will remember a harbour of refuge beside the bookstall, protected by the buffers of the Highland siding on one side and a breakwater of luggage on the other, and persons within this shelter could see the storming of the train to great advantage. Carmichael, the young Free Kirk minister of Drumtochty, who had been tasting the

CARMICHAEL HAD TAKEN HIS TURN.

civilisation of Muirtown overnight and was waiting for the Dunleith train, leant against the back of the bookstall, watching the scene with frank, boyish interest. Rather under six feet in height, he passed for more, because he stood so straight and looked so slim, for his limbs were as slender as a woman's, while women (in Muirtown) had envied his hands and feet. But in chest measure he was only two inches behind Saunders Baxter, the grieve of Drumsheugh, who was the standard of manhood by whom all others were tried and (mostly) condemned in Drumtochty. Chancing to come upon Saunders putting the stone one day with the bothy lads, Carmichael had taken his turn, with the result that his stone lay foremost in the final heat by an inch exactly. MacLure saw them kneeling together to measure, the Free Kirk minister and the ploughmen all in a bunch, and went on his way rejoicing to tell the Free Kirk folk that their new minister was a man of his hands. His hair was fair, just touched with gold, and he wore it rather long, so that in the excitement of preaching a lock sometimes fell down on his forehead, which he would throw back with a toss of his head — a gesture Mrs. Macfadyen, our critic, thought very taking. His dark blue eyes used to enlarge with passion in the Sacrament and grow so tender, the healthy tan disappeared and left his cheeks so white, that the mothers were terrified lest he should die early, and sent offerings of cream on Monday morning. For though his name was Carmichael, he had Celtic blood in him, and was full of all kinds of emotion, but mostly those that were brave and pure and true. He had done well at the University, and was inclined to be philosophical, for he knew little of himself and nothing of the world. There were times when he allowed himself to be

supercilious and sarcastic ; but it was not for an occasional jingle of cleverness the people loved him, or, for
that matter, any other man. It was his humanity that
won their hearts, and this he had partly from his mother,
partly from his training. Through a kind providence
and his mother's countryness, he had been brought
up among animals — birds, mice, dormice, guinea-pigs,
rabbits, dogs, cattle, horses, till he knew all their ways,
and loved God's creatures as did St. Francis d'Assisi,
to whom every creature of God was dear, from Sister
Swallow to Brother Wolf. So he learned, as he grew
older, to love men and women and little children, even
although they might be ugly, or stupid, or bad-tempered,
or even wicked, and this sympathy cleansed away many
a little fault of pride and self-conceit and impatience and
hot temper, and in the end of the days made a man of
John Carmichael. The dumb animals had an instinct
about this young fellow, and would make overtures to
him that were a certificate for any situation requiring
character. Horses by the wayside neighed at his
approach, and stretched out their velvet muzzles to be
stroked. Dogs insisted upon sitting on his knees, unless
quite prevented by their size, and then they put their
paws on his chest. Hillocks was utterly scandalised by
his collie's familiarity with the minister, and brought him
to his senses by the application of a boot, but Carmichael waived all apologies. "Rover and I made
friends two days ago on the road, and my clothes will
take no injury." And indeed they could not, for Carmichael, except on Sundays and at funerals, wore a
soft hat and suit of threadbare tweeds, on which a micro-
scopist could have found traces of a peat bog, moss of
dykes, the scale of a trout, and a tiny bit of heather.

His usual fortune befell him that day in Muirtown Station, for two retrievers, worming their way through the luggage, reached him, and made known their wants.

"Thirsty? I believe you. All the way from England, and heat enough to roast you alive. I 've got no dish, else I 'd soon get water.

" Inverness? Poor chaps, that 's too far to go with your tongues like a lime-kiln. Down, good dogs; I 'll be back in a minute."

You can have no idea, unless you have tried it, how much water a soft clerical hat can hold — if you turn up the edges and bash down the inside with your fist, and fill the space to the brim. But it is difficult to convey such a vessel with undiminished content through a crowd, and altogether impossible to lift one's eyes. Carmichael was therefore quite unconscious that two new-comers to the shelter were watching him with keen delight as he came in bareheaded, flushed, triumphant — amid howls of welcome — and knelt down to hold the cup till — drinking time about in strict honour — the retrievers had reached the maker's name.

" Do you think they would like a biscuit? " said a clear, sweet, low voice, with an accent of pride and just a flavour of amusement in its tone. Carmichael rose in much embarrassment, and was quite confounded.

They were standing together — father and daughter, evidently — and there was no manner of doubt about him. A spare man, without an ounce of superfluous flesh, straight as a rod, and having an air of command, with keen grey eyes, close-cropped hair turning white, a clean-shaven face except where a heavy moustache covered a firm-set mouth — one recognised in him a retired army man of rank, a colonel at least, it might be a general; and the bronze on his face suggested long Indian service. But he might have been dressed in Rob Roy tartan, or been a naval officer in full uniform, for all Carmichael knew. A hundred thousand faces pass before your eyes and are forgotten, mere physical impressions; you see one, and it is in your heart for ever, as you saw it the first time. Wavy black hair, a low, straight forehead, hazel eyes with long eyelashes, a perfectly-shaped Grecian nose, a strong mouth, whose upper lip had a curve of softness, a clear-cut chin with one dimple, small ears set high in the head, and a rich creamy complexion — that was what flashed upon Carmichael as he turned from the retrievers. He was a man so unobservant of women that he could not have described a woman's dress to save his life or any other person's; and now that he is married — he is a middle-aged man now and threatened with stoutness — it is his wife's reproach that he does not know when she wears her new spring bonnet for the first time. Yet he took in this young woman's dress, from the smart hat, with a white bird's wing on the side, and the close-fitting tailor made jacket, to the small, well-gloved hand in dogskin, the grey tweed skirt, and one shoe, with a tip on it, that peeped out below her frock. Critics might have hinted that her shoulders were too square, and that her figure wanted somewhat in softness of outline; but it seemed to Carmichael that he had never seen so winsome or high-bred a woman; and so it has also seemed to many who have gone farther afield in the world than the young minister of Drumtochty.

Carmichael was at that age when a man prides himself on dressing and thinking as he pleases, and had quite scandalised a Muirtown elder — a stout gentleman, who had come out in '43, and could with difficulty be weaned from Dr. Chalmers — by making his appearance on the preceding evening in amazing tweeds and a grey flannel shirt. He explained casually that for a fifteen-mile walk flannels were absolutely necessary, and that he was rather pleased to find that he had come from door to door in four hours and two minutes exactly. His host was at a loss for words, because he was comparing this unconventional youth with the fathers, who wore large white stocks and ambled along at about two and a half miles an hour, clearing their throats also in a very impressive way, and seasoning the principles of the Free Kirk with snuff of an excellent fragrance. It was hard even for the most generous charity to identify the spirit of the Disruption in such a figure, and the good elder grew so proper and so didactic that Carmichael went from bad to worse.

"Well, you would find the congregation in excellent order. The Professor was a most painstaking man, though retiring in disposition, and his sermons were thoroughly solid and edifying. They were possibly just a little above the heads of Drumtochty, but I always enjoyed Mr. Cunningham myself," nodding his head as one who understood all mysteries.

"Did you ever happen to hear the advice Jamie Soutar gave the deputation from Muirtown when they came up to see whether Cunningham would be fit for the North Kirk, where two Bailies stand at the plate every day, and the Provost did not think himself good enough to be an elder?" for Carmichael was full of wickedness that day, and earning a judgment.

His host indicated that the deputation had given in a very full and satisfactory report — he was, in fact, on the

Session of the North himself — but that no reference had been made to Jamie.

"Well, you must know," and Carmichael laid himself out for narration, "the people were harassed with raids from the Lowlands during Cunningham's time, and did their best in self-defence. Spying makes men cunning, and it was wonderful how many subterfuges the deputations used to practise. · They would walk from Kildrummie as if they were staying in the district, and one retired tradesman talked about the crops as if he was a farmer, but it was a pity that he did n't know the difference between the cereals.

"'Yon man that wes up aifter yir minister, Elspeth,' Hillocks said to Mrs. Macfadyen, 'hesna hed muckle money spent on his eddication. "A graund field o' barley," he says, and as sure as a 'm stannin' here, it wes the haugh field o' aits.'

"'He 's frae Glaisgie,' was all Elspeth answered, 'and by next Friday we 'll hae his name an' kirk. He said . he wes up for a walk an' juist dropped in, the wratch.'

"Some drove from Muirtown, giving out that they were English tourists, speaking with a fine East Coast accent, and were rebuked by Lachlan Campbell for breaking the Sabbath. Your men put up their trap at the last farm in Netheraird — which always has grudged Drumtochty its ministers and borne their removal with resignation — and came up in pairs, who pretended they did not know one another.

"Jamie was hearing the Professor's last lecture on Justification, and our people asked him to take charge of the strangers. He found out the town from their hats, and escorted them to the boundaries of the parish, assisting their confidences till one of your men — I

think it was the Provost — admitted that it had taken
them all their time to follow the sermon.

"'A 'm astonished at ye,' said Jamie, for the Netheraird man let it out; 'yon wes a sermon for young fouk,
juist milk, ye ken, tae the ordinar' discoorses. Surely,' as
if the thought had just struck him, 'ye werena thinkin'
o' callin' Maister Cunningham tae Muirtown.

"'Edinboorgh, noo; that micht dae gin the feck o'
the members be professors, but Muirtown wud be clean
havers. There's times when the Drumtochty fouk
themsels canna understand the cratur, he's that deep.
As for Muirtown' — here Jamie allowed himself a brief
rest of enjoyment; 'but ye 've hed a fine drive, tae say
naethin' o' the traivel.' "

Then, having begun, Carmichael retailed so many of
Jamie's most wicked sayings, and so exalted the Glen as
a place "where you can go up one side and down the
other with your dogs, and every second man you meet
will give you something to remember," that the city
dignitary doubted afterwards to his wife "whether this
young man was . . . quite what we have been accustomed to in a Free Church minister." Carmichael ought
to have had repentances for shocking a worthy man, but
instead thereof laughed in his room and slept soundly,
not knowing that he would be humbled in the dust by
mid-day to-morrow.

It seemed to him on the platform as if an hour passed
while he, who had played with a city father, stood, clothed
with shame, before this commanding young woman.
Had she ever looked upon a more abject wretch? and
Carmichael photographed himself with merciless accuracy, from his hair that he had not thrown back to an
impress of dust which one knee had taken from the

platform, and he registered a resolution that he would never be again boastfully indifferent to the loss of a button on his coat. She stooped and fed the dogs, who did her homage, and he marked that her profile was even finer — more delicate, more perfect, more bewitching—than her front face; but he still stood holding his shapeless hat in his hand, and for the first time in his life had no words to say.

"They are very polite dogs," and Miss Carnegie gave Carmichael one more chance; "they make as much of a biscuit as if it were a feast; but I do think dogs have such excellent manners, they are always so un-self-conscious."

"I wish I were a dog," said Carmichael, with much solemnity, and afterwards was filled with thankfulness that the baggage behind gave way at that moment, and that an exasperated porter was able to express his mind freely.

"Dinna try tae lift that box for ony sake, man. Sall, ye 're no' feared," as Carmichael, thirsting for action, swung it up unaided; and then, catching sight of the merest wisp of white, "A' didna see ye were a minister, an' the word cam oot sudden."

"You would find it a help to say Northumberland, Cumberland, Westmoreland, and Durham," and with a smile to Carmichael, still bareheaded and now redder than ever, Miss Carnegie went along the platform to see the Hielant train depart. It was worth waiting to watch the two minutes' scrimmage, and to hear the great man say, as he took off his cap with deliberation and wiped his brow, "That 's anither year ower; some o' you lads see tae that Dunleith train." There was a day when Carmichael would have enjoyed the scene to the full, but now he had eyes for nothing but that tall, slim figure and the white bird's wing.

When they disappeared into the Dunleith train, Carmichael had a wild idea of entering the same compartment, and in the end had to be pushed into the last second by the guard, who knew most of his regular people and every one of the Drumtochty men. He was so much engaged with his own thoughts that he gave two English tourists to understand that Lord Kilspindie's castle, standing amid its woods on the bank of the Tay, was a recently erected dye work, and that as the train turned off the North trunk line for Dunleith they might at any moment enter the pass of Killiecrankie.

CHAPTER II.

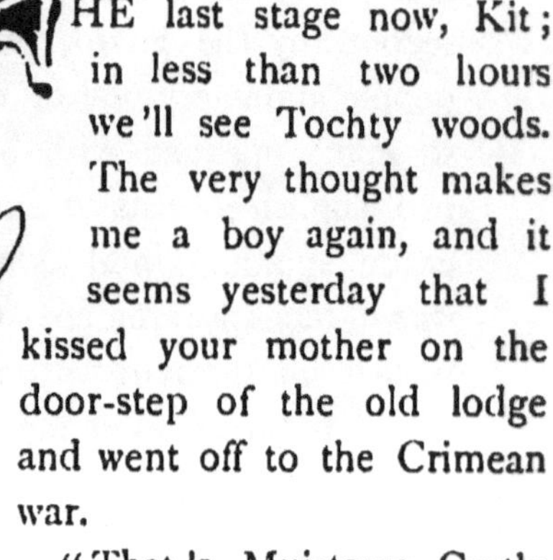

THE last stage now, Kit; in less than two hours we'll see Tochty woods. The very thought makes me a boy again, and it seems yesterday that I kissed your mother on the door-step of the old lodge and went off to the Crimean war.

"That's Muirtown Castle over there in the wood — a grand place in its way, but nothing to our home, lassie. Kilspindie — he was Viscount Hay then — joined me at Muirtown, and we fought through the weary winter. He left the army after the war, with lots of honour. A good fellow was Hay, both in the trenches and the messroom.

"I've never seen him since, and I dare say he's forgotten a battered old Indian. Besides, he's the big swell in this district, and I'm only a poor Hielant laird, with a wood and a tumble-down house and a couple of farms."

" You are also a shameless hypocrite and deceiver, for you believe that the Carnegies are as old as the Hays, and you know that, though you have only two farms, you have twelve medals and seven wounds. What does money matter? it simply makes people vulgar."

" Nonsense, lassie ; if a Carnegie runs down money, it's because he has got none and wishes he had. If you and I had only a few hundreds a year over the half-pay to rattle in our pockets, we should have lots of little pleasures, and you might have lived in England, with all sorts of variety and comfort, instead of wandering about India with a gang of stupid old chaps who have been so busy fighting that they never had time to read a book."

" You mean like yourself, dad, and V. C. and Colonel Kinloch ? Where could a girl have found finer company than with my Knights of King Arthur ? And do you dare to insinuate that I could have been content away from the regiment, that made me their daughter after mother died, and the army?

" Pleasure ! " and Kate's cheek flushed. " I 've had it since I was a little tot and could remember anything —the bugles sounding reveille in the clear air, and the sergeants drilling the new drafts in the morning, and the regiment coming out with the band before and you at its head, and hearing ' God save the Queen ' at a review, and seeing the companies passing like one man before the General.

" Don't you think that 's better than tea-drinking, and gossiping, and sewing meetings, and going for walks in some stupid little hole of a country town ? Oh, you wicked, aggravating dad. Now, what more will money do ? "

"Well," said the General, with much gravity, "if you were even a moderate heiress there is no saying but that we might pick up a presentable husband for you among the lairds. As it is, I fancy a country minister is all you could expect.

"Don't . . . my ears will come off some day; one was loosened by a cut in the Mutiny. No, I 'll never do the like again. But some day you will marry, all the same," and Kate's father rubbed his ears.

"No, I 'm not going to leave you, for nobody else could ever make a curry to please; and if I do, it will not be a Scotch minister — horrid, bigoted wretches, V. C. says. Am I like a minister's wife, to address mothers' meetings and write out sermons? By the way, is there a kirk at Drumtochty, or will you read prayers to Janet and Donald and me?"

"When I was a lad there was just one minister in Drumtochty, Mr. Davidson, a splendid specimen of the old school, who, on great occasions, wore gaiters and a frill with a diamond in the centre; he carried a gold-headed stick, and took snuff out of a presentation box.

"His son Sandie was my age to a year, and many a ploy we had together; there was the jackdaw's nest in the ivy on the old tower we harried together," and the General could only indicate the delightful risk of the exploit. "My father and the minister were pacing the avenue at the time, and caught sight of us against the sky. 'It 's your rascal and mine, Laird,' we heard the minister say, and they waited till we got down, and then each did his duty by his own for trying to break his neck; but they were secretly proud of the exploit, for I caught my father showing old Lord Kilspindie the spot, and next time Hay was up he tried to reach the place, and stuck where the wall hangs over. I 'll point out the hole this evening; you can see it from the other side of the den quite plain.

"Sandie went to the church —I wish every parson were as straight—and Kilspindie appointed him to succeed the old gentleman, and when I saw him in his study last month, it seemed as if his father stood before you, except the breeches and the frill; but Sandie has a marvellous stock — what havers I 'm deivin' you with, lassie."

"Tell me about Sandie this minute — did he remember the raiding of the jackdaws?"

"He did," cried the General, in great

"MANY A PLOY WE HAD TOGETHER."

spirits; "he just looked at me for an instant — no one knew of my visit — and then he gripped my hands, and do you know, Kit, he was . . . well, and there was a lump in my throat too; it would be about thirty years, for one reason and another, since we met."

"What did he say? the very words, dad," and Kate held up her finger in command.

"'Jack, old man, is this really you?'—he held me at arm's length—'man, div ye mind the jackdaw's nest?'"

"Did he? And he's to be our padre. I know I'll love him at once. Go on, everything, for you've never told me anything about Drumtochty."

"We had a glorious time going over old times. We fished up every trout again, and we shot our first day on the moor again with Peter Stewart, Kilspindie's head keeper, as fine an old Highlander as ever lived. Stewart said in the evening, 'You're a pair of prave boys, as becometh your fathers' sons,' and Sandie gave him two and fourpence he had scraped for a tip, but I had only one and elevenpence — we were both kept bare. But he knew better than to refuse our offerings, though he never saw less than gold or notes from the men that shot at the lodge, and Sandie remembered how he touched his Highland bonnet and said, 'I will be much obliged to you both; and you will be coming to the moor another day, for I hef his lordship's orders.'

"Boys are queer animals, lassie; we were prouder that Peter accepted our poor little tip than about the muirfowl we shot, though I had three brace and Sandie four. Highlanders are all gentlemen by birth, and be sure of this, Kit, it's only that breed which can manage boys and soldiers. But where am I now?"

"With Sandie — I beg his reverence's pardon — with the Rev. the padre of Drumtochty," and Kate went over and sat down beside the General to anticipate any rebellion, for it was a joy to see the warrior turning into a boy before her eyes. "Well?"

"We had a royal dinner, as it seemed to me. Sandie has a couple of servants, man and wife, who rule him with a rod of iron, but I would forgive that for the cooking and the loyalty. After dinner he disappeared with a look of mystery, and came back with a cobwebbed bottle of the old shape, short and bunchy, which he carried as if it were a baby.

"'Just two bottles of my father's port left; we'll have one to-day to welcome you back, and we'll keep the other to celebrate your daughter's marriage.' He had one sister, younger by ten years, and her death in girlhood nearly broke his heart. It struck me from something he said that his love is with her; at any rate, he has never married. Sandie has just one fault — he would not touch a cheroot; but he snuffs handsomely out of his father's box.

"Of course, I can't say anything about his preaching, but it's bound to be sensible stuff."

"Bother the sermons; he's an old dear himself, and I know we shall be great friends. We'll flirt together, and you will not have one word to say, so make up your mind to submit."

"We shall have good days in the old place, lassie; but you know we are poor, and must live quietly. What I have planned is a couple of handy women or so in the house with Donald. Janet is going to live at the gate where she was brought up, but she will look after you well, and we'll always have a bed and a glass of wine for a friend. Then you can have a run up to London and get your things, Kit," and the General looked wistfully at his daughter, as one who would have given her a kingdom.

"Do you think your girl cares so much about luxuries

and dresses? Of course I like to look well! — every
woman does, and if she pretends otherwise she 's a hypocrite ; but money just seems to make some women
hideous. It is enough for me to have you all to myself
up in your old home, and to see you enjoying the rest
you have earned. We 'll be as happy as two lovers,'
dad," and Kate threw an arm round-her father's neck
and kissed him.

"We have to change here," as the train began to
slow ; "prepare to see the most remarkable railway in the
empire, and a guard to correspond." And then it came
upon them, the first sight that made a Drumtochty man's
heart warm, and assured him that he was nearing home.

An engine on a reduced scale, that had once served
in the local goods department of a big station, and then,
having grown old and asthmatic, was transferred on half-
pay, as it were, to the Kildrummie branch, where it
puffed between the junction and the terminus half a
dozen times a day, with two carriages and an occasional
coal truck. Times there were when wood was exported
from Kildrummie, and then the train was taken down in
detachments, and it was a pleasant legend that, one market
day, when Drumtochty was down in force,' the engine
stuck, and Drumsheugh invited the Glen to get out and
push. The two carriages were quite distinguished in
construction, and had seen better days. One consisted
of a single first-class compartment in the centre, with a
bulge of an imposing appearance, supported on either
side by two seconds. As no native ever travelled second,
one compartment had been employed as a reserve to the
luggage van, so that Drumtochty might have a convenient
place of deposit for calves, but the other was jealously
reserved by Peter Bruce for strangers with second-class

tickets, that his branch might not be put to confusion. The other carriage was three-fourths third class and one-fourth luggage, and did the real work ; on its steps Peter stood and dispensed wisdom, between the junction and Kildrummie.

But neither the carriages nor the engine could have made history without the guard, beside whom the guards of the main line — even of the expresses that ran to London — were as nothing — fribbles and weaklings. For the guard of the Kildrummie branch was absolute ruler, lording it over man and beast without appeal, and treating the Kildrummie stationmaster as a federated power. Peter was a short man of great breadth, like unto the cutting of an oak-tree, with a penetrating grey eye, an immovable countenance, and bushy whiskers. It was understood that when the line was opened, and the directors were about to fill up the post of guard from a number of candidates qualified by long experience on various lines, Peter, who had been simply wasting his time driving a carrier's cart, came in, and sitting down opposite the board — two lairds and a farmer — looked straight before him without making any application. It was felt by all in an instant that only one course was open, in the eternal fitness of things. Experience was well enough, but special creation was better, and Peter was immediately appointed, his name being asked by the chairman afterwards as a formality. From the beginning he took up a masterful position, receiving his human cargo at the junction and discharging it at the station with a power that even Drumtochty did not resist, and a knowledge of individuals that was almost comprehensive. It is true that, boasting one Friday evening concerning the " crooded " state of the train, he admitted with reluctance that "there 's a stranger in the second I canna mak oot," but it is understood that he solved the problem before the man got his luggage at Kildrummie.

Perhaps Peter's most famous achievement was his demolition of a south country bagman, who had made himself unpleasant, and the story was much tasted by our guard's admirers. This self-important and vivacious gentleman, seated in the first, was watching Peter's leisurely movements on the Kildrummie platform with much impatience, and lost all self-control on Peter going outside to examine the road for any distant passenger.

"Look here, guard, this train ought to have left five minutes ago, and I give you notice that if we miss our connection I 'll hold your company responsible."

At the sound of this foreign voice with its indecent clamour, Peter returned and took up his position opposite the speaker, while the staff and the whole body of passengers — four Kildrummie and three Drumtochty, quite sufficient for the situation — waited the issue. Not one word did Peter deign to reply, but he fixed the irate traveller with a gaze so searching, so awful, so irresistible, that the poor man fell back into his seat and pretended to look out at the opposite window. After a pause of thirty seconds, Peter turned to the engine-driver.

"They 're a' here noo, an' there 's nae use waitin' langer ; ca' awa', but ye needna distress the engine."

It was noticed that the foolhardy traveller kept the full length of the junction between himself and Peter till the Dunleith train came in, while his very back was eloquent of humiliation, and Hillocks offered his snuff-box ostentatiously to Peter, which that worthy accepted as a public tribute of admiration.

PETER WAS STANDING IN HIS FAVOURITE ATTITUDE.

"Look, Kate, there he is;" and there Peter was, standing in his favourite attitude, his legs wide apart and his thumbs in his armholes, superior, abstracted, motionless till the train stopped, when he came forward.

"Prood tae see ye, General, coming back at laist, an' the Miss wi' ye; it 'll no be the blame o' the fouk up by gin ye bena happy. Drumtochty hes an idea o' itsel', and peety the man 'at tries tae drive them, but they 're couthy.

"This wy, an' a 'll see tae yir luggage," and before Peter made for the Dunleith van it is said that he took off his cap to Kate; but if so, this was the only time he had ever shown such gallantry to a lady.

Certainly he must have been flustered by something, for he did not notice that Carmichael, overcome by shyness at the sight of the Carnegies in the first, had hid himself in the second, till he closed the doors; then the Carnegies heard it all.

"It 's I, Peter," very quietly; "your first has passengers to-day, and . . . I 'll just sit here."

"Come oot o' that," after a moment, during which Peter had simply looked; then the hat and the tweeds came stumbling into the first, making some sort of a bow and muttering an apology.

"A 'll tak' yir ticket, Maister Carmichael," with severity. "General," suddenly relaxing, "this is the Free Kirk minister of yir pairish, an' a 'm jidgin' he 'll no try the second again."

Carmichael lifted his head and caught Kate's eye, and at the meeting of humour they laughed aloud. Whereupon the General said, "My daughter, Miss Carnegie," and they became so friendly before they reached Kildrummie that Carmichael forgot his disgraceful appearance, and when the General offered him a lift up, simply clutched at the opportunity.

The trap was a four-wheeled dog-cart. Kate drove, with her father by her side and Carmichael behind, but he found it necessary to turn round to give information of names and places, and he so managed that he could catch Kate's profile half the time.

When he got down at the foot of the hill by Hillocks' farm, to go up the near road, instead thereof he scrambled along the ridge, and looked through the trees as the carriage passed below; but he did not escape.

"What 's he glowerin' at doon there?" Hillocks inquired of Jamie Soutar, to whom he was giving some directions about a dyke, and Hillocks made a reconnaissance. "A 'll warrant that 's the General and his dochter. She 's a weel-faured lassie an' speerity-lookin'."

"It cowes a'," said Jamie to himself; "the first day he ever saw her; but it 's aye the way, aince an' ever, or . . . never."

"What 's the Free Kirk, dad?" when Carmichael had gone. "Is it the same as the Methodists?"

"No, no, quite different. I 'm not up in those things, but I 've heard it was a lot of fellows who would not obey the laws, and so they left and made a kirk for themselves, where they do whatever they like. By the way, that was the young fellow we saw giving the dogs water at Muirtown. I rather like him; but why did he look such a fool, and try to escape us at the junction?"

"How should I know? I suppose because he is a . . . foolish boy. And now, dad, for the Lodge and Tochty woods."

CHAPTER III.

I'T was the custom of the former time to construct roads on a straight line, with a preference for uphill and down, and engineers refused to make a circuit of twenty yards to secure level ground. There were two advantages in this uncompromising principle of construction, and it may be doubtful which commended itself most to the mind of our fathers. Roads were drained after the simplest fashion, because a standing pool in the hollow had more than a compensation in the dryness of the ascent and descent, while the necessity of sliddering down one side and scrambling up the other reduced driving to the safe average of four miles an hour — horse-doctors forming a class by themselves, and being preserved in their headlong career by the particular Providence which has a genial regard for persons who have too little sense or have taken too much liquor. Degenerate descendants, anxious to obtain the maximum of speed with the minimum of exertion, have shown a quite wonderful ingenuity in circumventing hills, so the road between Drumtochty Manse and Tochty Lodge gate was duplicated, and the track that plunged into the hollow was now forsaken of wheeled traffic and overgrown with grass.

"This way, Kate; it's the old road, and the way I came to kirk with my mother. Yes, it's narrow, but we'll get through and down below — it is worth the seeing."

So they forced a passage where the overgrown hedges resisted the wheels, and the trees, wet with a morning shower, dashed Kate's jacket with a pleasant spray, and the rail of the dog-cart was festooned with tendrils of honeysuckle and wild geranium.

"'There is the parish kirk of Drumtochty," as they came out and halted on the crest of the hill, "and though it be not much to look at after the Norman churches of the south, it's a brave old kirk in our fashion, and well set in the Glen."

For it stood on a knoll, whence the ground sloped down to the Tochty, and it lay with God's acre round it in the shining of the sun. Half a dozen old beeches made a shadow in the summer-time, and beat off the winter's storms. One standing at the west corner of the kirkyard had a fuller and sweeter view of the Glen than could be got anywhere save from the beeches at the Lodge; but then nothing like unto that can be seen far or near, and I have marvelled why painting men have never had it on their canvas.

"Our vault is at the east end, where the altar was in the old days, and there our dead of many generations lie. A Carnegie always prayed to be buried with his people in Drumtochty, but as it happened, two out of three of our house have fallen on the field, and so most of us have not had our wish.

"Black John, my great-grandfather, was out in '45, and escaped to France. He married a Highland lassie orphaned there, and entered the French service, as many a Scot did before him since the days of the Scots Guards. But when he felt himself a-dying, he asked leave of the English government to come home, and he would not die till he laid himself down in his room in the tower. Then he gave directions for his funeral, how none were to be asked of the county folk but Drummonds and Hays and Stewarts from Blair Athole and such like that had been out with the Prince. And he made his wife promise that she would have him dressed for his coffin as he fought on Culloden field, for he had kept the clothes.

"Then he asked that the window should be opened that he might hear the lilting of the burn below; and he called for my grandfather, who was only a young lad, and commanded him to enter one of the Scottish regiments and be a loyal kingsman, since all was over with the Stewarts.

"He said a prayer and kissed his wife's hand, being a courtly gentleman, and died listening to the sound of the water running over the stones in the den below."

"It was as good as dying on the field," said Kate, her face flushing with pride; "that is an ancestor worth remembering; and did he get a worthy funeral?"

"More than he asked for; his old comrades gathered

from far and near, and some of the chiefs that were out of hiding came down, and they brought him up this very road, with the pipers playing before the coffin. Fifty gentlemen buried John Carnegie, and every man of them had been out with the Prince.

"When they gathered in the stone hall you 'll see soon, his friend-in-arms, Patrick Murray, gave three toasts. The first was 'the king,' and every man bared his head; the second was 'to him that is gone;' the third was 'to the friends that are far awa';' and then one of the chiefs proposed another, 'to the men of Culloden;' and after that every gentleman dashed his glass on the floor. Though he was only a little lad at the time, my grandfather never forgot the sight.

"He also told me that his mother never shed a tear, but looked prouder than he ever saw her, and before they left the hall she bade each gentleman good-bye, and to the chief she spoke in Gaelic, being of Cluny's blood and a gallant lady.

"Another thing she did also which the lad could not forget, for she brought down her husband's sword from the room in the turret, and Patrick Murray, of the House of Athole, fastened it above the big fireplace, where it hangs unto this day, crossed now with my father's, as you will see, Kate, unless we stand here all day going over old stories."

"They 're glorious stories, dad; why did n't you tell them to me before? I want to get into the spirit of the past and feel the Carnegie blood swinging in my veins before we come to the Lodge. What did they do afterwards, or was that all?"

"They mounted their horses in the courtyard, and as each man passed out of the gate he took off his hat and bowed low to the widow, who stood in a window I will show you, and watched till the last disappeared into the avenue; but my grandfather ran out and saw them ride down the road in order of threes, a goodly company of gentlemen. But this sight is better than horsemen and swords."

They were now in the hollow between the kirk and the Lodge, a cup of greenery surrounded by wood. Behind, they still saw the belfry through the beeches; before, away to the right, the grey stone of a turret showed among the trees. The burn that sang to Black John ran beneath them with a pleasant sound, and fifty yards of turf climbed up to the cottage where the old road joined the new and the avenue of the Lodge began. Over this ascent the branches met, through which the sunshine glimmered and flickered, and down the centre came a white and brown cow in charge of an old woman.

"It's Bell Robb, that lives in the cottage there among the bushes. I was at the parish school with her, Kate — she's just my age — for we were all John Tamson's bairns in those days, and got our learning and our licks together, laird's son and cottar's daughter.

"People would count it a queer mixture nowadays, but there were some advantages in the former parish school idea; there were lots of cleverer subalterns in the old regiment, but none knew his men so well as I did. I had played and fought with their kind. Would you mind saying a word to Bell . . . just her name or something?" for this was a new life to the pride of the regiment, as they called Kate, and Carnegie was not sure how she might take it. Kate was a lovable lass, but like every complete woman, she had a temper and a stock of prejudices. She was good comrade with all true men, although her heart was whole, and with a few women that did not mince their words or carry two faces; but Kate had claws inside the velvet, and once she so handled with her tongue a young fellow who offended her that he sent in his papers. What she said was not much, but it was memorable, and every word drew blood. Her father was never quite certain what she would do, although he was always sure of her love.

"Do you suppose, dad, that I 'm to take up with all your friends of the jackdaw days? You seem to have kept fine company." Kate was already out of the dog-cart, and now took Bell by the hand.

"I am the General's daughter, and he was telling me that you and he were playmates long ago. You 'll let me come to see you, and you 'll tell me all his exploits when he was John Carnegie?"

"To think he minded me, an' him sae lang awa' at the weary wars." Bell was between the laughing and the crying. "We 're lifted to know oor laird 's a General, and that he 's gotten sic honour. There 's nae bluid like the auld bluid, an' the Carnegies cud aye afford to be hamely.

"Ye 're like him," and Bell examined Kate carefully; "but a' can tell yir mither'. dochter, a weel-faured mettlesome lady as wes ever seen; wae 's me, wae 's me for the wars," at the sight of Carnegie's face; "but ye 'll come in to see Marjorie. A 'll mak her ready," and Bell hurried into the cottage.

"Marjorie has been blind from her birth. She was the pet of the school, and now Bell takes care of her. Davidson was telling me that she wanted to support Marjorie off the wages she earns as a field hand on the

"I AM THE GENERAL'S DAUGHTER."

farms, and the parish had to force half-a-crown a week on them ; but hear this."

" Never mind hoo ye look," Bell was speaking.   " A' canna keep them waitin' till ye be snoddit."

" Gie me ma kep, at ony rate, that the minister brocht frae Muirtown, and Drumsheugh's shawl ; it wudna be respectfu' to oor Laird, an' it his first veesit ; " and there was a note of refinement in the voice, as of one living apart.

" Yes, I 'm here, Marjorie," and the General stooped over the low bed where the old woman was lying, " and this is my daughter, the only child left me ; you would hear that all my boys were killed."

" We did that, and we were a' wae for ye ; a' thocht o' ye and a' saw ye in yir sorrow, for them 'at canna see ootside see the better inside.   But it 'll be some comfort to be in the hame o' yir people aince mair, and to ken ye 've dune yir wark weel.   It 's pleasant for us to think the licht 'll be burnin' in the windows o' the Lodge again, and that ye 're come back aifter the wars.

" Miss Kate, wull ye lat me pass ma hand ower yir face, an' then a 'll ken what like ye are better nor some 'at hes the joy o' seein' ye wi' their een. . . . The Glen 'll be the happier for the sicht o' ye ; a' thank ye for yir kindness to a puir woman."

" If you begin to pay compliments, Marjorie, I 'll tell you what I think of that cap ; for the pink is just the very shade for your complexion, and it 's a perfect shape."

" Ma young minister, Maister Carmichael, seleckit it in Muirtown, an' a' heard that he went ower sax shops to find one to his fancy ; he never forgets me, an' he wrote me a letter on his holiday.   A'body likes him for his bonnie face an' honest ways."

"Oh, I know him already, Marjorie, for he drove up with us, and I thought him very nice ; but we must go, for you know I 've not yet seen our home, and I 'm just tingling with curiosity."

"You 'll not leave without breakin' bread; it 's little we hae, but we can offer ye oat-cake an' milk in token o' oor loyalty ; " and then Bell brought the elements of Scottish food ; and when Marjorie's lips moved in prayer as they ate, it seemed to Carnegie and his daughter like a sacrament. So the two went from the fellowship of the poor to their ancient house.

They drove along the avenue between the stately beeches that stood on either side and reached out their branches, almost but not quite unto meeting, so that the sun, now in the south, made a train of light down which the General and Kate came home. At the end of the beeches the road wheeled to the right, and Kate saw for the first time the dwelling-place of her people. Tochty Lodge was of the fourth period of Scottish castellated architecture, and till it fell into disrepair was a very perfect example of the sixteenth century mansion-house, where strength of defence could not yet be dispensed with, for the Carnegies were too near the Highland border to do without thick walls or to risk habitation on the ground floor. The buildings had first been erected on the L plan, and then had been made into a quadrangle, so that on the left was the main part, with a tower at the south-west corner over the den, and a wing at the south-east coming out to meet the gate. On the north-east and north were a tower and rooms now in ruins, and along the west ran a wall some six feet high with a stone walk three feet from the top, whence you could look down on the burn. A big gateway, whose doors were of oak studded with nails, with a grated lattice for observation, gave entrance to the courtyard.   In the centre of the yard there was an ancient oak and a draw well whose water never failed.   The eastern face was bare of ivy, except at the north corner, where stood the jackdaws' tower; but the rough grey stone was relieved by the tendrils and red blossoms of the hardy tropæolum which despises the rich soil of the south and the softer air, and grows luxuriantly on our homely northern houses.   As they came to the gateway, the General bade Kate pull up and read the scroll above, which ran in clear-cut letters —

TRY AND THEN

TRVST · BETTER GVDE

ASSVRANCE

BOT TRUST NOT

OR · YE · TRY · FOR · FEAR

OF · REPENTANCE.

" We 've been a slow dour race, Kit, who never gave our heart lightly, but having given it, never played the traitor.   Fortune has not favoured us, for acre after acre has gone from our hands, but, thank God, we 've never had dishonour."

" And never will, dad, for we are the last of the race."

Janet Macpherson was waiting in the deep doorway of the tower, and gave Kate welcome as one whose ancestors had for four generations served the Carnegies, since the day Black John had married a Macpherson.

" Calf of my heart," she cried, and took Kate in her arms.   " It is your foster-mother that will be glad to see you in the home of your people, and will be praying that God will give you peace and good days."

JANET MACPHERSON WAS WAITING IN THE DEEP DOORWAY.

Then they went up the winding stone stair, with deep, narrow windows, and came into the dining-hall where the fifty Jacobites toasted the king and many a gathering had taken place in the olden time. It was thirty-five feet long by fifteen broad, and twenty-two feet high. The floor was of flags over arches below, and the bare stone walls showed at the windows and above the black oak panelling which reached ten feet from the round. The fireplace was six feet high, and so wide that two could sit on either side within. Upon the mantelpiece the Carnegie arms stood out in bold relief under the two crossed swords. One or two portraits of dead Carnegies and some curious weapons broke the monotony of the walls, and from the roof hung a finely wrought iron candelabra. The western portion of the hall was separated by a screen of open woodwork, and made a pleasant dining-room. A door in the corner led into the tower, which had a library, with Carnegie's bedroom above, and higher still Kate's room, each with a tiny dressing closet. For the Carnegies always lived together in this tower, and their guests at the other end of the hall. The library had two windows. From one you could look down and see nothing but the foliage of the den, with a gleam of water where the burn made a pool, and from the other you looked over a meadow with big trees to the Tochty sweeping round a bend, and across to the high opposite banks covered with brush-wood. First they visited Carnegie's room.

"Here have we been born, and died if we did not fall in battle, and it 's not a bad billet after all for an old soldier. Yes, that is your mother when we were married, but I like this one better," and the General touched his breast, for he carried his love next his heart in a silver locket of Indian workmanship.

Three fine deerskins lay on the floor, and one side of the room was hung with tapestry; but the most striking piece of furnishing in the room was an oak cupboard, sunk a foot into the wall.

"I'll show you something in that cabinet after luncheon, Kate; but now let's see your room."

"How beautiful, and how cunning you have been," and then she took an inventory of the furniture, all new, but all in keeping with the age of the room. "You have spent far too much on a very self-willed and bad-tempered girl, and all I can do is to make you promise that you will come up here sometimes and let me give you tea in this window-seat, where we can see the woods and the Tochty."

"Well, Donald," said the General at table to his faithful servant, "how do you think Drumtochty will suit you?"

"Any place where you and Miss Kate will be living iss a good place for me, and there are six or maybe four men I hef been meeting that hef the language, but not good Gaelic — just poor Perthshire talk," for Donald was a West Highlander, and prided himself on his better speech.

"And what about a kirk, Donald? Are n't you Free like Janet?"

"Oh, yes, I am Free; but it iss not to that kirk I will be going most here, and I am telling Janet that she will be caring more about a man that hass a pleasant way with him than about the truth."

"What's wrong with things, Donald, since we lay in Edinburgh twenty years ago, and you used to give me bits of the Free Kirk sermons?"

"It iss all wrong that they hef been going these last

years, for they stand to sing and they sit to pray, and they will be using human himes.   And it iss great pieces of the Bible they hef cut out, and I am told that they are not done yet, but are going from bad to worse," and Donald invited questioning.

"What more are they after, man?"

"It will be myself that has found it out, and it iss only what might be expected, but I am not saying that you will be believing me."

"Out with it, Donald; let 's hear what kind of people we 've come amongst."

"They 've been just fairly left to themselves, and the godless bodies hef taken to watering the whisky."

CHAPTER IV.

"THE cabinet now, dad, and at once," when they went up the stairs and were standing in the room. " Just give me three guesses about the mystery; but first let me examine."

It was pretty to see Kate opening the doors, curiously carved with hunting scenes, and searching the interior, tapping with her knuckles and listening for a hollow sound.

" Is it a treasure we are to find? Then that 's one point. Not in the cabinet? I have it; there is a door into some other place; am n't I right?"

"Where could it be? We 're in a tower cut off from the body of the Lodge, with a room above and a room below;" and the General sat down to allow full investigation.

After many journeys up and down the stair, and many questions that brought no light, Kate played a woman's trick up in her room.

"The General wishes to show me the concealed room in this tower, Janet, or whatever you call it. Would you kindly tell us how to get entrance? You need n't come down; just explain to me;" and Kate was very pleasant indeed.

"Yes, I am hearing there iss a room in the tower, Miss Kate, that strangers will not be able to find; and it would be very curious if the Carnegies did not have a safe place for an honest gentleman when he wass in a little trouble. All the good houses will have their secret places, and it will not be easy to find some of them. Oh no; now I will remember one at Glamis Castle. . . . "

"Never mind Glamis, nurse, for the General is waiting. Where is the spring? is it in the oak cabinet?"

"It will be good for the General to be resting himself after his luncheon, and he will be thinking many things in his room. Oh yes," continued Janet, settling herself down to narrative, and giving no heed to Kate's beguiling ways, "old Mary that died near a hundred would be often telling me stories of the old days when I wass a little girl, and the one I liked best wass about the hiding of the Duke of Perth."

"You will tell me that to-morrow, when I come down to see your house, Janet, and to-day you 'll tell me how to open the spring."

"But it would be a pity not to finish the story about the Duke of Perth, for it goes well, and it will be good for a Carnegie to hear it." And Kate flung herself into the window-seat, but was hugely interested all the same.

"Mary wass sitting at her door in the evening, and that would be three days after Culloden, for the news had been sent by a sure hand from the Laird, when a man came riding along the road, and as soon as Mary saw him she knew he wass somebody; but perhaps it will be too long a story," and Janet began to arrange dresses in a wardrobe.

" No, no ; as you have begun it, I want to hear the end ; but quick, for there 's the room to see and the rest of the Lodge before it grows dark. What like was he ? "

" He wass a man that looked as if he would be commanding, but his clothes were common grey, and stained with the road. He wass very tired, and could hardly hold himself up in the saddle, and his horse wass covered with foam. ' Is this Tochty Lodge ? ' he asked, softening his voice as one trying to speak humbly. ' I am passing this way, and have a message for Mistress Carnegie ; think you that I can have speech of her quietly ? '

" So Mary will go up and tell the lady that one wass waiting to see her, and that he seemed a noble gentleman. When they came down to the courtyard he had drawn water for his horse from the well, and wass giving him to drink, thinking more of the beast that had borne him than of his own need, as became a man of birth.

" At the sight of the lady he took off his bonnet and bowed low, and asked if he might hef a private audience, to which Mistress Carnegie replied, ' We are private here,' and asked, ' Have you been with my son ? '

" ' We fought together for the Prince three days since — my name is Perth. I am escaping for my life, and desire a brief rest, if it please you, and bring no danger to your house.'

" ' Ye had been welcome, my Lord Duke,' and Mary used to show how her mistress straightened herself,

' though you were the poorest soldier that had drawn his sword for the good cause, and ye will stay here till it be safe for you to escape to France.'

" He wass four weeks hidden in the room, and although the soldiers searched all the house, they could never find the place, and Mrs. Carnegie put scorn upon them, asking why they did her so much honour and whom they sought. Oh yes, it wass a cunning place for the bad times, and you will be pleased to see it."

" And the secret, Janet," cried Kate, her hand upon the door; " you know it quite well."

" So does the General, Catherine of my heart," said Janet, " and he will be liking to show it himself."

So Kate departed in a rage, and gave orders that there be no more delay, for she would not spend an afternoon seeking for rat-holes.

" No rat-hole, Kit, but a very fair chamber for a hunted man ; it is twenty years and more since this door opened last, for none knows the trick of it save Janet and myself. There it goes."

A panel in the back of the cabinet slid aside behind its neighbour and left a passage through which one could squeeze himself with an effort.

" We go up a stair now, and must have light; a candle will do; the air is perfectly pure, for there 's plenty of ventilation ; " and then they crept up by steps in the thickness of the walls, till they stood in a chamber under six feet high, but otherwise as large as the bed-room below. The walls were lined with wood, and there were two tiny slits that gave air, but hardly any light. The only furniture in the room was an oaken chest, clasped with iron and curiously locked.

" Our plate chest, Kit; but there 's not much silver and

gold in it, worse luck for you, lassie; in fact, we're a pack of fools to set store by it. There's nothing in the kist but some old clothes, and perhaps some buckles and such like. I dare say there is a lock of hair also. Some day we will have a look inside."

"IT'S A DIFFICULT KEY TO TURN."

"To-day, instantly," and Kate shook her father. "You are a dreadful hypocrite, for I can see that you would rather Tochty were burned down than this box be lost. Are there any relics of Prince Charlie in it? Quick."

"Be patient; it's a difficult key to turn; there now;" but there was not much to see—only pieces of woollen cloth tightly folded down.

"Call Janet, Kate, for she ought to see this opening, and we'll carry everything down to my room, for no one could tell what like things are in this gloom. Yes, Perth lived here for weeks, and used to go up to the gallery where Black John's mother sat with her maid; but the son was hiding in the North, and never reached his house till he came to die."

First of all they came upon a ball dress of the former time, of white silk, with a sash of Macpherson tartan, besides much fine lace.

"That is the dress your great-grandmother wore as a bride at the Court of Versailles in the fifties. She was only a lassie, and seemed like her husband's daughter. The Prince danced with her, and they counted the dress something to be kept, and that night Locheil and Cluny also had a reel with Sheena Carnegie, while Black John looked like a young man, for he had been too sorely wounded to be able to dance with her himself." And then the General carried down with his own hands a Highland gentleman's evening dress, trews of the Royal tartan, and a velvet coat with silver buttons, and a light plaid of fine cloth.

"And this was her husband's dress that night; but why the Stewart tartan?"

"No, lassie, that is the suit the Prince wore at Holyrood, where he gave a great ball after Prestonpans, and danced with the Edinburgh ladies. It was smuggled across to France at last with other things of the Prince's, and he gave it to Carnegie. 'It will remind you of our great days,' he said, 'when the Stewarts saw their friends in Maiy's Palace.'"

Last of all, the General lifted out a casket and laid it on his table. Within it was a brooch, such as might once have been worn either by a man or a woman; diamonds set in gold, and in the midst a lock of fair hair.

"Is it really, father? . . . " And Kate took the jewel in her hand.

" Yes, the Prince's hair — his wedding present to Sheena Macpherson."

Kate kissed it fervently, and passed it to Janet, who placed it carefully in the box, while the General made believe to laugh.

"Your mother wore the brooch on great occasions, and you will do the same, Kit, for auld lang syne. There are two or three families left in Perthshire that will like to see it on your breast."

"Yes, and there will maybe be more than two or three that will like to see the lady that wears it." This from Janet.

"Your compliments are a little late, and you may keep them to yourself, Janet; it would have been kinder to tell me. . . ."

"Tell you what?" And the General looked very provoking.

" I hate to be beaten." Kate first looked angry, and then laughed. " What else is there to see?"

" There is the gallery, which is the one feature in our poor house, and we will try to reach it from the Duke's hiding-place, for it was a cleverly designed hole, and had its stair up as well as down." And then they all came out into one of the strangest rooms you could find in Scotland, and one that left a pleasant picture in their minds who had seen it lit of a winter night, and the wood burning on the hearth, and Kate dancing a reel with Lord Hay or some other brisk young man, while the General looked on from one of the deep window recesses.

The gallery extended over the hall and Kate's drawing-room, and measured fifty feet long from end to end.
The upper part of the walls was divided into compart-
ments by an arcading, made of painted pilasters and flat
arches. Each compartment had a motto, and this was
on one side of the fireplace :

> A · nice · wyfe · and
> A · back · doore
> Oft · maketh · a rich
> Man · poore.

And on the other : —

> Give liberalye
> To neidfvl · folke ·
> Denye · nane · of ·
> Them · al · for · litle
> Thow · knawest · heir
> In · this lyfe · of what
> Chaunce · may · the
> Befall.

· The glory of the gallery, however, was its ceiling,
which was of the seventeenth century work, and so wonderful that many learned persons used to come and study
it. After the great disaster when the Lodge was sold
and allowed to fall to pieces, this fine work went first,
and now no one examining its remains could have imagined how wonderful it was, and in its own way how
beautiful. This ceiling was of wood, painted, and semi-
elliptical in form, and one wet day, when we knew not
what else to do, Kate and I counted more than three
hundred panels. It was an arduous labour for the neck,
and the General refused to help us; but I am sure that
we did not make too many, for we worked time about,
while the General took note of the figures, and our plan

was that each finished his tale of work at some amazing
beast, so that we could make no mistake. Some of the
panels were circles, and they were filled in with coats-of-
arms; some were squares and they contained a bestiary
of that day. It was hard indeed to decide whether the
circles or the squares were more interesting. The former
had the arms of every family in Scotland that had the
remotest connection with the Carnegies, and besides
swept in a wider field, comprising David, King of Israel,
who was placed near Hector of Troy, and Arthur of
Brittany not far from Moses — all of whom had appropriate crests and mottoes. In the centre were the arms
of our Lord Christ as Emperor of Judea, and the chief
part of them was the Cross. But it came upon one with
a curious shock to see this coat among the shields of
Scottish nobles. There were beasts that could be recognised at once, and these were sparingly named; but
others were astounding, and above them were inscribed
titles such as these: Shoe-lyon, Musket, Ostray; and
one fearsome animal in the centre was designated the
Ram of Arabia. This display of heraldry and natural
history was reinforced by the cardinal virtues in seventeenth century dress: Charitas as an elderly female of
extremely forbidding aspect, receiving two very imper-
fectly clad children; and Temperantia as a furious-
looking person — male on the whole rather than female
— pouring some liquor — surely water — from a jug into
a cup, with averted face, and leaving little to be desired.
The afternoon sun shining in through a western window
and lingering among the black and white tracery, so
that the marking of a shield came into relief or a beast
suddenly glared down on one, had a weird, old-world
effect.

"It 's half an armoury and half a menagerie," said Kate, "and I think we 'll have tea in the library with the windows open to the Glen." And so they sat together in quietness, with books of heraldry and sport and ancient Scottish classics and such like round them, while Janet went out and in.

"So Donald has been obliged to leave his kirk;" for Kate had not yet forgiven Janet. "He says it 's very bad here; I hope you won't go to such a place."

"What would Donald Macdonald be saying against it?" inquired Janet, severely.

"Oh, I don't remember — lots of things. He thought you were making too much of the minister."

"The minister iss a good man, and hass some Highland blood in him, though he hass lost his Gaelic, and he will be very pleasant in the house. If I wass seeing a sheep, and it will be putting on this side and that, and quarrelling with everybody, do you know what I will be thinking?"

"That 's Donald, I suppose; well?"

"I will say to myself, that sheep iss a goat." And Janet left the room with the laurels of victory.

CHAPTER V.

T is one of the miseries of modern life, for which telephones are less than compensation, that ninety out of a hundred city folk have never known the comfort and satisfaction of dwelling in a house. When the sashes are flying away from the windows and the skirting boards from the floor, and the planks below your feet are a finger breadth apart, and the pipes are death-traps, it does not matter that the walls are covered by art papers and plastered over with china dishes. This erection, wherein human beings have to live and work and fight their sins and prepare for eternity, is a fraud and a lie. No man compelled to exist in such an environment of unreality can respect himself or other people ; and if it come to pass that he holds cheap views of life, and reads smart papers, and does sharp things in business, and that his talk be only a clever jingle, then a plea in extenuation will be lodged for him at the Great Assize. Small wonder that he comes to regard the world of men as an empty show and is full of cynicism, who has shifted at brief intervals from one shanty to an-

other and never had a fit dwelling-place all his years.
When a prophet cometh from the Eternal to speak unto
modern times as Dante did unto the Middle Ages, and
constructs the other world before our eyes, he will have
one circle in his hell for the builders of rotten houses,
and doubtless it will be a collection of their own works,
so that their sin will be its punishment, as is most fitting
and the way of things.

Surely there will also be some corner of heaven kept
for the man who, having received a charge to build the
shell wherein two people were to make a home, laid its
foundations deep and raised strong walls that nothing
but gunpowder could rend in pieces, and roofed it over
with oaken timber and lined it with the same, so that
many generations might live therein in peace and
honour. Such a house was the Lodge in those days,
although at last beginning to show signs of decay, and it
somehow stirred up the heroic spirit of the former time
within a man to sit before the big fire in the hall, with
grim Carnegies looking down from the walls and daring
you to do any meanness, while the light blazing out from
a log was flung back from a sword that had been drawn
in the '15. One was unconsciously reinforced in the
secret place of his manhood, and inwardly convinced
that what concerneth every man is not whether he fail
or succeed, but that he do his duty according to the light
which may have been given him until he die. It was also
a regeneration of the soul to awake in a room of the eastern tower, where the Carnegies' guests slept, and fling
up the window, with its small square panes, to fill one's
lungs with the snell northern air, and look down on the
woods glistening in every leaf, and the silver Tochty just
touched by the full risen sun. Miracles have been

wrought in that tower, for it happened once that an Edinburgh advocate came to stay at the Lodge, who spake after a quite marvellous fashion, known neither in England nor Scotland; and being himself of pure bourgeois blood, the fifth son of a factor, felt it necessary to despise his land, from its kirk downwards, and had a collection of japes at Scottish ways, which in his provincial simplicity he offered to the Carnegies. It seemed to him certain that people of Jacobite blood and many travels would have relished his clever talk, for it is not given to a national decadent to understand either the people he has deserted or the ancient houses at whose door he stands. Carnegie was the dullest man living in the matter of sneering, and Kate took an instant dislike to the mincing little man, whom she ever afterwards called the Popinjay, and so handled him with her tongue that his superiority was mightily shaken. But there was good stuff in the advocate, besides some brains, and after a week's living in the Lodge, he forgot to wear his eyeglass, and let his r's out of captivity, and attempted to make love to Kate, which foolishness that masterful damsel brought to speedy confusion. It was also said that when he went back to the Parliament House, every one could understand what he said, and that he got two briefs in one week, which shows how good it is to live in an ancient house with honest people.

"Is there a ghost, dad?" They were sitting before the fire in the hall after dinner — Kate in her favourite posture, leaning forward and nursing her knee. The veterans and I thought that she always looked at her best so, with her fine eyes fixed on the fire, and the light bringing her face into relief against the shadow. We saw her feet then — one lifted a little from the ground —

and V. C. declared they were the smallest you could find for a woman of her size.

"She knows it, too," he used to say, "for when a

KATE IN HER FAVOURITE POSITION.

woman has big feet she always keeps them tucked in below her gown. A woman with an eight-size glove and feet to correspond is usually a paragon of modesty, and strong on women's rights."

"Kate's glove is number six, and I think it's a size too big," broke in the Colonel — we were all lying in the sun on a bank below the beeches at the time, and the Colonel was understood to be preparing a sermon for some meeting — "but it's a strong little hand, and a steady; she used to be able to strike a shilling in the air at revolver practice."

"Ghost, lassie. Oh, in the Lodge, a Carnegie ghost — not one I've ever heard of; so you may sleep in peace, and I'm below if you feel lonely the first night."

"You are most insulting; one would think I were a milksop. I was hoping for a ghost — a white lady by choice. Did no Carnegie murder his wife, for instance, through jealousy or quarrelling?"

"The Carnegies have never quarrelled," said the General, with much simplicity; "you see the men have generally been away fighting, and the women had never time to weary of them."

"No woman ever wearies of a man unless he be a fool and gives in to her — then she grows sick of him. Life might be wholesome, but it would have no smack; it would be like meat without mustard. If a man cannot rule, he ought not to marry, for his wife will play the fool in some fashion or other like a runaway horse, and he has half the blame. Why did he take the box-seat?" and Kate nodded to the fire. "What are you laughing at?"

"Perhaps I ought to be shocked, but the thought of any one trying to rule you, Kit, tickles me immensely. I have had the reins since you were a bairn, and you have been a handful. You were a 'smatchit' at six years old, and a 'trimmie' at twelve, and you are qualifying for the highest rank in your class."

"What may that be, pray? it seems to me that the Scottish tongue is a perfect treasure-house for impertinent people. How Scots must congratulate themselves that they need never be at a loss when they are angry or even simply frank."

"If it comes to downright swearing, you must go to Gaelic," said the General, branching off. "Donald used to be quite contemptuous of any slight efforts at profanity in the barrack yard, although they sickened me. 'Toots, Colonel; ye do not need to be troubling yourself with such poor little words, for they are just nothing at all, and yet the bodies will be saying them over and over again like parrots. Now a Lochaber man could hef been saying what he wass wanting for fifteen minutes, and nefer hef used the same word twice, unless he had been forgetting his Gaelic. It's a peautiful language, the Gaelic, when you will not be fery well pleased with a man.'"

"That is very good, dad, but I think we were speaking in Scotch, and you have not told me that nice complimentary title I am living to deserve. Is 'cutty' the disreputable word? for I think I've passed that rank already; it sounds quite familiar."

"No, it's a far more fetching word than 'cutty,' or even than 'randy' (scold), which you may have heard."

"I have," replied Kate instantly, "more than once, and especially after I had a difference in opinion with Lieutenant Strange. You called me one or two names then, dad — in fact you were quite eloquent; but you know that he was a bad fellow, and that the regiment was well rid of him; but I'm older now, and I have not heard my promotion."

"It's the most vigorous word that Scots have for a particular kind of woman."

"Describe her," demanded Kate.

"One who has a mind of her own," began the General, carefully, "and a way, too, who is not easily cowed or managed, who is not . . ."

"A fool," suggested Kate.

"Who is not conspicuously soft in manner," pursued the General, with discretion, "who might even have a temper."

"Not a tame rabbit, in fact. I understand what you are driving at, and I know what a model must feel when she is being painted. And now kindly pluck up courage and name the picture." And Kate leant back, with her hand behind her head, challenging the General — if he dared. "Well?"

"Besom." And he was not at all ashamed, for a Scot never uses this word without a ring of fondness and admiration in his voice, as of one who gives the world to understand that he quite disapproves of this audacious woman, wife or daughter of his, but is proud of her all the time. It is indeed a necessity of his nature for a Scot to have husks of reproach containing kernels of compliment, so that he may let out his heart and yet preserve his character as an austere person, destitute of vanity and sentiment.

"Accept your servant's thanks, my General. I am highly honoured." And Kate made a sweeping courtesy, whereupon they both laughed merrily ; and a log blazing up suddenly made an old Carnegie smile who had taken the field for Queen Mary, and was the very man to have delighted in a besom.

"When I was here in June" — and the General

stretched himself in a deep red leather chair — " I stood a while one evening watching a fair-haired, blue-eyed little maid who was making a daisy chain and singing to herself in a garden. Her mother came out from the cottage, and, since she did not see me, devoured the child with eyes of love. Then something came into her mind — perhaps that the good man would soon be home for supper; she rushed forward and seized the child, as if it had been caught in some act of mischief. 'Come into the hoose, this meenut, ye little beesom, an' say yir carritches. What 's the chief end o' man?'"

" Could she have been so accomplished at that age?" Kate inquired, with interest. " Are you sure about the term of endearment? Was the child visibly flattered ? "

" She caught my eye as they passed in, and flung me a smile like one excusing her mother's fondness. But Davidson hears better things, for as soon as he appears the younger members of a family are taken from their porridge and set to their devotions.

" ' What are ye glowerin' at there, ye little cutty? Toom (empty) yir mooth this meenut and say the twenty-third Psalm to the minister.' "

" Life seems full of incident, and the women make the play. What about the men? Are they merely a chorus ? "

" A stranger spending a week in one of our farm-houses would be ready to give evidence in a court of justice that he had never seen women so domineering or men so submissive as in Drumtochty.

" And why? Because the housewife who sits in church as if butter would n't melt in her mouth speaks with much fluency and vigour at home, and the man says nothing. His normal state is doing wrong and being scolded from morning till night — for going out without his breakfast, for not cleaning his boots when he comes in, for spoiling chairs by sitting on them with wet clothes, for spilling his tea on the tablecloth, for going away to market with a dusty coat, for visiting the stable with his Sunday coat, for not speaking at all to visitors, for saying things he ought n't when he does speak — till the long-suffering man, raked fore and aft, rushes from the house in desperation, and outside remarks to himself, by way of consolation, ' Losh keep 's ! there 's nae livin' wi' her the day; her tongue 's little better than a threshing-mill.' His confusion, however, is neither deep nor lasting, and in a few minutes he has started for a round of the farm in good heart, once or twice saying ' Sall ' in a way that shows a lively recollection of his wife's gifts."

" Then the men love to be ruled," began Kate, with some contempt; " it does not give me a higher idea of the district."

" Wait a moment, young woman, for all that goes for nothing except to show that the men allow the women to be supreme in one sphere."

" In the dairy, I suppose? "

" Perhaps; and a very pleasant kingdom, too, as I remember it, when a hot, thirsty, tired laddie, who had been fishing or ferreting, was taken into the cool, moist, darkened place, and saw a dish of milk creamed for his benefit by some sonsy housewife. Sandie and I used to think her omnipotent, and heard her put the gude man through his facings with awe, but by-and-by we noticed that her power had limits. When the matter had to do with anything serious, sowing or reaping or kirk or market, his word was law.

" He said little, but it was final, and she never contradicted ; it was rare to hear a man call his wife by name ; it was usually ' gude wife,' and she always referred to him as the ' maister.' And without any exception, these silent, reserved men were ' maister ; ' they had a look of authority."

" They gave way in trifles, to rule in a crisis, which is just my idea of masculine government," expatiated Kate. " A woman likes to say what she pleases and have her will in little things ; she has her way, and if a man corrects her because she is inaccurate, and nags at her when she does anything he does not approve, then he is very foolish and very trying, and if she is not quite a saint, she will make him suffer.

" Do you remember Dr. Pettigrew, that prim little effigy of a man, and his delightful Irish wife, and how conversation used to run when he was within hearing ? "

" Glad to have a tasting, Kit," and the General lay back in expectation.

" ' Oi remember him, as foine an upstanding young officer as ye would wish to see, six feet in his boots.'

" ' About five feet ten, I believe, was his exact height, my dear.'

" ' Maybe he was n't full grown then, but he was a good-looking man, and as pretty a rider as ever sat on a horse. Well, he was a Warwickshire man . . .'

" ' Bucks, he said himself.'

" ' He was maybe born in both counties for all you know.'

" ' Alethea,' with a cough and reproving look.

" ' At any rate Oi saw him riding in a steeplechase in the spring of '67, at Aldershot.'

"'It must, I think, have been '66. We were at Gibraltar in '67. Please be accurate.'

"'Bother your accuracy, for ye are driving the pigs through my story. Well, Oi was telling ye about the steeplechase Jimmy Brook rode. It was a mile, and he had led for half, and so he was just four hundred yards from the post.'

"'A half would be eight hundred and eighty yards.'

"'Oi wish from my heart that geography, arithmetic, memory, and accuracy, and every other work of Satan were drowned with Moses in the Red Sea. Go, for any sake, and bring me a glass of irritated water.'"

"Capital," cried the General. "I heard that myself, or something like it. Pettigrew was a tiresome wretch, but he was devoted to his wife in his own way."

"Which was enough to make a woman throw things at him, as very likely Alethea did when they were alone. What a fool he was to bother about facts; the charm of Lithy was that she had none — dates and such like would have made her quite uninteresting. The only dates I can quote myself are the Rebellion and the Mutiny, and I'll add the year we came home. I don't like datey women ; but then it's rather cheap for one to say that who doesn't know anything," and Kate sighed very becomingly at the contemplation of her ignorance.

"Except French, which she speaks like a Parisian," murmured the General.

"That's a fluke, because I was educated at the Scotch convent with these dear old absurd nuns who were Gordons, and Camerons, and Macdonalds, and didn't know a word of English."

"Who can manage her horse like a rough-rider," continued the General, counting on his finger, "and dance

like a Frenchwoman, and play whist like a half-pay officer, and — "

" That 's not education ; those are simply the accomplishments of a besom.   You know, dad, I 've never read
a word of Darwin, and I got tired of George Eliot and
went back to Scott."

" I 've no education myself," said the General, ruefully,
"except the Latin the old dominie thrashed into me, and
some French which all our set in Scotland used to have,
and . . . I can hold my own with the broadsword.
When I think of all those young officers know, I wonder
we old chaps were fit for anything."

" Well, you see, dad," and Kate began to count also,
"you were made of steel wire, and were never ill ; you
could march for a day and rather enjoy a fight in the
evening ; you would go anywhere, and the men followed
just eighteen inches behind ; you always knew what the
enemy was going to do before he did it, and you always
did what he did n't expect you to do.   That 's not half
the list of your accomplishments, but they make a good
beginning for a fighting man."

" It will be all mathematics in the future, Kit, and
there will be no fighting at close quarters.   The officers
will wear gloves and spectacles — but where are we now,
grumbling as if we were sitting in a club window?   Besides, these young fellows can fight as well as pass exams.
You were saying that it was a shame of a man to complain of his wife flirting," and the General studied the
ceiling.

" You know that I never said anything of the kind ;
some women are flirty in a nice way, just as some are
booky, and some are dressy, and some are witty, and
some are horsey ; and I think a woman should be herself.

I should say the right kind of man would be proud of his wife's strong point, and give her liberty."

" He is to have none, I suppose, but just be a foil to throw her into relief. Is he to be allowed any opinions of his own? . . . It looks hard, that cushion, Kit, and I 'm an old broken-down man."

"You deserve leather, for you know what I think about a man's position quite well. If he allow himself to be governed by his wife in serious matters, he is not worth calling a man."

" Like poor Major MacIntosh."

" Exactly. What an abject he was before that woman, who was simply —"

" Not a besom, Kate," interrupted the General, anxiously — afraid that a classical word was to be misused.

" Certainly not, for a besom must be nice, and at bottom a lady — in fact, a woman of decided character."

" Quite so. You 've hit the bull's-eye, Kit, and paid a neat compliment to yourself. Have you a word for Mrs. MacIntosh?"

" A vulgar termagant " — the General indicated that would do — " who would call her husband an idiot aloud before a dinner-table, and quarrel like a fishwife with people in his presence.

" Why, he dare n't call his soul his own; he belonged to the kirk, you know, and there was a Scotch padre, but she marched him off to our service, and if you had seen him trying to find the places in the Prayer-book. If a man has n't courage enough to stand by his faith, he might as well go and hang himself. Don't you think the first thing is to stick by your religion, and the next by your country, though it cost one his life?"

" That 's it, lassie ; every gentleman does."

" She was a disgusting woman," continued Kate, " and jingling with money ; I never saw so many precious stones wasted on one woman ; they always reminded me of a jewel in a swine's snout."

" Kate ! " remonstrated her father, " that 's . . ."

" Rather coarse, but it 's her blame ; and to hear Mrs. MacIntosh calculating what each officer had — I told her we would live in a Lodge at home and raise our own food. My opinion is that her father was a publican, and I 'm sure she had once been a Methodist."

" Why ? "

" Because she was so Churchy, always talking about celebrations and vigils, and explaining that it was a sin to listen to a Dissenting chaplain."

" Then, Kate, if your man — as they say here — tried to make you hold his views ? "

" I would n't, and I 'd hate him."

" And if he accepted yours ? "

" I 'd despise him," replied Kate, promptly.

" You are a perfect contradiction."

" You mean I 'm a woman, and a besom, and therefore I don't pretend to be consistent or logical, or even fair, but I am right."

Then they went up the west tower to the General's room, and looked out on the woods and the river, and on a field of ripe corn upon the height across the river, flooded with the moonlight.

" Home at last, lassie, you and I, and another not far off, maybe."

Kate kissed her father, and said, " One in love, dad . . . and faith."

CHAPTER VI.

A PLEASAUNCE.

HE General read Morning Prayers in brief, omitting the Psalms and lessons, and then after breakfast, with much gossip and ancient stories from Donald, the father and daughter went out to survey their domain, and though there be many larger, yet there can be few more romantic in the north. That Carnegie had a fine eye and a sense of things who, out of all the Glen — for the Hays had little in Drumtochty in those days — fastened on the site of the Lodge and planted three miles of wood, birch and oak, and beech and ash, with the rowan tree, along the river that goes out and in seven times in that distance, so that his descendants might have a fastness for their habitation and their children might grow up in kindly woods on which the south sun beats from early spring till late autumn, and within the sight and sound of clean, running water. No wonder they loved their lonely home with tenacious hearts, and left it only because it was in their blood to be fighting.

They had been out at Langside and Philiphaugh, in the '15 and the '45, and always on the losing side. The Lodge had never been long without a young widow and a fatherless lad, but family history had no warning for him — in fact, seemed rather to be an inspiration in the old way — for no sooner had the young laird loved and married than he would hear of another rebellion, and ride off some morning to fight for that ill-fated dynasty whose love was ever another name for death. There was always a Carnegie ready as soon as the white cockade appeared anywhere in Scotland, and each of the house fought like the men before him, save that he brought fewer at his back and had less in his pocket. Little was left to the General and our Kate, and then came the great catastrophe that lost them the Lodge, and so the race has now neither name nor house in Scotland, save in the vault in Drumtochty Kirk. It is a question whether one is wise to revisit any place where he has often been in happier times and see it desolate. For me, at least, it was a mistake, and the melancholy is still upon me. The deserted house falling at last to pieces, the over-grown garden, the crumbling paths, the gaping bridges over the little burns, and the loneliness, chilled one's soul. There was no money to spare in the General's time, but it is wonderful what one gardener, who has no hours, and works for love's sake, can do, even in a place that needed half a dozen. Then he was assisted unofficially by Donald, who declared that working in the woods was " fery healthy and good for one or two small cuts I happened to get in India," and Kate gave herself to the garden. The path by the river was kept in repair, and one never knew when Kate might appear round the corner. Once I had come down from the cottage on a fine February day to

ONE GARDENER WHO . . . WORKS FOR LOVE'S SAKE.

see the snowdrops in the sheltered nooks, for there were
little dells white as snow at that season in Tochty woods,
and Kate, hearing that I had passed, came of her kindness to take me back to luncheon.   She had on a jacket

of sealskin that we greatly admired, and a felt hat with three grouse feathers on the side, and round her throat a red satin scarf. The sun was shining on the bend of the path, and she came into the light singing " Jack o' Hazeldean," walking, as Kate ever did in song, with a swinging step like soldiers on a march. It seemed to me that day that she was born to be the wife either of a noble or a soldier, and I still wish at times within my heart she were Countess of Kilspindie, for then the Lodge had been a fair sight to-day, and her father had died in his own room. And other times I have imagined myself Kilspindie, who was then Lord Hay, and questioned whether I should have ordered Tochty to be dismantled and left a waste as it is this day, and would have gone away to the wars, or would not have loved to keep it in order for her sake, and visited it in the springtime when the primroses are out, and the autumn when the leaves are blood-red. Then I declare that Hay, being of a brave stock, and having acted as a man of honour — for that is known to all now — ought to have put a good face on his disappointment; but all the time I know one man who would have followed Lord Hay's suit, and who regrets that he ever again saw Tochty Lodge.

" First of all," said the General as they sallied forth, " we shall go to the Beeches, and see a view for which one might travel many days, and pay a ransom."

So they went out into the court with its draw-well, from which they must needs have a draught. Suddenly the General laid down the cup like a man in sudden pain, for he was thinking of Cawnpore, and they passed quickly through the gateway and turned into a path that wound among great trees that had been planted, it was said, by the Carnegie who rode with Montrose. They were walking on a plateau stretching out beyond the line of the Lodge, and therefore commanding the Glen, if one had eyes to see and the trees were not in the way. Kate laid her hand on the General's arm beneath an ancient beech, and they stood in silence to receive the blessing of the place, for surely never is the soul so open to the voice of nature as by the side of running water and in the heart of a wood. The fretted sunlight made shifting figures of brightness on the ground; above the innumerable leaves rustled and whispered; a squirrel darted along a branch and watched the intruders with bright, curious eyes; the rooks cawed from the distance; the pigeons cooed in sweet, sad cadence close at hand. They sat down on the bare roots at their feet and yielded themselves to the genius of the forest — the god who will receive the heart torn and distracted by the fierce haste and unfinished labours and vain ambitions of life, and will lay its fever to rest and encompass it with the quietness of eternity.

" Father," whispered Kate, after a while, as one wishing to share confidences, for there must be something to tell, " where are you? "

" You wish to know? Well, all day I 've been fishing down the stream, and am coming home, very tired, very dirty, very happy, and I meet my mother just outside those trees. I am boasting of the fish that I have caught, none of which, I 'm sure, can be less than half a pound. She is rating me for my appearance and beseeching me to keep at a distance. Then I go home and down into the vaulted kitchen, where Janet's mother gives me joyous welcome, and produces dainties saved from dinner for my eating. The trouts are now at biggest only a quarter of a pound, for they have to be cooked as a final course, but those that were hooked and escaped are each a pound, except one in the hole below Lynedoch Bridge, which was two pounds to an ounce. Afterwards I make a brave attempt to rehearse the day in the gun-room to Sandie, who first taught me to cast a line, and fall fast asleep, and, being shaken up, sneak off to bed, creeping slowly up the stair, where the light is falling, to the little room above yours, where, as I am falling over, I seem to hear my mother's voice as in this sighing of the wind. Ah me, what a day it was! And you, Kit?"

"Oh, I was back in the convent with my nuns, and Sister Flora was trying to teach me English grammar in good French, and I was correcting her in bad French, and she begins to laugh because it is all so droll. 'I am Scotch, and I teach you English all wrong, and you tell me what I ought to say in French which is all wrong; let us go into the garden,' for she was a perfect love, and always covered my faults. I am sitting in the arbour, and the Sister brings a pear that has fallen. 'I do not think it is wicked,' she says, and I say it is simply a duty to eat up fallen pears, and we laugh again. As we sit, they are singing in the chapel, and I hear 'Ave Maria, ora pro nobis.' Then I think of you, and the tears will come to my eyes, and I try to hide my face, but the Sister understands and comforts me. 'Your father is a gallant gentleman, and the good God pities you, and will keep him in danger,' and I fondle the Sister, and wonder whether any more pears have fallen. How peaceful it is within that high wall, which is rough and forbidding outside, but inside it is hung with green-ery, and among the leaves I see pears and peaches. But I missed you, dad," and Kate touched her father, for they had a habit of just touching each other gently when together.

"Do you really think we have been in India, and that you have a dozen medals, and I am . . . an old maid?"

"Certainly not, Kit, a mere invention — we are boy and girl, and . . . we'll go on to the view."

Suddenly they came out from the shade into a narrow lane of light, where some one of the former time, with an eye and a soul, had cleared a passage among the trees, so that one standing at the inner end and looking outwards could see the whole Glen, while the outstretched branches of the beeches shaded his eyes. Morning in the summer-time about five o'clock was a favourable hour, because one might see the last mists lift, and the sun light up the face of Ben Urtach, and evening-tide was better, because the Glen showed wonderfully tender in the soft light, and the Grampians were covered with glory. But it was best to take your first view towards noon, for then you could trace the Tochty upwards as it appeared and reappeared, till it was lost in woods at the foot of Glen Urtach, with every spot of interest on either side. Below the kirk it ran broad and shallow, with a bank of brushwood on one side and a meadow on the other, fringed with low bushes from behind which it was possible to drop a fly with some prospects of success, while in quite unprotected situations the Drumtochty fish laughed at the tempter, and departed with contemptuous whisks of the tail. Above the haughs was a little mill, where flax was once spun and its lade still remained, running between the Tochty and the steep banks down which the glen descended to the river. Opposite this mill the Tochty ran with strength, escaping from the narrows of the bridge, and there it was that

Weelum MacLure drove across Sir George in safety, because the bridge was not for use that day. Whether that bridge was really built by Marshall Wade in his great work of pacifying the Highlands is very far from certain, but Drumtochty did not relish any trifling with its traditions, and had a wonderful pride in its solitary bridge, as well it might, since from the Beeches nothing could well be more picturesque. Its plan came nearly to an inverted V, and the apex was just long enough to allow the horses to rest after the ascent, before they precipitated themselves down the other side. During that time the driver leant on the ledge, and let his eye run down the river, taking in the Parish Kirk above and settling on the Lodge, just able to be seen among the trees where the Tochty below turned round the bend. What a Drumtochty man thought on such occasions he never told, but you might have seen even Whinnie nod his head with emphasis. The bridge stood up clear of banks and woods, grey, uncompromising, unconventional, yet not without some grace of its own in its high arch and abrupt descents. One with good eyes and a favouring sun could see the water running underneath, and any one caught its sheen higher up, before a wood came down to the water's edge and seemed to swallow up the stream. Above the wood it is seen again, with a meal mill on the Tochty left nestling in among the trees, and one would call it the veriest burn, but it was there that Posty lost his life to save a little child. And then it dwindles into the thinnest thread of silver, and at last is seen no more from the beeches. From the Tochty the eye makes its raids on north and south. The dark, massy pine-woods on the left side of the glen are broken at intervals by fields as they threaten to come down upon the river, and their shelter lends an air of comfort and warmth to the glen. On the right the sloping land is tilled from the bank above the river up to the edge of the moor that swells in green and purple to the foot of the northern rampart of mountains, but on this side also the glen here and there breaks into belts of fir, which fling their kindly arms round the scattered farm-houses, and break up the monotony of green and gold with squares of dark green foliage and the brown of the tall, bare trunks. Between the meandering stream and the cultivated land and the woods and the heather and the distant hills, there was such a variety as cannot be often gathered into the compass of one landscape.

"And all our own," cried Kate in exultation; "let us congratulate ourselves."

"I only wish it were, lassie. Why, did n't you understand we have only these woods and a few acres of ploughed land now?"

"You stupid old dad; I begin to believe that you have had no education. Of course the Hays have got the land, but we have the view and the joy of it. This is the only place where one can say to a stranger, 'Behold Drumtochty,' and he will see it at a flash and at its best."

"You 're brighter than your father, Kit, and a contented lassie to boot, and for that word I 'll take you straight to the Pleasaunce."

"What a charming name; it suggests a fairy world, with all sorts of beautiful things and people."

"Quite right, Kit"—leading the way down to a hollow, surrounded by wood and facing the sun, the General opened a door in an ivy-covered wall — "for there is just one Pleasaunce on the earth, and that is a garden."

AMONG THE GREAT TREES.

It had been a risk to raise certain people's expectations and then bring them into Tochty garden, for they can be satisfied with no place that has not a clean-shaven lawn and beds of unvarying circles, pyrethrum, calceolaria, and geranium, and brakes of rare roses, and glass-houses with orchids worth fifty pound each, which is a garden in high life, full of luxury, extravagance, weariness. As Kate entered, a moss rose which wandered at its will caught her skirt, and the General cut a blossom which she fastened in her breast, and surely there is no flower so winsome and fragrant as this homely rose.

"Like yourself, Miss Carnegie," and the General rallied his simple wit for the occasion, "very sweet and true, with a thorn, too, if one gripped it the wrong way."

Whereat he made believe to run, and had the better speed because there were no gravel walks with boxwood borders here, but alleys of old turf that were pleasant both to the touch and the eye. In the centre where all the ways met he capitulated with honours of war, and explained that he had intended to compare Kate to a violet, which was her natural emblem, but had succumbed to the temptation of her eyes, "which make men wicked, Kit, with the gleam that is in them."

"Is n't it a tangle?" Which it was, and no one could look upon it without keen delight, unless he were a horticultural pedant in whom the appreciation of nature had been killed by parterres. There was some principle of order, and even now, when the Pleasaunce is a wilderness, the traces can be found. A dwarf fruit tree stood at every corner, and between the trees a three-foot border of flowers kept the peas and potatoes in their places. But the borders were one sustained, elaborate, glorified disorder. There were roses of all kinds that have ever gladdened poor gardens and simple hearts — yellow tea roses, moss roses with their firm, shapely buds, monthly roses that bore nearly all the year in a warm spot, the white briar that is dear to north country people, besides standards in their glory, with full round purple blossom. Among the roses, compassing them about and jostling one another, some later, some earlier in bloom, most of them together in the glad summer days, one could find to his hand wall-flowers and primroses, sweet-william and dusty-miller, daisies red and white, forget-me-nots and pansies, pinks and carnations, marigolds and phloxes of many varieties. The confusion of colours was preposterous, and showed an utter want of æsthetic sense. In fact, one may confess that the Lodge garden was only one degree removed from the vulgarity and prodigality of nature. There was no taste, no reserve, no harmony about that garden. Nature simply ran riot and played according to her will like a child of the former days, bursting into apple blossom and laburnum gold and the bloom of peas and the white strawberry flower in early summer, and then, later in the year, weaving garlands of blazing red, yellow, white, purple, round beds of stolid roots and brakes of currant bushes. There was a copper beech, where the birds sang, and from which they raided the fruit with the skill of Highland caterans. The Lodge bees lived all day in this garden, save when they went to reinforce their sweetness from the heather bloom. The big trees stood round the place and covered it from every wind except the south, and the sun was ever blessing it. There was one summer-house, a mass of honeysuckle, and there they sat down as those that had come back to Eden from a wander year.

"Well, Kit?"

"Thank God for our Pleasaunce." And they would have stayed for hours, but there was one other spot that had a fascination for the General neither years nor wars had dulled, and he, who was the most matter-of-fact and romantic of men, must see and show it to his daughter before they ceased.

"A mile and more, Kit, but through the woods and by the water all the way."

Sometimes they went down a little ravine made by a small burn fighting and wearing its way for ages to the Tochty, and stood on a bridge of two planks and a hand-rail thrown over a tiny pool, where the water was resting on a bed of small pebbles. The oak copse covered the sides of the tiny glen and met across the streamlet, and one below could see nothing but greenery and the glint of the waterfall where the burn broke into the bosky den from the bare heights above. Other times the path, that allowed two to walk abreast if they wished very much and kept close together, would skirt the face of the high river bank, and if you peeped down through the foliage of the clinging trees you could see the Tochty running swiftly, and the overhanging branches dipping in their leaves. Then the river would make a sweep and forsake its bank, leaving a peninsula of alluvial land between, where the geranium and the hyacinth and the iris grew in deep, moist soil. One of these was almost clear of wood and carpeted with thick, soft turf, and the river beside it was broad and shining.

"We shall go down here," said the General, "and I will show you something that I count the finest monu-ment in Perthshire, or maybe in broad Scotland."

In the centre of the sward, with trees just touching it with the tips of their branches, was a little square, with a simple weather-beaten railing. And the General led Kate to the spot, and stood for a while in silence.

"Two young Scottish lassies, Kate, who died two hundred years ago, and were buried here, and this is the ballad —

> "'Bessie Bell and Mary Grey
> They were twa bonnie lassies,
> They biggit a hoose on yonder brae
> And theikit it ower wi' rashes.'"

Then the General and Kate sat down by the river edge, and he told her the deathless story, — how in the plague of 1666 they fled to this district to escape infection; how a lover came to visit one of them and brought death in his kiss; how they sickened and died; how they were laid to rest beside the Tochty water; and generations have made their pilgrimage to the place, so wonderful and beautiful is love. They loved, and their memory is immortal.

Kate rested her chin on her hand and gazed at the running water, which continued while men and women live and love and die.

"He ought not to have come; it was a cowardly, selfish act, but I suppose," added the General, "he could not keep away."

"Be sure she thought none the less of him for his coming, and I think a woman will count life itself a small sacrifice for love," and Kate went over to the grave.

A thrush was singing as they turned to go, and nothing was said on the way home till they came near the Lodge.

"Who can that be going in, Kate? He seems a padre."

"I do not know, unless it be our fellow traveller from Muirtown; but he has been redressing himself, and is not improved.

"Father," and Kate stayed the General, as they crossed the threshold of their home, "we have seen many beautiful things to-day, for which I thank you; but the greatest was love."

CHAPTER VII

A WOMAN OF THE NEW DISPENSATION.

CARMICHAEL'S aunt, who equipped his house, was determined on one point, and would not hear of a clerical housekeeper for her laddie. Margaret Meiklewham — a woman of a severe countenance, and filled with the spirit of the Disruption — who had governed the minister of Pitscowrie till his decease, and had been the terror of callow young probationers, offered herself, and gave instances of her capability.

"Gin ye leave yir nephew in my hands, ye needna hae ony mair concern. A 'll manage him fine, an' haud him on the richt road. Ye may lippen tae 't, a' wesna five and thirty year wi' Maister MacWheep for naethin'.

"He wes a wee fractious and self-willed at the off-go, an' wud be wantin' this an' that for his denner, but he sune learned tae tak' what wes pit afore him ; an' as for gaein' oot withoot tellin' me, he wud as sune hae thocht o' fleein' ; when he cam' in he keepit naethin' back at his tea.

"Preachin' wes kittle wark in Pitscoorie, for the fouk were awfu' creetics, though they didna maybe think sae muckle o' themselves as Drumtochty. A' aye githered their jidgment through the week, an' gin he hed made a slip meddling wi' warks or sic-like in his sermon, it wes pit richt next Sabbath, and sovereignty whuppit in at the feenish.

"Ye ken the Auld Kirk hes tae be watchit like a cat wi' a moose, an' though a' say it as sudna, Maister Mac-Wheep wud hae made a puir job o' the business himsel'. The pairish meenister wes terrible plausible, an' askit oor man tae denner afore he wes settled in his poopit, an' he wes that simple, he wud hae gaen," and Margaret indicated by an uplifting of her eyebrows the pitiable inno-cence of MacWheep.

"Ye guidit him, nae doot?" inquired Carmichael's aunt, with interest.

"'Maister MacWheep,' says I," and Miss Meikle-wham's lips were very firm, "'a'll no deny that the Auld Kirk is Christian, an' a've never said that a Mod-erate cudna be savit, but the less trokin' (trafficking) ye hae wi' them the better. There's maybe naethin' wrang wi' a denner, but the next thing 'll be an exchange o' poopits, and the day ye dae that ye may close the Free Kirk.'

"And the weemen"—here the housekeeper paused as one still lost in amazement at the audacity with which they had waylaid the helpless MacWheep—"there wes ae madam in Muirtown that hed the face tae invite her-sel' oot tae tea wi' three dochters, an' the way they wud flatter him on his sermons wes shamefu'.

"If they didna begin askin' him tae stay wi' them on Presbytery days, and Mrs. MacOmish hed the face tae peety him wi' naebody but a hoosekeeper. He lat oot tae me though that the potatoes were as hard as a stone at denner, an' that he hed juist ae blanket on his bed, which wesna great management for four weemen."

As Carmichael's aunt seemed to be more and more impressed, Margaret moistened her lips and rose higher.

"So the next time ma lady comes oot tae see the spring flowers," she said, "a' explained that the minister wes sae delicate that a' didna coont it richt for him tae change his bed, and a' thocht it wud be mair comfortable for him tae come hame on the Presbytery nichts, an' safer.

"What said she? No a word," and Miss Meiklewham recalled the ancient victory with relish. "She lookit at me, and a' lookit at her, an' naething passed; but that wes the laist time a' saw her at the manse. A 've hed experience, and a 'm no feared tae tak' chairge o' yi · nephew."

Carmichael's aunt was very deferential, complimenting the eminent woman on her gifts and achievements, and indicating that it would be hard for a young Free Kirk minister to obtain a better guardian; but she had already made arrangements with a woman from the south, and could not change.

Drumtochty was amazed at her self-will, and declared by the mouth of Kirsty Stewart that Carmichael's aunt had flown in the face of Providence. Below her gentle simplicity she was however a shrewd woman, and was quite determined that her nephew should not be handed over to the tender mercies of a clerical housekeeper, who is said to be a heavier yoke than the Confession of Faith, for there be clever ways of escape from confessions, but none from Margaret Meiklewham; and

while all the churches are busy every year in explaining
that their Articles do not mean what they say, Miss
Meiklewham had a snort which was beyond all she said,
and that was not by any means restricted.

"John," said Carmichael's aunt, one day after they
had been buying carpets, "I 've got a housekeeper for
you that will keep you comfortable and can hold her
tongue," but neither then nor afterwards, neither to her
nephew nor to Drumtochty, did Carmichael's aunt tell
where she secured Sarah.

"That 's my secret, John," she used to say, with much
roguishness, "an' ye maun confess that there 's ae thing
ye dinna ken. Ye 'll hae the best-kept manse in the
Presbytery, an' ye 'll hae nae concern, sae be content."

Which he was, and asked no questions, so that he
knew no more of Sarah the day she left than the night
she arrived; and now he sometimes speculates about her
history, but he has no clue.

She was an event in the life of the parish, and there
are those who speak of her unto this day with exaspera-
tion. The new housekeeper was a subject of legitimate
though ostentatiously veiled curiosity, and it was expected that a full biography by Elspeth Macfadyen
would be at the disposal of the kirkyard, as well as the
Free Kirk gate, within ten days of her arrival; it might
even be on the following Sabbath, although it was felt
that this was asking too much of Elspeth.

It was on the Friday evening Mrs. Macfadyen called,
with gifts of butter and cream for the minister, and was
received with grave, silent courtesy. While they played
with the weather, the visitor made a swift examination,
and she gave the results on Sabbath for what they were
worth.

—

"A tall, black wumman, spare an' erect, no ill-faured nor ill-made ; na, na, a 'll alloo that ; a trig, handy cummer, wi' an eye like a hawk an' a voice like pussy ; nane o' yir gossipin', haverin', stravaigin' kind. He 'll be clever 'at gets onything out o' her or maks much o' a bargain wi' her.

"Sall, she 's a madam an' nae mistak'. If that waefu', cunnin', tramping wratch Clockie didna come tae the door, where I was sittin', an' askit for the new minister. Ye ken he used tae come an' hear Maister Cunningham on the principles o' the Disruption for an 'oor, givin' oot that he wes comin' roond tae the Free Kirk view; then he got his denner an' a suit o' claithes."

" A' mind o' Clockie gettin' five shillin's ae day," remarked Jamie Soutar, who was at the Free Kirk that morning ; "he hed started Dr. Chalmers wi' the minister ; Dr. Guthrie he coontit to be worth aboot half-a-croon ; but he aince hed three shillin's oot o' the Cardross case. He wes graund on the doctrine o' speeritual independence, and terrible drouthy ; but a 'm interruptin' ye, Elspeth."

"' The minister is at dinner,' says she, ' and can't be disturbed ; he sees no one at the door.'

" ' It 's reeligion a 'm come aboot,' says Clockie, stickin' in his foot tae keep the door open, ' an' a 'll juist wait at the fire.'

" ' It 's more likely to be whisky from your breath, and you will find a public-house in the village ; we give nothing to vagrants here.' Then she closed the door on his foot, and the language he used in the yard wesna connectit wi' reeligion."

Drumtochty admitted that this showed a woman of vigour—although our conventions did not allow us to treat Clockie or any known wastrel so masterfully — and there was an evident anxiety to hear more.

"Her dress wes black an' fittit like a glove, an' wes set aff wi' a collar an' cuffs, an' a' saw she hedna come frae the country, so that wes ae thing settled ; yon 's either a toon dress or maybe her ain makin' frae patterns.

"It micht be Edinburgh or Glesgie, but a' began tae jalouse England aifter hearin' her hannel Clockie, sae a' watchit for a word tae try her tongue."

"Wurk is a gude handy test," suggested Jamie ; "the English hae barely ae r, and the Scotch hae aboot sax in 't."

"She wudna say 't, Jamie, though a' gied her a chance, speakin' aboot ae wumman daein' a'thing in the manse, sae a' fell back on church, an' that brocht oot the truth. She didna say 'chich,' so she 's no English born, and she didna say 'churrrch,' so she 's been oot o' Scotland. It wes half and between, and so a' said it wud be pleasant for her tae be in her ain country again, aifter livin' in the sooth."

Her hearers indicated that Elspeth had not fallen beneath herself, and began to wonder how a woman who had lived in London would fit into Drumtochty.

"What div ye think she said tae me?" Then Drumtochty understood that there had been an incident, and that Elspeth as a conversationalist, if not as a raconteur, had found her equal.

"'You are very kind to think of my movements, but'"—and here Mrs. Macfadyen spoke very slowly—"'I 'm afraid they don't teach home geography at your school. Paisley is not out of Scotland.'"

"Ye 've met yir match, Elspeth," said Jamie, with a hoarse chuckle, and the situation was apparent to all.

It was evident that the new housekeeper was minded to hide her past, and the choice of her last residence was a stroke of diabolical genius. Paisley is an ancient town inhabited by a virtuous and industrious people, who used to make shawls and now spin thread, and the atmosphere is so literary that it is believed every tenth man is a poet. Yet people do not boast of having been born there, and natives will pretend they came from Greenock. No one can mention Paisley without a smile, and yet no one can say what amused him. Certain names are the source of perennial laughter, in which their inhabitants join doubtfully, as persons not sure whether to be proud or angry. They generally end in an apology, while the public, grasping vaguely at the purpose of such a place, settle on it every good tale that is going about the world unprovided for and fatherless. So a name comes to be bathed in the ridiculous, and a mere reference to it passes for a stroke of supreme felicity.

"Paisley"—Jamie again tasted the idea—"she 'll be an acqueesition tae the Glen."

It was Sarah's first stroke of character to arrive without notice—having utterly baffled Peter at the Junction—and to be in complete possession of the manse on the return of Carmichael and his aunt from pastoral visits.

"Sarah," cried the old lady in amazement at the sight of the housekeeper in full uniform, calm and self-possessed, as one having been years in this place, "when did ye come?"

"Two hours ago, m'am, and I think I understand the house. Shall I bring tea into the dining-room, or would you rather have it in the study?" But she did not once glance past his aunt to Carmichael, who was gazing in

silence at this composed young woman in the doorway.

"This is Sarah, John, who hes come to keep yir
house," and his aunt stepped back. "Sarah, this is my
dear laddie, the minister."

Perhaps because her eyes were of a flashing black that
pierced one like a steel blade, Sarah usually looked down
in speaking to you, but now she gave Carmichael one
swift, comprehensive look that judged him soul and
body, then her eyes fell, and her face, always too hard
and keen, softened.

"I will try, sir, to make you comfortable, and you will
tell me anything that is wrong."

"You took us by surprise, Sarah," and Carmichael,
after his hearty fashion, seized his housekeeper's hand;
"let me bid you welcome to the manse. I hope you
will be happy here, and not feel lonely."

But the housekeeper only bowed, and turned to his aunt.

"Dinner at six? As you were not in, and it did not
seem any use consulting the woman that was here, I am
preparing for that hour."

"Well, ye see, Sarah, we have just been taking tea,
with something to it, but if—"

"Gentlemen prefer evening dinner, ma'am."

"Quite right, Sarah," burst in Carmichael in great
glee; "tea-dinner is the most loathsome meal ever invented, and we'll never have it in the Free Manse.   ·

"That is an admirable woman, auntie," as Sarah disappeared, "with sound views on important subjects.
I'll never ask again where she came from; she is her
own testimonial."

"You mauna be extravagant, John; Sarah hes never
seen a manse before, and I must tell her not to—"

" Ruin me, do you mean, by ten courses every evening, like the dinners West-end philanthropists used to give our men to show them how to behave at table? We 'll be very economical, only having meat twice a week — salt fish the other days — but it will always be dinner."

" What ails you at tea-dinner, John? it's very tasty and homely."

" It 's wicked, auntie, and has done more injury to religion than drinking. No, I 'm not joking — that is a childish habit — but giving utterance to profound truth, which ought to be proclaimed on the house-tops, or perhaps in the kitchens.

"Let me explain, and I 'll make it as plain as day — all heresy is just bad thinking, and that comes from bad health, and the foundation of health is food. A certain number of tea-dinners would make a man into a Plymouth brother. It 's a mere question of time.

"You see if a man's digestion is good he takes a cheerful view of things ; but if he is full of bile, then he is sure that everybody is going to be lost except himself and his little set, and that 's heresy. Apologetics is just dietetics ; now there 's an epigram made for you on the spot, and you don't know what it means, so we 'll have a walk instead."

His aunt knew what was coming, but was too late to resist, so she was twice taken round the room for exercise, till she cried out for mercy, and was left to rest while Carmichael went out to get an appetite for that dinner.

Nothing was said during its progress, but when Sarah had finally departed after her first triumph, won under every adverse circumstance of strangeness and limited resources, Carmichael took his aunt's hand and kissed it.

" It is an illuminated address you deserve, auntie, for

such a paragon ; as it is, I shall be the benefactor of a
Presbytery, asking the men up by turns on fast-days, and
sending them home speechless with satisfaction."

"Sarah was always a clever woman ; if she had only
— " But Carmichael heard not, in his boyish excitement of householding.

"Clever is a cold word for such genius. Mark my
words, there is not a manse in Perthshire that shall not
sound with the praise of Sarah. I vow perpetual celibacy
on the spot. No man would dream of marrying that had
the privilege of such a housekeeper."

"Ye 're a silly laddie, John ; but some day a fair face
will change a' yer life, an' if she be a good wumman like
your mother, I 'll thank God."

"No woman can be compared with her," and the
minister sobered. "You and she have spoiled me for
other women, and now you have placed me beyond
temptation with such a cook."

So it came to pass that Carmichael, who knew nothing
about fine cooking till Sarah formed his palate with her
cunning sauces, and, after all, cared as little what he ate as
any other healthy young man, boasted of his housekeeper
continually by skilful allusions, till the honest wives of
his fathers and brethren were outraged and grew feline,
as any natural woman will if a servant is flung in her face
in this aggravating fashion.

"I 'm glad to hear you 're so well pleased, Mr. Carmichael," Mrs. MacGuffie would say, who was full of
advice, and fed visitors on the produce of her garden,
"but no man knows comfort till he marries. It 's a chop
one day and a steak the next all the year round — nothing tasty or appetising ; and as for his shirts, most
bachelors have to sew on their own buttons. Ah, you

all pretend to be comfortable, but I know better, for Mr. MacGuffie has often told me what he suffered."

Whereat Carmichael would rage furiously, and then, catching sight of MacGuffie, would bethink him of a Christian revenge. MacGuffie was invited up to a day of humiliation — Sarah receiving for once *carte blanche* — and after he had powerfully exhorted the people from the words, " I am become like a bottle in the smoke," he was conducted to the manse in an appropriately mournful condition, and set down at the table. He was inclined to dwell on the decadence of Disruption principles during soup, but as the dinner advanced grew wonderfully cheerful, and being installed in an arm-chair with a cup of decent coffee beside him, sighed peacefully, and said, " Mr. Carmichael, you have much cause for thankfulness." Mr. MacGuffie had not come to the age of sixty, however, without learning something, and he only gave his curious spouse to understand that Carmichael had done all in his power to make his guest comfortable, and was not responsible for his servant's defects.

Ladies coming with their husbands to visit the manse, conceived a prejudice against Sarah on the general ground of dislike to all housekeepers as a class of servants outside of any mistress's control, and therefore apt to give themselves airs, and especially because this one had a subtle suggestion of independent personality that was all the more irritating because it could not be made plain to the dull male intelligence, which was sadly deceived.

" What a lucky man Carmichael is on his first venture ! " Even Dr. Dowbiggin, of St. Columba's, Muirtown, grew enthusiastic to his wife in the privacy of their bedchamber on a sacramental visit, and every one knows

that the Doctor was a responsible man, ministering to
four bailies and making "overtures" to the Assembly,

"MR. CARMICHAEL, YOU HAVE MUCH CAUSE FOR
THANKFULNESS."

beginning with "Whereas" and ending with "Venerable House." "I am extremely pleased to see . . .
everything so nice."

"You mean, James, that you have had a good dinner, far too ambitious for a young minister's table. Did you ever see an entrée on a Disruption table, or dessert with finger glasses? I call it sinful — for the minister of Drumtochty, at least; and I don't believe he was ever accustomed to such ways. If she attended to his clothes, it would set her better than cooking French dishes. Did you notice the coat he was wearing at the station? — just like a gamekeeper. But it is easy for a woman to satisfy a man; give him something nice to eat, and he 'll ask no more."

"So far as my recollection serves me, Maria" — the Doctor was ruffled, and fell into his public style — " I made no reference to food, cooked or uncooked, and perhaps I may be allowed to say that it is not a subject one thinks of . . . at such seasons. What gave me much satisfaction was to see one of our manses so presentable; as regards the housekeeper, so far as I had an opportunity of observing, she seemed a very capable woman indeed," and the Doctor gave one of his coughs, which were found most conclusive in debate.

" It 's easy to be a man's servant," retorted Mrs. Dowbiggin, removing a vase of flowers from the dressing-table with contempt, " for they never look below the surface. Did you notice her hands, as white and smooth as a lady's? You may be sure there 's little scrubbing and brushing goes on in this manse."

"How do you know, Maria?" — the Doctor was weakening. "You have never been in the house before."

" We 'll soon see that, James, though I dare say it would never occur to a man to do such a thing. Did you ever look below the bed?"

" Never," replied the Doctor, promptly, who was not

constructed to stoop, " and I am not going to begin after
that . . . ah . . . this evening, with work before me to-
morrow.   But I would be glad to see you."

" I have done so every night of my life for fear of
robbers, and the dust I 've seen in strange houses —
it 's there you can tell a good servant," and Mrs. Dowbiggin nodded with an air of great sagacity.

" Well," demanded the Doctor, anxiously watching
the operation, " guilty or not guilty ? "

"She knew what I would do. I hate those sharp
women ; " and then the Doctor grew so eloquent over
uncharitable judgments and unreasonable prejudices that
his wife denounced Sarah bitterly as a " cunning woman
who got on the blind side of gentlemen."

Her popularity with Carmichael's friends was beyond
question, for though she was a reserved woman, with no
voluntary conversation, they all sent messages to her,
inquired for her well-being at Fast-days, and brought
her gifts of handkerchiefs, gloves, and such like. When
they met at Theologicals and Synods they used to talk of
Sarah with unction — till married men were green with
envy — being simple fellows and helpless in the hands
of elderly females of the Meiklewham genus. For there
are various arts by which a woman, in Sarah's place, wins
a man's gratitude, and it may be admitted that one is
skilful cooking. Sensible and book-reading men do not
hunger for six courses, but they are critical about their
toast and . . . nothing more, for that is the pulse.
Then a man also hates to have any fixed hour for breakfast
— never thinking of houses where they have prayers at
7.50 without a shudder — but a man refuses to be kept
waiting five minutes for dinner. If a woman will find
his belongings, which he has scattered over three rooms

and the hall, he invests her with many virtues, and if she packs his portmanteau, he will associate her with St. Theresa.   But if his hostess be inclined to discuss problems with him, he will receive her name with marked coldness ; and if she follow up this trial with evil food, he will conceive a rooted dislike for her, and will flee her house.   So simple is a man.

When Sarah proposed to Carmichael that she should prepare breakfast after he rung for his hot water, and when he never caught a hint of reproach on her face though he sat up till three and came down at eleven, he was lifted, hardly believing that such humanity could be found among women, who always seem to have a time table they are carrying out the livelong day.

"The millennium is near at hand," said MacQueen, when the morning arrangements of the Free Kirk manse of Drumtochty were made known to him — MacQueen, who used to arrive without so much as a nightshirt, having left a trail of luggage behind him at various junctions, and has written books so learned that no one dares to say that he has not read them.   Then he placed an ounce of shag handly, and Carmichael stoked the fire, and they sat down, with Beaton, who could refer to the Summa of St. Thomas Aquinas from beginning to end, and they discussed the Doctrine of Scripture in the Fathers, and the formation of the Canon, and the authorship of the Pentateuch till two in the study.   Afterwards they went to MacQueen's room to hear him on the Talmud, and next adjourned to Beaton's room, who offered a series of twelve preliminary observations on the Theology of Rupert of Deutz, whereupon his host promptly put out his candle, leaving that man of supernatural memory to go to bed in the dark ; and as Carmichael

pulled up the blind in his own room, the day was breaking and a blackbird had begun to sing. Next afternoon
Beaton had resumed his observations on Rupert, but now
they were lying among the heather on the side of Glen
Urtach, and Carmichael was asleep, while MacQueen
was thinking that they would have a good appetite for
dinner that evening.

Sarah had only one fault to find with her master, and
that was his Bohemian dress; but since it pleased him
to go one button less through studied carelessness, she
let him have his way; and as for everything else, she
kept her word to his aunt, and saw that he wanted for
nothing, serving him with perpetual thoughtfulness and
swift capacity.

Little passed between them except a good-natured
word or two from him and her courteous answer, but she
could read him as a book, and when he came home that
day from Muirtown she saw he was changed. He was
slightly flushed, and he could not sit still, wandering in
and out his study till dinner-time. He allowed the soup
to cool, and when she came in with sweets he had barely
touched his cutlet.

" It is the sauce you like, sir," with some reproach in
her voice.

" So it is, Sarah — and first rate." Then he added
suddenly, " Can you put a button on this coat to-night,
and give it a good brush?"

In the evening Sarah went down to post a letter, and
heard the talk, how Miss Carnegie had come home with
the General, and was worthy of her house; how the
minister also had driven up with her from Muirtown; and
on her return she did her best by the coat, handling it very
kindly, and singing softly to herself " Robin Adair."

Next morning he came down in his blacks — the worst-made suit ever seen on a man, ordered to help a village tailor at his home — and announced his intention of starting after lunch for Saunderson's manse, beyond Tochty woods, where he would stay all night. .

" He will call on the way down, and, if he can, coming back," Sarah said to herself, as she watched him go, " but it 's a pity he should go in such a coat ; it might have been put together with a pitchfork. It only makes the difference greater, and 't is wider than he knows already. And yet a woman can marry beneath her without loss ; but for a man it is ruin."

She went up to his room and made it neat, which was ever in disorder on his leaving, and then she went to a western window and looked into the far distance.

CHAPTER VIII.

A WOMAN OF THE OLD DISPENSATION.

VERY Sabbath at eleven o'clock, or as soon thereafter as the people were seated — consideration was always shown to distant figures coming down from the high glen — Carmichael held what might be called High Mass in the Free Kirk. Nothing was used in praise but the Psalms of David, with an occasional Paraphrase sanctioned by usage and sound teaching. The prayers were expected to be elaborate in expression and careful in statement, and it was then that they prayed for the Queen and Houses of Parliament. And the sermon was the event to which the efforts of the minister and the thoughts of the people had been moving for the whole week. No person was absent except through sore sickness or urgent farm duty; nor did rain or snow reduce the congregation by more than ten people, very old or very young. Carmichael is now minister of a West End kirk, and, it is freely rumoured in Drumtochty, has preached before Lords of Session; but he has never been more nervous than facing that handful of quiet, impenetrable, critical faces in his first kirk.   When the service was over, the people broke into little bands that disappeared along the west road, and over the moor, and across the Tochty.   Carmichael knew each one was reviewing his sermon head by head, and, pacing his garden, he remembered the missing points with dismay.

It was the custom of the Free Kirk minister to go far afield of a summer evening, and to hold informal services in distant parts of the parish.   This was the joy of the day to him, who was really very young and hated all conventionalities even unto affectation.   He was never weary of complaining that he had to wear a gown, which was continually falling back and being hitched over with impatient motions, and the bands, which he could never tie, and were, he explained to a horrified beadle in Muirtown, an invention of Satan to disturb the preacher's soul before his work.   Once, indeed, he dared to appear without his trappings, on the plea of heat, but the visible dismay and sorrow of the people was so great — some failing to find the Psalm till the first verse had been sung — that he perspired freely and forgot the middle head of his discourse.

"It's a mercy," remarked Mrs. Macfadyen to Burnbrae afterward, "that he didna play that trick when there wes a bairn tae be baptised.   It wudna hae been lichtsome for its fouk; a'body wants a properly ordained minister.   Ye'll gie him a hint, Burnbrae, for he's young and fordersome (rash), but gude stuff for a' his pliskies (frolics)."

No one would have liked to see the sacred robes in

the places of evening worship, and Carmichael threw all forms to the winds — only drawing the line, with great regret and some searchings of heart, at his tweed jacket. His address for these summer evening gatherings he studied as he went through the fragrant pine woods or over the moor by springy paths that twisted through the heather, or along near cuts that meant leaping little burns and climbing dykes whose top stones were apt to follow your heels with embarrassing attachment. Here and there the minister would stop as a trout leapt in a pool, or a flock of wild duck crossed the sky to Loch Sheuchie, or the cattle thrust inquisitive noses through some hedge, as a student snatches a mouthful from some book in passing. For these walks were his best study; when thinking of his people in their goodness and simplicity, and touched by nature at her gentlest, he was freed from many vain ideas of the schools and from artificial learning, and heard the Galilean speak as He used to do among the fields of corn. He came on people going in the same direction, but they only saluted, refraining even from the weather, since the minister's thoughts must not be disturbed, and they were amazed to notice that he stooped to pluck a violet in the wood. His host would come a little way to meet him and explain the arrangements that had been made for a kirk. Sometimes the meeting-place was the granary of the farm, with floor swept clean and the wooden shutters opened for light, where the minister preached against a mixed background of fanners, corn measures, piles of sacks, and spare implements of the finer sort; and the congregation, who had come up a ladder cautiously like hens going to roost — being severally warned about the second highest step — sat on bags stuffed with straw, boards resting on upturned pails, while a few older folk were accommodated with chairs, and some youngsters disdained not the floor. It was pleasanter in the barn, a cool, lofty, not unimpressive place of worship, with its mass of golden straw and its open door through which various kindly sounds of farm life came in and strange visitors entered. The collies, most sociable of animals, would saunter in and make friendly advances to Carmichael reading a chapter; then, catching their master's eye and detecting no encouragement, would suddenly realise that they were at kirk, and compose themselves to sleep — " juist like ony Christian," as Hillocks once remarked with envy, his own plank allowing no liberties — and never taking any part except in a hymn like

> " See the mighty host advancing,
> Satan leading on,"

which they regarded as recreation rather than worship.

It was also recalled for years that a pet lamb came into Donald Menzies's barn and wandered about for a while, and Carmichael told that pretty legend of St. Francis, how he saw a white lamb among the kids, and burst into tears at the sight, because it reminded him of Jesus among the sinners. Indeed, these services were very extemporaneous, with hymns instead of psalms, and sermons without divisions. Carmichael also allowed himself illustrations from the life around, and even an anecdote at a time, which was all the more keenly relished that it would have been considered a confession of weakness in a regular sermon. 'He has been heard to say that he came nearer the heart of things once or twice in the barns than he has ever done since, not even excepting that famous course of sermons every one talked about last year, the "Analysis of Doubt," which almost converted two professors to Christianity, and were heard by the editor of the *Caledonian* in the disguise of a street preacher. It was also pleasantly remembered for long in the parish that Dr. Davidson appeared one evening in Donald Menzies's barn and joined affably in the "Sweet By-and-Bye." Afterward, being supplied with a large arm-chair, he heard the address with much attention — nodding approval four times, if not five — and pronouncing the benediction with such impressiveness that Donald felt some hesitation in thrashing his last stack in the place next day. The Doctor followed up this visit with an exhortation from the pulpit on the following Sabbath, in which he carefully distinguished such services by an ordained minister, although held in a barn, from unlicensed Plymouthistic gatherings held in corn rooms — this at Milton's amateur efforts — and advised his people in each district to avail themselves of "my friend Mr. Carmichael's excellent ministrations," which Papal Bull, being distributed to the furthest corner of the parish before nightfall, greatly lifted the Free Kirk and sweetened the blood of the Glen for years. It seemed to me, watching things in Drumtochty during those days with an impartial mind, that the Doctor, with his care for the poor, his sympathy for the oppressed, his interest in everything human, his shrewd practical wisdom, and his wide toleration, was the very ideal of the parish clergyman. He showed me much courtesy while I lived in the Cottage, although I did not belong to his communion, and as my imagination reconstructs the old parish of a winter night by the fire, I miss him as he used to be on the road, in the people's homes, in his pulpit, among his books — ever an honourable and kind-hearted gentleman.

One evening a woman came into Donald Menzies's barn just before the hour of service, elderly, most careful in her widow's dress, somewhat austere in expression, but very courteous in her manner. No one recognised her at the time, but she was suspected to be the forerunner of the Carnegie household, and Donald offered her a front seat. She thanked him for his good-will, but asked for a lower place, greatly delighting him by a reference to the parable wherein the Master rebuked the ambitious Pharisees who scrambled for chief seats. Their accent showed of what blood they both were, and that their Gaelic had still been mercifully left them, but they did not use it because of their perfect breeding, which taught them not to speak a foreign tongue in this place. So the people saw Donald offer her a hymn-book and heard her reply :

"It iss not a book that I will be using, and it will be a peety to take it from other people ; " nor would she stand at the singing, but sat very rigid and with closed lips. When Carmichael, who had a pleasant tenor voice and a good ear, sang a solo, then much tasted in such meetings, she arose and left the place, and the minister thought he had never seen anything more uncompromising than her pale set face.

It was evident that she was Free Kirk and of the Highland persuasion, which was once over-praised and then has been over-blamed, but is never understood by the Lowland mind ; and as Carmichael found that she had come to live in a cottage at the entrance to the Lodge, he looked in on his way home. She was sitting at a table reading the Bible, and her face was more hostile than in the meeting ; but she received him with much politeness, dusting a chair and praying him to be seated.

CARMICHAEL SANG A SOLO.

"You have just come to the district to reside, I think? I hope you will like our Glen."

"It wass here that I lived long ago, but I hef been married and away with my mistress many years, and there are not many that will know me."

"But you are not of Drumtochty blood?" inquired the minister.

"There iss not one drop of Sassenach blood in my veins"—this with a sudden flash. "I am a Macpherson and my husband wass a Macpherson; but we hef served the house of Carnegie for four generations."

"You are a widow, I think, Mrs. Macpherson?" and Carmichael's voice took a tone of sympathy. "Have you any children?"

"My husband iss dead, and I had one son, and he iss dead also; that iss all, and I am alone;" but in her voice there was no weakening.

"Will you let me say how sorry I am?" pleaded Carmichael; "this is a great grief, but I hope you have consolations."

"Yes, I will be having many consolations; they both died like brave men with their face to the enemy. There were six that did not feel fery well before Ian fell; he could do good work with the sword as well as the bayonet, and he wass not bad with the dirk at a time."

Neither this woman nor her house were like anything in Drumtochty, for in it there was a buffet for dishes, and a carved chest and a large chair, all of old black oak; and above the mantelpiece two broadswords were crossed, with a circle of war medals beneath on a velvet ground, flanked by two old pistols.

"I suppose those arms have belonged to your people, Mrs. Macpherson; may I look at them?"

"'They are not anything to be admiring, and it wass not manners that I should hef been boasting of my men. It iss a pleasant evening and good for walking."

"You were at the meeting, I think?" and Carmichael tried to get nearer this iron woman. "We were sorry you had to go out before the end. Did you not feel at home?"

"I will not be accustomed to the theatre, and I am not liking it instead of the church."

"But surely there was nothing worse in my singing alone than praying alone?" and Carmichael began to argue like a Scotsman, who always fancies that people can be convinced by logic, and forgets that many people, Celts in especial, are ruled by their heart and not by their head; "do you see anything wrong in one praising God aloud in a hymn, as the Virgin Mary did?"

"It iss the Virgin Mary you will be coming to next, no doubt, and the Cross and the Mass, like the Catholics, although I am not saying anything against them, for my mother's cousins four times removed were Catholics, and fery good people. But I am a Presbyterian, and do not want the Virgin Mary."

Carmichael learned at that moment what it was to argue with a woman, and he was to make more discoveries in that department before he came to terms with the sex, and would have left in despair had it not been for an inspiration of his good angel.

"Well, Mrs. Macpherson, I did n't come to argue about hymns, but to bid you welcome to the Glen and to ask for a glass of water, for preaching is thirsty work."

"It iss black shame I am crying on myself for sitting here and offering you neither meat nor drink," and she was stung with regret in an instant. "It iss a little spirits you will be tasting, and this iss Talisker which I will be keeping for a friend, for whisky iss not for women."

She was full of attention, but when Carmichael took milk instead of whisky, her suspicions revived, and she eyed him again.

"You are not one of those new people I am hearing of in the Lowlands that are wiser than the fery Apostles?"

"What people?" and Carmichael trembled for his new position.

"'Total abstainers' they will call themselves," and the contempt in her accent was wonderful.

"No, I am not," Carmichael hastened to reassure his hostess; "but there are worse people than abstainers in the world, and it would be better if we had a few more. I will stick to the milk, if you please."

"You will take what you please," and she was again mollified; "but the great ministers always had their tasting after preaching; and I hef heard one of them say that it wass a sin to despise the Lord's mercies. You will be taking another glass of milk and resting a little."

"This hospitality reminds me of my mother, Mrs. Macpherson." Carmichael was still inspired, and was, indeed, now in full sail. "She was a Highland woman, and had the Gaelic. She sometimes called me Ian instead of John."

"When you wass preaching about the shepherd finding the sheep, I wass wondering how you had the way to the heart, and I might have been thinking, oh yes, I might hef known"—all the time Janet was ever bringing something new out of the cupboard, though

Carmichael only sipped the milk. "And what wass your mother's name?"

"Farquharson; her people came from Braemar; but they are all dead now, and I am the last of the race."

"A good clan," cried Janet, in great spirits, "and a loyal; they were out with the Macphersons in the '45. Will you happen to know whether your ancestor suffered?"

"That he did, for he shot an English officer dead on his doorstep, and had to flee the country; it was not a pretty deed."

"Had the officer broken bread with him?" inquired Janet, anxiously.

"No, he had come to quarter himself and his men on him, and said something rude about the Prince."

"Your ancestor gave him back his word like a gentleman; but he would maybe hef to stay away for a while. Wass he of the chief's blood?"

"Oh no, just a little laird, and he lost his bit of land, and we never saw the place again."

"He would be a Dunniewassal, and proud it iss I am to see you in my house; and the Gaelic, will you hef some words?"

"Just the sound of it, Mrs. Macpherson," and he repeated his three sentences, all that he had learned of his mother, who had become a Scotswoman in her speech.

"Call me Janet, my dear; and it iss the good Gaelic your mother must have had, and it makes my heart glad to think my minister iss a Farquharson, by the mother's side."

"We sing nothing but Psalms at church, Mrs. . . . . Janet, so you will be pleased, and we stand to pray and sit to sing."

"Tuts, tuts, I am not minding about a bit hime at a time from a friend, but it iss those Lowlanders meddling with everything I do not like, and I am hoping to hear you sing again, for it wass a fery pretty tune;" and the smith, passing along the road when Carmichael left that evening, heard Janet call him "my dear," and invoke a thousand blessings on his head.

When he called again in the end of the week to cement the alliance and secure her presence on Sabbath, Janet was polishing the swords, and was willing enough to give their history.

"This wass my great-grandfather's, and these two nicks in the blade were made on the dragoons at Prestonpans; and this wass my husband's sword, for he wass sergeant-major before he died, a fery brave man, good at the fighting and the praying too.

"Maybe I am wrong, and I do not know what you may be thinking, but things come into my mind when I am reading the Bible, and I will be considering that it wass maybe not so good that the Apostles were fishing people."

"What ails you at fishermen, Janet?"

"Nothing at all but one thing; they are clever at their nets and at religion, but I am not hearing that they can play with the sword or the dirk.

"It wass a fery good intention that Peter had that night, no doubt, and I will be liking him for it when he took his sword to the policeman, but it wass a mighty poor blow. If Ian or his father had got as near as that, it would not have been an ear that would have been missing."

"Perhaps his head," suggested Carmichael.

"He would not have been putting his nose into honest

people's business again, at any rate," and Janet nodded her head as one who could see a downright blow that left no regrets; "it hass always made me ashamed to read about that ear.

"It wass not possible, and it iss maybe no good speaking about it now"—Janet felt she had a minister now she could open her mind to—"but it would hef been better if our Lord could hef had twelve Macphersons for His Apostles."

"You mean they would have been more brave and faithful?"

"There wass a price of six thousand pounds, or it might be four, put on Cluny's head after Culloden, and the English soldiers were all up and down the country, but I am not hearing that any clansman betrayed his chief.

"Thirty pieces of silver wass a fery small reward for such a dirty deed, and him one of the Chief's tail too; it wass a mistake to be trusting to fisher folk instead of Glen's men.

"There iss something I hef wished," concluded Janet, who seemed to have given her mind to the whole incident, "that Peter or some other man had drawn his skean-dhu and slippit it quietly into Judas. We would hef been respecting him fery much to-day, and it would hef been a good lesson—oh yes, a fery good lesson—to all traitors."

As they got more confidential, Janet began to speak of signs and dreams, and Carmichael asked her if she had the second sight.

"No; it iss not a lie I will be telling you, my dear, nor will I be boasting. I have not got it, nor had my mother, but she heard sounds, oh yes, and knew what wass coming to pass.

"'Janet,' she would say, 'I have heard the knock three times at the head of the bed; it will be your Uncle Alister, and I must go to see him before he dies.'"

"And was she —"

"Oh yes, she wass in time, and he wass expecting her; and once she saw the shroud begin to rise on her sister, but no more; it never covered the face before her eyes; but the knock, oh yes, many times."

"Have you known any one that could tell what was happening at a distance, and gave warning of danger?" for the latent Celt was awakening in Carmichael, with his love of mystery and his sense of the unseen.

"Listen, my dear" — Janet lowered her voice as one speaking of sacred things — "and I will tell you of Ina Macpherson, who lived to a hundred and two, and had the vision clear and sure.

"In the great war with Russia I wass staying in the clachan of my people, and then seven lads of our blood were with the Black Watch, and every Sabbath the minister would pray for them and the rest of the lads from Badenoch that were away at the fighting.

"One day Ina came into my sister's house, and she said, 'It iss danger that I am seeing,' and my heart stood still in my bosom for fear that it wass my own man Hamish.

"'No,' and she looked at me, 'not yet, and not to-day,' but more she would not say about him. 'Is it my son Ronald?' my sister cried, and Ina only looked before her. 'It's a sore travail, and round a few black tartans I see many men in grey, pressing them hard; ochone, ochone.'

"'It's time to pray,' I said, and there wass a man in

the clachan that wass mighty in prayer. and we gathered into his kitchen, four and twenty women and four men, and every one had a kinsman in the field.

"It iss this minute that I hear Dugald crying to the Almighty, 'Remember our lads, and be their help in the day of battle, and give them the necks of their enemies,' and he might be wrestling for half an hour, when Ina rose from her knees and said, 'The prayer is answered, for the tartans have the field, and I see blood on Ronald, but it is not his own.'"

"And did you ever hear—"

"Wait, my dear, and I will tell you, for the letter came from my nephew, and this is what he wrote:

"'It wass three to one, and the gloom came on me, for I thought that I would never see Glenfeshie again, nor the water of the loch, nor the deer on the side of the hill. Then I wass suddenly strengthened with all might in the inner man, and it iss five Russians that I hef killed to my own hands.'

"And so it wass, and a letter came from his captain, who wass of Cluny's blood, and it will be read in church, and a fery proud woman wass my sister."

These were the stories that Janet told to her minister in the days before the Carnegies came home, as well as afterwards, and so she prepared him to be an easier prey to a soldier's daughter.

CHAPTER IX.

A DAUGHTER OF DEBATE.

HEY met under the arch of the gate, and Carmichael returned with the Carnegies, Kate making much of him and insisting that he should stay to luncheon.

"You are our first visitor, Mr. Carmichael, and the General says that we need ·not expect more than six, so we mean to be very kind to them. Do you live far from here?"

"Quite near — just two miles west. I happened to be passing; in fact, I 'm going down to the next parish, and I . . . I thought that I would like to call and . . . and bid you welcome;" for Carmichael had not yet learned the art of conversation, which stands mainly in touching details lightly and avoiding the letter I.

"It is very cruel of you to be so honest and dispel our flattering illusions " — Kate marvelled at his mendacity — "we supposed you had come 'anes errand' — I 'm picking up Scotch — to call on your new neighbours. Does the high road pass the Lodge?"

"Oh no; the road is eight miles further; but the Drumtochty people take the near way through the woods; it's also much prettier. I hope you will not forbid us, General? two people a week is all the traffic."

"Forbid them — not I," said Carnegie, laughing. "A man is not born and bred in this parish without learning some sense. It would be a right of way case, and Drumtochty would follow me from court to court, and would never rest till they had gained or we were all ruined.

"Has it ever struck you, Mr. Carmichael, that one of the differences between a Highlander and a Scot is that each has got a pet enjoyment? With the one it's a feud, and with the other it's a lawsuit. A Scot dearly loves a 'ganging plea.'

"No, no; Tochty woods will be open so long as Kate and I have anything to say in the matter. The Glen and our people have not had the same politics, but we've lived at peace, as neighbours ought to do, with never a lawsuit even to give a fillip to life."

"So you see, Mr. Carmichael," said Kate, "you may come and go at all times through our territory; but it would be bare courtesy to call at the Lodge for afternoon tea."

"Or tiffin," suggested the General; "and we can always offer curry, as you see. My daughter has a capital recipe she wiled out of an old Hindoo rascal that cooked for our mess. You really need not take it on that account," as Carmichael was doing his best in much misery; "it is only meant to keep old Indians in fair humour — not to be a test of good manners. By the way, Janet has been sounding your praises; how have you won her heart?"

"Oh, very easily — by having some drops of Highland blood in my veins; and so I am forgiven all my faults, and am credited with all sorts of excellences."

"Then the Highlanders are as clannish as ever," cried the General. "Scotland has changed so much in the last half century that the Highlanders might have become quite unsentimental and matter-of-fact.

"Lowland civilisation only crossed the Highland line after '45, and it will take more than a hundred and thirty years to recast a Celt. Scottish education and theology are only a veneer on him, and below he has all his old instincts.

"So far as I can make out, a Celt will rather fish than plough, and be a gamekeeper than a workman; but if he be free to follow his own way, a genuine Highlander would rather be a soldier than anything else under the sun."

"What better could a man be?" and Kate's eyes sparkled; "they must envy the old times when their fathers raided the Lowlands and came home with the booty. It's a pity everybody is so respectable now, don't you think?"

"Certainly the police are very meddlesome," and Carmichael now devoted himself to Kate, without pretence of including the General; "but the spirit is not dead. A Celt is the child of generations of cattle-stealers, and the raiding spirit is still in the blood. May I offer an anecdote?"

"Six, if you have got so many, and they are all about Highlanders," and Kate leant forward and nursed her knee, for they had gone into the library.

"Last week I was passing the cattle market in Edinburgh, and a big Highland drover stopped me, begging for a little money.

"'It iss from Lochaber I hef come with some beasties, and to-morrow I will be walking back all the way, and it iss this night I hef no bed. I wass considering that the gardens would be a good place for a night, but they are telling me that the police will·be disturbing me.'

"He looked so simple and honest that I gave him half-a-crown and said that I was half a Highlander. I have three Gaelic sentences, and I reeled them off with my best accent.

"'Got forgive me,' he said, 'for thinking you to be a Sassenach body, and taking your money from you. You are a fery well-made man, and here iss your silver piece, and may you always hef one in your pocket.'

"'But what about your bed?'

"'Tuts, tuts, that will be all right, for I hef maybe got some six or five notes of my own that were profit on the beasties; but it iss a pity not to be taking anything that iss handy when a body happens to be in the south.'"

"Capital." Kate laughed merrily,. and her too rare laugh I used to think the gayest I ever heard. "It was the only opportunity left him of following his fathers. What a fine business it must have been, starting from Braemar one afternoon, a dozen men well armed, and getting down to Strathmore in the morning; then lying hid in some wood all day, and collecting a herd of fat cattle in the evening, and driving them up Glen Shee, not knowing when there might be a fight."

"Hard lines on the Scottish farmers, Kit, who might be very decent fellows, to lose their cattle or get a cut from a broadsword."

"Oh, they had plenty left; and seriously, dad, without joking, you know, what better could a Presbyterian Low-

"HERE ISS YOUR SILVER PIECE."

lander do than raise good beef for Highland gentlemen?
Mr. Carmichael, I beg pardon; you seem so good a
Celt, that I forgot you were not of our faith."

"We are not Catholics," the General explained,
gravely, "although many of our blood have been, and
my daughter was educated in a convent. We belong to
the Episcopal Church of Scotland, and will go into
Muirtown at a time, but mostly we shall attend the kirk
of my old friend Dr. Davidson. Every man is entitled
to his faith, and Miss Carnegie rather . . ."

"Forgot herself." Kate came to her father's relief.
"She often does; but one thing Miss Carnegie remem-
bers, and that is that General Carnegie likes his cheroot
after tiffin. Do you smoke, Mr. Carmichael? Oh, I
am allowed to stay, if you don't object, and have forgiven my rudeness."

"You make too much of a word, Miss Carnegie." Carmichael was not a man to take offence till his pride was
roused. "Very likely my drover was a true blue Presbyterian, and his minister as genuine a cateran as himself.

"Years ago I made the acquaintance of an old Highland minister called MacTavish, and he sometimes stays
with me on his way north in the spring. For thirty
years he has started at the first sign of snow, and spent
winter spoiling the good people of the south. Some
years he has gone home with three hundred pounds."

"But how does he get the money?" inquired the
General, "and what does he use it for?"

"He told me the history of his campaigns when he
passed in March, and it might interest you; it's our
modern raid, and although it's not so picturesque as a
foray of the Macphersons, yet it has points, and shows
the old spirit lives.

" ' She wass a goot woman, Janet Cameron, oh yes, Mr. John, a fery exercised woman, and when she wass dying she will be saying peautiful things, and one day she will be speaking of a little field she had beside the church.

" ' " What do you think I should be doing with that piece of ground," she will be saying, " for the end iss not far off, and it iss not earth I can be taking with me, oh no, nor cows."

" ' " No, Janet," I said, " but it iss a nice field, and lies to the sun.   It might be doing good after you are gone, if it wass not wasted on your mother's cousins twice removed in Inverness, who will be drinking every drop of it, and maybe going to the Moderate Kirk."

" ' It wass not for two months or maybe six weeks she died, and I will be visiting her every second day.   Her experiences were fery good, and I hef told them at sacraments in the north.   The people in the south are free with their money, but it iss not the best of my stories that I can give them ; they are too rich for their stomachs.

" ' Janet will often be saying to me, " Mister Dugald, it iss a thankful woman that I ought to be, for though I lost my man in the big storm and two sons in the war, I hef had mercies, oh yes.   There wass the Almighty and my cow, and between them I hef not wanted, oh no : they just did."

" ' " Janet, you will be forgetting your field that iss lying next the manse, and the people will be thinking that it iss a glebe ; but I am telling them that it iss Janet Cameron's, who iss a fery experienced woman, and hass nefer seen the inside of a Moderate Kirk since the Disruption."

" ' Maybe you will be astonished, Mister John, but when Janet's will will be read that piece of ground wass left to the Free Kirk, which wass fery kind and mindful of

Janet, and I made a sermon about her from the text of the " elect lady."

" ' It wass a good field, but it needed a dyke and some drains, and it wass not our people that had the money. So I made another sermon on the text, " The boar out of the wood doth waste it, and the wild beast of the field doth devour it," and went down to the south. It wass not a dyke and some drains, but enough to build a byre and a stable I came back with. That wass in '55, and before '60 there will be a new manse with twelve rooms that iss good for letting to the English people. But it wass ten years the church needed, and a year for the porch to keep it warm, for I am not liking stoves, and will not hef one in Crianshalloch.

" ' It iss wonderful how much money the bodies hef in Glasgow, and it iss good for them to be hearing sound doctrine at a time. There will be no Arminianism when I am preaching, and no joking; but maybe there will be some parables, oh yes, about the sheep coming in at the manse door for want of a fence, and the snow lying in the pulpit.'

" ' There is a cateran for you, and, mind you, a good fellow too. It 's not greed sends him out, but sheer love of spoil. Would you like to see MacTavish next time he passes up with the cattle? " for Carmichael was emboldened by the reception of his sketch.

" Nothing we should like better, for the General and I want to know all about Scotland; but don't you think that those ministers have injured the Highlanders? Janet, you know, has such gloomy ideas about religion."

" There is no doubt, Miss Carnegie, that a load of Saxon theology has been landed on the Celt, and it has disfigured his religion. Sometimes I have felt that the

Catholic of the west is a truer type of northern faith than the Presbyterian of Ross-shire."

"I am so glad to hear you say that," said Miss Carnegie, "for we had one or two west Catholics in the old regiment, and their superstitions were lovely. You remember, dad, the MacIvers."

"That was all well enough, Kit, but none of them could get the length of corporal; they were fearfully ignorant, and were reported at intervals for not keeping their accoutrements clean."

"That only showed how religious they were, did n't it, Mr. Carmichael? Had n't the early Christians a rooted objection to the bath? I remember our Padre saying that in a lecture."

"There are a good many modern Christians of the same mind, Miss Carnegie, and I don't think our poor Highlanders are worse than Lowlanders; but Catholic or Protestant, they are all subject to the gloom. I cannot give the Gaelic word.

"What is that? Oh, a southerner would call it depression, and assign it to the liver, for he traces all trouble to that source. But there is no word for this mood in English, because it is not an English experience. My mother fell under it at times, and I saw the effect."

"Tell us, please, if all this description does not weary you?" and Kate shone on Carmichael, who would have talked on the Council of Nice or the rotation of crops to prolong his privileges.

"It comes on quite suddenly, and is quite a spiritual matter — a cloud which descends and envelops the soul. While it lasts a Highlander will not laugh nor sing; he will hardly speak, and he loses all hope about everything. One of our men has the gloom at a time, and then he believes that he is . . . damned. I am speaking theologically."

"The regiment must have been fond of theology, dad Yes, we understand."

"Once he went out to the hill, and lay all night wrestling and agonising to be sure whether there was a God. You know he 's just a small farmer, and it seems to me splendid that such a man should give himself to the big problems of the universe. Do you know," and Carmichael turned to the General, who was smoking in great peace, "I believe that is the reason the Highlanders are such good fighting men. They fear God, and they don't fear any other person."

"I 'll vouch for one thing," said the veteran with emphasis; "our men put off the gloom, or whatever you call it, when they smelt powder; I never saw a panic in a Highland regiment in more than forty years' soldiering."

"What 's the reason of the gloom? I believe that I have a touch of it myself at times — don't stare at me, dad, it 's rude — just a thin mist, you know, but distinctly not indigestion. Is it a matter of race?"

"Of course, but that 's no explanation." Carmichael had fallen into his debating society style. "I mean one has to go further back; all our habits are shaped by environment."

"One moment, please. I have always wanted to ask some clever person what environment meant. I asked Colonel MacLeod once, dad, and he said it was out of the new book on tactics, and he was thankful he had retired. Now Mr. Carmichael will make it plain," and Kate was very demure.

"It is rather stupid to use the word so much as people do now," and Carmichael glanced dubiously at Kate; "scientific men use it for circumstances."

" Is that all? then do pray say environment. Such a word introduces one into good society, and gives one the feeling of being well dressed; now about a Highlander's environment, is it his kilt you are thinking of, or his house, or what? "

" His country " — and Carmichael's tone had a slight note of resentment, as of one ruffled by this frivolity — " with its sea lochs, and glens, and mists. Any one who has been bred and reared at the foot of one of our mountains will have a different nature and religion from one living in Kent or Italy. He has a sense of reverence, and surely that is a good thing."

" Nothing more needed nowadays," the General broke in with much spirit; " it seems to me that people nowadays respect nobody, neither the Queen nor Almighty God. As for that man Brimstone, he will never cease till he has ruined the Empire. You need n't look at me, Kate, for Mr. . . . Carmichael must know this as well as any other sensible man.

" Why, sir," and now the General was on his feet, " I was told on good authority at the club last week by a newspaper man — a monstrously clever man — that Mr. Brimstone, when he is going down to the House of Commons to disestablish the Church, or the army, or something, will call in at a shop and order two hundred silk hats to be sent to his house. What do you call that, sir? "

" I should call it a deliberate — "

" *Jeu d'esprit.* Of course it is, dad," and Kate threw an appealing glance to Carmichael, who had sprung to his feet and was standing stiffly behind his chair, for he was a fierce Radical.

"I SHOULD CALL IT A DELIBERATE —"

"Perhaps it was, lassie — those war correspondents used to be sad rascals — and, at any rate, politics are bad taste. Another cheroot, Mr. Carmichael? Oh, nonsense ; you must tell my daughter more about your Highlanders. They are a loyal set, at any rate, and we all admire that."

"Yes, they are," and Carmichael unbent again, "and will stick by their side whether it be right or wrong. They're something like a woman in their disposition."

"Indeed," said Kate, who did not think Carmichael had responded very courteously to her lead, "that is very interesting. They are, you mean, full of prejudices and notions."

"If a Highlander takes you into his friendship, you may say or do what you like, he will stand by you, and although his views are as different from yours as black from white, will swear he agrees with every one. If he's not your friend, he can see no good in anything you do, although you be on his own side."

"In fact, he has very little judgment and no sense of justice ; and I think you said," Kate went on sweetly, "his nature reminded you of a woman's?"

"You're sure that you like cheroots?" for the General did not wish this lad, Radical though he was, sacrificed on his first visit ; "some men are afraid of the opium in them."

"Please do not interrupt Mr. Carmichael when he is making a capital comparison," and Kate held him to the point.

"What I intend is really a compliment," went on Carmichael, "and shows the superior fineness and sensitiveness of a woman's mind."

Kate indicated that she was sure that was his meaning, but waited for details.

"You see," with the spirit of one still fresh to the pulpit, "a man is slower, and goes by evidence; a woman is quicker, and goes by her instincts."

"Like the lower animals," suggested Kate, sweetly, "by scent, perhaps. Well?"

"You are twisting my words, Miss Carnegie." Carmichael did not like being bantered by this self-possessed young woman. "Let me put it this way. Would a jury of women be as impartial as a jury of men? Why, a bad-looking man would have no chance, for they would condemn him at once, not for what he did, but for what they imagined he was."

"Which would save a lot of time and rid society of some precious scoundrels," with vivid recollections of her own efforts in this direction. "Then you grant that women have some intelligence, although no sense of justice, which is a want?"

"Far brighter than men," said Carmichael, eagerly; "just consider the difference between a man's and a woman's speech. A man arranges and argues from beginning to end, and is the slave of connection. He will labour every idea to exhaustion before he allows it to escape, and then will give a solemn cough by way of punctuating with a full stop, before he goes on to his next point. Of course the audience look at their watches and make for the door."

"What would a woman do?" Kate inquired with much interest.

"A lady was speaking lately at Muirtown for an orphanage at Ballyskiddle, and described how Patsy was rescued from starvation, and greatly affected us. 'Patsy

will never want bread again,' she concluded, and two
bailies wept aloud.

"Then she went on, and it seemed to me a stroke of
genius, 'Speaking about Patsy, has any lady present a
black dress suitable for a widow woman?' Before we
knew that we had left Patsy, the people were in a
widow's home, and the bailies were again overcome. I
mention them because it is supposed that a bailie is the
most important human being in Scotland, and he feels it
his duty not to yield to emotion.

"No, a woman speaker never sacrifices her capital;
she carries it with her from England to France in her
speech, and recognises no channel passage. In fact,"
and Carmichael plunged into new imagery, "a man's
progress is after the manner of a mole, while a woman
flits from branch to branch like a — "

"Squirrel — I know," came in Kate, getting tired.

"Bird, I meant. Why do you say squirrel?" and
Carmichael looked suspiciously at Kate.

"Because it's such a careless, senseless, irresponsible
little beast. Have you met many women, Mr. Carmichael? Really they are not all fools, as you have
been trying to suggest for the last ten minutes."

"Highlanders are a safer subject of conversation than
women," said the General, good-naturedly, as he bade
Carmichael good-bye. "And you must tell us more
about them next time you call, which I hope will be
soon."

Carmichael halted twice on his way through the
woods; once he stamped his foot and looked like a
man whose pride had been ruffled; the other time he
smiled to himself as one who was thinking of a future
pleasure.

It was dusk as he crossed Lynedoch Bridge, and he looked down upon the pool below where the trout were leaping. Half an hour passed, and then he started off at high speed for Kilbogie Manse. "Please God if 1 am worthy," he was saying to himself; "but I fear she is too high above me every way."

CHAPTER X.

A SUPRA-LAPSARIAN.

EREMIAH SAUNDERSON had remained in the low estate of a " probationer " for twelve years after he left the Divinity Hall, where he was reported so great a scholar that the Professor of Apologetics spoke to him deprecatingly, and the Professor of Dogmatics openly consulted him on obscure writers. He had wooed twenty-three congregations in vain, from churches in the black country where the colliers rose in squares of twenty and went out without ceremony, to suburban places of worship where the beadle, after due consideration of the sermon, would take up the afternoon notices and ask that they be read at once for purposes of utility, which that unflinching functionary stated to the minister with accuracy and much faithfulness. Vacant congregations desiring a list of candidates made one exception, and prayed that Jeremiah should not be let loose upon them, till at last it came home to the unfortunate scholar himself that he was an offence and a byeword. He began

to dread the ordeal of giving his name, and, as is still
told, declared to a household, living in the fat wheat
lands and without any imagination, that he was called
Magor Missabib. When a stranger makes a statement
of this kind with a sad seriousness, no one judges it
expedient to offer any remark, but it was skilfully arranged that Missabib's door should be locked from the
outside, and one member of the household sat up all
night. The sermon next day did not tend to confidence
— having seven quotations in unknown tongues — and
the attitude of the congregation was one of alert vigilance ; but no one gave any outward sign of uneasiness,
and six able-bodied men collected in a pew below the
pulpit knew their duty in an emergency.

Saunderson's election to the Free Church of Kilbogie
was therefore an event in the ecclesiastical world, and a
consistent tradition in the parish explained its inwardness
on certain grounds, complimentary both to the judgment
of Kilbogie and the gifts of Mr. Saunderson. On Saturday evening he was removed from the train by the
merest accident, and left the railway station in such a
maze of meditation that he ignored the road to Kilbogie
altogether, although its sign post was staring him in the
face, and continued his way to Drumtochty. It was half-
past nine when Jamie Soutar met him on the high road
through our Glen, still travelling steadily west, and being
arrested by his appearance, beguiled him into conversation, till he elicited that Saunderson was minded to reach
Kilbogie. For an hour did the wanderer rest in Jamie's
kitchen, during which he put Jamie's ecclesiastical history
into a state of thorough repair — making seven distinct
parallels between the errors that had afflicted the Scottish Church and the early heretical sects — and then

Jamie gave him in charge of a ploughman who was court-ing in Kilbogie and was not averse to a journey that seemed to illustrate the double meaning of charity. Jere-miah was handed over to his anxious hosts at a quarter to one in the morning, covered with mud, somewhat fatigued, but in great peace of soul, having settled the place of election in the prophecy of Habakkuk as he came down with his silent companion through Tochty woods.

Nor was that all he had done. When they came out from the shadow and struck into the parish of Kilbogie — whose fields, now yellow unto harvest, shone in the moonlight — his guide broke silence and enlarged on a plague of field-mice which had quite suddenly appeared and had sadly devastated the grain of Kilbogie. Saun-derson awoke from study and became exceedingly curi-ous, first of all demanding a particular account of the coming of the mice, their multitude, their habits, and their determination. Then he asked many questions about the moral conduct and godliness of the inhabitants of Kilbogie, which his companion, as a native of Drum-tochty, painted in gloomy colours, although indicating that even in Kilbogie there was a remnant. Next morn-ing the minister rose at daybreak, and was found wander-ing through the fields in such a state of excitement that he could hardly be induced to look at breakfast. When the "books" were placed before him, he turned promptly to the ten plagues of Egypt, which he expounded in order as preliminary to a full treatment of the visitations of Providence.

" He cowes (beats) a' ye ever saw or heard," the farmer of Mains explained to the elders at the gate. " He gaed tae bed at half twa and wes oot in the fields

by four, an' a 'm dootin' he never saw his bed. He 's
lifted abune the body a'thegither, an' can hardly keep
himsel' awa' frae the Hebrew at his breakfast. Ye 'll
get a sermon the day, or ma name is no Peter Pitillo."
Mains also declared his conviction that the invasion of
mice would be dealt with after a Scriptural and satisfying
fashion. The people went in full of expectation, and to
this day old people recall Jeremiah Saunderson's trial
sermon with lively admiration. Experienced critics were
suspicious of candidates who read lengthy chapters from
both Testaments and prayed at length for the Houses of
Parliament, for it was justly held that no man would take
refuge in such obvious devices for filling up the time
unless he was short of sermon material. One unfortunate, indeed, ruined his chances at once by a long peti-
tion for those in danger on the sea — availing himself
with some eloquence of the sympathetic imagery of the
107th Psalm — for this effort was regarded as not only
the most barefaced padding, but also as evidence of an
almost incredible blindness to circumstances. " Did he
think Kilbogie wes a fishing village? " Mains inquired
of the elders afterwards, with pointed sarcasm. Kilbogie
was not indifferent to a well-ordered prayer — although
its palate was coarser in the appreciation of felicitous
terms and allusions than that of Drumtochty — and
would have been scandalised if the Queen had been
omitted ; but it was by the sermon the young man must
stand or fall, and Kilbogie despised a man who post-
poned the ordeal.

Saunderson gave double pledges of capacity and fulness before he opened his mouth in the sermon, for he
read no Scripture at all that day, and had only one
prayer, which was mainly a statement of the Divine

Decrees and a careful confession of the sins of Kilbogie;
and then, having given out his text from the prophecy of
Joel, he reverently closed the Bible and placed it on the
seat behind him. His own reason for this proceeding
was a desire for absolute security in enforcing his subject,
and a painful remembrance of the disturbance in a south
country church when he landed a Bible — with clasps —
on the head of the precentor in the heat of a discourse
defending the rejection of Esau. Our best and simplest actions — and Jeremiah was as simple as a babe —
can be misconstrued, and the only dissentient from Saunderson's election insisted that the Bible had been deposited on the floor, and asserted that the object of this
profanity was to give the preacher a higher standing in
the pulpit. This malignant reading of circumstances
might have wrought mischief — for Saunderson's gaunt
figure did seem to grow in the pulpit — had it not been
for the bold line of defence taken up by Mains.

" Gin he wanted tae stand high, wes it no tae preach
the word? an' gin he wanted a soond foundation for his
feet, what better could he get than the twa Testaments?
Answer me that."

It was seen at once that no one could answer that,
and the captious objector never quite recovered his position in the parish, while it is not the least of Kilbogie's
boasting, in which the Auld Kirk will even join against
Drumtochty, that they have a minister who not only does
not read his sermons and does not need to quote his
texts, but carries the whole book in àt least three languages in his head, and once, as a proof thereof, preached
with it below his feet.

Much was to be looked for from such a man, but even
Mains, whetted by intercourse with Saunderson, was

astonished at the sermon. It was a happy beginning to draw a parallel between the locusts of Joel and the mice of Kilbogie, and gave the preacher an opportunity of describing the appearance, habits, and destruction of the locusts, which he did solely from Holy Scripture, translating various passages afresh and combining lights with marvellous ingenuity. This brief preface of half an hour, which was merely a stimulant for the Kilbogie appetite, led up to a thorough examination of physical judgments, during which both Bible and Church history were laid under liberal contribution. At this point the minister halted, and complimented the congregation on the attention they had given to the facts of the case, which were his first head, and suggested that before approaching the doctrine of visitations they might refresh themselves with a Psalm. The congregation were visibly impressed, and many made up their minds while singing:

" That man hath perfect blessedness ; "

and while others thought it due to themselves to suspend judgment till they had tasted the doctrine, they afterwards confessed their confidence. It goes without saying that he was immediately beyond the reach of the ordinary people on the second head, and even veterans in theology panted after him in vain, so that one of the elders, nodding assent to an exposure of the Manichæan heresy, suddenly blushed as one who had played the hypocrite. Some professed to have noticed a doctrine that had not been touched upon, but they never could give it a name, and it excited just admiration that a preacher, starting from a plague of mice, should have made a way by strictly scientific methods into the secret places of theology. Saunderson allowed his hearers a brief rest after the second head, and cheered them with the assurance that what was still before them would be easy to follow. It was the application of all that had gone before to the life of Kilbogie, and the preacher proceeded to convict the parish under each of the ten commandments — with the plague of mice ever in reserve to silence excuses —· till the delighted congregation could have risen in a body and taken Saunderson by the hand for his fearlessness and faithfulness. Perhaps the extent and thoroughness of this monumental sermon can be best estimated by the fact that Claypots, father of the present tenant, who always timed his rest to fifty minutes exactly, thus overseeing both the introduction and application of the sermon, had a double portion, and even a series of supplementary dozes, till at last he sat upright through sheer satiety. It may also be offered as evidence that the reserve of peppermint held by mothers for their bairns was pooled, doles being furtively passed across pews to conspicuously needy families, and yet the last had gone before Saunderson finished.

Mains reported to the congregational meeting that the minister had been quiet for the rest of the day, but had offered to say something about Habakkuk to any evening gathering, and had cleared up at family worship some obscure points in the morning discourse. He also informed the neighbours that he had driven his guest all the way to Muirtown, and put him in an Edinburgh carriage with his own hands, since it had emerged that Saunderson, through absence of mind, had made his down journey by the triangular route of Dundee. It was quite impossible for Kilbogie to conceal their pride in electing such a miracle of learning, and their bearing in Muirtown was distinctly changed; but indeed they

did not boast vainly about Jeremiah Saunderson, for his
career was throughout on the level of that monumental
sermon. When the Presbytery in the gaiety of their
heart examined Saunderson to ascertain whether he was
fully equipped for the work of the ministry, he professed
the whole Old Testament in Hebrew, and MacWheep of
Pitscowrie, who always asked the candidate to read the
twenty-third Psalm, was beguiled by Jeremiah into the
Book of Job, and reduced to the necessity of asking
questions by indicating verbs with his finger. His Greek
examination led to an argument between Jeremiah and
Dr. Dowbiggin on the use of the aorist, from which the
minister-elect of Kilbogie came out an easy first; and
his sermons were heard to within measurable distance
of the second head by an exact quorum of the exhausted
court, who were kept by the clerk sitting at the door,
and preventing MacWheep escaping. His position in
the court was assured from the beginning, and fulfilled
the function of an Encyclopædia with occasional amazing results, as when information was asked about some
Eastern sect for whose necessities the Presbytery were
asked to collect, and to whose warm piety affecting
allusion was made, and Jeremiah showed clearly, with
the reporters present, that the Cappadocians were guilty
of a heresy beside which Morisonianism was an un-
sullied whiteness. His work as examiner-in-general for
the court was a merciful failure, and encouraged the
students of the district to return to their district court,
who on the rumour of him had transferred themselves
in a body to a Highland Presbytery, where the standard
question in Philosophy used to be, " How many horns
has a dilemma, and distinguish the one from the other."
No man knew what the minister of Kilbogie might not
ask — he was only perfectly certain that it would be

beyond his knowledge; but as Saunderson always gave the answer himself in the end, and imputed it to the student, anxiety was reduced to a minimum. Saunderson, indeed, was in the custom of passing all candidates and reporting them as marvels of erudition, whose only fault was a becoming modesty — which, however, had not concealed from his keen eye hidden treasures of learning. Beyond this sphere the good man's services were not used by a body of shrewd ecclesiastics, as the inordinate length of an ordination sermon had ruined a dinner prepared for the court by " one of our intelligent and large-hearted laymen," and it is still pleasantly told how Saunderson was invited to a congregational *soirée* — an ancient meeting where the people ate oranges and the speaker rallied the minister on being still unmarried — and discoursed — as a carefully chosen subject — on the Jewish feasts, with illustrations from the Talmud, till some one burst a paper bag and allowed the feelings of the people to escape. When this history was passed round Muirtown Market, Kilbogie thought still more highly of their minister, and indicated their opinion of the other parish in severely theological language.

Saunderson's reputation for unfathomable learning and saintly simplicity was built up out of many incidents, and grew with the lapse of years to a solitary height in the big strath, so that no man would have dared to smile had the Free Kirk minister of Kilbogie appeared in Muirtown in his shirt sleeves, and Kilbogie would only have been a trifle more conceited. Truly he was an amazing man, and, now that he is dead and gone, the last of his race, I wish some man of his profession had written his life, for the doctrine he taught and the way he lived will not be believed by the new generation. The arrival of his goods was more than many sermons to Kilbogie, and I had it from Mains's own lips. It was the kindly fashion of those days that the farmers carted the new minister's furniture from the nearest railway station, and as the railway to Kildrummie was not yet open, they had to go to Stormont Station on the north line; and a pleasant procession they made passing through Pitscowrie, ten carts in their best array, and drivers with a semi-festive air. Mr. Saunderson was at the station, having reached it by some miracle without mistake, and was in a condition of abject nervousness about the handling and conveyance of his belongings.

"You will be careful — exceeding careful," he implored; "if one of the boxes were allowed to descend hurriedly to the ground, the result to what is within would be disastrous. I am much afraid that the weight is considerable, but I am ready to assist;" and he got ready.

"Dinna pit yirsel' intae a ferry farry (commotion)," but Mains was distinctly pleased to see a little touch of worldliness, just enough to keep the new minister in touch with humanity. "It 'll be queer stuff oor lads canna lift, an' a 'll gie ye a warranty that the' 'll no be a cup o' the cheeny broken;" and then Saunderson conducted his congregation to the siding.

"Dod, man," remarked Mains to the station-master, examining a truck with eight boxes; "the manse 'll no want for dishes at ony rate; but let 's start on the furniture; whar hae ye got the rest o' the plenishing?

"Naething mair? havers, man, ye dinna mean tae say they pack beds an' tables in boxes; a' doot there 's a truck missin'." Then Mains went over where the minister was fidgeting beside his possessions.

"No, no," said Saunderson, when the situation was put before him, "it's all here. I counted the boxes, and I packed every box myself. That top one contains the fathers — deal gently with it; and the Reformation divines are just below it. Books are easily injured, and they feel it. I do believe there is a certain life in them, and . . . and . . . they don't like being ill-used," and Jeremiah looked wistfully at the ploughmen.

"Div ye mean tae say," as soon as Mains had recovered, "that ye 've brocht naethin' for the manse but bukes, naither bed nor bedding? Keep's a'," as the situation grew upon him, "whar are ye tae sleep, and what are ye to sit on? An' div ye never eat? This croons a';" and Mains gazed at his new minister as one who supposed that he had taken Jeremiah's measure and had failed utterly.

"*Mea culpa* — it's . . . my blame," and Saunderson was evidently humbled at this public exposure of his incapacity; "some slight furnishing will be expedient, even necessary, and I have a plan for book-shelves in my head; it is ingenious and convenient, and if there is a worker in wood . . ."

"Come awa' tae the dog-cart, sir," said Mains, realising that even Kilbogie did not know what a singular gift they had obtained, and that discussion on such sublunary matters as pots and pans was useless, not to say profane. So eight carts got a box each; one, Jeremiah's ancient kist of moderate dimensions; and the tenth — that none might be left unrecognised — a handbag that had been on the twelve years' probation with its master. The story grew as it passed westwards, and when it reached us we were given to understand that the Free Kirk minister of Kilbogie had come to his parish with his clothing in a paper parcel and twenty-four packing cases filled with books, in as many languages — half of them dating from the introduction of printing, and fastened by silver clasps — and that if Drumtochty seriously desired to hear an intellectual sermon at a time, we must take our way through Tochty woods.

Mrs. Pitillo took the minister into her hands, and compelled him to accompany her to Muirtown, where she had him at her will for some time, so that she equipped the kitchen (fully), a dining-room (fairly), a spare bedroom (amply), Mr. Saunderson's own bedroom (miserably), and secured a table and two chairs for the study. This success turned her head. Full of motherly forethought, and having a keen remembrance that probationers always retired in the afternoon at Mains to think over the evening's address, and left an impress of the human form on the bed when they came down to tea, Mrs. Pitillo suggested that a sofa would be an admirable addition to the study. As soon as this piece of furniture, of a size suitable for his six feet, was pointed out to the minister, he took fright, and became quite unmanageable. He would not have such an article in his study on any account, partly because it would only feed a tendency to sloth — which, he explained, was one of his besetting sins — and partly because it would curtail the space available for books, which, he indicated, were the proper furniture of any room, but chiefly of a study. So great was his alarm that he repented of too early concessions about the other rooms, and explained to Mrs. Pitillo that every inch of space must be rigidly kept for the overflow from the study, which he expected — if he were spared — would reach the garrets. Several times on their way back to Kilbogie, Saunderson looked wistfully at Mrs. Pitillo, and once opened his mouth as if to speak, from which she gathered that he was grateful for her kindness, but dared not yield any farther to the luxuries of the flesh.

What this worthy woman endured in securing a succession of reliable housekeepers for Mr. Saunderson and overseeing the interior of that remarkable home, she was never able to explain to her own satisfaction, though she made many honest efforts, and one of her last intelligible utterances was a lamentable prophecy of the final estate of the Free Church manse of Kilbogie. Mr. Saunderson himself seemed at times to have some vague idea of her painful services, and once mentioned her name to Carmichael in feeling terms. There had been some delay in providing for the bodily wants of the visitor after his eight miles' walk from Drumtochty, and it seemed likely that he would be obliged to take his meal standing for want of a chair.

"While Mrs. Pitillo lived, I have a strong impression, almost amounting to certainty, that the domestic arrangements of the manse were better ordered; she had the episcopal faculty in quite a conspicuous degree, and was, I have often thought, a woman of sound judgment.

"We were not able at all times to see eye to eye, as she had an unfortunate tendency to meddle with my books and papers, and to arrange them after an artificial fashion. This she called tidying, and, in its most extreme form, cleaning.

"With all her excellencies, there was also in her what I have noticed in most women, a certain flavour of guile, and on one occasion, when I was making a brief journey through Holland and France in search of comely editions of the fathers, she had the books carried out

"SHE HAD AN UNFORTUNATE TENDENCY TO MEDDLE WITH MY BOOKS."

to the garden and dusted. It was the space of two years before I regained mastery of my library again, and unto this day I cannot lay my hands on the service book of King Henry VIII., which I had in the second edition, to say nothing of an original edition of Rutherford's *Lex Rex*.

" It does not become me, however, to reflect on the efforts of that worthy matron, for she was by nature a good woman, and if any one could be saved by good works, her place is assured. I was with her before she died, and her last words to me were, 'Tell Jean tae dust yir bukes aince in the sax months, and for ony sake keep ae chair for sittin' on.' It was not the testimony one would have desired in the circumstances, but yet, Mr. Carmichael, I have often thought that there was a spirit of . . . of unselfishness, in fact, that showed the working of grace." Later in the same evening Mr. Saunderson's mind returned to his friend's spiritual state, for he entered into a long argument to show that while Mary was more spiritual, Martha must also have been within the Divine Election.

CHAPTER XI.

IN THE GLOAMING.

UGUST is our summer time in the north, and Carmichael found it pleasant walking from Lynedoch bridge to Kilbogie. The softness of the gloaming, and the freshness of the falling dew, and the scent of the honeysuckle in the hedge, and the smell of the cut corn in the fields — for harvest is earlier down there than with us — and the cattle chewing the cud, and the sheltering shadow of old beech trees, shed peace upon him and touched the young minister's imagination. Fancies he may have had in early youth, but he had never loved any woman except his mother and his aunt. There had been times when he and his set declared they would never marry, and one, whose heart was understood to be blighted, had drawn up the constitution of a celibate Union. It was never completed — and therefore never signed — because the brotherhood could not agree about the duration of the vows — the draftsman, who has been twice married since then, standing stiffly for their perpetuity, while the others considered that a dispensing power might be lodged in the Moderator of Assembly.

This railing against marriage on the part of his friends was pure boyishness, and they all were engaged on the mere prospect of a kirk, but Carmichael had more of a mind on the matter. There was in him an ascetic bent, inherited from some Catholic ancestor, and he was almost convinced that a minister would serve God with more abandonment in the celibate state. As an only child, and brought up by a mother given to noble thoughts, he had learned to set women in a place by themselves, and considered marriage for ordinary men to flavour of sacrilege. His mother had bound it as a law upon him that he was never to exercise his tongue on a woman's failings, never to argue with a woman unto her embarrassment, never to regard her otherwise than as his superior. Women noticed that Carmichael bore himself to them as if each were a Madonna, and treated him in turn according to their nature. Some were abashed, and could not understand the lad's shyness; those were saints. Some were amused, and suspected him of sarcasm; those were less than saints. Some horrified him unto confusion of face because of the shameful things they said. One middle-aged female, whose conversation oscillated between physiology and rescue work, compelled Carmichael to sue for mercy on the ground that he had not been accustomed to speak about such details of life with a woman, and ever afterwards described him as a prude. It seemed to Carmichael that he was disliked by some women because he thought more highly of them than they thought of themselves.

Carmichael was much tried by the baser of his fellow-students, especially a certain class of smug, self-contented, unctuous men, who neither had endured hardship to get to college, nor did any work at college. They were described in reports as the "fruits of the revival," and had been taken from behind counters and sent to the University, not because they had any love of letters, like Domsie's lads at Drumtochty, but because rich old ladies were much impressed by the young men's talk, and the young men were perfectly aware that they would be better off in the ministry than in any situation they could gain by their own merits. As Carmichael grew older, and therefore more charitable, he discovered with what faulty tools the work of the world and even of kirks is carried on, and how there is a root of good in very coarse and common souls. When he was a young judge — from whom may the Eternal deliver us all — he was bitter against the "fruits," as he called them, because they did their best to escape examinations, and spoke in a falsetto voice, and had no interest in dogs, and because they told incredible tales of their spiritual achievements. But chiefly did Carmichael's gorge rise against those unfortunates because of the mean way they spoke of marriage, and on this account, being a high-spirited young fellow, he said things which could hardly be defended, and of which afterwards he honestly repented.

"Yes, religion is profitable for both worlds," one of them would exhort by the junior common-room fire, "and if you doubt it, look at me; five-and-twenty shillings a week as a draper's assistant was all I had, and no chance of rising. Now I 'm a gentleman " — here Carmichael used to look at the uncleanly little man and snort — "and in two years I could ask any girl in religious society, and she would take me. A minister can marry any woman, if he be evangelical. Ah," he would conclude, with a fine strain of piety, "the Gospel is its own reward."

What enraged Carmichael as he listened in the distance to these pæans of Pharisaism was the disgusting fact that the "fruits" did carry off great spoil in the marriage field, so that to a minister without culture, manners, or manliness, a middle-class family would give their pet daughter, when they would have refused her to a ten times better man fighting his way up in commerce. If she died, then this enterprising buccaneer would achieve a second and third conquest, till in old age he would rival the patriarchs in the number of his wives and possessions. As for the girl, Carmichael concluded that she was still under the glamour of an ancient superstition, and took the veil after a very commonplace and squalid Protestant fashion. This particular "fruit" against whom Carmichael in his young uncharitableness especially raged, because he was more self-complacent and more illiterate than his fellows, married the daughter of a rich self-made man, and on the father's death developed a peculiar form of throat disease, which laid him aside from the active work of the ministry — a mysterious providence, as he often explained — but allowed him to enjoy life with a guarded satisfaction. What Carmichael said to him about his ways and his Gospel was very unpleasant and quite unlike Carmichael's kindly nature, but the only revenge the victim took was to state his conviction that Scotland would have nothing to do with a man that was utterly worldly, and in after years to warn vacant churches against one who did not preach the Cross.

After one of those common-room encounters, Carmichael used to fling himself out into the east wind and greyness of Edinburgh, fuming against the simplicity of good people, against the provincialism of his college, against the Pharisaism of his church, against the Philistinism of Scottish life. He would go down to Holyrood and pity Queen Mary, transported from the gay court of France to Knox's Scotland, divided between theology and bloodshed. In the evening he would sweep his table clean of German books on the Pentateuch, and cover it with prints of the old masters, which he had begun to collect, and ancient books of Catholic devotion, and read two letters to his mother from her uncle, who had been a Vicar-General, and died in an old Scottish convent in Spain. There was very little in the letters beyond good wishes, and an account of the Vicar-General's health, but they seemed to link a Free Kirk divinity student on to the Holy Catholic Church. Mother Church cast her spell over his imagination, and he envied the lot of her priests, who held a commission no man denied and administered a world-wide worship, whom a splendid tradition sanctioned, whom each of the arts hastened to aid; while he was to be the minister of a local sect and work with the "fruits," who knew nothing of Catholic Christianity, but supposed their little eddy, whereon they danced like rotten sticks, to be the main stream. Next day a reaction would set in, and Carmichael would have a fit of Bohemianism, and resolve to be a man of letters. So the big books on theology would again be set aside, and he would write an article for *Ferrier's Journal*, that kindliest of all journals to the young author, which he would receive back in a week " with thanks." The Sunday night came, and Carmichael sat down to write his weekly letter to his mother — she got notes

between, he found them all in her drawers, not a scrap
missing — and as he wrote, his prejudices, and petu-
lances, and fancies, and unrest passed away.   Before he

MOTHER CHURCH CAST HER SPELL OVER HIS
IMAGINATION.

had told her all that happened to him during the week —
touching gently on the poor Revivalist — although his
mother had a saving sense of humour, and was a quite
wonderful mimic — and saying nothing of his evening

with St. Francis de Sales — for this would have alarmed
her at once — he knew perfectly well that he would be
neither a Roman nor a reporter, but a Free Kirk minister, and was not utterly cast down ; for notwithstanding
the yeasty commotion of youth and its censoriousness,
he had a shrewd idea that a man is likely to do his life-
work best in the tradition of his faith and blood. Next
morning his heart warmed as he went in through the
college gates, and he would have defended Knox unto
the death, as the maker of Scotland. His fellow-students
seemed now a very honest set of men, as indeed they
were, although a trifle limited in horizon, and he hoped
that one of the " fruits " was " satisfied with his Sunday's
work," which shows that as often as a man of twenty-one
gets out of touch with reality, he ought straightway to
sit down and write to his mother. Carmichael indeed
told me one evening at the Cottage that he never had
any mystical call to the ministry, but only had entered
the Divinity Hall instead of going to Oxford because his
mother had this for her heart's desire, and he loved her.
As a layman it perhaps did not become me to judge
mysteries, but I dared to say that any man might well
be guided by his mother in religion, and that the closer
he kept to her memory the better he would do his work.
After which both of us smoked furiously, and Carmichael,
two minutes later, was moved to remark that some Turk-
ish I had then was enough to lure a man up Glen Urtach
in the month of December.

The young minister was stirred on the way to Kilbogie, and began to dream dreams in the twilight. Love
had come suddenly to him, and after an unexpected
fashion. Miss Carnegie was of another rank and another
faith, nor was she even his ideal woman, neither con-

spicuously spiritual nor gentle, but frank, outspoken, fearless, self-willed. He could also see that she had been spoiled by her father and his friends, who had given her *carte blanche* to say and do what she pleased. Very likely — he could admit that even in the first blush of his emotion — she might be passionate and prejudiced on occasion, even a fierce hater. This he had imagined in the Tochty woods, and was not afraid, for her imperfections seemed to him a provocation and an attraction. They were the defects of her qualities — of her courage, candour, generosity, affection. Carmichael leant upon a stile, and recalled the carriage of her head, the quick flash of her eye, the tap of her foot, the fascination of her manner. She was free from the affectations, gaucheries, commonplaces, wearinesses of many good women he had known. St. Theresa had been the woman enshrined in the tabernacle of his heart, but life might have been a trifle tiresome if a man were married to a saint. The saints have no humour, and do not relax. Life with a woman like Miss Carnegie would be effervescent and stimulating, full of surprises and piquancy. No, she was not a saint, but he felt by an instinct she was pure, loyal, reverent, and true at the core. She was a gallant lass, and . . . he loved her.

What an absurdity was this revery, and Carmichael laughed aloud at himself. Twice he had met Miss Carnegie — on one occasion she had found him watering strange dogs out of his hat, and on the other he had given her to understand that women were little removed from fools. He had made the worst of himself, and this young woman who had lived with smart people must have laughed at him. Very likely she had made him into a story, for as a raconteur himself he knew the temptation to work up raw material, or perhaps Miss Carnegie had forgotten long ago that he had called. Suppose that he should call to-morrow on his way home and say, "General Carnegie, I think it right to tell you that I admire your daughter very much, and should like your permission to pay my addresses. I am Free Church minister in Drumtochty, and my stipend is £200 a year" . . . his laugh this time was rather bitter. The Carnegies would be at once admitted into the county set, and he would only meet them at a time . . . Lord Hay was a handsome and pleasant young fellow. He would be at Glen Urtach House for the shooting in a few days . . . that was a likely thing to happen . . . the families were old friends . . . there would be great festivities in the Glen . . . perhaps he would be asked to propose the bride's health . . . It really seemed a providence that Saunderson should come along the road when he was playing the fool like a puling boy, for if any man could give a douche to love-sickness it was the minister of Kilbogie.

Carmichael was standing in the shadow as Saunderson came along the road, and the faint light was a perfect atmosphere for the dear old bookman. Standing at his full height he might have been six feet, but with much poring over books and meditation he had descended some three inches. His hair was long, not because he made any conscious claim to genius, but because he forgot to get it cut, and with his flowing, untrimmed beard, was now quite grey. Within his clothes he was the merest skeleton, being so thin that his shoulder-blades stood out in sharp outline, and his hands were almost transparent. The redeeming feature in Saunderson was his eyes, which were large and eloquent, of a trustful, wistful hazel, the beautiful eyes of a dumb animal. Whether he was expounding doctrines of an incredible disbelief in humanity or exalting, in rare moments, the riches of a divine love in which he did not expect to share, or humbly beseeching his brethren to give him information on some point in scholarship no one knew anything about except himself, or stroking the hair of some little child sitting upon his knee, those eyes were ever simple, honest, and most pathetic. Young ministers coming to the Presbytery full of self-conceit and new views were arrested by their light shining through the glasses, and came in a year or two to have a profound regard for Saunderson, curiously compounded of amusement at his ways, which for strangeness were quite beyond imagination, admiration for his knowledge, which was amazing for its accuracy and comprehensiveness, respect for his honesty, which feared no conclusion, however repellent to flesh and blood, but chiefly of love for the unaffected and shining goodness of a man in whose virgin soul neither self nor this world had any part. For years the youngsters of the Presbytery knew not how to address the minister of Kilbogie, since any one who had dared to call him Saunderson, as they said "Carmichael" and even "MacWheep," though he was elderly, would have been deposed, without delay, from the ministry — so much reverence at least was in the lads — and "Mister" attached to this personality would be like a silk hat on the head of an Eastern sage. Jenkins of Pitrodie always considered that he was inspired when he one day called Saunderson "Rabbi," and unto the day of his death Kilbogie was so called. He made protest against the title as being forbidden in the Gospels, but the lads insisted that it must be understood in

the sense of scholar, whereupon Saunderson disowned it
on the ground of his slender attainments. The lads saw
the force of this objection, and admitted that the
honourable word belonged by rights to MacWheep, but
it was their fancy to assign it to Saunderson — whereat
Saunderson yielded, only exacting a pledge that he
should never be so called in public, lest all concerned be
condemned for foolishness. When it was announced
that the University of Edinburgh had resolved to confer
the degree of D. D. on him for his distinguished learning
and great services to theological scholarship, Saunderson,
who was delighted when Dowbiggin of Muirtown got the
honour for being an ecclesiastic, would have refused it
for himself had not his boys gone out in a body and
compelled him to accept. They also purchased a
Doctor's gown and hood, and invested him with them in
the name of Kilbogie two days before the capping.
One of them saw that he was duly brought to the Tol-
booth Kirk, where the capping ceremonial in those days
took place. Another sent a list of Saunderson's articles
to British and foreign theological and philological re-
views, which filled half a column of the *Caledonian*, and
drew forth a complimentary article from that exceedingly
able and caustic paper, whose editor lost all his hair
through sympathetic emotion the morning of the Disruption, and ever afterwards pointed out the faults of the
Free Kirk with much frankness. The fame of Rabbi
Saunderson was so spread abroad that a great cheer went
up as he came in with the other Doctors elect, in which
he cordially joined, considering it to be intended for his
neighbour, a successful West-end clergyman, the author
of a *Life of Dorcas* and other pleasing booklets. For
some time after his boys said " Doctor " in every third

sentence, and then grew weary of a too common title, and fell back on Rabbi, by which he was known unto the day of his death, and which is now engraved on his tombstone.

The Rabbi was tasting some morsel of literature as he came along, and halted opposite Carmichael, whom he did not see in the shadow, that he might enjoy it aloud.

"That is French verse, Rabbi, I think, but it sounds archaic; is it from a Huguenot poet?"

"Assuredly," replied the Rabbi, not one whit astonished that a man should come out from a hedge on Kilbogie road and recognise his quotation; "from Clement Marot, whom, as you remember, there is good evidence Queen Mary used to read. It is you, John Carmichael." The Rabbi awoke from the past, and held Carmichael's hand in both of his. "This was very mindful. You were going home from Pitscowrie and turned aside to visit me.

"It is unfortunate that I am hastening to a farm called the Mains, on the border of Pitscourie parish, to expound the Word; but you will go on to the Manse and straitly charge Barbara to give you food, and I will hasten to return." And the Rabbi looked forward to the night with great satisfaction.

"No, I am not coming from Pitscowrie, and you are not going there, as far as one can see. Why, you are on your way to Tochty woods; you are going west instead of east; Rabbi, tell the truth, have you been snuffing?"

This was a searching question, and full of history. When the Rabbi turned his back against the wind to snuff with greater comfort, he was not careful to resume his original position, but continued cheerfully in the new direction. This weakness was so well known that the

school bairns would watch till he had started, and stand
in a row on the road to block his progress. Then there
would be a parley, which would end in the Rabbi capit-
ulating and rewarding the children with peppermints,
whereupon they would see him fairly off again and go on
their way — often looking back to see that he was safe,
and somehow loving him all the more for his strange
ways. So much indeed was the Rabbi beloved that a
Pitscowrie laddie, who described Saunderson freely as a
"daftie" to Mains' grandson, did not see clearly for
a week, and never recovered his lost front tooth.

"That," remarked young Mains, " 'll learn Pitscowrie
tae set up impidence aboot the minister."

"There is no doubt that I snuffed — it was at
Claypots steading — but there was no wind that I
should turn. This is very remarkable, John, and . . .
disconcerting.

"These humiliations are doubtless a lesson," resumed
the Rabbi as they hurried to Mains, "and a rebuke.
Snuffing is in no sen.e a necessity, and I have long
recognised that the habit requires to be restricted —
very carefully restricted. For some time I have had
fixed times — once in the forenoon, once in the afternoon, and again in the evening. Had I restrained myself till my work was over and I had returned home
this misadventure would not have occurred, whereby I
have been hindered and the people will have been kept
waiting for their spiritual food.

"It is exactly twenty years to-night since I began this
meeting in Mains," the Rabbi explained to Carmichael,
"and I have had great pleasure in it and some profit.
My subject has been the Epistle to the Romans, and by
the goodness of God we are approaching the last chap-

ters. The salutations will take about a year or so;
Rufus, chosen in the Lord, will need careful treatment;
and then I thought, if I were spared, of giving another
year to a brief review of the leading points of doctrine;
eh?"

Carmichael indicated that the family at Mains would
almost expect something of the sort, and inquired
whether there might not be a few passages requiring
separate treatment at fuller length than was possible in
this hurried commentary.

"Quite so, John, quite so; no one is more bitterly
conscious of the defects of this exposition than myself—
meagre and superficial to a degree, both in the patristic
references and the experimental application; but we are
frail creatures, John, and it is doubtful whether the exposition of any book should extend unto a generation.
It has always caused me regret that Mains — I mean the
father of the present tenant — departed before we had
come to the comfort of the eighth chapter."

The Rabbi's mind was much affected by this thought,
and twice in the kitchen his eye wandered to the chair
where his friend had sat, with his wife beside him. From
Priscilla and Aquila he was led into the question of hospitality, on which he spoke afterwards till they came to
the Manse, where he stationed Carmichael on the door-
step till he secured a light.

"There is a parcel of books on the floor, partially
opened, and the way of passing is narrow and somewhat
dangerous in the darkness."

CHAPTER XII.

INISTERS there were in the great strath so orderly that they kept their sealing-wax in one drawer and their string in another, while their sermons were arranged under the books of the Bible, and tied with green silk. Dr. Dowbiggin, though a dull man and of a heavy carriage, could find in an instant the original draft of a motion on instrumental music he made in the Presbytery of Muirtown in the year '59, and could also give the exact page in the blue-books for every word he had uttered in the famous case when he showed that the use of a harmonium to train MacWheep's choir was a return to the bondage of Old Testament worship. His collection of pamphlets was supposed to be unique, and was a terror to controversialists, no man knowing when a rash utterance on the bottomless mystery of "spiritual independence" might not be produced from the Doctor's coat-tail pocket. He retired to rest at 10.15, and rose at six, settling the subject of his next sermon on Sabbath evening, and finishing the first head before breakfast on Monday morning. He had three hats — one for funerals, one for marriages, one for ordinary occasions — and has returned from the Presbytery door to brush his coat. Morning prayers in Dr. Dowbiggin's house were at 8.05, and the wrath of the Doctor was so dangerous that one probationer staying at the manse, and not quite independent of influence, did not venture to undress, but snatched a fearful doze sitting upright on a cane-bottomed chair, lest he should not be in at the psalm. Young ministers of untidy habits regarded Dr. Dowbiggin's study with despair, and did not recover their spirits till they were out of Muirtown. Once only did this eminent man visit the manse of Kilbogie, and in favourable moments after dinner he would give his choicer experiences.

"It is my invariable custom to examine the bed to see that everything is in order, and any one sleeping in Kilbogie Manse will find the good of such a precaution. I trust that I am not a luxurious person — it would ill become one who came out in '43 — but I have certainly become accustomed to the use of sheets. When I saw there were none on the bed, I declined to sleep without them, and I indicated my mind very distinctly on the condition of the manse.

"Would you believe it?" the Doctor used to go on. "Saunderson explained, as if it were a usual occurrence, that he had given away all the spare linen in his house to a girl that had to marry in . . . urgent circumstances, and had forgotten to get more. And what do you think did he offer as a substitute for sheets?" No one could even imagine what might not occur to the mind of Saunderson.

"Towels, as I am an honourable man ; a collection of towels, as he put it, 'skilfully attached together, might make a pleasant covering.' That is the first and last time I ever slept in the Free Church Manse of Kilbogie. As regards Saunderson's study, I will guarantee that the like of it cannot be found within Scotland," and at the very thought of it that exact and methodical ecclesiastic realised the limitations of language.

His boys boasted of the Rabbi's study as something that touched genius in its magnificent disorderliness, and Carmichael was so proud of it that he took me to see it as to a shrine. One whiff of its atmosphere as you entered the door gave an appetite and raised the highest expectations. For any bookman can estimate a library by scent — if an expert he could even write out a catalogue of the books and sketch the appearance of the owner. Heavy odour of polished mahogany, Brussels carpets, damask curtains and tablecloths ; then the books are kept within glass, consist of sets of standard works in half calf, and the owner will give you their cost wholesale to a farthing. Faint fragrance of delicate flowers, and Russia leather, with a hint of cigarettes ; prepare yourself for a marvellous wall-paper, etchings, bits of oak, limited editions, and a man in a velvet coat. Smell of paste and cloth binding and general newness means yesterday's books and a man racing through novels with a paper knife. Those are only book-rooms by courtesy, and never can satisfy any one who has breathed the sacred air. It is a rich and strong spirit, not only filling the room, but pouring out from the door and possessing the hall, redeeming an opposite dining-room from grossness, and a more distant drawing-room from frivolity, and even lending a goodly flavour to bedrooms on upper floors. It is distilled from curious old duodecimos packed on high shelves out of sight, and blows over folios, with large clasps, that once stood in monastery libraries, and gathers a subtle sweetness from parchments that were illuminated in ancient scriptoriums, that are now grass grown, and is fortified with good old musty calf. The wind was from the right quarter on the first day I visited Kilbogie Manse, and as we went up the garden walk the Rabbi's library already bade us welcome, and assured us of our reward for a ten miles' walk.

Saunderson was perfectly helpless in all manner of mechanics — he could not drive a tack through anything except his own fingers, and had given up shaving at the suggestion of his elders — and yet he boasted, with truth, that he had got three times as many books into the study as his predecessor possessed in all his house. For Saunderson had shelved the walls from the floor to the ceiling, into every corner and over the doors, and above the windows, as well as below them. The wright had wished to leave the space clear above the mantelpiece.

"Ye'll be hanging Dr. Chalmers there, or maybe John Knox, and a bit clock 'll be handy for letting ye ken the 'oors on Sabbath."

The Rabbi admitted that he had a Knox, but was full of a scheme for hanging him over his own history, which he considered both appropriate and convenient. As regards time, it was the last thing of which that worthy man desired to be reminded — going to bed when he could no longer see for weariness, and rising as soon as he awoke, taking his food when it was brought to him, and being conducted to church by the beadle after the last straggler was safely seated. He even cast covetous eyes upon the two windows, which were absurdly large, as he considered, but compromised matters by removing the shutters and filling up the vacant space with slender works

"YE 'LL BE HANGING DR. CHALMERS THERE."

of devotion. It was one of his conceits that the rising sun smote first on an À Kempis, for this he had often noticed as he worked of a morning.

Book-shelves had long ago failed to accommodate

Rabbi's treasures, and the floor had been bravely utilised. Islands of books, rugged and perpendicular, rose on every side; long promontories reached out from the shore, varied by bold headlands; and so broken and varied was that floor that the Rabbi was pleased to call it the Ægean Sea, where he had his Lesbos and his Samos. It is absolutely incredible, but it is all the same a simple fact, that he knew every book and its location, having a sense of the feel as well as the shape of his favourites. This was not because he had the faintest approach to orderliness — for he would take down twenty volumes and never restore them to the same place by any chance. It was a sort of motherly instinct by which he watched over them all, even loved prodigals that wandered over all the study and then set off on adventurous journeys into distant rooms. The restoration of an emigrant to his lawful home was celebrated by a feast in which, by a confusion of circumstances, the book played the part of the fatted calf, being read afresh from beginning to end. During his earlier and more agile years the Rabbi used to reach the higher levels of his study by wonderful gymnastic feats, but after two falls — one with three Ante-Nicene fathers in close pursuit — he determined to call in assistance. This he did after an impressive fashion. When he attended the roup at Pitfoodles — a day of historical prices — and purchased in open competition, at three times its value, a small stack ladder, Kilbogie was convulsed, and Mains had to offer explanations.

"He 's cuttit aff seevin feet, and rins up it tae get his tapmaist bukes, but that 's no a'," and then Mains gave it to be understood that the rest of the things the minister had done with that ladder were beyond words. For in order that the rough wood might not scar the sensitive backs of the fathers, the Rabbi had covered the upper end with cloth, and for that purpose had utilised a pair of trousers. It was not within his ability in any way to reduce or adapt his material, so that those interesting garments remained in their original shape, and, as often as the ladder stood reversed, presented a very impressive and diverting spectacle. It was the inspiration of one of Carmichael's most successful stories — how he had done his best to console a woman on the death of her husband, and had not altogether failed, till she caught sight of the deceased's nether garments waving disconsolately on a rope in the garden, when she refused to be comforted. "Toom (empty) breeks tae me noo," and she wept profusely, "toom breeks tae me."

One of the great efforts of the Rabbi's life was to seat his visitors, since, beyond the one chair, accommodation had to be provided on the table, wheresoever there happened to be no papers, and on the ledges of the book-cases. It was pretty to see the host suggesting from a long experience those coigns of vantage he counted easiest and safest, giving warnings also of unsuspected danger in the shape of restless books that might either yield beneath one's feet or descend on one's head. Carmichael, however, needed no such guidance, for he knew his way about in the marvellous place, and at once made for what the boys called the throne of the fathers. This was a lordly seat, laid as to its foundation in mediæval divines of ponderous content, but excellently finished with the Benedictine edition of St. Augustine, softened by two cushions, one for a seat and another for a back. Here Carmichael used to sit in great content, smoking and listening while the Rabbi hunted an idea through Scripture with many authorities, or defended the wildest Calvinism with strange, learned arguments; from this place he would watch the Rabbi searching for a lost note on some passage of Holy Writ amid a pile of papers two feet deep, through which he burrowed on all fours, or climbing for a book on the sky-line, to forget his errand and to expound some point of doctrine from the top of the ladder.

"You're comfortable, John, and you do not want to put off your boots after all that travelling to and fro? then I will search for Barbara, and secure some refreshment for our bodies," and Carmichael watched the Rabbi depart with pity, for he was going on a troublous errand.

Housekeepers are, after beadles, the most wonderful functionaries in the ecclesiastical life of Scotland, and every species could be found within a day's journey of Drumtochty. Jenkins, indeed, suggested that a series of papers on Church Institutions read at the clerical club should include one on housekeepers, and offered to supply the want, which was the reason why Dr. Dowbiggin refused to certify him to a vacancy, speaking of him as "frivolous and irresponsible." The class ranged from Sarah of Drumtochty, who could cook and knew nothing about ecclesiastical affairs, to that austere damsel, Margaret Meiklewham of Pitscowrie, who had never prepared an appetising meal in her life, but might have sat as an elder in the Presbytery.

Among all her class, Barbara MacCluckie stood an easy worst, being the most incapable, unsightly, evil-tempered, vexatious woman into whose hands an unmarried man had ever been delivered. MacWheep had his own trials, but his ruler saw that he had sufficient food and some comfort, but Barbara laid herself out to make the Rabbi's life a misery. He only obtained his meals as a favour, and an extra blanket had to be won by a week's abject humiliation. Fire was only allowed him at times, and he secured oil for his lamp by stratagems. Latterly he was glad to send strange ministers to Mains, and his boys alone forced lodgment in the manse. The settlement of Barbara was the great calamity of the Rabbi's life, and was the doing of his own good nature. He first met her when she came to the manse one evening to discuss the unlawfulness of infant baptism and the duty of holding Sunday on Saturday, being the Jewish Sabbath. His interest deepened on learning that she had been driven from twenty-nine situations through the persecution of the ungodly; and on her assuring him that she had heard a voice in a dream bidding her take charge of Kilbogie Manse, the Rabbi, who had suffered many things at the hands of young girls given to lovers, installed Barbara, and began to repent that very day. A tall, bony, forbidding woman, with a squint and a nose turning red, as she stated, from chronic indigestion, let it be said for her that she did not fall into the sins of her predecessors. It was indeed a pleasant jest in Kilbogie for four Sabbaths that she allowed a local Romeo, who knew not that his Juliet was gone, to make his adventurous way to her bedroom window, and then showed such an amazing visage that he was laid up for a week through the suddenness of his fall. What the Rabbi endured no one knew, but his boys understood that the only relief he had from Barbara's tyranny was on Sabbath evening, when she stated her objections to the doctrine, and threatened henceforward to walk into Muirtown in order to escape from unsound doctrine. On such occasions the Rabbi laid himself out

A TALL, BONY, FORBIDDING WOMAN.

for her instruction with much zest, and he knew when he
had produced an impression, for then he went supperless
to bed.   Between this militant spirit and the boys there

was an undying feud, and Carmichael was not at all hurt
to hear her frank references to himself.

"What need he come stravagin' doon frae Drumtochty
for? it wud set him better tae wait on his ain fouk. A
licht-headed fellow, they say as kens; an' as for his
doctrine — weel, maybe it 'll dae for Drumtochty.

"Tea? Did ye expect me tae hae biling water at this
'oor o' the nicht? My word, the money wud flee in this
hoose gin a' wesna here. Milk 'll dae fine for yon
birkie : he micht be gled tae get onything, sorning on a
respectable manse every ither week."

"You will pardon our humble provision"—this is
how the Rabbi prepared Carmichael; "we have taken
my worthy Abigail unawares, and she cannot do for us
what in other circumstances would be her desire. She
has a thorn in the flesh which troubles her, and makes
her do what she would not; but I am convinced that her
heart is right."

That uncompromising woman took no notice of Drumtochty, but busied herself in a search for the Rabbi's
bag, which he insisted had been brought home from Muirtown that morning, and which was at last found covered
with books.

"Do not open it at present, Barbara; you can identify the contents later if it be necessary, but I am
sure they are all right," and the Rabbi watched Barbara's
investigations with evident anxiety.

"Maybe ye hae brocht back what ye started wi', but
gin ye hev, it 's the first time a' can mind. Laist sacrament at Edinburgh ye pickit up twal books, ae clothes
brush, an' a crochet cover for a chair, an' left a'thing
that belonged tae ye."

"It was an inadvertence; but I obtained a drawer for

my own use this time, and I was careful to pack its contents into the bag, leaving nothing." But the Rabbi did not seem over-confident.

"There's nae question that ye hev filled the pack," said Barbara, with much deliberation and an ominous calmness; "but whether wi' yir ain gear or some ither body's, a 'll leave ye tae judge yirsel'. A 'll juist empty the bag on the bukes;" and Barbara selected a bank of Puritans for the display of her master's spoil.

"Ae slipbody (bodice), well hemmed and gude stuff — ye didna tak' that wi' ye, at ony rate; twa pillow slips — they 'll come in handy, oor ain are wearin' thin; ae pair o' sheets — 'll juist dae for the next trimmie that ye want tae set up in her hoose; this 'll be a bolster slip, a 'm judgin' — "

"It must be the work of Satan," cried the poor Rabbi, who constantly saw the hand of the great enemy in the disorder of his study. "I cannot believe that my hands packed such garments in place of my own."

"Ye 'll be satisfied when ye read the name; it 's plain eneuch; ye needna gang dodderin' aboot here and there lookin' for yir glasses; there 's twa pair on your head already;" for it was an hour of triumph to Barbara's genial soul.

"It 's beyond understanding," murmured the Rabbi. "I must have mistaken one drawer for another in the midst of meditation;" and then, when Barbara had swept out of the room with the varied linen on her arm, "this is very humiliating, John, and hard to bear."

"Nonsense, Rabbi; it 's one of the finest things you have ever done. Half a dozen journeys of that kind would refurnish the manse; it 's just a pity you can't annex a chair;" but he saw that the good man was sorely vexed.

"You are a good lad, John, and it is truly marvellous what charity I have received at the hands of young men who might have scorned and mocked me. God knows how my heart has been filled with gratitude, and I . . . have mentioned your names in my unworthy prayers that God may do to you all according to the kindness ye have shown unto me."

It was plain that this lonely, silent man was much moved, and Carmichael did not speak.

"People consider that I am ignorant of my failings and weaknesses, and I can bear witness with a clear conscience that I am not angry when they smile and nod the head; why should I be? But, John, it is known to myself only and Him before whom all hearts are open how great is my suffering in being among my neighbours as a sparrow upon the housetop.

"May you never know, John, what it is to live alone and friendless till you lose the ways of other men and retire within yourself, looking out on the multitude passing on the road as a hermit from his cell, and knowing that some day you will die alone, with none to . . . give you a draught of water."

"Rabbi, Rabbi " — for Carmichael was greatly distressed at the woe in the face opposite him, and his heart was tender that night — "why should you have lived like that? Do not be angry, but . . . did God intend . . . it cannot be wrong . . . I mean . . . God did give Eve to Adam."

"Laddie, why do ye speak with fear and a faltering voice? Did I say aught against that gracious gift or the holy mystery of love, which is surely the sign of the union betwixt God and the soul, as is set forth after a mystical shape in the Song of Songs? But it was not for me — no, not for me. I complain not, neither have I vexed my soul. He doeth all things well."

" But, dear Rabbi" — and Carmichael hesitated, not knowing where he stood.

" Ye ask me why" — the Rabbi anticipated the question — " and I will tell you plainly, for my heart has ever gone forth to you. For long years I found no favour in the eyes of the Church, and it seemed likely I would be rejected from the ministry as a man useless and unprofitable. How could I attempt to win the love of any maiden, since it did not appear to be the will of God that I should ever have a place of habitation? It consisted not with honour, for I do hold firmly that no man hath any right to seek unto himself a wife till he have a home."

" But . . . "

" Afterwards, you would say. Ah, John, then had I become old and unsightly, not such a one as women could care for. It would have been cruel to tie a maid for life to one who might only be forty years in age, but was as seventy in his pilgrimage, and had fallen into unlovely habits."

Then the Rabbi turned on Carmichael his gentle eyes, that were shining with tears.

" It will be otherwise with you, and so let it be. May I live to see you rejoicing with the wife of your youth."

So it came to pass that it was to this unlikely man Carmichael told his new-born love, and he was amazed at the understanding of the Rabbi, as well as his sympathy and toleration.

" A maid of spirit — and that is an excellent thing; and any excess will be tamed by life. Only see to it that ye agree in that which lieth beneath all churches and maketh souls one in God. May He prosper you in your wooing as He did the patriarch Jacob, and far more abundantly."

Very early in the morning Carmichael awoke, and being tempted by the sunrise, arose and went downstairs. As he came near the study door he heard a voice in prayer, and knew that the Rabbi had been all night in intercession.

"Thou hast denied me wife and child; deny me not Thyself. . . . A stranger Thou hast made me among men; refuse me not a place in the City. . . . Deal graciously with this lad who has been to me as a son in the Gospel. . . . He has not despised an old man; put not his heart to confusion. . . ."

Carmichael crept upstairs again, but not to sleep, and at breakfast he pledged the Rabbi to come up some day and see Kate Carnegie.

CHAPTER XIII.

NGLISH folk have various festivals in the religious year, as becometh a generous country, but in our austere and thrifty Glen there was only one high day, and that was Sacrament Sabbath. It is rumoured — but one prefers not to believe scandals — that the Scottish Kirk nowadays is encouraging a monthly Sacrament, after which nothing remains in the way of historical declension except for people to remain for the Sacrament as it may occur to them, and for men like Drumsheugh to get up at meetings to give their religious experiences, when every one that has any understanding will know that the reserve has gone out of Scottish character, and the reverence from Scottish faith. Dr. Davidson's successor, a boisterous young man of bourgeois manners, elected by popular vote, has got guilds, where Hillocks' granddaughter reads papers on Emerson and refers to the Free Kirk people as Dissenters, but things were different in the old days before the Revolution. The Doctor had such unquestioning confidence in himself that he considered his very presence a sufficient defence for the Kirk, and was of such perfect breeding that he regarded other Kirks with unbroken charity. He was not the man to weary the parish with fussy little schemes, and he knew better than level down the Sacrament. It was the summit of the year to which the days climbed, from which they fell away, and it was held in the middle of August. Then nature was at her height in the Glen, and had given us of her fulness. The barley was golden, and, rustling in the gentle wind, wearied for the scythe; the oats were changing daily, and had only so much greenness as would keep the feathery heads firm for the handling; the potatoes having received the last touch of the plough, were well banked up and flowering pleasantly; the turnips, in fine levels, like Hillocks', or gently sloping fields, like Menzies', were so luxuriant that a mere townsman could not have told the direction of the drills; the hay had been gathered into long stacks like unto the shape of a two-storied house, and the fresh aftermath on the field was yielding sweet morsels for the horses of an evening; the pasture was rich with the hardy white clover, and one could hear from the road the cattle taking full mouthfuls; young spring animals, like calves and lambs, were now falling into shape and beginning independent life, though with an occasional hankering after the past, when the lambs would fall a-bleating for their mothers, and calves would hang about the gate at evening, where they had often fought shamelessly to get a frothy nose once more into the milk-pail.

Our little gardens were full a-blow, a very blaze and maze of colour and foliage, wherein the owner wandered of an evening examining flowers and fruit with many and prolonged speculations — much aided by the smoke of tobacco — as to the chance of gaining a second at our horticultural show with his stocks, or honourable mention

GATHERING HER BERRY HARVEST.

for a dish of mixed fruit. The good wife might be seen of an afternoon about that time, in a sun-bonnet and a gown carefully tucked up, gathering her berry harvest for preserves, with two young assistants, who worked at a

modest distance from their mother, very black as to
their mouths, and preserving the currants, as they
plucked them, by an instantaneous process of their own
invention. Next afternoon a tempting fragrance of boiling sugar would make one's mouth water as he passed,
and the same assistants, never weary in well-doing,
might be seen setting saucers of black jam upon the
window-sill to "jeel," and receiving, as a kind of black-
mail, another saucerful of "skim," which, I am informed,
is really the refuse of the sugar, but, for all that, wonderfully
toothsome. Bear with a countryman's petty foolishness,
ye mighty people who live in cities, and whose dainties
come from huge manufactories. Some man reading
these pages will remember that red-letter day of the
summer-time long ago, and the faithful hands that
plucked the fruit, and the old kitchen, with its open
beams, and the peat fire glowing red, and the iron arm
that held the copper-lined pan — much lent round the
district — and the smack of the hot, sweet berries, more
grateful than any banquet of later days.

The bees worked hard in this time of affluence, and
came staggering home with spoil from the hills, but it was
holiday season on the farms. Between the last labours
on the roots and the beginning of harvest there was no
exacting demand from the land, and managing farmers
invented tasks to fill up the hours. An effort was made
to restore carts and implements to their original colour,
which was abruptly interrupted by the first day of cutting, so that one was not surprised to see a harvest cart
blue on one side and a rich crusted brown on the other.
Drumsheugh would even send his men to road-making,
and apologise to the neighbours — "juist reddin' up aboot
the doors" — while Saunders the foreman and his staff

laboured in a shamefaced manner like grown-ups playing at a children's game. Hillocks used to talk vaguely about going to see a married sister in Glasgow, and one year got as far as Kildrummie, where he met Piggie Walker, and returned to have a deal in potatoes with that enterprising man. More than once Drumsheugh — but then his position was acknowledged — set off on the Monday for Carnoustie with a large carpet bag containing, among other things, two pounds of butter and two dozen eggs, and announced his intention of spending a fortnight at the " saut water." The kirkyard would bid him good-bye, and give him a united guarantee that Sabbath would be kept at Drumtochty during his absence, but the fathers were never astonished to see the great man drop into Muirtown market next Friday on his way west — having found four days of unrelieved gaiety at that Scottish Monaco enough for flesh and blood.

This season of small affairs was redeemed by the Sacrament, and preparations began far off with the cleaning of the kirk. As early as June our beadle had the face of one with something on his mind, and declined to pledge himself for roups of standing corn, where his presence was much valued, not on business grounds, but as an official sanction of the proceedings. Drumtochty always felt that Dr. Davidson was fully represented by his man, and John could no longer disentangle the two in his own mind — taking a gloomy view of the parish when he was laid up by lumbago and the Doctor had to struggle on single-handed, and regarding the future when both would be gone with despair.

" Ay, ay, Hillocks," he once remarked to that worthy, " this 'll be a queer-like place when me an' the Doctor 's awa'.

"Na, na, a' daurna promise for the roup, but ye can cairry it on whether a 'm there or no; prices dinna hang on a beadle, and they're far mair than appearances. A'm juist beginning tae plan the reddin' up for the Saicrament, an' a 've nae speerit for pleesure; div ye ken, Hillocks, a' wud actually coont a funeral distrackin'."

"Ye hev an awfu' responsibility, there's nae doot o' that, John, but gin ye juist jined the fouk for ae field, it wud be an affset tae the day, an' the auctioneer wud be lifted."

With the beginning of July, John fairly broke ground in the great effort, and was engaged thereon for six weeks, beginning with the dusting of the pulpit and concluding with the beating of Drumsheugh's cushion. During that time the Doctor only suggested his wants to John, and the fathers themselves trembled of a Sabbath morning lest in a moment of forgetfulness they might carry in some trace of their farms with them and mar the great work. It was pretty to see Whinnie labouring at his feet in a grassy corner, while John watched him from the kirk door with an unrelenting countenance.

The elders also had what might be called their cleaning at this season, examining into the cases of any who had made a "mistak'" since last August, and deciding whether they should be allowed to "gang forrit." These deliberations were begun at the door, where Drumsheugh and Domsie stood the last five minutes before the Doctor appeared, and were open to the congregation, who from their places within learned the offenders' prospects.

"The Doctor 'll dae as he considers richt, an' he's juist ower easy pleased wi' onybody 'at starts a-greetin', but yon 's ma jidgment, Dominie."

"I do not wish to dispute with you, Drumsheugh"—
Domsie always spoke English on such occasions—"and
the power of the keys is a solemn charge. But we
must temper a just measure of severity with a spirit of
mercy."

"Ye may temper this or temper that," said Drumsheugh, going to the root of the matter, "but a' tell ye,
Dominie, there's ower mony o' thae limmers in the
country juist noo, an' a 'm for making an example o'
Jean Ferguson."

So Jean did not present herself for a token on the
approaching Fast-day, and sat out with the·children during the Sacrament with as becoming an expression of
penitence as her honest, comely face could accomplish.
Nor did Jean or her people bear any grudge against the
Doctor or the Session for their severity. She had gone
of her own accord to confess her fault, and was willing
that her process of cleansing should be thorough before
she received absolution. When a companion in misfortune spoke of the greater leniency of Pitscowrie, Jean
expressed her thankfulness that she was of Drumtochty.

"Nane o' yir loose wys for me — gie me a richt minister as dis his duty;" which showed that whatever might
be her deflections in practice, Jean's ideas of morals
were sound.

Preparations in the parish at large began two weeks
before the Sacrament, when persons whose attendance
had been, to say the least, irregular slipped in among the
fathers without ostentation, and dropping into a conversation on the weather, continued, as it were, from last
Sabbath, used it skilfully to offer an apology for past
failures in church observance.

"It's keepit up wonderfu' through the week, for a'

never like ower bricht mornin's," old Sandie Ferguson would remark casually, whose arrival, swallow-like, heralded the approach of the great occasion. "The roads are graund the noo frae the heich (high glen) ; we 've hed an awfu' winter, neeburs, up oor wy — clean blockit up. Them 'at lives ablow are michty favoured, wi' the kirk at their door."

"It 's maist extraordinar' hoo the seasons are changin' " — Jamie Soutar could never resist Sandie's effrontery — "A' mind when Mairch saw the end o' the snow, an' noo winter is hangin' aboot in midsummer. A 'm expeckin' tae hear, in another five year, that the drifts last through the Sacrament in August. It 'll be a sair trial for ye, Sandie, a wullin' kirkgoer — but ye 'll hae the less responsibility."

"Millhole 's here, at ony rate, the day, an' we 're gled tae see him " — for Drumsheugh's pride was to have a large Sacrament — and so Sandie would take his place at an angle to catch the Doctor's eye, and pay such rapt attention to the sermon that any one not knowing the circumstances might have supposed that he had just awaked from sleep.

Ploughmen who on other Sabbaths slept in the forenoon and visited their sweethearts the rest of the day, presented themselves for tokens on the Fast-day, and made the one elaborate toilette of the year on Saturday evening, when they shaved in turns before a scrap of glass hung outside the bothy door, and the foreman, skilled in the clipping of horses, cut their hair, utilising a porridge bowl with much ingenuity to secure a round cut. They left early on the Sabbath morning, and formed themselves into a group against the gable of the kirk, — being reviewed with much satisfaction by Drumsheugh,

who had a keen eye for absentees from the religious function of the year. At the first sound of the bell the ploughmen went into kirk a solid mass, distributing themselves in
the servants' pews attached to the farmers' pews, and main-
taining an immovable countenance through every part of
the service, any tendency to somnolence being promptly
and effectually checked by the foreman, who allowed himself some ease when alone on other days, but on Sacrament
Sabbath realised his charge and never closed an eye. The
women and children proceeded to their places on arrival,
and the fathers followed them as the bell gave signs of
ceasing. Drumsheugh and Domsie then came in from
the plate and the administration of discipline, and the
parish waited as one man for the appearance of John with
the Bible, the Doctor following, and envied those whose
seat commanded the walk from the manse down which
the procession came every Sabbath with dignity, but once
a year with an altogether peculiar majesty.

Drumtochty exiles meeting in London or other foreign
places and recalling the Glen, never part without lighting
on John and passing contempt on all officials beside him.
"Ye mind John?" one will say, wagging his head with
an amazement that time and distance has in no wise
cooled, and his fellow glensman will reply, "Ay, ye
may traivel the warld ower or ye see his marrow."
Then they will fall into a thoughtful silence, and each
knows that his neighbour is following John as he comes
down the kirkyard on the great day. "Comin' in at the
door lookin' as if he didna ken there wes a body in the
kirk, a' aye coontit best," but his friend has another
preference. "It wes fine, but, man, tae see him set the
bukes doon on the pulpit cushion, and then juist gie ae
glisk roond the kirk as much as tae say, 'What think ye

o' that?' cowed a' thing." It has been given to myself amid other privileges to see (and store in a fond memory) the walk of a University mace-bearer, a piper at the Highland gathering, a German stationmaster (after the war), and an alderman (of the old school), but it is bare justice to admit, although I am not of Drumtochty, but only as a proselyte of the gate, that none of those efforts is at all to be compared with John's achievement. Within the manse the Doctor was waiting in pulpit array, grasping his father's snuff-box in a firm right hand, and it was understood that, none seeing them, and as a preparation for the strain that would immediately be upon them, both the minister and his man relaxed for a minute.

"Is there a respectable attendance, John?" and the Doctor would take a preliminary pinch. "Drumsheugh does not expect many absentees."

"Naebody 's missin' that a' cud see, sir, except that ill gettit wratch, Tammie Ronaldson, and a' coont him past redemption. A' gaed in as a' cam doon, and gin he wesna lyin' in his bed sleepin' an' snorin' like a heathen."

"Well, John, did you do your duty as an officer of the church?"

"A' stood ower him, Doctor, an' a' juist said tae masel', 'Shall a' smite wi' the sword?' but a' left him alane for this time." And so they started — John in front with the books, and the Doctor a pace behind, his box now in the left hand, with a handkerchief added, and the other holding up his gown, both dignitaries bare-headed, unself-conscious, absorbed in their office.

The books were carried level with the top button of John's waistcoat — the Psalm-book being held in its place by the two extended thumbs — and neither were allowed to depart from the absolute horizontal by an eighth of an inch, even going up the pulpit stairs. When they had been deposited in their place, and slightly patted, just to settle them, John descended to make way for the Doctor, who had been waiting beneath in a commanding attitude. He then followed the minister up, and closed the door — not with a bang, but yet so that all might know he had finished his part of the work. If any one had doubted how much skill went to this achievement, he had his eyes opened when John had the lumbago, and the smith arrived at the kirk door three yards ahead of the Doctor, and let the Psalm-book fall on the pulpit floor.

"We 're thankfu' tae hae ye back, John," said Hillocks. "Yon wes a temptin' o' Providence."

Once only had I the privilege of seeing John in this his glory, and the sight of him afflicted me with a problem no one has ever solved. It might, indeed, be made a branch of scientific investigation, and would then be called the Genesis of Beadles. Was a beadle ever a baby? What like was he before he appeared in his office? Was he lying as a cardinal in petto till the right moment, and then simply showed himself to be appointed as one born unto this end? No one dared to hint that John had ever followed any other avocation, and an effort to connect John with the honourable trade of plumbing in the far past was justly regarded as a disgraceful return of Tammie Ronaldson's for much faithful dealing. Drumtochty refused to consider his previous history, if he had any, and looked on John in his office as a kind of Melchizedek, a mysterious, isolated work of Providence.

He was a mere wisp of a man, with a hard, keen face, iron-grey hair brushed low across his forehead, and clean-shaven cheeks.

"A 've naething tae say against a beard," on being once consulted, "an' a 'm no prepared tae deny it maun

HE WAS A MERE WISP OF A MAN.

be in the plan o' Providence. In fact, gin a' wes in a private capaucity, a' michtna shave, but in ma public capaucity, a 've nae alternative. It wud be a fine story tae gang roond the Presbytery o' Muirtown that the Beadle o' Drumtochty hed a beard."

His authority was supreme under the Doctor, and never was disputed by man or beast save once, and John himself admitted that the circumstances were quite peculiar. It was during the Doctor's famous continental tour, when Drumsheugh fought with strange names in the kirkyard, and the Presbytery supplied Drumtochty in turn. The minister of St. David's, Muirtown, was so spiritual that he left his voice at the foot of the pulpit stairs, and lived in the Song of Solomon, with occasional excursions into the Lamentations of Jeremiah, and it was thoughtless not to have told Mr. Curlew that two or three dogs — of unexceptionable manners — attended our kirk with their masters. They would no more have thought of brawling in church than John himself, and they knew the parts of the service as well as the Doctor, but dogs have been so made by our common Creator that they cannot abide falsetto, and Mr. Curlew tried them beyond endurance. When he lifted up his voice in " Return, return, O Shulamite, return, return," a long wail in reply, from below a back seat where a shepherd was slumbering, proclaimed that his appeal had not altogether failed. " Put out that dog," said the preacher in a very natural voice, with a strong suggestion of bad temper, " put that dog out immediately ; it 's most disgraceful that such . . . eh, conduct should go on in a Christian church. Where is the church officer ? "

" A 'm the Beadle o' Drumtochty " — standing in his place — " an' a 'll dae yir pleesure ; " and the occasion was too awful for any one, even the dog's master, to assist, far less to laugh.

So Laddie was conducted down the passage — a dog who would not condescend to resist — and led to the outer gate of the kirkyard, and John came in amid a dead silence — for Mr. Curlew had not yet got his pulpit note again — and faced the preacher.

" The dog 's oot, sir, but a' tak this congregation tae witness, ye begood (began) it yirsel', " and it was said that Mr. Curlew's pious and edifying chant was greatly restricted in country kirks from that day.

It was not given to the beadle to sit with the elders in that famous court of morals which is called the Kirk Session, and of which strange stories are told by Southern historians, but it was his to show out and in the culprits with much solemnity. He was able to denote the exact offence in the language of Kirk law, and was considered happy in his abbreviations for technical terms. As a familiar of the Inquisition, he took oversight of the district, and saw that none escaped the wholesome discipline of the Church.

"Ye 're back," he said, arresting Peter Ferguson as he tried to escape down a byroad, and eyeing the prodigal sternly, who had fled from discipline to London, and there lost a leg; "the' 'll be a meetin' o' Session next week afore the Saicrament; wull a' tell the Doctor ye 're comin'?"

"No, ye 'll dae naething o' the kind, for a 'll no be there. A 've nae suner got hame aifter ma accident but ye 're tormentin' me on the verra road wi' yir Session. Ye drave me awa' aince, an' noo ye wud harry (hunt) me aff again."

"A weel, a weel"—and John was quite calm—"dinna pit yirsel' in a feery farry (excitement); ye 'll gang yir ain wy and earn yir ain jidgment. It wes for yir gude a' spoke, and noo a 've dune ma pairt, an' whatever comes o't, ye 'll no hae me or ony ither body tae blame."

"What think ye 'll happen?"—evidently sobered by John's tone, yet keeping up a show of defiance. "Ye wud think the Session wes the Sheriff o' Perthshire tae hear ye blawin' and threatenin'."

"It 's no for me tae say what may befa' ye, Peter Ferguson, for a 'm no yir jidge, but juist 'a frail mortal, beadle though I be; but a' may hev ma thochts.

"Ye refused the summons sax month syne, and took yir wys tae London — that wes contumacy added tae yir ither sin. Nae doot ye made certain ye hed escapit, but hed ye? A' leave it tae yirsel', for the answer is in yir body," and John examined Peter's wooden leg with an austere interest.

"Ay, ay, ma man," he resumed — for Peter was now

quite silenced by this uncompromising interpretation of the ways of Providence — " ye aff tae London, an' the Lord aifter ye, an' whuppit aff ae leg. Noo ye declare ye 'll be as countermacious as ever, an' a 'm expeckin' the Lord 'll come doon here an' tak the ither leg, an' gin that disna dae, a' that remains is tae stairt on yir airms ; and, man Peter, ye 'll be a bonnie-like sicht before a' 's dune."

This was very faithful dealing, and it had its desired effect, for Peter appeared at next meeting, and in due course was absolved, as became an obedient son of the Church.

John did not, however, always carry the sword, but bore himself gently to young people so long as they did not misbehave in church, and he had a very tender heart toward probationers, as being callow members of that great ecclesiastical guild in which he was one of the heads.

When one of those innocents came to take the Doctor's place, John used to go in to visit them in the dining-room on Saturday evening, partly to temper the severity of his wife, Dr. Davidson's housekeeper, who dealt hardly with the lads, and partly to assist them with practical hints regarding pulpit deportment and the delivery of their sermons. One unfortunate was so nervous and clinging that John arranged his remarks for him into heads — with an application to two classes — and then, having suggested many points, stopped under the yew arch that divided the kirkyard from the manse garden, and turned on the shaking figure which followed.

" Ae thing mair ; aifter ye 're dune wi' yir sermon, whether ye 're sweatin' or no, for ony sake fa' back in yir seat and dicht (wipe) yir broo," which being done by the exhausted orator, made a great impression on the people, and was so spread abroad that a year afterwards it won for him the parish of Pitscowrie.

CHAPTER XIV.

A MODERATE.

S a matter of fact, Dr. Davidson, minister of Drumtochty, stood exactly five feet nine in his boots, and was therefore a man of quite moderate height; but this is not what you had dared to state to any loyal and self-respecting person in the parish. For "the Doctor"—what suggestions of respect and love were in that title on a Drumtochty tongue—was so compactly made and bore himself with such dignity, both in walk and conversation, that Drumsheugh, although not unaccustomed to measurement and a man of scrupulous accuracy, being put into the witness-box, would have sworn that Dr. Davidson was "aboot sax feet aff and on—maybe half an inch mair, standin' at his full hicht in the pulpit." Which fond delusion seemed to declare abroad, as in a parable, the greatness of the Doctor.

Providence had dealt bountifully with Dr. Davidson, and had bestowed on him the largest benefit of heredity. He was not the first of his house to hold this high place of parish minister—the only absolute monarchy in the land—and he must not receive over-praise for not falling into those personal awkwardnesses and petty tyrannies which are the infallible signs of one called suddenly to the throne. His were the pride of blood, the inherent sense of authority, the habit of rule, the gracious arts of manner, the conviction of popular devotion, the grasp of affairs, the interest in the people's life, which are the marks and aids of a royal caste. It was not in the nature of things that the Doctor should condescend to quarrel with a farmer or mix himself up with any vulgar squabble, because his will was law in ninety cases in a hundred, and in the other ten he skilfully anticipated the people's wishes. When the minister of Nether Pitfoodles — who had sermons on "Love, Courtship, and Marriage," and was much run after in Muirtown — quarrelled with his elders about a collection, and asked the interference of the Presbytery, Dr. Davidson dealt severely with him in open court as one who had degraded the ministry and discredited government. It was noticed also that the old gentleman would afterward examine Nether Pitfoodles curiously for minutes together in the Presbytery, and then shake his head.

"Any man," he used to say to his reverend brother of Kildrummie, as they went home from the Presbytery together, "who gets into a wrangle with his farmers about a collection is either an upstart or he is a fool, and in neither case ought he to be a minister of the Church of Scotland." And the two old men would lament the decay of the ministry over their wine in Kildrummie Manse — being both of the same school, cultured, clean-living, kind-hearted, honourable, but not extravagantly evangelical clergymen. They agreed in everything except the matter of their after-dinner wine, Dr. Davidson having a partiality for port, while the minister of

Kildrummie insisted that a generous claret was the hereditary drink of a Scottish gentleman. This was only, however, a subject of academic debate, and was not allowed to interfere with practice — the abbé of Drumtochty taking his bottle of claret, in an appreciative spirit, and the curé of Kildrummie disposing of his two or three glasses of port with cheerful resignation.

If Drumtochty exalted its minister above his neighbours, it may be urged in excuse that Scottish folk are much affected by a man's birth, and Dr. Davidson had a good ancestry. He was the last of his line, and represented a family that for two centuries had given her sons to the Kirk. Among those bygone worthies, the Doctor used to select one in especial for honourable mention. He was a minister of Dunleith, whose farmers preferred to play ball against the wall of the kirk to hearing him preach, and gave him insolence on his offering a pious remonstrance. Whereupon the Davidson of that day, being, like all his race, short in stature, but mighty in strength, first beat the champion player one Sabbath morning at his own game to tame an unholy pride, and then thrashed him with his fist to do good to his soul. This happy achievement in practical theology secured an immediate congregation, and produced so salutary an effect on the schismatic ball-player that he became in due course an elder, and was distinguished for his severity in dealing with persons absenting themselves from public worship, or giving themselves overmuch to vain amusements.

At the close of the last century the Doctor's grandfather was minister of the High Kirk, Muirtown, where he built up the people in loyalty to Kirk and State, and himself recruited for the Perthshire Fencibles. He also delivered a sermon entitled "The French Revolution the just judgment of the Almighty on the spirit of insubordination," for which he received a vote of thanks from the Lord Provost and Bailies of Muirtown in council assembled, as well as a jewel from the Earl of Kilspindie, the grandfather of our lord, which the Doctor inherited and wore on the third finger of his left hand. Had Carmichael or any other minister decked himself after this fashion, it had not fared well with him, but even the Free Kirk appreciated a certain pomp in Dr. Davidson, and would have resented his being as other men. He was always pleased to give the history of the ring, and generally told a story of his ancestor, which he had tasted much more frequently than the sermon. A famous judge had asked him to dinner as he made his circuit, and they had disputed about the claret, till at last its excellence compelled respect at the close of the first bottle.

"'Now, Reverend Sir,' said the judge, 'this wine has been slandered and its fair fame taken away without reason. I demand that you absolve it from the scandal.'

"'My Lord,' said my worthy forbear, 'you are a great criminal lawyer, but you are not well read in Kirk law, for no offender can be absolved without three appearances.'

"My grandfather," the Doctor used to conclude, "had the best of that jest besides at least two bottles of claret, for in those days a clergyman took more wine than we would now think seemly, although, mark you, the old gentleman always denounced drunkenness on two grounds: first, because it was an offence against religion, and second, because it was a sign of weakness."

Some old folk could remember the Doctor's father, who never attained to the Doctorate, but was a commanding personage. He published no sermons, but as the first Davidson in Drumtochty, he laid the foundations of good government. The Kilspindie family had only recently come into the parish — having purchased the larger part of the Carnegies' land — and Drumtochty took a thrawn fit, and among other acts of war pulled down time after time certain new fences. The minister was appealed to by his lordship, and having settled the rights of the matter, he bade the factor wait in patience till the Sacrament, and Drumsheugh's father used to tell unto the day of his death, as a historical event, how the Doctor's father stood at the communion-table and debarred from the Sacrament evil livers of all kinds, and that day in especial all who had broken Lord Kilspindie's fences, — which was an end of the war. There was a picture of him in the Doctor's study, showing a very determined gentleman, who brought up both his parish and his family upon the stick, and with undeniable success.

With such blood in his veins it was not to be expected that our Doctor should be after the fashion of a modern minister. No one had ever seen him (or wished to see him) in any other dress than black cloth, and a broad-brimmed silk hat, with a white stock of many folds and a bunch of seals depending from some mysterious pocket. His walk, so assured, so measured, so stately, was a means of grace to the parish, confirming every sound and loyal belief, and was crowned, so to say, by his stick, which had a gold head, and having made history in the days of his father, had reached the position of a heredi-tary sceptre. No one could estimate the aid and comfort that stick gave to the Doctor's visits, but one quite understood the force of the comparison Hillocks once drew, after the Doctor's death, between the coming to his house of the Doctor and a "cry" from his energetic successor under the new *régime*.

"He 's a hard-workin' body, oor new man, aye rin rinnin', fuss fussin' roond the pairish, an' he 's a pop'lar hand in the pulpit, but it 's a puir business a veesit frae him.

"It 's juist in an' oot like a cadger buyin' eggs, nae peace an' nae solemnity. Of coorse it 's no his blame that he 's naethin' tae look at, for that 's the wy he wes made, an' his father keepit a pig (china) shop, but at ony rate he micht get a wise-like stick.

"Noo, there wes the Doctor 'at 's dead an' gone ; he didna gang scrammelin' an' huntin' aifter the fouk frae Monday tae Saiturday. Na, na, he didna lower himsel' preachin' an' paiterin' like a missionary body. He announced frae the pulpit whar he wes gaein' and when he wes comin'.

"'It 's my purpose,'" and Hillocks did his best to imitate the Doctor, "'to visit the farm of Hillocks on Wednesday of this week, and I desire to meet with all persons living thereon ;' it wes worth callin' an intimation, an' gied ye pleesure in yir seat.

"On Tuesday aifternoon John wud juist drap in tae see that a'thing wes ready, and the next aifternoon the Doctor comes himsel', an' the first thing he dis is tae lay the stick on the table an' gin he hed never said a word, tae see it lyin' there wes a veesitation. But he 's a weel-meanin' bit craturie, Maister Peebles, an' handy wi' a magic lantern. Sall," and then Hillocks became incapable of speech, and you knew that the thought of Dr. Davidson explaining comic slides had quite overcome him.

This visitation counted as an event in domestic life,

and the Doctor's progress through the Glen was noted
in the kirkyard, and any special remark duly reported.
Nothing could be more perfect than his manner on such
occasions, being leisurely, comprehensive, dignified, gracious. First of all he saluted every member of the family
down to the bairns by name, for had he not at least
married the heads of the household, and certainly baptised all the rest? Unto each he made some kindly remark also — to the good man a commendation of his
careful farming, to the good-wife a deserved compliment
on her butter; the eldest daughter was praised for the
way in which she was sustaining the ancient reputation
of Hillocks' dairy; there was a word to Hillocks' son on
his masterly ploughing; and some good word of Dominie Jamieson's about the little lassie was not forgotten.
After which the Doctor sat down — there was some difficulty in getting the family to sit in his presence — and
held a thorough review of the family history for the last
year, dwelling upon the prospects of Charlie, for whom the
Doctor had got a situation, and Jean, the married daughter,
whose husband might one day have a farm with four pair
of horses in the carse of Gowrie. The Doctor would
then go out to give his opinion on the crops, which was
drawn from keen practical knowledge — his brochure on
"The Potato Disease : Whence it Came and How it is
to be Met " created much stir in its day — and it was
well known that the Doctor's view on bones or guano as
a preferable manure was decisive. On his return the
servants came in — to whom also he said a word — and
then from the head of the table he conducted worship
— the ploughmen looking very uneasy and the children
never taking their eyes off his face, while the gude-wife
kept a watchful eye on all. At the prayer she was care-

ful to be within arm's reach of Hillocks, since on one memorable occasion that excellent man had remained in an attitude of rapt devotion after the others had risen from their knees, which sight profoundly affected. the family, and led the Doctor to remark that it was the only time he had seen Hillocks play the Pharisee in public. The Doctor's favourite passages were the eulogium on the model housewife in Proverbs, the parable of the Good Samaritan, and the 12th chapter of Romans, from which he deduced many very searching and practical lessons on diligence, honesty, mercy, and hospitality. Before he left, and while all were under the spell of his presence, the Doctor would approach the delicate subject of Hillocks' "tout-mout" (dispute) with Gormack over a purchase at a roup, in which it was freely asserted that Gormack had corrupted the Kildrummie auctioneer, a gentleman removed above pecuniary bribes, but not unaffected by liquid refreshment. So powerfully did the Doctor appeal to Hillocks' neighbourliness that he took snuff profusely, and authorised the Doctor to let it be understood at Gormack that the affair was at an end, which treaty was confirmed by the two parties in Kildrummie train, when Hillocks lent Gormack his turnip-sowing machine and borrowed in turn Gormack's water-cart. Mr. Curlew had more than once hinted in the Presbytery of Muirtown that Dr. Davidson was not so evangelical as might be desired, and certainly Mr. Curlew's visitation was of a much more exciting nature ; but St. David's congregation was never without a quarrel, while the Doctor created an atmosphere in Drumtochty wherein peace and charity flourished exceedingly.

Whatever might be urged in praise of his visitation, surely the Doctor could never be more stately or fatherly

than on Sacrament Sabbath, as he stood in his place to
begin service. His first act was to wipe elaborately
those gold eye-glasses, without which nothing would have
been counted a sermon in Drumtochty Kirk, and then,
adjusting them with care, the Doctor made a deliberate survey of the congregation, beginning at his right
hand and finishing at his left. Below him sat the elders
in their blacks, wearing white stocks that had cost them
no little vexation that morning, and the precentor, who
was determined no man, neither Saunders Baxter nor
another, should outsing him that day in Coleshill.
Down the centre of the kirk ran a long table, covered
with pure white linen, bleached in the June showers
and wonderfully ironed, whereon a stain must not be
found, for along that table would pass the holy bread and
wine. Across the aisle on either side, the pews were
filled with stalwart men, solemn beyond their wonted
gravity, and kindly women in simple finery, and rosy-
cheeked bairns. The women had their tokens wrapped
in snowy handkerchiefs, and in their Bibles they had
sprigs of apple-ringy and mint, and other sweet-scented
plants. By-and-by there would be a faint fragrance of
peppermint in the kirk — the only religious and edifying sweet, which flourishes wherever sound doctrine is
preached and disappears before new views, and is therefore now confined to the Highlands of Wales and Scotland, the last home of our fathers' creed. The two back
seats were of black oak, richly carved. In the one sat the
General and Kate, and across the passage Viscount Hay,
Lord Kilspindie's eldest son, a young man of noble build
and carriage, handsome and debonair, who never moved
during the sermon save twice, and then he looked at the
Carnegies' pew.

When the Doctor had satisfied himself that none were missing of the people, he dropped his eye-glass — each act was so closely followed that Drumsheugh below could tell where the Doctor was — and took snuff after the good old fashion, tapping the box twice, selecting a pinch, distributing it evenly, and using first a large red bandana and then a delicate white cambric handkerchief. When the cambric disappeared, each person seized his Bible, for the Doctor would say immediately with a loud, clear voice, preceded by a gentlemanly clearance of the throat, " Let us compose our minds for the worship of Almighty God by singing to His praise the first Psalm.

> " ' That man hath perfect blessedness
> Who walketh not astray — ' "

Then Peter Rattray, of the high Glen, would come in late, and the Doctor would follow him with his eye till the unfortunate man reached his pew, where his own flesh and blood withdrew themselves from him as if he had been a leper, and Peter himself wished that he had never been born.

" Five minutes earlier, Peter, would have prevented this unseemly interruption — ahem.

> " ' In counsel of ungodly men,
> Nor stands in sinners' way.' "

Before the Sacrament the Doctor gave one of his college sermons on some disputed point in divinity, and used language that was nothing short of awful.

" Grant me those premises," he would say, while the silence in the kirk could be felt, " and I will show to any reasonable and unprejudiced person that those new theories are nothing but a resuscitated and unjustifiable Pelagianism." Such passages produced a lasting impression in the parish, and once goaded Drumsheugh's Saunders into voluntary speech.

"Yon wes worth ca'in' a sermon. Did you ever hear sic words out o' the mouth o' a man? Noo that bleatin' cratur Curlew 'at comes frae Muirtown is jist pittin' by the time. Sall, ae sermon o' the Doctor's wud last yon body for a year."

After the sermon the people sang,

"'T was on that night when doomed to know,"

and the elders, who had gone out a few minutes before, entered the kirk in procession, bearing the elements, and set them before the Doctor, now standing at the table. The people came from their pews and took their seats, singing as they moved, while the children were left to their own devices, tempered by the remembrance that their doings could be seen by the Doctor, and would receive a just recompense of reward from their own kin in the evening. Domsie went down one side and Drumsheugh the other, collecting the tokens, whose clink, clink in the silver dish was the only sound.

"If there be any other person who desires to take the Sacrament at this the first table" (for the Sacrament was given then to detachments), "let him come without delay."

"Let us go, dad," whispered Kate. "He is a dear old padre, and . . . they are good people and our neighbours."

"But they won't kneel, you know, Kit; will you . . . ?"

"We 'll do as they do; it is not our Sacrament." So the father and daughter went up the kirk and took their places on the Doctor's left hand. A minute later Lord Hay rose and went up his aisle, and sat down opposite the Carnegies, looking very nervous, but also most modest and sincere.

The Doctor gave the cup to the General, who passed it to Kate, and from her it went to Weelum MacLure, and another cup he gave to Hay, whom he had known from a child, and he handed it to Marget Howe, and she to Whinnie, her man; and so the two cups passed down from husband to wife, from wife to daughter, from daughter to servant, from lord to tenant, till all had shown forth the Lord's death in common fellowship and love as becometh Christian folk. In the solemn silence the sunshine fell on the faces of the communicants, and the singing of the birds came in through the open door with the scent of flowers and ripe corn. Before the congregation left, the Doctor addressed a few words of most practical advice, exhorting them, in especial, to live in the spirit of the Sermon on the Mount, and to be good neighbours. It was on one of those occasions that he settled a dispute between masters and men — whether the cutting of grass for the horses' breakfast should be included in the day's work — and ended the only bitterness known in Drumtochty.

At the kirk gate Hay introduced himself to his father's friend, and the General looked round to find his daughter, but Kate had disappeared. She had seen the face of Marget Howe after the Sacrament as the face of one in a vision, and she had followed Marget to the road.

"Will you let me walk with you for a little? I am General Carnegie's daughter, and I would like to speak to you about the Sacrament; it was lovely."

"Ye dae me much honour, Miss Carnegie," and Marget slightly flushed, "an' much pleasure, for there is

"WILL YOU LET ME WALK WITH YOU FOR A LITTLE?"

naething dearer tae me than keeping the Sacrament; it is my joy every day and muckle comfort in life."

"But I thought you had it only once a year?" questioned Kate.

"With bread and wine in outward sign that is once, and maybe eneuch, for it makes ane high day for us all, but div ye not think, Miss Carnegie, that all our life should be ane Sacrament?"

"Tell me," said Kate, looking into Marget's sweet, spiritual face.

"Is it no the picture of His Luve, who thocht o' everybody but Himsel', an' saved everybody but Himsel', an' didna He say we maun drink His cup and live His life?"

Kate only signed that Marget should go on.

"Noo a 'm judgin' that ilka ane o's is savit juist as we are baptised intae the Lord's death, and ilka time ane o's keeps back a hot word, or humbles a proud heart, or serves anither at a cost, we have eaten the Body and drunk the Blood o' the Lord."

"You are a good woman," cried Kate, in her impulsive way, so quick to be pleased or offended. "May I come to see you some day?"

"Dinna think me better than I am : a woman who had many sins tae fecht and needit many trials tae chasten her; but ye will be welcome at Whinny Knowe for yir ain sake and yir people's, an' gin it ever be in ma pooer tae serve ye, Miss Carnegie, in ony wy, it wull be ma joy."

Twice as she came through the woods Kate stopped; once she bit her lip, once she dashed a tear from her eye.

"Where did you go to, lassie?" and the General met Kate at the gateway. "Lord Hay came to the drive with me, and was quite disappointed not to meet you — a very nice lad indeed, manly and well-mannered."

"Never mind Lord Hay, dad; I 've been with the most delightful woman I 've ever seen."

"Do you mean she was in kirk?"

"Yes, sitting across the table—she is a farmer's wife, and a better lady than we saw in India.

"Oh, dad," and Kate kissed her father, "I wish I had known my mother; it had been better for me, and . . . happier for you."

CHAPTER XV.

JOINT POTENTATES.

AMONG all the houses in a Scottish parish the homeliest and kindliest is the manse, for to its door some time in the year comes every inhabitant, from the laird to the cottar woman. Within the familiar and old-fashioned study, where the minister's chair and writing-table could not be changed without discomposing the parish, and where there are fixed degrees of station, so that the laird has his chair and the servant lass hers, the minister receives and does his best for all the folk committed to his charge. Here he consults with the factor about some improvement in the arrangements of the little commonwealth, he takes counsel with a farmer about his new lease and promises to say a good word to his lordship, he confirms the secret resolution of some modest gifted lad to study for the holy ministry, he hears the shamefaced confession of some lassie whom love has led astray, he gives good advice to a son leaving the Glen for the distant dangerous world, he comforts the mother who has received bad news from abroad. Generations have come in their day to this room, and generations still unborn will come in their joys and sorrows, with their trials and their affairs, while the manse stands and human life runs its old course. And when, as was the case with Dr. Davidson in Drumtochty, the minister is ordained to the parish in his youth, and, instead of hurrying hither and thither, preaching in vacancies, scheming and intriguing, he dwells all his days among his own people, he himself knows three generations, and accumulates a store of practical wisdom for the help of his people. What may be the place of the clergyman in an English parish, and what associations of sympathy and counsel the rectory may have for the English farm-labourer, it is not permitted to a northern man to know, but it is one good thing at least in our poor land that the manse is another word for guidance and good cheer, so that Jean advises Jock in their poor little perplexity about a new place to "slip doon an' see the Doctor," and Jock, although appearing to refuse, does "gie a cry at the manse," and comes home to the gude-wife mightily comforted.

The manse builders of the ancient days were men of a shrewd eye and much wisdom. If anywhere the traveller in the north country sees a house of moderate size peeping from among a clump of trees in the lap of a hill where the north-easter cannot come and the sun shines full and warm, then let him be sure that is the manse, with the kirk and God's acre close beside, and that the fertile little fields around are the glebe, which the farmers see are ploughed and sown and reaped first in the parish. Drumtochty Manse lay beneath the main road, so that the cold wind blowing from the north went over its chimneys, and on the east it was sheltered by the Tochty woods. Southwards it overlooked the fields that sloped towards the river, and westwards, through some ancient trees, one study window had a peep of the west, although it was not given to the parish manse to lie of an evening in the glory of the setting sun, as did the Free Kirk. Standing at the gate and looking down beneath the beeches that stood as sentinels on either side of the little drive, one caught a pleasant glimpse of the manse garden, with its close-cut lawn and flower-beds and old summer-house and air of peace. No one troubled the birds in that place, and they had grown shameless in their familiarity with dignities — a jackdaw having once done his best to steal the Doctor's bandana handkerchief and the robins settling on his hat. Irreverence has limits, and in justice to a privileged friend it ought to be explained that the Doctor wore on these occasions an aged wide-awake and carried no gold-headed stick. His dog used to follow him step by step as he fed the birds and pottered among the flowers, and then it always ended in the old man sitting down on a seat at the foot of the lawn, with Skye at his feet, and looking across the Glen where he had been born and where for nearly half a century he had ministered. Kate caught him once in this attitude, and was so successful in her sketch that some have preferred it to the picture in oils that was presented to the Doctor by the Presbytery of Muirtown, and was painted by an R. A. who spent a fortnight at the manse and departed with some marvellous heads, still to be identified in certain councillors and nobles of the past. Both are hanging in the same house now, far from Drumtochty, and there they call one " Public Capaucity " and the other " Private Capaucity," and you require to have seen both to know our kindly, much-loved Moderate.

As John grew old with his master and mellowed, he would make believe to work close by, so that at times

"PRIVATE CAPAUCITY."

they might drop into talk, recalling names that had died out of the Glen, shrewd sayings that fell from lips now turned to dust, curious customs that had ceased forever, all in great charity. Then there would come a pause, and John would say, "Ay, ay," and go away to the bees. Under the influence of such reminiscences John used to become depressed, and gently prepare Rebecca for the changes that were not far off, when Drumtochty would have a new minister and a new beadle.

"The Doctor's failin', Becca, an' it 's no tae be expeckit that a 'll be lang aifter him; it wudna be fittin', an' a 'm no wantin' 't. Aifter ye 've carried the bukes afore ae minister for five and thirty year, ye 're no anxious for a change ; naebody 'll ever come doon the kirkyaird like the Doctor, an' a' cudna brak ma step ; na, na, there 's no mony things a' michtna learn, but a' cudna brak ma step."

Rebecca went on with her dinner in silence; even capable men had weaknesses somewhere, and she was accustomed to those moralisings.

"A 'm the auldest beadle in the Presbytery o' Muirtown — though a' say it as sudna — an' the higher the place the mair we 'll hae tae answer for, Becca. Nae man can hold the poseetion a 'm in withoot anxieties. Noo there wes the 'Eruption' in '43 — it could not be ignorance which made John cling to this word, and so we supposed that the word was adopted in the spirit of historical irony — "that wes a crisis. Did a' ever tell ye, Rebecca, that there wes juist ae beadle left the next morning tae cairry on the Presbytery of Muirtown?"

"Ay, forty times an' mair," replied that uncompromising woman, "an' it wud set ye better tae be servin' the Doctor's lunch than sittin' haverin' an' blawin' there."

No sane person in Drumtochty would have believed that any human being dared to address John after this fashion, and it is still more incredible that the great man should have risen without a word and gone about his duty. Such a surprising and painful incident suggests the question whether a beadle or any other person in high position ought to be married, and so be exposed to inevitable familiarities. Hillocks took this view strongly in the kirkyard at the time of John's marriage — although neither he nor any one knew with how much reason — and he impressed the fathers powerfully.

"Becca cam frae Kilspindie Castle near thirty year syne, and John 's took the bukes aboot the same time; they 've agreed no that ill for sic a creetical poseetion a' that time, him oot an' her in, an' atween them the Doctor 's no been that ill-servit; they micht hae lat weel alane.

"She 's no needin' a man tae keep her," and Hillocks proceeded to review the situation, "for Becca 's hed a gude place, an' she disna fling awa' her siller on dress. As for John, a' canna mak him oot, for he gets his stockin's darned and his white stock dune as weel an' maybe better than if he wes mairried."

The kirkyard could see no solution of the problem, and Hillocks grew pessimistic.

"It 'll be a doon-come tae him, a 'm judgin', an' 'll no be for the gude o' the parish. He 's never been crossed yet, an' he 'll no tak weel wi' contradickin' . . ."

· "She wudna daur," broke in Whinny, "an' him the beadle."

"Ye ken little aboot weemen," retorted Hillocks, "for yir gude-wife is by hersel' in the pairish, an' micht be a sanct; the maist o' them are a camsteary lot. A 'm no sayin'," he summed up, "that Becca 'll gie the beadle the word back or refuse to dae his biddin', but she 'll be pittin' forrit her ain opeenions, an' that 's no what he 's been accustomed tae in Drumtochty."

They were married one forenoon in the study, with Drumsheugh and Domsie for witnesses — the address given by the Doctor could hardly be distinguished from an ordination charge — and John announced his intention of accompanying his master that afternoon to the General Assembly, while Rebecca remained in charge of the manse.

"It wudna be wise-like for us twa," exclaimed the beadle, "tae be stravagin' ower the country for three or fower days like wild geese, but the pairish micht expect something. Noo, a 've hed ma share o' a Presbytery an' a Synod, tae say naethin' o' Kirk Sessions, but a 've never seen an Assembly.

"Gin you cud get a place, a' wud spend ma time considering hoo the officer comes in, and hoo he lays doon the buke an' sic-like; a' micht get a hint," said John, with much modesty.

So John went alone for his wedding tour, and being solemnly introduced to Thomas, the chief of all beadles, discussed mysteries with him unto great edification; but he was chiefly impressed by the Clerk of the Free Kirk Assembly — into which he had wandered on an errand of exploration — who was a fiery-faced old gentleman with a stentorian voice and the heart of a little child.

"Ye never heard him cry, 'Officer, shut the door,' afore a vote?" he inquired of the Doctor. "Weel, ye 've missed a real pleesure, sir; gin ye stude on Princes Street, wi' the wind frae the richt airt, ye micht hear him. A' never heard onything better dune; hoo ony man wi' sic a face and voice cud be content ootside the Auld Kirk passes me."

John was so enamoured of this performance that after

much cogitation he unburdened his mind to the Doctor, and showed how such a means of grace might be extended to Drumtochty.

"Noo, if there wes nae objection in order, aifter ye hed settled in the pulpit, an' hed yir first snuff, ye micht say, 'Officer, shut the door.' Then a' wud close the kirk door deleeberately in sicht o' the hale congregation an' come back tae ma place, an' Peter Rattray himsel' wudna daur tae show his face aifter that. Ye hae the voice an' the manner, Doctor, an' it's no richt tae wyste them."

In public John defended the Doctor's refusal as a proof of his indulgence to the prodigals of the parish, but with his intimates he did not conceal his belief that the opportunity had been 'lost of bringing the service in Drumtochty Kirk to absolute perfection. John's own mind still ran on the mighty utterance, and so it came to pass that the question of mastery in the kitchen of the manse under the new *régime* was settled within a week after his ecclesiastical honeymoon.

"Rebecca" — this with a voice of thunder from the fireplace, where the beadle was reading the *Muirtown Advertiser* — "shut the door."

The silence was so imperative that John turned round, and saw his spouse standing with a half-dried dish in her hand.

"Ma name is Rebecca," as she recovered her speech, "an' there's nae ither wumman in the hoose, but a'm judgin' ye werena speakin' tae me or" — with awful severity — "ye've made a mistak', an' the suner it's pit richt the better for baith you an' me an' the manse o' Drumtochty.

"For near thirty year ye've gane traivellin' in an' oot

STANDING WITH A HALF-DRIED DISH IN HER HAND.

o' this kitchen withoot cleanin' yir feet, and ye 've pit yir shoon on the fender, an' hung up yir weet coat on the back o' the door, an' commandit this an' that as if ye were the Doctor himsel', an' a' cud dae naethin', for ye were beadle o' Drumtochty.

"So a' saw there wes nae ither wy o't but tae mairry ye an' get some kind of order in the hoose; noo ye 'll understand the poseetion an' no need anither tellin'; ootside in the kirk an' pairish ye 're maister, an' a 'll never conter ye, for a' ken ma place as a kirk member an' yir place as beadle; inside in this hoose a 'm maister, an' ye 'll dae what ye 're bid, always in due submission tae the Doctor, wha 's maister baith in an' oot. Tak yir feet aff that steel bar this meenut" — this by way of practical application; and when after a brief pause, in which the fate of an empire hung in the balance, John obeyed, the two chief officials in the parish had made their covenant.

Perhaps it is unnecessary to add that they carefully kept their bounds, so that Becca would no more have thought of suggesting a new attitude to John as he stood at the foot of the pulpit stair waiting for the Doctor's descent than John would have interfered with the cooking of the Doctor's dinner. When the glass was set at fair, they even exchanged compliments, the housekeeper expressing her sense of unworthiness as she saw John in his high estate, while he would indicate that the Doctor's stock on Sacrament Sabbath reached the highest limits of human attainment. The Doctor being left to the freedom of his own will, laboured at a time to embroil the powers by tempting them to cross one another's frontiers, but always failed, because they foresaw the consequences with a very distinct imagination. If he asked

Rebecca to convey a message to Drumsheugh, that cautious woman would send in John to receive it from the Doctor's own lips, and if the Doctor gave some directions regarding dinner to John, Rebecca would appear in a few minutes to learn what the Doctor wanted. It was an almost complete delimitation of frontiers, and the Doctor used to say that he never quite understood the Free Kirk theory of the relation between Church and State till he considered the working agreement of his two retainers. It was, he once pleasantly said to the minister of Kildrummie, a perfect illustration of " co-ordinate jurisdiction with mutual subordination." It is just possible that some one may not fully grasp those impressive words, in which case let him appreciate other people's accomplishments and mourn his ignorance, for they were common speech in Drumtochty, and were taught at their porridge to the Free Kirk children.

It is an unfortunate circumstance, however, that even a scientific frontier wavers at places, and leaves a piece of doubtful territory that may at any moment become a cause of war. Surely there is not on the face of the Scottish earth a more unoffending, deferential, conciliatory person than a " probationer," who on Saturdays can be seen at every country junction, bag in hand, on his patient errand of " supply," and yet it was over his timid body the great powers of the manse twice quarrelled disastrously. As a guest in the manse, to be received on Saturday evening, to be conducted to his room, to be fed and warmed, to go to his bed at a proper hour — ten on Saturday and ten-thirty on Sabbath — to be sent away on Monday morning in good time for the train, he was within the province of Rebecca. As a

minister to be examined, advised, solemnised, encouraged, to be got ready on Sabbath morning and again dis-
robed, to be edified with suitable conversation and generally made as fit as possible for his work, he was
evidently within John's sphere of influence. It was certainly the beadle's business to visit the dining-room on
Saturday evening, where the young man was supposed to
be meditating against the ordeal of the morrow, to get
the Psalms for the precentor, to answer strictly profes-
sional questions, and generally to advise the neophyte
about the sermon that would suit Drumtochty, and the
kind of voice to be used. One thing John knew perfectly well he ought not to do, and that was to invite a
probationer to spend the evening in the Doctor's study,
for on this point Rebecca was inexorable.

"A' dinna say that they wud read the Doctor's letters,
an' a' dinna say they wud tak a buke as a keepsake, but
a' can never forget ane o' them — he hed a squint and
red hair — comin' oot frae the cupboard as a' opened
the door.

"'There 's juist ae wy oot o' the room, an' it 's by the
door ye cam in at,' a' said; 'maybe ye wud like tae
come an' sit in the dinin'-room; ye 'll be less dis-
trackit.'" And Rebecca charged John that no probationer should in future be allowed to enter the Doctor's
sanctum on any consideration.

John's excuse for his solitary fault was that the lad
thought that he could study his sermon better with
books round him, and so Rebecca found the young gentleman seated in the Doctor's own chair and working
with the Doctor's own pen, unblushing and shameless.

"Gin ye want Cruden's *Concordance*" — this was
when Rebecca had led him out a chastened man — "or

Matthew Henry tae fill up yir sermon, the books 'll be brocht by the church officer."

Rebecca's intrusion, in turn, into John's sphere was quite without excuse, and she could only explain her conduct by a general reference to the foolishness of the human heart. It came out through the ingenuousness of the probationer, who mentioned casually that he was told Drumtochty liked four heads in the sermon.

"May I ask the name of yir adviser?" said the beadle, with awful severity. "The hoosekeeper? A' thocht so, an' a' wud juist gie ye due intimation that the only person qualified an' entitled tae gie ye information on sic subjects is masel', an' ony ither is unjustified an' unwarranted.

"Fower heads? Three an' an application is the Doctor's invariable rule, an' gin a probationer gied oot a fourth, a' winna undertake tae say what michtna happen. Drumtochty is no a pairish tae trifle wi', an' it disna like new-fangled wys. Fower!" and the scorn for this unorthodox division was withering.

Rebecca realised the gravity of the situation in the kitchen, and humbled herself greatly.

"It wes as a hearer that he askit ma opinion, an' no as an authority. He said that the new wy wes tae leave oot heads, an' a' saw a' the hay spread oot across the field, so a' told him tae gither it up intae ' coles ' (hay-cocks), an' it wud be easier lifted. Maybe a' mentioned fower — a 'll no deny it; but it 's the first time a' ever touched on heads, an' it 'll be the laist."

Upon those terms of penitence, John granted pardon, but it was noticed on Sabbath that when Becca got in the way of the retiring procession to the manse, the beadle was heard in the kirkyard, " Oot o' ma road, wumman," in a tone that was full of judgment, and that Rebecca withdrew to the grass as one justly punished.

This excellent woman once accomplished her will, however, in spite of John, and had all her days the pleasant relish of a secret triumph. Her one unfulfilled desire was to see the Doctor in his court dress which he wore as Moderator of the Kirk of Scotland during the Assembly time, and which had lain ever since in a box with camphor and such preservatives amid the folds. It was aggravating to hear Drumsheugh and Hillocks — who had both gone to the Assembly that year for the sole purpose of watching the Doctor enter and bow to the standing house — enlarging on his glory in velvet and lace and silver buckles, and growing in enthusiasm with the years.

"It's little better than a sin," she used to insist, "tae see the bonnie suit gien the Doctor by the Countess o' Kilspindie, wi' dear knows hoo much o' her ain auld lace on 't, lyin' useless, wi' naebody tae get a sicht o't on his back.   Dinna ye think, man " — this with much persuasiveness — " that ye cud get the Doctor tae pit on his velvets on an occasion, maybe a Saicrament?   The pairish wud be lifted ; an' ye wud look weel walkin' afore him in his lace."

"Dinna plead wi' me, wumman ; a' wud gie a half-year's wages tae see him in his grandeur ; but it 's offeecial, div ye no see, an' canna be used except by a Moderator.   Na, na, ye can dust and stroke it, but ye 'll never see yon coat on the Doctor."

This was little less than a challenge to a woman of spirit, and Rebecca simply lived from that day to clothe the Doctor in embroidered garments.   Her opportunity arrived when Kate's birthday came round, and the

Doctor insisted on celebrating it by a party of four. By the merest accident his housekeeper met Miss Carnegie on the road, and somehow happened to describe the excellent glory of the Doctor's full dress, whereupon that wilful young woman went straight to the manse, nor left till the Doctor had promised to dine in ruffles, in which case she pledged herself that the General would come in uniform, and she would wear the family jewels, so that everything would be worthy of the Doctor's dinner.

"Hoo daur ye," began John, coming down from the Doctor's room, where the suit was spread upon the bed; but his wife did not allow him to continue, explaining that the thing was none of her doing, and that it was only becoming that honour should be shown to Miss Carnegie when she dined for the first time at the manse of Drumtochty.

DRIED ROSE LEAVES.

OWNSPEOPLE are so clever, and know so much, that it is only just something should be hidden from their sight, and it is quite certain that they do not understand the irresistible and endless fascination of the country. They love to visit us in early autumn, and are vastly charmed with the honeysuckle in the hedges, and the corn turning yellow, and the rivers singing in the sunlight, and the purple on the hill-side. It is then that the dweller in cities resolves to retire, as soon as may be, from dust and crowds and turmoil and hurry, to some cottage where the scent of roses comes in at the open window, and one is wakened of a morning by the birds singing in the ivy. When the corn is gathered into the stack-yard, and the leaves fall on the road, and the air has a touch of frost, and the evenings draw in, then the townsman begins to shiver and bethink him of his home. He leaves the fading glory with a sense of relief, like one escaping from approaching calamity, and as often as his thoughts turn thither, he pities us in our winter solitude. "What a day this will be in Drumtochty," he says, coming in from the slushy streets, and rubbing his hands before the fire.

This good man is thankful to Providence for very slight mercies, since he knows only one out of the four seasons that make our glorious year. He had been wise to visit us in the summer-time, when the light hardly dies out of the Glen, and the grass and young corn presents six shades of green, and the scent of the hay is everywhere, and all young creatures are finding themselves with joy. Perhaps he had done better to have come north in our spring-time, when nature, throwing off the yoke of winter, bursts suddenly into an altogether indescribable greenery, and the primroses are blooming in Tochty woods, and every cottage garden is sweet with wallflowers, and the birds sing of love in every wood, and the sower goes forth to sow. And though this will appear quite incredible, it had done this comfortable citizen much good to have made his will, and risked his life with us in the big snowstorm that used to shut us up for fourteen days every February. One might well endure many hardships to stand on the side of Ben Urtach, and see the land one glittering expanse of white on to the great strath on the left, and the hills above Dunleith on the right, to tramp all day through the dry, crisp snow, and gathering round the wood fire of an evening, tell pleasant tales of ancient days, while the wind powdered the glass with drift, and roared in the chimney. Then a man thanked God that he was not confined to a place where the pure snow was trodden into mire, and the thick fog made it dark at mid-day.

This very season of autumn, which frightened the townsfolk, and sent them home in silence, used to fill our hearts with peace, for it was to us the crown and triumph of the year. We were not dismayed by the leaves that fell with rustling sound in Tochty woods, nor by the bare stubble fields from which the last straw had been raked by thrifty hands, nor by the touch of cold in the north-west wind blowing over Ben Urtach, nor by the greyness of the running water. The long toil of the year had not been in vain, and the harvest had been safely gathered. The clump of sturdy little stacks, carefully thatched and roped, that stood beside each homestead, were the visible fruit of the long year's labour, and the assurance of plenty against winter. Let it snow for a week on end, and let the blast from the mouth of Glen Urtach pile up the white drift high against the outer row of stacks, the horses will be put in the mill-shed, and an inner stack will be forked into the threshing loft, and all day long the mill will go with dull, rumbling sound that can be heard from the road, while within the grain pours into the corn-room, and the clean yellow straw is piled in the barn. Hillocks was not a man given to sentiment, yet even he would wander among the stacks on an October evening, and come into the firelight full of moral reflections. A vague sense of rest and thankfulness pervaded the Glen, as if one had come home from a long journey in safety, bringing his possessions with him.

The spirit of October was on the Doctor as he waited for his guests in the drawing-room of the manse. The Doctor had a special affection for the room, and would often sit alone in it for hours in the gloaming. Once Rebecca came in suddenly, and though the light was dim and the Doctor was seated in the shadow by the piano, she was certain that he had been weeping. He would not allow any change to be made in the room, even the shifting of a table, and he was very particular about its good keeping. Twice a year Rebecca polished the old-fashioned rosewood furniture, and so often a man came from Muirtown to tune the piano, which none in the district could play, and which the Doctor kept locked. Two little pencil sketches, signed with a childish hand, Daisy Davidson, the minister always dusted himself, as also a covered picture on the wall, and the half-yearly cleaning of the drawing-room was concluded when he arranged on the backs of two chairs one piece of needlework showing red and white roses, and another whereon was wrought a posy of primroses. The room had a large bay window opening on the lawn, and the Doctor had a trick of going out and in that way, so that he often had ten minutes in its quietness; but no visitor was taken there, except once a year, when the wife of the Doctor's old friend, Lord Kilspindie, drove up to lunch, and the old man escorted her ladyship round the garden and brought her in by the window. On that occasion, but only then, the curtain was lifted from the picture, and for a brief space they stood in silence. Then he let the silken veil fall and gently arranged its folds, and offering her his arm with a very courtly bow, led the Countess into the dining-room, where Rebecca had done her best, and John waited in fullest Sabbath array.

The Doctor wandered about the room — looking out on the garden, mysterious in the fading light, changing the position of a chair, smoothing the old-fashioned needlework with caressing touch, breaking up a log in the grate. He fell at last into a revery before the fire

THE OLD MAN ESCORTED HER LADYSHIP.

— which picked out each bit of silver on his dress and shone back from the black velvet — and heard nothing, till John flung open the door and announced with immense majesty, "General Carnegie and Miss Carnegie."

"Welcome, Kate, to the house of your father's friend, and welcome for your own sake, and many returns of this day. May I say how that white silk and those rubies become you? It is very kind to put on such beautiful things for my poor little dinner. As for you, Jack, you are glorious," and the Doctor must go over Carnegie's medals till that worthy and very modest man lost all patience.

"No more of this nonsense; but, Sandie, that is a desperately becoming get-up of yours; does n't he suit it well, Kit? I never saw a better calf on any man."

"You are both 'rael bonnie,' and ought to be very grateful to me for insisting on full dress. I 'm sorry that there is only one girl to admire two such handsome men; it's a poor audience, but at any rate it is very appreciative and grateful," and Kate courtsied to each in turn, for all that evening she was in great good-humour.

"By the way, there will be one more to laugh at us, for I 've asked the Free Kirk minister to make a fourth for our table. He is a nice young fellow, with more humanity than most of his kind; but did not I hear that he called at the Lodge to pay his respects?"

"Certainly he did," said the General, "and I rather took a fancy to him. He has an honest eye and is not at all bad-looking, and tells a capital story. But Kit fell upon him about something, and I had to cover him. It's a wonder that he ever came near the place again."

"He has been at the Lodge eight times since then," explained Kate, with much composure; "but he will on no account be left alone with the head of the household.

The General insulted him on politics, and I had to interfere; so he looks on me as a kind of protector, and I walk him out to the Beeches lest he be massacred."

"Take care, my dear Catherine," for the Doctor was a shrewd old gentleman; "protecting comes perilously near loving, and Carmichael's brown eyes are dangerous."

"They are dark blue." Kate was off her guard, and had no sooner spoken than she blushed, whereat the Doctor laughed wickedly.

"You need not be afraid for Kate," said the General, cheerfully; "no man can conquer her; and as for the poor young padres, she made their lives miserable."

"They were so absurd," said Kate, "so innocent, so ignorant, so authoritative, that it was for their good to be reduced to a proper level. But I rather think your guest has forgotten his engagement. He will be so busy with his book that even a manse dinner will have no attraction." The Doctor looked again at Kate, but now she wore an air of great simplicity.

It was surely not Carmichael's blame that he was late for Dr. Davidson's dinner, since he had thought of nothing else since he rose, which was at the unearthly hour of six. He went out for a walk, which consisted of one mile east and another west from the village, and, with pauses, during which he rested on gates and looked from him, lasted two hours. On his return he explained to Sarah that his health had received much benefit, and that she was not to be surprised if he went out every morning at or before daybreak. He also mentioned casually that he was to dine at the manse that day, and Sarah, who had been alarmed lest this unexpected virtue might mean illness, was at rest. His habit was to linger over breakfast, propping a book against the sugar basin, and taking it and his rasher slice about, which was, he insisted, the peculiar joy of a bachelor's breakfast; but this morning Sarah found him at ten o'clock still at table, gazing intently at an untouched cutlet, and without any book. He swallowed two mouthfuls hurriedly and hastened to the study, leaving her to understand that he had been immersed in a theological problem. It seemed only reasonable that a man should have one pipe before settling down to a forenoon of hard study, but there is no doubt that the wreaths of smoke, as they float upwards, take fantastic shapes, and lend themselves to visions. Twelve o'clock — it was outrageous — six hours gone without a stroke of work. Sarah is informed that, as he has a piece of very stiff work to do, luncheon must be an hour later, and that the terrier had better go out for a walk. Then Carmichael cleared his table and set himself down to a new German critic, who was doing marvellous things with the Prophet Isaiah. In three thick volumes — paper bound and hideous to behold — and in a style of elaborate repulsiveness, Schlochenboshen showed that the book had been written by a syndicate, on the principle that each member contributed one verse in turn, without reference to his neighbours. It was, in fact, the simple plan of a children's game, in which you write a noun and I an adjective, and the result greatly pleases the company; and the theory of the eminent German was understood to throw a flood of light on Scripture. Schlochenboshen had already discovered eleven alternating authors, and as No. 4 would occasionally, through pure perversity and just contrary to rules, pool his contribution with No. 6, several other interesting variations were introduced. In such circumstances one must fix the list of authors in his head, and this can be conveniently done by letters of the alphabet. Carmichael made a beginning with four, KATE, and then he laid down his pen and went out for a turn in the garden. When he came in with a resolute mind, he made a precis of the Professor's introduction, and it began, "Dear Miss Carnegie," after which he went to lunch and ate three biscuits. As for some reason his mind could not face even the most fascinating German, Carmichael fell back on the twelve hundredth book on Mary Queen of Scots, which had just come from the library, and which was to finally vindicate that very beautiful, very clever, and very perplexing young woman. An hour later Carmichael was on the moor, full of an unquenchable pity for Chatelard, who had loved the sun and perished in his rays. The cold wind on the hill braced his soul, and he returned in a heroic mood. He only was the soldier of the Cross, who denied himself to earthly love and hid a broken heart. And now he read À Kempis and the *Christian Year*. Several passages in the latter he marked in pencil with a cross, and when his wife asked him the reason only last week, he smiled, but would give no answer. Having registered anew his vow of celibacy, he spent an hour in dressing, an operation, he boasted, which could be performed in six minutes, and which, on this occasion, his housekeeper determined to review.

With all the women in the Glen, old and young, she liked the lad, for a way that he had and the kindness of his heart, and was determined that he should be well dressed for once in his life. It was Sarah, indeed, that kept Carmichael late, for she not only laid out his things for him with much care and judgment, but on sight of the wisp of white round his neck she persuaded him to

accept her services, and at last she was satisfied. He
also lost a little time as he came near the manse, for he
grew concerned lest his tie was not straight, and it takes
time to examine yourself in the back of your watch,
when the light is dimming and it is necessary to retire
behind a hedge lest some keen Drumtochty eye should
detect the roadside toilet.

John had brought in the lamp before Carmichael
entered, and his confusion was pardonable, for he had
come in from the twilight, and none could have expected
such a sight.

"Glad to see you, Carmichael " — the Doctor hastened
to cover his embarrassment. " It is very good of you to
honour my little party by your presence. You know the
General, I think, and Miss Carnegie, whose first birthday
in Drumtochty we celebrate to-night.

" No wonder you are astonished," for Carmichael was
blushing furiously ; "and I must make our defence, eh,
Carnegie? else it will be understood in Free Kirk circles
that the manse is mad. We seem, in fact, a pair of old
fools, and you can have your jest at us ; but there is an
excuse even for our madness.

"It is long since we have had a young lady in our
Glen, and now that she has come to live among us —
why, sir, we must just do her bidding.

 " Our Queen has but a little court, but her courtiers
are leal and true ; and when she ordered full dress, it
was our joy to obey. And if you choose to laugh, young
sir — why, you may ; we are not ashamed with such a
Queen, and I do her homage."

The Doctor stooped and kissed Kate's hand in the
grand manner which is now lost, after which he drew out
his snuff-box and tapped it pleasantly, as one who had

taken part in a state function; but there was the suspicion of a tear in his eye, for these things woke old memories.

"Kate's a wilfu' lassie," said the General, fondly, "and she has long ruled me, so I suppose her father must do likewise."   And the General also kissed Kate's hand.

"You are both perfectly absurd to-night," said Kate, confused and red, "but no Queen ever had truer hearts to love her, and if I cannot make you knights, I must reward you as I can."   And Kate, ignoring Carmichael, kissed first her father and then the Doctor. Then she turned on him with a proud air, "What think you of my court, Mr. Carmichael?"

"It is the best in Christendom, Miss Carnegie"—and his voice trembled with earnestness—"for it has the fairest Queen and two gentlemen of Christ for its servants."

"Very prettily said"—the Doctor thought the little scene had gone far enough—"and as a reward for that courteous speech you shall take Her Majesty in to dinner, and we old battered fellows shall follow in attendance." There was a moment's silence, and then Carmichael spoke.

"If I had only known, Miss Carnegie, that I might have . . . put on something to do you honour too, but I have nothing except a white silk hood. I wish I had been a Militiaman or . . . a Freemason."

"This is your second remarkable wish in my hearing," and Kate laughed merrily; "last time you wished you were a dog on Muirtown platform. Your third will be your last, I suppose, and one wonders what it will be."

"It is already in my heart"—Carmichael spoke low —"and some day I will dare to tell it to you."

"Hush," replied Kate quickly, lifting her hand; "the padre is going to say grace." As this was an official function in John's eyes, that worthy man allowed himself to take a general view, and he was pleased to express his high approval of the company, enlarging especially on Carmichael, whom, as a Free Kirkman, he had been accustomed rather to belittle.

"Of coorse," he explained loyally, "he 's no tae be compared wi' the Doctor, for there 's nae minister ootside the Auld Kirk can hae sic an air, and he 's no set up like the General, but he lookit weel an' winsome.

"His hair wes flung back frae his forehead, his een were fair dancin', an' there wes a bit o' colour in his cheek. He hes a wy wi' him, a 'll no deny, 'at taks wi' fouk.

"A 'm no sure that he 's been at mony denners though, Becca, for he hardly kent what he wes daein'. A' juist pit the potatoes on his plate, for he never lat on he saw me; an' as for wine, a' cudna get a word oot o' him."

"Ye 're lifted above ordinary concerns, John, an' it 's no tae be expeckit that a beadle sud notice the way o' a lad wi' a lass," and Becca nodded her head with much shrewdness.

"Div ye mean that, Rebecca? That cowes a'; but it 's no possible. The General's dochter an' a Free Kirk minister, an' her an Esculopian — "

"Love kens naither rank nor creeds; see what ye did yersel', and you beadle o' Drumtochty;" and John — every man has some weak point — swallowed the compliment with evident satisfaction.

Meanwhile they had fallen on this very subject of creeds in the dining-room, and Kate was full of curiosity.

"Will you two padres do me a favour? I knew you would. Well, I want to know for certain what is the difference between the two Kirks in Drumtochty. Now which of you will begin?" and Kate beamed on them both.

"Whatever you wish we will do, Kate," said the Doctor; "but you will have me excused in this matter, if you please, and hear my friend. I am tired of controversy, and he has a fair mind, and, as I know well, a pleasant wit. Tell Miss Carnegie how your people left the Kirk of Scotland."

"Well, the dispute began "— and Carmichael faced his task manfully —"about the appointment of clergymen, whether it should lie with a patron or the people. Lord Kilspindie had the nomination of Drumtochty, and if every patron had been as wise as our house, then there had been no Disruption."

The Doctor bowed, and motioned to Carnegie to fortify himself with port.

"Other patrons had no sense, and put in unsuitable men, and the people rebelled, since it is a sad thing for a country parish to have a minister who is not . . ."

"A gentleman? or straight? Quite so," chimed in Kate; "it must be beastly."

"So a party fought for the rights of the people," resumed Carmichael, "and desired that the parish should have a voice in choosing the man who was to take charge of . . . their souls."

"Is n't that like soldiers electing their officers?" inquired the General, doubtfully.

"Go on, Carmichael; you are putting your case capitally; don't plunge into theology, Jack, whatever you do . . . it is Sandeman's — a sound wine."

"Then what happened?" and Kate encouraged Carmichael with her eyes.

"Four hundred clergymen threw up their livings one day and went out to begin a Free Kirk, where there are no patrons.

"You have no idea — for I suppose you never heard of this before — how ministers suffered, living and dying in miserable cottages — and the people met for service on the sea-shore or in winter storms — all for conscience sake."

Carmichael was glowing, and the Doctor sipped his port approvingly.

"Perhaps they ought not to have seceded, and perhaps their ideas were wrong; but it was heroism, and a good thing for the land."

"It was splendid!" Kate's cheek flushed. "And Drumtochty?"

"Ah, something happened here that was by itself in Scotland. Will you ask Dr. Davidson not to interrupt or browbeat me? Thank you; now I am safe.

"Some one of influence went to old Lord Kilspindie, who had no love to the Free Kirk, and told him that a few of his Drumtochty men wanted to get a site for a Free Kirk, and that he must give it. And he did."

"Now, Carmichael," began the Doctor, who had scented danger; but Kate held up her hand with an imperious gesture, and Carmichael went on : —

"The same person used to send to the station for the Free Kirk probationer, and entertain him after a lordly fashion — with port, if he were worthy — and send him on his way rejoicing — men have told me. But," concluded Carmichael, averting his face from the foot of the table, "wild horses will not compel me to give that good Samaritan's name."

"Was it you, Davidson, that sanctioned such a proceeding? Why, it was mutiny."

"Of course he did, dad," cried Kate; "just the very thing he would do; and so, I suppose, the Free Kirk love him as much as they do yourself, sir?"

"As much? far more . . . "

"Had I known what downright falsehood the Free Kirk minister of Drumtochty was capable of, I would never have allowed him to open his mouth."

"Well, I am satisfied, at any rate," said Kate, "and I propose to retire to the drawing-room, and I know who would love a rubber of whist by-and-by. We are just the number."

A minute later Carmichael asked leave to join Kate, as he believed she was to have him for partner, and he must understand her game.

"How adroit he is to-night, Jack;" but the General rather pitied the lad, with whom he imagined Kate was playing as a cat with a mouse.

"Have you ever seen the face below the veil?" for they did not talk long about whist in the drawing-room. "I do not think it would be wrong to look, for the padre told me the story.

"Yes, a very winning face. His only sister, and he simply lived for her. She was only twelve when she died, and he loves her still, although he hardly ever speaks of her."

They stood together before the happy girl-face enshrined in an old man's love. They read the inscription: "My dear sister Daisy."

"I never had a sister," and Carmichael sighed.

"And I have now no brother." Their hands met as they gently lowered the veil.

"Well, have you arranged your plans?" and the Doctor came in intent on whist.

"Only one thing. I am going to follow Miss Carnegie's lead, and she is always to win," said the Free Kirk minister of Drumtochty.

CHAPTER XVII

SMOULDERING FIRES.

T is the right of every Scot — secured to him by the Treaty of Union and confirmed by the Disruption — to criticise his minister with much freedom, but this privilege is exercised with a delicate charity. When it is not possible for a conscientious hearer to approve a sermon, he is not compelled to condemnation. "There wes naething wrang wi' the text," affords an excellent way of escape, and it is open to suggest efficiency in another department than the pulpit. "Mister MacWheep michtna be a special preacher, but there 's nae doot he wes a graund veesitor." Before Carmichael left the West Kirk, Edinburgh, where he served his apprenticeship as an assistant, a worthy elder called to bid him good-bye, and spoke faithfully, to the lad's great delight.

"You have been very acceptable, wonderfully so for a young man, and we shall follow your career with much interest. It is right, however, to add, and you will accept this in a right spirit, that it was not by preaching that you commended yourself to our people, but by your visiting. Your sermons are what I might call . . . hazy — you will get a hold of the truth by-and-by, no doubt — but you have a gift for visitation."

The exact quality and popularity of this gift was excellently stated by the wife of a working man, who referred with enthusiasm to the edifying character of the assistant's conversation.

"Tammas misses Maister Carmichael juist terrible, for he wud come in on a forenicht an' sit, an' smoke, an' haver wi' the gude man by the 'oor. He wes the maist divertin' minister a' ever saw in the West Kirk."

It will be evident that Carmichael's visitation belonged to a different department of art from that of Dr. Davidson. He arrived without intimation by the nearest way that he could invent, clothed in a shooting jacket and a soft hat, and accompanied by at least two dogs. His coming created an instant stir, and Carmichael plunged at once into the life of the household. It is kept on fond record, and still told by the surviving remnant of his flock, that on various occasions and in the course of pastoral visitation he had turned the hay in summer, had forked the sheaves in harvest-time, had sacked the corn for market, and had driven a gude wife's churn. After which honourable toil he would eat and drink anything put before him   except boiled tea, against which he once preached with power — and then would sit indefinitely with the family before the kitchen fire, telling tales of ancient history, recalling the old struggles of Scottish men, describing foreign sights, enlarging on new books, till he would remember that he had only dropped in for

an hour, and that two meals must be waiting for him at
the manse. His visits were understood to be quite
unfinished, and he left every house pledged to return
and take up things at the point where he had been
obliged to break off, and so he came at last in this
matter of visitation into a condition of hopeless insolv-
ency. His adventures were innumerable and always
enjoyable — falling off the two fir trees that made a
bridge over our deeper burns, and being dried at the
next farm-house — wandering over the moor all night
and turning up at a gamekeeper's at daybreak, covered
with peat and ravening with hunger — fighting his way
through a snowstorm to a marriage, and digging the
bridegroom out of a drift — dodging a herd of Highland
cattle that thought he had come too near their calves, or
driving off Drumsheugh's polled Angus bull with con-
tumely when he was threatening Mrs. Macfadyen. If
he met the bairns coming from school, the Glen rang
with the foolery. When Willie Harley broke his leg,
Carmichael brought his dog Jackie — I could tell things
of that dog — and devised dramatic entertainments of
such attraction that Jamie Soutar declared them no better
than the theatre, and threatened Carmichael with a skep
of honey as a mark of his indignation. As for the old
women of the Glen, he got round them to that extent that
they would gossip with him by the hour over past days,
and Betty Macfarlane was so carried by the minister's
sympathy that she brought out from hidden places some
finery of her youth, and Carmichael was found by Miss
Carnegie arranging a faded Paisley shawl on Betty's
shoulders. And was it not this same gay Free Kirkman
who trained an eleven to such perfection on a field of
Drumsheugh's that they beat the second eleven of Muir-

town gloriously? on which occasion Tammas Mitchell, by
the keenness of his eye and the strength of his arm, made
forty-four runs; and being congratulated by Drumtochty
as he carried his bat, opened his mouth for the first time
that day, saying, " Awa wi' ye."

WOULD GOSSIP WITH HIM BY THE HOUR.

So it came to pass that notwithstanding his unholy
tendency to Biblical criticism and other theological
pedantry, Drumtochty loved Carmichael because he
was a man; and Dr. Davidson, lighting upon him in
Hillocks' garden, with the family round him full of joy,
would threaten him with a prosecution for poaching

under the ecclesiastical Game Laws, and end by insisting
upon him coming to dinner at the manse, when he
might explain his conduct. Drumtochty loved him for
his very imperfections, and follows his career unto this
day with undying interest, recalling his various escapades
with huge delight, and declaring to strangers that even in
his callow days they had discovered that Carmichael was
a preacher.

Carmichael had occasional fits of order, when he repented of his desultory ways, and began afresh with
much diligence, writing out the names of the congregation with full details — he once got as far as Menzies
before he lost the book — mapping the parish into
districts, and planning an elaborate visitation. It may
have been an accident that the district he chose for
experiment embraced Tochty Lodge — where the Carnegies had just settled — but it was natural that his first
effort should be thorough. There were exactly ten Free
Kirk families from Tochty Lodge eastwards, and some of
these still speak with feeling of the attention they received, which exceeded all they had ever known before
or since.

" It wesna that he sat sae lang as a 've heard o' him
daein' in the heich Glen, but it wes the times he cam', "
Mrs. Stirton used to expatiate, " maybe twice a week for
a month. He hed a wy o' comin' through Tochty
Wood — the shade helpit him tae study, he said — an'
jumpin' the dyke. Sall, gin he dinna mak a roadie for
himsel' through the field that year. A' wudna say," she
used to add in a casual tone, " but that he micht hae
gi'en a cry at the Lodge, but he cudna dae less, passin'
the door."

Carmichael was astonished himself at the number of

times he was obliged to see General Carnegie on business, of one kind or another. Sometimes it was about the Flower Show, of which the General had become a patron; sometimes it was the Highland Games, when the General's help would be of so much use; sometimes it was the idea of repairing the old bridge; sometimes— and Carmichael blushed when it came to this — to get the General's opinion on a military question in the Bible. The least he could do in laying such a tax on a good-natured man was to bring a book for his daughter's reading, or a curious flower he had picked up on the hill, or a story he had heard in his visiting. Miss Carnegie was generally gracious, and would see him on his way if the day were fine, or show him some improvements in the " Pleasaunce," or accompany him to Janet's cottage to have a taste of that original woman's conversation to-gether. It came upon Carmichael at a time that he was, inadvertently, calling too frequently at the Lodge, and for a week he would keep to the main road, or even pass the corner of the Lodge with an abstracted air — for he loathed the thought of being deflected from the path of duty by any personal attraction— and used to change the subject of conversation after Janet had spoken for half an hour on Kate.

People were speculating in a guarded manner regard-ing the possibility of news, and Janet had quarrelled furiously with Donald for laughing such unworthy rumours to scorn, when the parish was almost convulsed by the historic scene in the Free Kirk, and all hope of a roman-tic alliance was blasted. Archie Moncur, elder, and James Macfadyen, deacon, were counting the collection in the vestibule, and the congregation within were just singing the last verse of their first psalm, when General Carnegie and his daughter appeared at the door.

"Has service begun?" whispered Kate, while her father reverently bared his head. "I 'm so sorry we are late, but you will let us in, won't you, and we shall be as quiet as mice."

"A 'll open the door," and Archie explained the geography of the situation, "an' ye 'll juist slip intae the manse pew; it 's in the corner, wi' curtains roond it, an' naebody 'll see ye, naither minister nor people;" and so Carmichael went through the service, and had almost reached the end of his sermon before he knew that Kate was in the church.

She was very conscious of him and keenly observant of every detail — his white silk hood thrown into relief by the black Geneva gown, his fair, flushed face touched with tenderness and reverence, a new accent of affection in his voice as one speaking to his charge, and especially she noted in this Free Kirkman a certain fervour and high hope, a flavour also of subtle spirituality, that were wanting in Dr. Davidson. His hair might have been better brushed, and his whiskers were distinctly ragged — but those things could be easily put right; then she tossed her head in contempt of herself. It had come to a fine pass when a girl that had carried her heart un- touched through Simla should be concerned about the appearance of a Highland minister. The General was well acquainted with that proud motion, and began to regret that they had come. It was Davidson's blame, who had sent them to hear a good sermon for once, as he said, and now Kate would only find material for raillery. He tugged his moustache and wished that they were again in the open air.

When the sermon came, the occupants of the manse pew composed themselves for fifteen minutes' patient endurance, after the well-bred fashion of their Church, each selecting a corner with a skill born of long experience. They were not, however, to rest in peace and detachment of mind till the doxology (or its corresponding formula in the Scottish Kirk) summoned them back, for this was to be a quite memorable sermon for them and their fellow-hearers and all Drumtochty.

Carmichael had been lecturing through Old Testament history, and having come to the drama of Elijah and Jezebel, had laid himself out for its full and picturesque treatment. He was still at that age when right seems to be all on one side, and a particular cause can be traced down the centuries in all lands and under all conditions. For the most part of two days he had wandered over the moor in the bright, cold November weather reconstructing the scene in Israel on Scottish lines, and he entered the pulpit that morning charged with the Epic of Puritanism. Acute critics, like Elspeth Macfadyen, could tell from Carmichael's walk down the church that he was in great spirits, and even ordinary people caught a note of triumph in his voice as he gave out the first Psalm. For the first few sentences of his sermon he spoke quietly, as one reserving and restraining himself, and gave a historical introduction which allowed the General to revive some ancient memories of India without interruption. But Kate caught the imperial tone of one who had a message to deliver and was already commanding people to listen. She was conscious of a certain anxiety, and began to wish that she were in front and could see his face, instead of only the side of his head. Then Carmichael threw back his hair with the air of one taking off his coat, and plunged the congregation into the midst of the battle, describing Elijah's forgetfulness of self, pro-

found conviction of righteousness, high purpose for his
nation and devotion to the cause of Jehovah, till Burnbrae and the Free Kirkmen straightened themselves
visibly in their pews, and touching so skilfully on the
Tyrian princess in her beauty, her culture, her bigotry,
her wiles, her masterfulness, that several women —
greatly delighting in the exposure of such a " trimmie "
— nodded approval.   Kate had never given herself to the
study of Old Testament history, and would have had
some difficulty in identifying Elijah — there was a mare
called Jezebel of vicious temper — but she caught the
contagion of enthusiasm.   If the supreme success of a
sermon be to stimulate the hearer's mind, then Carmichael
ought to have closed at this point.   His people would
have been all the week fighting battles for conscience
sake, and resisting smooth, cunning temptation to the
farthest limits of their lives and in unimaginable ways.
Kate herself, although a person quite unaffected by
preaching, had also naturalised the sermon in her life
with much practical and vivid detail.   Carmichael was
Elijah, the prophet of the common people, with his
simple ways and old-fashioned notions and love of hardness, only far more gentle and courteous and amusing
than that uncompromising Jew; and she — why, she
would be Jezebel just for the moment, who had come
from . . . India into the Glen, and could bring Elijah
to her feet if she chose, and make him do her will, and
then . . .   The girls in the choir before the pulpit
noticed the look on Kate's face, and wondered whether
the Carnegies would join the Free Kirk.

Carmichael had an instinct that he ought to fling over
the remaining four pages of his sermon and close the
service with a war Psalm, and he told me when I was

staying with him last week that he sacrifices the last head
of his sermon almost every Sunday in his city pulpit.
But he was only a lad in Drumtochty, and besides was
full of a historical parallel, which after a scientific illustration is most irresistible to a young minister. No one
had ever seen it before, but of course Elijah was John
Knox, and Jezebel was Queen Mary of Scots, and then
Carmichael set to work afresh, with something less
than conspicuous success. Scottish people are always
ready for a eulogium on John Knox in church, or on
Robert Burns out of church, but the Reformer is rather
the object of patriotic respect and personal devotion.
Netherton snuffed in quite a leisurely way, and the women
examined the bonnet of the manse housekeeper, while
Knox stood in the breach for the liberties of Scotland,
and when Carmichael began to meddle with Mary, he
distinctly lost the sympathies of his audience and entered on dangerous ground. Scots allow themselves, at
times, the rare luxury of being illogical, and one of the
occasions is their fondness for Queen Mary. An austere
Puritan may prove that this young woman was French in
her ways, an enemy to the Evangel, a born and practised
flirt, and art and part in the murder of Darnley. A Scot
will not deny the evidence, and if he be thrust into the
box he may bring in the prisoner guilty, but his heart is
with the condemned, and he has a grudge against the
prosecutor. For he never forgets that Mary was of the
royal blood and a thorough Stewart, that her face turned
men's heads in every country she touched, that she had the
courage of a man in her, that she was shamefully used,
and if she did throw over that ill-conditioned lad,
well . . . " Puir lassie, she hed naebody tae guide her,
but sall, she focht her battle weel," and out of this judgment none can drive an honest Scot.

"Yon wes a graund discoorse the day, gude wife," Jeems hazarded to Elspeth on the way home, "but a' thocht the minister wes a wee hard on Queen Mary; there 's nae doot she wes a papist, an' micht hae gien Knox a bit twist wi' the screws gin she cud hae gruppit him, but a' dinna like her misca'd."

"A 've heard him wi' ma ain ears crackin' her up by the 'oor, an' a' canna mak' oot what set him against her the day; but he 's young," remarked Elspeth, sagely, "an' wi' his age it 's either saint or deevil, an' ae day the one an' the next day the ither; there 's nae medium. Noo, maist fouk are juist half an' between, an' Mary hed her faults.

"Ma word, Jeems," continued Elspeth with much relish, "Mary wud sune hae settled the minister gin she hed been in the kirk the day."

"Ay, ay," inquired Jeems, "noo what wud the hizzie hae dune?"

"She wud juist hae sent for him an' lookit wi' her een, an' askit him what ill he hed at her, an' gin that wesna eneuch she wud hae pit her handkerchief tae her face."

"Of coorse he cudna hae stude that; a' micht hae gien in masel'," admitted Jeems, "but Knox wes stiff."

"Maister Carmichael is no a Knox, naither are ye, Jeems, an' it 's a mercy for me ye arena. Mary wud hae twistit Maister Carmichael roond her finger, but a 'm judgin' he 'll catch it as it is afore mony days, or ma name 's no Elspeth Macfadyen. Did ye see Miss Carnegie rise an' gae oot afore he feenished?"

"Div ye mean that, Elspeth?" and her husband was amazed at such penetration. "Noo a' thocht it hed

been the heat ; a' never held wi' that stove ; it draws up
the air.   Hoo did ye jalouse yon ?"

"She wes fidgetin' in her seat when he yokit on
Mary, an' the meenut he named her 'our Scottish
Jezebel' the Miss rose an' opened the seat door that
calm, a' knew she wes in a tantrum, and she gied him a
look afore she closed the kirk door that wud hae brocht
ony man tae his senses.

"Jeems," went on Elspeth with solemnity, "a' coont
this a doonricht calamity, for a' wes houpin' he wud hae
pleased· them the day, an' noo a 'm sair afraid that the
minister hes crackit his credit wi' the Lodge."

"Div ye think, Elspeth, he saw her gang oot an' sus-
peckit the cause ?"

"It 's maist michty tae hear ye ask sic a question,
Jeems. What gared him mak' a hash o' the baptism
prayer, and return thanks that there wes a leevin' father,
instead o' mither, and gie oot the 103rd Paraphrase?
Tak' ma word for 't, he 's wishin' by this time that he 'd
lat puir Mary alane."

It was just above Hillocks' farm that the General overtook Kate, who was still blazing.

"Did you ever hear such vulgar abuse and . . . abom-
inable language from a pulpit? He 's simply a raging
fanatic, and not one bit better than his Knox. And I
. . . we thought him quite different . . . and a gentleman.
I 'll never speak to him again. Scottish Jezebel : I suppose he would call me Jezebel if it occurred to him."

"Very likely he would," replied the General, dryly,
" and I must say his talk about Queen Mary seemed
rather bad taste. But that 's not the question, Kate,
which is your conduct in leaving a place of worship in
such an . . . unladylike fashion."

" What ? " for this was new talk from her father.

" As no Carnegie ought to have done. You have forgotten yourself and your house, and there is just one thing for you to do, and the sooner the better."

" Father, I 'll never look at him again . . . and after that evening at Dr. Davidson's, and our talking . . . about Queen Mary, and . . . lots of things."

" Whether you meet Mr. Carmichael again or not is your own affair, but this touches us both, and you . . . must write a letter of apology."

" And if I don't? " said Kate, defiantly.

" Then I shall write one myself for you. A Carnegie must not insult any man, be he one faith or the other, and offer him no amends."

So Donald handed in this letter at the Free Kirk Manse that evening, and left without an answer.

Tochty Lodge.

Sir, — Your violent and insolent attack on a martyred Queen caused me to lose self-control in your church to-day, and I was unable to sit longer under such language.

It has been pointed out to me that I ought not to have left church as I did, and I hereby express regret.

The books you were so good as to lend me I have sent back by the messenger. — Yours truly,

Catherine Carnegie.

When Carmichael called next day, Donald informed him with unconcealed satisfaction that Lord Hay was lunching with the family, and that the General and Miss Carnegie were going to Muirtown Castle to-morrow for a visit ; but Janet had not lost hope.

" Do not be taking this to heart, my dear, for I will be asking a question. What will be making Miss Kate so very angry? it is not every man she would be minding, though he spoke against Queen Mary all the day. When a woman does not care about a man she will not take the trouble to be angry. That is what I am thinking; and it is not Lord Hay that has the way, oh no, though he be a proper man and good at shooting."

CHAPTER XVIII.

OLLEGE friends settled in petty lowland towns, and meeting Carmichael on sacramental occasions, affected to pity him, inquiring curiously what were his means of conveyance after the railway ceased, what time a letter took to reach him, whether any foot ever crossed his door from October to May, whether the great event of the week was not the arrival of the bread cart. Those were exasperating gibes from men who could not take a walk without coming on a coal pit, nor lift a book in their studies without soiling their hands, whose windows looked on a street and commanded the light of a grocer's shop instead of a sunset. It ill became such miserables to be insolent, and Carmichael taught them humility when he began to sound the praises of Drumtochty; but he could not make townspeople understand the unutterable satisfaction of the country minister, who even from old age and great cities looks back with fond regret to his first parish on the slope of the Grampians. Some kindly host wrestles with him to stay a few days more in civilisation, and pledges him to run up whenever he wearies of his exile, and the ungrateful rustic can hardly conceal the joy of his escape. He shudders on the way to the station at the drip of the dirty sleet and the rags of the shivering poor, and the restless faces of the men and the unceasing roar of the traffic. Where he is going the white snow is falling gently on the road, a cart full of sweet-smelling roots is moving on velvet, the driver stops to exchange views with a farmer who has been feeding his sheep, within the humblest cottage the fire is burning clearly. With every mile northwards the Glenman's heart lifts; and as he lands on his far-away little station, he draws a deep breath of the clean, wholesome air. It is a long walk through the snow, but there is a kindly, couthy smell from the woods, and at sight of the squares of light in his home, weariness departs from a Drumtochty man. Carmichael used to say that a glimpse of Archie Moncur sitting with his sisters before the fire as he passed, and the wild turmoil of his dogs within the manse as the latch of the garden gate clicked, and the flood of light pouring out from the open door on the garden, where every branch was feathered with snow, and to come into his study, where the fire of pine logs was reflected from the familiar titles of his loved books, gave him a shock of joy such as he has never felt since, even in the days of his prosperity.

"The city folk are generous with their wealth," he was saying to me only last week, when I was visiting him in his West End manse and we fell a-talking of the Glen, "and they have dealt kindly by me; they are also full of ideas, and they make an inspiring audience for a preacher. If any man has a message to deliver from the Eternal, then he had better leave the wilderness and come to the city, and if he has plans for the helping of his fellow men, let him come where he can get his work and his labourers.

THE DRIVER STOPS TO EXCHANGE VIEWS.

" No, I do not repent leaving the Glen, for the Divine Hand thrust me forth and has given me work to do, and I am not ungrateful to the friends I have made in the city; but God created me a countryman, and "— here Carmichael turned his back to me — "my heart goes back to Drumtochty, and the sight of you fills me with . . . longing.

"Ah, how this desiderium, as the Rabbi would have said, comes over one with the seasons as they come and go. In spring they send me the first snowdrops from the Glen, but it is a cruel kindness, for I want to be where they are growing in Clashiegar den. When summer comes people praise the varied flower-beds of the costly city parks, but they have not seen Tochty woods in their glory. Each autumn carries me to the harvest field, till in my study I hear the swish of the scythe and feel the fragrance of the dry, ripe grain. And in winter I see the sun shining on the white sides of Glen Urtach, and can hardly keep pen to paper in this dreary room.

"What nonsense this is," pulling himself together; "yes, that is the very chair you sat in, and this is the table we stuck between us with our humble flask of Moselle of a winter's night . . . let's go to bed; we 'll have no more good talk to-night."

When he had left me, I flung open my window in search of air, for it seemed as if the city were choking me. A lamp was flaring across the street, two cabs rattled past with revellers singing a music-hall song, a heavy odour from many drains floated in, the multitude of houses oppressed one as with a weight. How sweet and pure it was now at the pool above Tochty mill, where the trout were lying below the stones and the ash boughs dipping into the water.

Carmichael once, however, lost all love of the Glen, and that was after Kate flung herself out of the Free Kirk and went on a visit to Muirtown Castle. He was completely disenchanted and saw everything at its poorest. Why did they build the manse so low that an able-bodied man could touch the ceiling of the lower rooms with an effort and the upper rooms easily? What possessed his predecessor to put such an impossible paper on the study and to stuff the room with bookshelves? A row of Puritan divines offended him — a wooden, obsolete theology — but he also pitched a defence of Queen Mary into a cupboard — she had done enough mischief already. The garden looked squalid and mean, without flowers, with black patches peeping through the thin covering of snow, with a row of winter greens opposite the southern window. He had never noticed the Glen so narrow and bare before, nor how grey and unlovely were the houses. Why had not the people better manners and some brightness? they were not always attending funerals and making bargains. What an occupation for an educated man to spend two hours in a cabin of a vestry with a dozen labouring men, considering how two pounds could be added to the Sustentation Fund, or preaching on Sunday to a handful of people who showed no more animation than stone gods except when the men took snuff audibly. Carmichael was playing the spoiled child — not being at all a mature or perfect character, then or now — and was ready to hit out at anybody. His bearing was for the first and only time in his life supercilious, and his sermons were a vicious attack on the doctrines most dear to the best of his people. His elders knew not what had come over him, although Elspeth Macfadyen was mysteriously apologetic, and in moments of sanity he despised himself. One day he came to a good resolution suddenly, and went down to see Rabbi Saunderson

TWO TRAMPS HELD CONFERENCE

—the very thought of whose gentle, patient, selfless life
was a rebuke and a tonic.

When two tramps held conference on the road, and

one indicated to the other visibly that any gentleman in temporary distress would be treated after a Christian fashion at a neighbouring house, Carmichael, who had been walking in a dream since he passed the lodge, knew instantly that he must be near the Free Kirk manse of Kilbogie. The means of communication between the members of the nomadic profession is almost perfect in its frequency and accuracy, and Saunderson's manse was a hedge-side word. Not only did all the regular travellers by the north road call on their going up in spring and their coming down in autumn, but habitués of the east coast route were attracted and made a circuit to embrace so hospitable a home, and even country vagrants made their way from Dunleith and down through Glen Urtach to pay their respects to the Rabbi. They had particular directions to avoid Barbara — expressed forcibly on five different posts in the vicinity and enforced in picturesque language, of an evening — and they were therefore careful to waylay the Rabbi on the road, or enter his study boldly from the front. The humbler members of the profession contented themselves with explaining that they had once been prosperous tradesmen, and were now walking to Muirtown in search of work — receiving their alms, in silence, with diffidence and shame ; but those in a higher walk came to consult the Rabbi on Bible difficulties, which were threatening to shake their faith, and departed much relieved — with a new view of Lot's wife, as well as a suit of clothes the Rabbi had only worn three times.

"You have done kindly by me in calling" — the vagabond had finished his story and was standing, a very abject figure, among the books — " and in giving me the message from your friend. I am truly thankful that he is now labouring — in iron, did you say? and I hope he may be a cunning artificer.

" You will not set it down to carelessness that I cannot quite recall the face of your friend, for, indeed, it is my privilege to see many travellers, and there are times when I may have been a minister to them on their journeys, as I would be to you also if there be anything in which I can serve you. It grieves me to say that I have no clothing that I might offer you; it happens that a very worthy man passed here a few days ago most insufficiently clad and . . . but I should not have alluded to that; my other garments, save what I wear, are . . . kept in a place of . . . safety by my excellent housekeeper, and she makes their custody a point of conscience; you might put the matter before her. . . . Assuredly it would be difficult, and I crave your pardon for putting you in an . . . embarrassing position; it is my misfortune to have to-day neither silver nor gold," catching sight of Carmichael in the passage, "this is a Providence. May I borrow from you, John, some suitable sum for our brother here who is passing through adversity?"

" Do not be angry with me, John " — after the tramp had departed, with five shillings in hand and much triumph over Carmichael on his face — " nor speak bitterly of our fellow men. Verily theirs is a hard lot who have no place to lay their head, and who journey in weariness from city to city. John, I was once a stranger and a wayfarer, wandering over the length and breadth of the land. Nor had I a friend on earth till my feet were led to the Mains, where my heart was greatly refreshed, and now God has surrounded me with young men of whose kindness I am not worthy, wherefore it becometh me to show mercy unto others," and the Rabbi looked at Carmichael with such sweetness, that the lad's sullenness began to yield, although he made no sign.

"Moreover," and the Rabbi's voice took a lower tone, "as often as I look on one of those men of the highways, there cometh to me a vision of Him who was an outcast of the people, and albeit some may be as Judas, peradventure one might beg alms of me, a poor sinful man, some day, and lo it might be . . . the Lord Himself in a saint," and the Rabbi bowed his head and stood awhile much moved.

"Rabbi," after a pause, during which Carmichael's face had changed, "you are incorrigible. For years we have been trying to make you a really good and wise man, both by example and precept, and you are distinctly worse than when we began — more lazy, miserly, and uncharitable. It is very disheartening.

"Can you receive another tramp and give him a bed, for I am in low spirits, and so, like every other person in trouble, I come to you, you dear old saint, and already I feel a better man."

"Receive you, John? It is doubtless selfish, but it is not given to you to know how I weary to see your faces, and we shall have much converse together — there are some points I would like your opinion on — but first of all, after a slight refreshment, we must go to Mains: behold the aid to memory I have designed " — and the Rabbi pointed to a large square of paper hung above Chrysostom, with " Farewell, George Pitillo, 3 o'clock."
" He is the son's son of my benefactor, and he leaves his father's house this day to go into a strange land across the sea: I had a service last night at Mains, and

expounded the departure of Abraham, but only slightly, being somewhat affected through the weakness of the flesh. There was a covenant made between the young man and myself, that I should meet him at the crossing of the roads to-day, and it is in my mind to leave a parable with him against the power of this present world."

Then the Rabbi fell into a meditation till the dog-cart came up, Mains and his wife in the front and George alone in the back, making a brave show of indifference.

"George," said the Rabbi, looking across the field and speaking as to himself, "we shall not meet again in this world, and in a short space they will bury me in Kilbogie kirkyard, but it will not be in me to lie still for thinking of the people I have loved. So it will come to pass that I may rise — you have ears to understand, George — and I will inquire of him that taketh charge of the dead about many and how it fares with them."

"And George Pitillo, what of him, Andrew?"

"'Oh, it's a peety you didna live langer, Mr. Saunderson, for George hes risen in the warld and made a great fortune.'"

"How does it go with his soul, Andrew?"

"'Well, you see, Mister Saunderson, George hes hed many things to think about, and he maybe hasna hed time for releegion yet, but nae doot he'll be turnin' his mind that wy soon.'"

"Poor George, that I baptised and admitted to the sacrament and . . . loved : exchanged his soul for the world."

The sun was setting fast, and the landscape — bare stubble fields, leafless trees, still water, long, empty road

—was of a blood-red colour fearsome to behold, so that no one spake, and the horse chafing his bit made the only sound.

Then the Rabbi began again.

"And George Pitillo — tell me, Andrew?"

"'Weel, ye see, Mister Saunderson, ye wud be sorry for him, for you and he were aye chief; he's keepit a gude name an' workit hard, but hesna made muckle o' this warld.'"

"And his soul, Andrew?"

"'Oo, that's a' richt; gin we a' hed as gude a chance for the next warld as George Pitillo we micht be satisfied.'"

"That is enough for his old friend; hap me over again, Andrew, and I'll rest in peace till the trumpet sound."

Carmichael turned aside, but he heard something desperately like a sob from the back of the dog-cart, and the Rabbi saying, "God be with you, George, and as your father's father received me in the day of my sore discouragement, so may the Lord God of Israel open a door for you in every land whithersoever you go, and bring you in at last through the gates into the city." The Rabbi watched George till the dog-cart faded away into the dusk of the winter's day, and they settled for the night in their places among the books before the Rabbi spoke.

It was with a wistful tenderness that he turned to Carmichael and touched him slightly with his hand, as was a fashion with the Rabbi.

"You will not think me indifferent to your welfare because I have not inquired about your affairs, for indeed this could not be, but the going forth of this lad has tried my heart. Is there aught, John, that it becometh you to tell me, and wherein my years can be of any avail? "

" It is not about doctrine I wished to speak to you, Rabbi, although I am troubled thus also, but about . . . you remember our talk."

"About the maid, surely; I cannot forget her, and indeed often think of her since the day you brought me to her house and made me known unto her, which was much courtesy to one who is fitter for a book-room than a woman's company.

"She is fair of face and hath a pleasant manner, and surely beauty and a winsome way are from God; there seemed also a certain contempt of baseness and a strength of will which are excellent. Perhaps my judgment is not even because Miss Carnegie was gracious to me, and you know, John, it is not in me to resist kindness, but this is how she seems to me. Has there been trouble between you?"

" Do not misunderstand me, Rabbi; I have not spoken one word of love to . . . Miss Carnegie, nor she to me; but I love her, and I thought that perhaps she saw that I loved her. But now it looks as if . . . what I hoped is never to be," and Carmichael told the Queen Mary affair.

"Is it not marvellous," mused the Rabbi, looking into the fire, " how one woman who was indeed at the time little more than a girl did carry men, many of them wise and clever, away as with a flood, and still divideth scholars and even . . . friends?

" It was not fitting that Miss Carnegie should have left God's house in heat of temper, and it seemeth to us that she hath a wrong reading of history, but it is surely good that she hath her convictions, and holdeth them fast like a brave maid.

"Is it not so, John, that friends and doubtless also . . . lovers have been divided by conscience and have been on opposite sides in the great conflict, and doth not this show how much of conscience there is among men?

"It may be this dispute will not divide you — being now, as it were, more an argument of the schools than a matter of principle, but if it should appear that you are far apart on the greater matters of faith, then . . . you will have a heavy cross to carry. But it is my mind that the heart of the maiden is right, and that I may some day see her . . . in your home, whereat my eyes would be glad."

The Rabbi was so taken up with the matter that he barely showed Carmichael a fine copy of John of Damascus he had secured from London, and went out of his course at worship to read, as well as to expound with much feeling, the story of Ruth the Moabitess, showing conclusively that she had in her a high spirit, and that she was designed of God to be a strength to the house of David. He was also very cheerful in the morning, and bade Carmichael good-bye at Tochty woods with encouraging words. He also agreed to assist his boy at the Drumtochty sacrament.

It was evident that the Rabbi's mind was much set on this visit, but Carmichael did not for one moment depend upon his remembering the day, and so Burnbrae started early on the Saturday with his dog-cart to bring Saunderson up and deposit him without fail in the Free Kirk manse of Drumtochty. Six times that day did the minister leave his "action" sermon and take his way to the guest room, carrying such works as might not be quite unsuitable for the old scholar's perusal, and arranging a lamp of easy management, that the night hours might not be lost. It was late in the afternoon before the Rabbi was delivered at the manse, and Burnbrae gave explanations next day at the sacramental dinner.

"It wes just ten when a' got tae the manse o' Kilbogie, an' his hoosekeeper didna ken whar her maister wes ; he micht be in Kildrummie by that time, she said, or half wy tae Muirtown. So a' set oot an' ransackit the parish till a' got him, an' gin he wesna sittin' in a bothie takin' brose wi' the plowmen an' expoundin' Scripture a' the time. .

"He startit on the ancient martyrs afore we were half a mile on the road, and he gied ae testimony aifter anither, an' he wesna within sicht o' the Reformation when we cam tae the hooses ; a 'll no deny that a' let the mare walk bits o' the road, for a' cud hae heard him a' nicht ; ma bluid 's warmer yet, freends."

The Rabbi arrived in great spirits, and refused to taste meat till he had stated the burden of his sermon for the morrow.

"If the Lord hath opened our ears the servant must declare what has been given him, but I prayed that the message sent through me to your flock, John, might be love. It hath pleased the Great Shepherd that I should lead the sheep by strange paths, but I desired that it be otherwise when I came for the first time to Drumtochty.

"Two days did I spend in the woods, for the stillness of winter among the trees leaveth the mind disengaged for the Divine word, and the first day my soul was heavy as I returned, for this only was laid upon me, 'vessels of wrath, fitted to destruction.' And, John, albeit God would doubtless have given me strength according to His will, yet I was loath to bear this awful truth to the people of your charge.

"Next day the sun was shining pleasantly in the wood and it came to me that clouds had gone from the face of God, and as I wandered among the trees a squirrel sat on a branch within reach of my hand and did not flee. Then I heard a voice, ' I have loved thee with an everlasting love, therefore with loving kindness have I drawn thee.'

"It was, in an instant, my hope that this might be God's word by me, but I knew not it was so till the Evangel opened up on all sides, and I was led into the outgoings of the eternal love after so moving a fashion that I dared to think that grace might be effectual even with me . . . with me.

"God opened my mouth on Sabbath on this text unto my own flock, and the word was not void. It is little that can be said on sovereign love in two hours and it may be a few minutes ; yet even this may be more than your people are minded to bear. So I shall pretermit certain notes on doctrine ; for you will doubtless have given much instruction on the purposes of God, and very likely may be touching on that mystery in your action sermon."

During the evening the Rabbi was very genial — tasting Sarah's viands with relish, and comparing her to Rebecca, who made savoury meat, urging Carmichael to smoke without scruple, and allowing himself to snuff three times, examining the bookshelves with keen appreciation, and finally departing with three volumes of modern divinity under his arm, to reinforce the selection in his room, "lest his eyes should be held waking in the night watches." He was much overcome by the care that had been taken for his comfort, and at the door of his room blest his boy: "May the Lord give you the sleep of His beloved, and strengthen you to declare all His truth on the morrow." Carmichael sat by his study fire for a while and went to bed much cheered, nor did he dream that there was to be a second catastrophe in the Free Kirk of Drumtochty which would be far sadder than the first, and leave in one heart life-long regret.

CHAPTER XIX.

THE FEAR OF GOD.

T was the way of the Free Kirk that the assisting minister at the Sacrament should sit behind the Communion Table during the sermon, and the congregation, without giving the faintest sign of observation, could estimate its effect on his face. When Doctor Dowbiggin composed himself to listen as became a Church leader of substantial build — his hands folded before him and his eyes fixed on the far window — and was so arrested by the opening passage of Cunningham's s e r m o n on Justification by Faith that he visibly started, and afterward sat sideways with his ears cocked, Drumtochty, while doubtful whether any Muirtown man could appreciate the subtlety of their minister, had a higher idea of the Doctor; and when the Free Kirk minister of Kildrummie — a stout man and given to agricultural pursuits — went fast asleep under a masterly discussion of the priesthood of Melchisedek, Drumtochty's opinion of the intellectual condition of Kildrummie was confirmed beyond argument.

During his ministry of more than twenty years the Rabbi had never preached at Drumtochty — being fearful that he might injure the minister who invited him, or might be so restricted in time as to lead astray by ill-balanced statements — and as the keenest curiosity would never have induced any man to go from the Glen to worship in another parish, the Free Kirk minister of Kilbogie was still unjudged in Drumtochty. They were not sorry to have the opportunity at last, for they had suffered not a little at the hands of Kilbogie in past years, and the coming event disturbed the flow of business at Muirtown market.

"Ye 're tae hae the Doctor at laist," Mains said to Netherton — letting the luck-penny on a transaction in seed-corn stand over — "an' a 'm jidgin' the time 's no been lost. He 's plainer an' easier tae follow then he wes at the affgo. Ma word " — contemplating the exercise before the Glen — "but ye 'll aye get eneuch here and there tae cairry hame." Which shows what a man the Rabbi was, that on the strength of his possession a parish like Kilbogie could speak after this fashion to Drumtochty.

"He 'll hae a fair trial, Mains " — Netherton's tone was distinctly severe — "an' mony a trial he 's hed in his day, they say: wes 't three an' twenty kirks he preached in, afore ye took him? But mind ye, length 's nae standard in Drumtochty; na, na, it 's no hoo muckle wind a man hes, but what like is the stuff that comes. It 's bushels doon bye, but it 's wecht up bye."

Any prejudice against the Rabbi, created by the boasting of a foolish parish not worthy of him, was reduced by his venerable appearance before the pulpit, and quite dispelled by his unfeigned delight in Carmichael's con-

duct of the " preliminaries." Twice he nodded approval
to the reading of the hundredth Psalm, and although he
stood with covered face during the prayer, he emerged
full of sympathy.   As his boy read the fifty-third of Isaiah
the old man was moved well-nigh to tears, and on the
giving out of the text from the parable of the Prodigal
Son, the Rabbi closed his eyes with great expectation, as
one about to be fed with the finest of the wheat.

Carmichael has kept the sermon unto this day, and as
often as he finds himself growing hard or supercilious,
reads it from beginning to end.   It is his hair shirt, to be
worn from time to time next his soul for the wrongness in
it and the mischief it did.   He cannot understand how he
could have said such things on a Sacrament morning and
in the presence of the Rabbi, but indeed they were
inevitable.   When two tides meet there is ever a cruel
commotion, and ships are apt to be dashed on the rocks,
and Carmichael's mind was in a "jabble" that day.
The new culture, with its wider views of God and man,
was fighting with the robust Calvinism in which every
Scot is saturated, and the result was neither peace nor
charity.   Personally the lad was kindly and good-
natured, intellectually he had become arrogant, intolerant,
acrid, flinging out at old-fashioned views, giving quite
unnecessary challenges, arguing with imaginary antagon-
ists.   It has ever seemed to me, although I suppose that
history is against me, that if it be laid on any one to
advocate a new view that will startle people, he ought
of all men to be conciliatory and persuasive ; but Carmichael was, at least in this time of fermentation, very
exasperating and pugnacious, and so he drove the Rabbi
to the only hard action of his life, wherein the old man
suffered most, and which may be said to have led to his
death.

Carmichael, like the Rabbi, had intended to preach that morning on the love of God, and thought he was doing so with some power. What he did was to take the Fatherhood of God and use it as a stick to beat Pharisees with, and under Pharisees he let it be seen that he included every person who still believed in the inflexible action of the moral laws and the austere majesty of God. Many good things he no doubt said, but each had an edge, and it cut deeply into people of the old school. Had he seen the Rabbi, it would not have been possible for him to continue, but he only was conscious of Lachlan Campbell, with whom he had then a feud, and who, he imagined, had come to criticise him. So he went on his rasping way that Sacrament morning, as when one harrows the spring earth with iron teeth, exciting himself with every sentence to fresh crudities of thought and extravagances of opposition. But it only flashed on him that he had spoken foolishly when he came down from the pulpit, and found the Rabbi a shrunken figure in his chair before the Holy Table.

Discerning people, like Elspeth Macfadyen, saw the whole tragedy from beginning to end, and felt the pity of it keenly. For a while the Rabbi waited with fond confidence — for was not he to hear the best-loved of his boys — and he caught eagerly at a gracious expression, as if it had fallen from one of the fathers. Anything in the line of faith would have pleased the Rabbi that day, who was as a little child and full of charity, in spite of his fierce doctrines. By-and-by the light died away from his eyes as when a cloud comes over the face of the sun and the Glen grows cold and dreary. He opened his eyes and was amazed — looking at the people and questioning them what had happened to their minister. Suddenly he flushed as a person struck by a friend, and then, as one blow followed another, he covered his face with both hands, sinking lower and lower in his chair, till even that decorous people were almost shaken in their attention.

When Carmichael gave him the cup in the Sacrament the Rabbi's hand shook and he spilled some drops of the wine upon his beard, which all that day showed like blood on the silvery whiteness. Afterwards he spake in his turn to the communicants, and distinguished the true people of God from the multitude — to whom he held out no hope — by so many and stringent marks, that Donald Menzies refused the Sacrament with a lamentable groan. And when the Sacrament was over and the time came for Carmichael to shake hands with the assisting minister in the vestry, the Rabbi had vanished, and he had no speech with him till they went through the garden together — very bleak it seemed in the winter dusk — unto the sermon that closed the services of the day.

"God's hand is heavy in anger on us both this day, John," and Carmichael was arrested by the awe and sorrow in the Rabbi's voice, "else . . . you had not spoken as you did this forenoon, nor would necessity be laid on me to speak . . . as I must this night.

"His ways are all goodness and truth, but they are oftentimes encompassed with darkness, and the burden He has laid on me is . . . almost more than I can bear ; it will be heavy for you also.

"You will drink the wine of astonishment this night, and it will be strange if you do not . . . turn from the hand that pours it out, but you will not refuse the truth or . . . hate the preacher," and at the vestry door the Rabbi looked wistfully at Carmichael.

During the interval the lad had been ill at ease, suspecting from the Rabbi's manner at the Table, and the solemnity of his address, that he disapproved of the action sermon, but he did not for a moment imagine that the situation was serious. It is one of the disabilities of good-natured and emotional people, without much deepness of earth, to belittle the convictions and resolutions of strong natures, and to suppose that they can be talked away by a few pleasant, coaxing words.

The Rabbi had often yielded to Carmichael and his other boys in the ordinary affairs of life — in meat and drink and clothing, even unto the continuance of his snuffing. He had been most manageable and pliable — as a child in their hands — and so Carmichael was quite confident that he could make matters right with the old man about a question of doctrine as easily as about the duty of a midday meal. Certain bright and superficial people will only learn by some solitary experience that faith is reserved in friendship, and that the most heroic souls are those which count all things loss — even the smile of those they love — for the eternal. For a moment Carmichael was shaken as if a new Rabbi were before him ; then he remembered the study of Kilbogie and all things that had happened therein, and his spirits rose.

" How dare you suggest such wickedness, Rabbi, that any of us should ever criticise or complain of anything you say? Whatever you give us will be right, and do us good, and in the evening you will tell me all I said wrong."

Saunderson looked at Carmichael for ten seconds as one who has not been understood, and sighed. Then he went down the kirk after the beadle, and the people marked how he walked like a man who was afraid he might fall, and, turning a corner, he supported himself on the end of a pew. As he crept up the pulpit stairs Elspeth gave James a look, and, although well accustomed to the slowness of his understanding, was amazed that he did not catch the point. Even a man might have seen that this was not the same minister that came in to the Sacrament with hope in his very step.

"A'm no here tae say 'that a' kent what wes comin'" — Elspeth, like all experts, was strictly truthful — "for the like o' that wes never heard in Drumtochty, and noo that Doctor Saunderson is awa, will never be heard again in Scotland. A' jaloused that vials wud be opened an' a' wesna wrang, but ma certes " — and that remarkable woman left you to understand that no words in human speech could even hint at the contents of the vials.

When the Rabbi gave out his text, "Vessels of wrath," in a low, awestruck voice, Carmichael began to be afraid, but after a little he chid himself for foolishness. During half an hour the Rabbi traced the doctrine of the Divine Sovereignty through Holy Scripture with a characteristic wealth of allusion to Fathers ancient and reforming, and once or twice he paused as if he would have taken up certain matters at greater length, but restrained himself, simply asserting the Pauline character of St. Augustine's thinking, and exposing the looseness of Clement of Alexandria with a wave of the hand as one hurrying on to his destination.

"Dear old Rabbi" — Carmichael congratulated himself in his pew — "what need he have made so many apologies for his subject? He is going to enjoy himself, and he is sure to say something beautiful before he is done." But he was distinctly conscious all the same of a wish that the Rabbi were done and all . . . well.

uncertainty over. For there was a note of anxiety, almost of horror, in the Rabbi's voice, and he had not let the Fathers go so lightly unless under severe constraint. What was it? Surely he would not attack their minister in face of his people. . . . The Rabbi do that, who was in all his ways a gentleman? Yet . . . and then the Rabbi abruptly quitted historical exposition and announced that he would speak on four heads. Carmichael, from his corner behind the curtains, saw the old man twice open his mouth as if to speak, and when at last he began he was quivering visibly, and he had grasped the outer corners of the desk with such intensity that the tassels which hung therefrom — one of the minor glories of the Free Kirk — were held in the palm of his hand, the long red tags escaping from between his white wasted fingers. A pulpit lamp came between Carmichael and the Rabbi's face, but he could see the straining hand, which did not relax till it was lifted in the last awful appeal, and the white and red had a gruesome fascination. It seemed as if one had clutched a cluster of full, rich, tender grapes and was pressing them in an agony till their life ran out in streams of blood, and dripped upon the heads of the choir sitting beneath, in their fresh, hopeful youth. And it also came to Carmichael with pathetic conviction even then that every one was about to suffer, but the Rabbi more than them all together. While the preacher was strengthening his heart for the work before him, Carmichael's eye was attracted by the landscape that he could see through the opposite window. The ground sloped upwards from the kirk to a pine-wood that fringed the great moor, and it was covered with snow on which the moon was beginning to shed her faint, weird light. Within, the light from the upright lamps was falling on the ruddy, contented faces of men and women and little children, but without it was one cold, merciless whiteness, like unto the justice of God, with black shadows of judgment.

"This is the message which I have to deliver unto you in the name of the Lord, and even as Jonah was sent to Nineveh after a strange discipline with a word of mercy, so am I constrained against my will to carry a word of searching and trembling.

"First"—and between the heads the Rabbi paused as one whose breath had failed him—"every man belongs absolutely to God by his creation.

"Second. The purpose of God about each man precedes his creation.

"Third. Some are destined to Salvation, and some to Damnation.

"Fourth"—here the hard breathing became a sob—"each man's lot is unto the glory of God."

It was not only skilled theologians like Lachlan Campbell and Burnbrae, but even mere amateurs, who understood that they were that night to be conducted to the farthest limit of Calvinism, and that whoever fell behind through the hardness of the way, their guide would not flinch.

As the Rabbi gave the people a brief space wherein to grasp his heads in their significance, Carmichael remembered a vivid incident in the Presbytery of Muirtown, when an English evangelist had addressed that reverend and austere court with exhilarating confidence—explaining the extreme simplicity of the Christian faith, and showing how a minister ought to preach. Various good men were delighted, and asked many questions of the evangelist—who had kept a baby-linen shop for twenty years, and was unspoiled by the slightest trace of theology — but the Rabbi arose and demolished his " teaching," convicting him of heresy at every turn, till there was not left one stone upon another.

" But surely fear belongs to the Old Testament dispensation," said the unabashed little man to the Rabbi afterwards. " ' Rejoice,' you know, my friend, ' and again I say rejoice.' "

" If it be the will of God that such a man as I should ever stand on the sea of glass mingled with fire, then this tongue will be lifted with the best, but so long as my feet are still in the fearful pit it becometh me to bow my head."

" Then you don't believe in assurance ? " but already the evangelist was quailing before the Rabbi.

" Verily there is no man that hath not heard of that precious gift, and none who does not covet it greatly, but there be two degrees of assurance " — here the Rabbi looked sternly at the happy, rotund little figure — " and it is with the first you must begin, and what you need to get is assurance of your damnation."

One of the boys read an account of this incident — thinly veiled — in a reported address of the evangelist, in which the Rabbi — being, as it was inferred, beaten in scriptural argument — was very penitent and begged his teacher's pardon with streaming tears. What really happened was different, and so absolutely conclusive that Doctor Dowbiggin gave it as his opinion " that a valuable lesson had been read to unauthorised teachers of religion."

Carmichael recognised the same note in the sermon and saw another man than he knew, as the Rabbi, in a low voice, without heat or declamation, with frequent pauses and laboured breathing, as of one toiling up a hill, argued the absolute supremacy of God and the utter helplessness of man. One hand ever pressed the grapes, but with the other the old man wiped the perspiration that rolled in beads down his face. A painful stillness fell on the people as they felt themselves caught in the meshes of this inexorable net and dragged ever nearer to the abyss. Carmichael, who had been leaning forward in his place, tore himself away from the preacher with an effort, and moved where he could see the congregation. Campbell was drinking in every word as one for the first time in his life perfectly satisfied. Menzies was huddled into a heap in the top of his pew as one justly blasted by the anger of the Eternal. Men were white beneath the tan, and it was evident that some of the women would soon fall a-weeping. Children had crept close to their mothers under a vague sense of danger, and a girl in the choir watched the preacher with dilated eyeballs like an animal fascinated by terror.

"It is as a sword piercing the heart to receive this truth, but it is a truth and must be believed. There are hundreds of thousands in the past who were born and lived and died and were damned for the glory of God. There are hundreds of thousands in this day who have been born and are living and shall die and be damned for the glory of God. There are hundreds of thousands in the future who shall be born and shall live and shall die and shall be damned for the glory of God. All according to the will of God, and none dare say nay nor change the purpose of the Eternal." For some time the oil in the lamps had been failing — since the Rabbi had been speaking for nigh two hours — and as he came to an end of this passage the light began to flicker and die.

First a lamp at the end of Burnbrae's pew went out and then another in the front. The preacher made as though he would have spoken, but was silent, and the congregation watched four lamps sink into darkness at intervals of half a minute. There only remained the two pulpit lamps, and in their light the people saw the Rabbi lift his right hand for the first time.

"Shall . . . not . . . the . . . Judge . . . of all the earth . . . do . . . right?" The two lamps went out together and a great sigh rose from the people. At the back of the kirk a child wailed and somewhere in the front a woman's voice — it was never proved to be Elspeth Macfadyen — said audibly, " God have mercy upon us." The Rabbi had sunk back into the seat and buried his face in his hands, and through the window over his head the moonlight was pouring into the church like unto the far-off radiance from the White Throne.

When Carmichael led the Rabbi into the manse he could feel the old man trembling from head to foot, and he would touch neither meat nor drink, nor would he speak for a space.

" Are you there, John?" — and he put out his hand to Carmichael, who had placed him in the big study chair, and was sitting beside him in silence.

" I dare not withdraw nor change any word that I spake in the name of the Lord this day, but . . . it is my infirmity . . . I wish I had never been born."

" It was awful," said Carmichael, and the Rabbi's head again fell on his breast.

" John," — and Saunderson looked up, — " I would give ten thousand worlds to stand in the shoes of that good man who conveyed me from Kilbogie yesterday,

WRESTLING IN DARKNESS OF SOUL.

and with whom I had very pleasant fellowship concerning the patience of the saints.

"It becometh not any human being to judge his neighbour, but it seemed to me from many signs that he was within the election of God, and even as we spoke of Polycarp and the martyrs who have overcome by the blood of the Lamb, it came unto me with much power, 'Lo, here is one beside you whose name is written in the Lamb's Book of Life, and who shall enter through the gates into the city;' and grace was given me to rejoice in his joy, but I . . . "—and Carmichael could have wept for the despair in the Rabbi's voice.

"Dear Rabbi!"—for once the confidence of youth was smitten at the sight of a spiritual conflict beyond its depth—"you are surely . . . depreciating yourself . . . Burnbrae is a good man, but compared with you . . . is not this like to the depression of Elijah?" Carmichael knew, however, he was not fit for such work, and had better have held his peace.

"It may be that I understand the letter of Holy Scripture better than some of God's children, although I be but a babe even in this poor knowledge, but such gifts are only as the small dust of the balance. He will have mercy on whom He will have mercy.

"John," said the Rabbi suddenly, and with strong feeling, "was it your thought this night as I declared the sovereignty of God that I judged myself of the elect, and was speaking as one himself hidden for ever in the secret place of God?"

"I . . . did not know," stammered Carmichael, whose utter horror at the unrelenting sermon had only been tempered by his love for the preacher.

"You did me wrong, John, for then had I not dared to speak at all after that fashion ; it is not for a vessel of mercy filled unto overflowing with the love of God to exalt himself above the vessels . . . for whom there is no mercy. But he may plead with them who are in like case with himself to . . . acknowledge the Divine Justice."

Then the pathos of the situation overcame Carmichael, and he went over to the bookcase and leant his head against certain volumes, because they were weighty and would not yield.   Next day he noticed that one of them was a Latin Calvin that had travelled over Europe in learned company, and the other a battered copy of Jonathan Edwards that had come from the house of an Ayrshire farmer.

" Forgive me that I have troubled you with the concerns of my soul, John " — the Rabbi could only stand with an effort — " they ought to be between a man and his God. There is another work laid to my hand for which there is no power in me now.   During the night I shall ask whether the cup may not pass from me, but if not, the will of God be done."

Carmichael slept but little, and every time he woke the thought was heavy upon him that on the other side of a narrow wall the holiest man he knew was wrestling in darkness of soul, and that he had added to the bitterness of the agony.

CHAPTER XX.

INTER has certain mornings which redeem weeks of misconduct, when the hoar frost during t h e night has r e-s i l v e r e d every branch and braced the s n o w u p o n the g r o u n d, and the sun rises in ruddy strength and drives out of sight every cloud and mist, and moves all day through an expanse of unbroken blue, and is reflected from the dazzling whiteness of the earth as from a mirror. Such a sight calls a man from sleep with authority, and makes his blood tingle, and puts new heart in him, and banishes the troubles of the night. Other mornings winter joins in the conspiracy of principalities and powers to daunt and crush the human soul. No sun is to be seen, and the grey atmosphere casts down the heart, the wind moans and whistles in fitful gusts, the black clouds hang low in threatening masses, now and again a flake of snow drifts in the wind. A storm is near at hand, not the thunder-shower of summer, with warm rain and the kindly sun in ambush, but dark and blinding snow, through which even a gamekeeper cannot see six yards, and in which weary travellers lie down to rest and die.

The melancholy of this kind of day had fallen on Saunderson, whose face was ashen, and who held Carmichael's hand with such anxious affection that it was impossible to inquire how he had slept, and it would have been a banalité to remark upon the weather. After the Rabbi had been compelled to swallow a cup of milk by way of breakfast, it was evident that he was ready for speech.

"What is it, Rabbi?" as soon as they were again settled in the study. "If you did not . . . like my sermon, tell me at once. You know that I am one of your boys, and you ought to . . . help me." Perhaps it was inseparable from his youth, with its buoyancy and self-satisfaction, and his training in a college whose members only knew by rumour of the existence of other places of theological learning, that Carmichael had at that moment a pleasing sense of humility and charity. Had it been a matter of scholastic lore, of course neither he nor more than six men in Scotland could have met the Rabbi in the gate. With regard to modern thought, Carmichael knew that the good Rabbi had not read *Ecce Homo*, and was hardly, well . . . up to date. He would not for the world hint such a thing to the dear old man, nor even argue with him; but it was flattering to remember that the attack could be merely one of blunderbusses, in which the modern thinker would at last intervene and save the ancient scholar from humiliation.

"Well, Rabbi?" and Carmichael tried to make it easy.

"Before I say what is on my heart, John, you will grant an old man who loves you one favour. So far as in you lies you will bear with me if that which I have to say, and still more that which my conscience will compel me to do, is hard to flesh and blood."

"Did n't we settle that last night in the vestry?" and Carmichael was impatient; "is it that you do not agree with the doctrine of the Divine Fatherhood? We younger men are resolved to base Christian doctrine on the actual Scriptures, and to ignore mere tradition."

"An excellent rule, my dear friend," cried the Rabbi, wonderfully quickened by the challenge, "and with your permission and for our mutual edification we shall briefly review all passages bearing on the subject in hand — using the original, as will doubtless be your wish, and you correcting my poor recollection."

About an hour afterwards, and when the Rabbi was only entering into the heart of the matter, Carmichael made the bitter discovery — without the Rabbi having even hinted at such a thing — that his pet sermon was a mass of boyish crudities, and this reverse of circumstances was some excuse for his pettishness.

"It does not seem to me that it is worth our time to haggle about the usage of Greek words or to count texts: I ground my position on the general meaning of the Gospels and the sense of things," and Carmichael stood on the hearthrug in a very superior attitude.

"Let that pass then, John, and forgive me if I appeared to battle about words, as certain scholars of the olden time were fain to do, for in truth it is rather about the hard duty before me than any imperfection in your teaching I would speak," and the Rabbi glanced nervously at the young minister.

"We are both Presbyters of Christ's Church, ordained after the order of primitive times, and there are laid on us certain heavy charges and responsibilities from which we may not shrink, as we shall answer to the Lord at the great day."

Carmichael's humiliation was lost in perplexity, and he sat down, wondering what the Rabbi intended.

"If any Presbyter should see his brother fall into one of those faults of private life that do beset us all in our present weakness, then he doth well and kindly to point it out unto his brother; and if his brother should depart from the faith as they talk together by the way, then it is a Presbyter's part to convince him of his error and restore him."

The Rabbi cast an imploring glance, but Carmichael had still no understanding.

"But if one Presbyter should teach heresy to his flock in the hearing of another . . . even though it break the other's heart, is not the path of duty fenced up on either side, verily a straight, narrow way, and hard for the feet to tread?"

"You have spoken to me, Rabbi, and . . . cleared yourself" — Carmichael was still somewhat sore — "and I 'll promise not to offend you again in an action sermon."

"Albeit you intend it not so, yet are you making it harder for me to speak. . . . See you not . . . that I . . . that necessity is laid on me to declare this matter to my brother Presbyters in court assembled . . . but not in hearing of the people?" Then there was a stillness in the room, and the Rabbi, although he had closed his eyes, was conscious of the amazement on the young man's face.

" Do you mean to say," speaking very slowly, as one taken utterly aback, " that our Rabbi would come to my . . . to the Sacrament and hear me preach, and . . . report me for heresy to the Presbytery? Rabbi, I know we don't agree about some things, and perhaps I was a little . . . annoyed a few minutes ago because you . . . know far more than I do, but that is nothing. For you to prosecute one of your boys and be the witness yourself. . . . Rabbi, you can't mean it. . . . Say it's a mistake."

The old man only gave a deep sigh.

" If it were Dowbiggin or . . . any man except you, I would n't care one straw, rather enjoy the debate, but you whom we have loved and looked up to and boasted about, why, it's like . . . a father turning against his sons."

The Rabbi made no sign.

" You live too much alone, Rabbi," and Carmichael began again as the sense of the tragedy grew on him, " and nurse your conscience till it gets over tender ; no other man would dream of . . . prosecuting a . . . fellow minister in such circumstances. You have spoken to me like a father, surely that is enough," and in his honest heat the young fellow knelt down by the Rabbi's chair and took his hand.

A tear rolled down the Rabbi's cheek, and he looked fondly at the lad.

" Your words pierce me as sharp swords, John ; spare me, for I can do none otherwise ; all night I wrestled for release, but in vain."

Carmichael had a sudden revulsion of feeling, such as befalls emotional and ill-disciplined natures when they are disappointed and mortified.

"Very good, Doctor Saunderson"—Carmichael rose awkwardly and stood on the hearthrug again, an elbow on the mantelpiece—"you must do as you please and as you think right. I am sorry that I . . . pressed you so far, but it was on grounds of our . . . friendship.

" Perhaps you will tell me as soon as you can what you propose to do, and when you will bring . . . this matter before the Presbytery. My sermon was fully written and . . . is at your disposal."

While this cold rain beat on the Rabbi's head he moved not, but at its close he looked at Carmichael with the appeal of a dumb animal in his eyes.

" The first meeting of Presbytery is on Monday, but you would no doubt consider that too soon; is there anything about dates in the order of procedure for heresy?" and Carmichael made as though he would go over to the shelves for a law book.

"John," cried the Rabbi—his voice full of tears—rising and following the foolish lad, "is this all you have in your heart to say unto me? Surely, as I stand before you, it is not my desire to do such a thing, for I would rather cut off my right hand.

"God hath not been pleased to give me many friends, and He only knows how you and the others have comforted my heart. I lie not, John, but speak the truth, that there is nothing unto life itself I would not give for your good, who have been as the apple of my eye unto me."

Carmichael hardened himself, torn between a savage sense of satisfaction that the Rabbi was suffering for his foolishness and the inclination of his better self to respond to the old man's love.

"If there be a breach between us, it will not be for you as it must be for me. You have many friends, and may God add unto them good men and faithful, but I shall lose my one earthly joy and consolation, when your feet are no longer heard on my threshold and your face no longer brings light to my room. And, John, even this thing which I am constrained to do is yet of love, as . . . you shall confess one day."

Carmichael's pride alone resisted, and it was melting fast. Had he even looked at the dear face, he must have given way, but he kept his shoulder to the Rabbi, and at that moment the sound of wheels passing the corner of the manse gave him an ungracious way of escape.

"That is Burnbrae's dog-cart . . . Doctor Saunderson, and I think he will not wish to keep his horse standing in the snow, so unless you will stay all night, as it's going to drift. . . . Then perhaps it would be better. . . . Can I assist you in packing?" How formal it all sounded, and he allowed the Rabbi to go upstairs alone, with the result that various things of the old man's are in Carmichael's house unto this day.

Another chance was given the lad when the Rabbi would have bidden him good-bye at the door, beseeching that he should not come out into the drift, and still another when Burnbrae, being concerned about his passenger's appearance, who seemed ill-fitted to face a storm, wrapt him in a plaid; and he had one more when the old man leant out of the dog-cart and took Carmichael's hand in both of his, but only said, "God bless you for all you 've been to me, and forgive me for all wherein I have failed you." And they did not meet again till that never-to-be-forgotten sederunt of the Free

Kirk Presbytery of Muirtown, when the minister of Kilbogie accused the minister of Drumtochty of teaching the Linlathen heresy of the Fatherhood of God in a sermon before the Sacrament.

Among all the institutions of the North a Presbytery is the most characteristic, and affords a standing illustration of the contradictions of a superbly logical people. It is so anti-clerical a court that for every clergyman there must be a layman — country ministers promising to bring in their elder for great occasions, and instructing him audibly how to vote — and so fiercely clerical that if the most pious and intelligent elder dared to administer a sacrament he would be at once tried and censured for sacrilege. So careful is a Presbytery to prevent the beginnings of Papacy that it insists upon each of its members occupying the chair in turn, and dismisses him again into private life as soon as he has mastered his duties, but so imbued is it with the idea of authority that whatever decision may be given by some lad of twenty-five in the chair — duly instructed, however, by the clerk below — will be rigidly obeyed. When a Presbytery has nothing else to do, it dearly loves to pass a general condemnation on sacerdotalism, in which the tyranny of prelates, and the foolishness of vestments will be fully exposed, but a Presbytery wields a power at which a bishop's hair would stand on end, and Doctor Dowbiggin once made Carmichael leave the Communion Table and go into the vestry to put on his bands.

When a Presbytery is in its lighter moods, it gives itself to points of order with a skill and relish beyond the Southern imagination. It did not matter how harmless, even infantile, might be the proposal placed before the court by such a man as MacWheep of Pitscowrie, he has hardly got past an apology for his presumption in venturing to speak at all, before a member of Presbytery — who had reduced his congregation to an irreducible minimum by the woodenness of his preaching — inquires whether the speech of " our esteemed brother is not *ultra vires* " or something else as awful. MacWheep at once sits down with the air of one taken red-handed in arson, and the court debates the point till every authority has taken his fill, when the clerk submits to the Moderator, with a fine blend of deference and infallibility, that Mr. MacWheep is perfectly within his rights; and then, as that estimable person has, by this time, lost any thread he ever possessed, the Presbytery passes to the next business — with the high pirit of men returning from a holiday. Carmichael u d, indeed, to relate how in a great stress of business omeone moved that the Presbytery should adjourn for dinner, and the court argued for seventy minutes, with many precedents, whether such a motion — touching as it did the standing orders — could even be discussed, and with an unnecessary prodigality of testimony he used to give perorations which improved with every telling.

The love of law diffused through the Presbytery became incarnate in the clerk, who was one of the most finished specimens of his class in the Scottish Kirk. His sedate appearance, bald, polished head, fringed with pure white hair, shrewd face, with neatly cut side whiskers, his suggestion of ur rring accuracy and inexhaustible memory, his attitud , for exposition, — holding his glasses in his left hand and enforcing his decision with the little finger of the right hand — carried conviction even to the most disorderly. Ecclesiastical radicals, boiling over with new schemes, and boasting to admiring circles of MacWheeps

that they would not be brow-beaten by red tape officials
became ungrammatical before that firm gaze, and ended

HIS ATTITUDE FOR EXPOSITION.

in abject surrender. Self-contained and self-sufficing, the
clerk took no part in debate, save at critical moments to
lay down the law, but wrote his minutes unmoved through

torrents of speech on every subject, from the Sustentation Fund to the Union between England and Scotland, and even under the picturesque eloquence of foreign deputies, whose names he invariably requested should be handed to him, written legibly on a sheet of paper.   On two occasions only he ceased from writing : when Dr. Dowbiggin discussed a method of procedure — then he watched him over his spectacles in hope of a nice point ; or when some enthusiastic brother would urge the Presbytery to issue an injunction on the sin of Sabbath walking — then the clerk would abandon his pen in visible despair, and sitting sideways on his chair and supporting his head by that same little finger, would face the Presbytery with an expression of reverent curiosity on his face why the Almighty was pleased to create such a man. His preaching was distinguished for orderliness, and was much sought after for Fast days.   It turned largely on the use of prepositions and the scope of conjunctions, so that the clerk could prove the doctrine of Vicarious Sacrifice from " for," and Retribution from " as " in the Lord's prayer, emphasising and confirming everything by that wonderful finger, which seemed to be designed by Providence for delicate distinctions, just as another man's fist served for popular declamation.   His pulpit masterpiece was a lecture on the Council of Jerusalem, in which its whole deliberations were reviewed by the rules of the Free Kirk Book of Procedure, and a searching and edifying discourse concluded with two lessons. First : That no ecclesiastical body can conduct its proceedings without officials.   Second :   That such men ought to be accepted as a special gift of Providence.

The general opinion among good people was that the clerk's preaching was rather for upbuilding than arous-

ing, but it is still remembered by the survivors of the old
Presbytery that when MacWheep organised a conference
on "The state of religion in our congregations," and it
was meandering in strange directions, the clerk, who
utilised such seasons for the writing of letters, rose amid
a keen revival of interest — it was supposed that he had
detected an irregularity in the proceedings — and offered
his contribution. "It did not become him to boast,"
he said, "but he had seen marvellous things in his day:
under his unworthy ministry three beadles had been converted to Christianity," and this experience was so final
that the conference immediately closed.

Times there were, however, when the Presbytery rose
to its height, and was invested with an undeniable spiritual dignity. Its members, taken one by one, consisted
of farmers, shepherds, tradesmen, and one or two profes-
sional men, with some twenty ministers, only two or
three of whom were known beyond their parishes. Yet
those men had no doubt that as soon as they were con-
stituted in the name of Christ, they held their authority
from the Son of God and Saviour of the world, and they
bore themselves in spiritual matters as His servants. No
kindly feeling of neighbourliness or any fear of man could
hinder them from inquiring into the religious condition
of a parish or dealing faithfully with an erring minister.
They had power to ordain, and laid hands on the bent
head of some young probationer with much solemnity;
they had also power to take away the orders they had
given, and he had been hardened indeed beyond hope
who could be present and not tremble when the Moderator, standing in his place, with the Presbytery around,
and speaking in the name of the Head of the Church,
deposed an unworthy brother from the holy ministry.

MacWheep was a "cratur," and much given to twaddle, but when it was his duty once to rebuke a fellow-minister for quarrelling with his people, he was delivered from himself, and spake with such grave wisdom as he has never shown before or since.

When the Presbytery assembled to receive a statement from Doctor Saunderson "*re* error in doctrine by a brother Presbyter," even a stranger might have noticed that its members were weighted with a sense of responsibility, and although a discussion arose on the attempt of a desultory member to introduce a deputy charged with the subject of the lost ten tribes, yet it was promptly squelched by the clerk, who intimated, with much gravity, that the court had met *in hunc effectum*, viz. to hear Doctor Saunderson, and that the court could not, in consistence with law, take up any other business, not even — here Carmichael professed to detect a flicker of the clerkly eyelids — the disappearance of the ten tribes.

It was the last time that the Rabbi ever spoke in public, and it is now agreed that the deliverance was a fit memorial of the most learned scholar that has been ever known in those parts. He began by showing that Christian doctrine has taken various shapes, some more and some less in accordance with the deposit of truth given by Christ and the holy Apostles, and especially that the doctrine of Grace had been differently conceived by two eminent theologians, Calvin and Arminius, and his exposition was so lucid that the clerk gave it as his opinion afterwards, that the two systems were understood by certain members of the court for the first time that day. Afterwards the Rabbi vindicated and glorified Calvinism from the Scriptures of the Old and New

Testament, from the Fathers, from the Reformation Divines, from the later creeds, till the brain of the Presbytery reeled through the wealth of allusion and quotation, all in the tongues of the learned. Then he dealt with the theology of Mr. Erskine of Linlathen, and showed how it was undermining the very foundations of Calvinism; yet the Rabbi spake so tenderly of our Scottish Maurice that the Presbytery knew not whether it ought to condemn Erskine as a heretic or love him as a saint. Having thus brought the court face to face with the issues involved, the Rabbi gave a sketch of a certain sermon he had heard while assisting "a learned and much-beloved brother at the Sacrament," and Carmichael was amazed at the transfiguration of this very youthful performance, which now figured as a profound and edifying discourse, for whose excellent qualities the speaker had not adequate words. This fine discourse was, however, to a certain degree marred, the Rabbi suggested, by an unfortunate, although no doubt temporary, leaning to the teaching of Mr. Erskine, whose beautiful piety, which was even to himself in his worldliness and unprofitableness a salutary rebuke, had exercised its just fascination upon his much more spiritual brother. Finally the Rabbi left the matter in the hands of the Presbytery, declaring that he had cleared his conscience, and that the minister was one — here he was painfully overcome — dear to him as a son, and to whose many labours and singular graces he could bear full testimony, the Rev. John Carmichael, of Drumtochty. The Presbytery was slow and pedantic, but was not insensible to a spiritual situation, and there was a murmur of sympathy when the Rabbi sat down — much exhausted, and never having allowed himself to look once at Carmichael.

Then arose a self-made man, who considered ortho-
doxy and capital to be bound up together, and especially identified any departure from sovereignty with that
pestilent form of Socialism which demanded equal chances
for every man. He was only a plain layman, he said,
and perhaps he ought not to speak in the presence of so
many reverend gentlemen, but he was very grateful to
Doctor Saunderson for his honourable and straightforward
conduct. It would be better for the Church if there
were more like him, and he would just like to ask Mr.
Carmichael one or two questions. Did he sign the Confession? — that was one ; and had he kept it? — that
was two ; and the last was, When did he propose to go?
He knew something about building contracts, and he
had heard of a penalty when a contract was broken.
There was just one thing more he would like to say —
if there was less loose theology in the pulpit there would
be more money in the plate. The shame of the Rabbi
during this harangue was pitiable to behold.

Then a stalwart arose on the other side, and a young
gentleman who had just escaped from a college debating
society wished to know what century we were living in,
warned the last speaker that the progress of theological
science would not be hindered by mercenary threats,
advised Doctor Saunderson to read a certain German,
called Ritschl, — as if he had been speaking to a babe
in arms, — and was refreshing himself with a Latin
quotation, when the Rabbi, in utter absence of mind,
corrected a false quantity aloud.

"Moderator," the old man apologised in much confusion, "I wot not what I did, and I pray my reverend
brother, whose interesting and instructive address I have
interrupted by this unmannerliness, to grant me his

pardon, for my tongue simply obeyed my ear." Which untoward incident brought the modern to an end, as by a stroke of ironical fate. It seemed to the clerk that little good to any one concerned was to come out of this debate, and he signalled to Doctor Dowbiggin, with whom he had dined the night before, when they concocted a motion over their wine. Whereupon that astute man explained to the court that he did not desire to curtail the valuable discussion, from which he personally had derived much profit, but he had ventured to draw up a motion, simply for the guidance of the House — it was said by the Rabbi's boys that the Doctor's success as an ecclesiastic was largely due to the skilful use of such phrases — and then he read : " Whereas the Church is set in all her courts for the defence of the truth, whereas it is reported that various erroneous doctrines are being promulgated in books and other public prints, whereas it has been stated that one of the ministers of this Presbytery has used words that might be supposed to give sanction to a certain view which appears to conflict with statements contained in the standards of the Church, the Presbytery of Muirtown declares first of all, its unshaken adherence to the said standards ; secondly, deplores the existence in any quarter of notions contradictory or subversive of said standards ; thirdly, thanks Doctor Saunderson for the vigilance he has shown in the cause of sound doctrine ; fourthly, calls upon all ministers within the bounds to have a care that they create no offence or misunderstanding by their teaching, and finally enjoins all parties concerned to cultivate peace and charity."

This motion was seconded by the clerk and carried unanimously, — Carmichael being compelled to silence by the two wise men for his own sake and theirs, — and was declared to be a conspicuous victory both by the self-made man and the modern, which was another tribute to the ecclesiastical gifts of Doctor Dowbiggin and the clerk of the Presbytery of Muirtown.

CHAPTER XXI.

THE Rabbi had been careful to send an abstract of his speech to Cármichael, with a letter enough to melt the heart even of a self-sufficient young clerical; and Carmichael had considered how he should bear himself at the Presbytery. His intention had been to meet the Rabbi with public cordiality and escort him to a seat, so that all men should see that he was too magnanimous to be offended by this latest eccentricity of their friend. This calculated plan was upset by the Rabbi coming in late and taking the first seat that offered, and when he would have gone afterwards to thank him for his generosity the Rabbi had disappeared. It was evident that the old man's love was as deep as ever, but that he was much hurt, and would not risk another repulse. Very likely he had walked in from Kilbogie, perhaps without breakfast, and had now started to return to his cheerless manse. It was a wetting spring rain, and he remembered that the Rabbi had no coat. A fit of remorse overtook Carmichael, and he scoured the streets of Muirtown to find the Rabbi, imagining

deeds of attention — how he would capture him unawares mooning along some side street hopelessly astray;
how he would accuse him of characteristic cunning and
deep plotting; how he would carry him by force to the
Kilspindie Arms and insist upon their dining in state;
how the Rabbi would wish to discharge the account and
find twopence in his pockets — having given all his silver to an ex-Presbyterian minister stranded in Muirtown
through peculiar circumstances; how he would speak
gravely to the Rabbi on the lack of common honesty,
and threaten a real prosecution, when the charge would
be "obtaining a dinner on false pretences;" how they
would journey to Kildrummie in high content, and —
the engine having whistled for a dog-cart — they would
drive to Drumtochty manse, the sun shining through the
rain as they entered the garden; how he would compass
the Rabbi with observances, and the old man would sit
again in the big chair full of joy and peace. Ah, the
kindly jests that have not come off in life, the gracious
deeds that never were done, the reparations that were
too late! When Carmichael reached the station the
Rabbi was already half way to Kilbogie, trudging along
wet and weary and very sad, because, although he had
obeyed his conscience at a cost, it seemed to him as if
he had simply alienated the boy whom God had given
him as a son in his old age, for even the guileless Rabbi
suspected that the ecclesiastics considered his action
foolishness and of no service to the Church of God.
Barbara's language on his arrival was vituperative to a
degree; she gave him food grudgingly, and when, in the
early morning, he fell asleep over an open Father, he
was repeating Carmichael's name, and the thick old
paper was soaked with tears.

His nemesis seized Carmichael so soon as he reached the Dunleith train in the shape of the Free Kirk minister of Kildrummie, who had purchased six pounds of prize seed potatoes, and was carrying the treasure home in a paper bag. This bag had done after its kind, and as the distinguished agriculturist had not seen his feet for years, and could only have stooped at the risk of apoplexy, he watched the dispersion of his potatoes with dismay, and hailed the arrival of Carmichael with exclamations of thankfulness. It is wonderful over what an area six pounds of (prize) potatoes can deploy on a railway platform, and how the feet of passengers will carry them unto far distances. Some might never have been restored to the bag had it not been for Kildrummie's comprehensive eye and the physical skill with which he guided Carmichael, till even prodigals that had strayed over to the neighbourhood of the Aberdeen express were restored to the extemporised fold in the minister's top-coat pockets. Carmichael had knelt on that very platform six months or so before, but then he stooped in the service of two most agreeable dogs and under the approving eyes of Miss Carnegie ; that was a different experience from hunting after single potatoes on all fours among the feet of unsympathetic passengers, and being prodded to duty by the umbrella of an obese Free Kirk minister. As a reward for this service of the aged, he was obliged to travel to Kildrummie with his neighbour — in whom for the native humour that was in him he had often rejoiced, but whose company was not congenial that day — and Kildrummie laid himself out for a pleasant talk. After the roots had been secured and their pedigree stated, Kildrummie fell back on the proceedings of Presbytery, expressing much admiration

for the guidance of Doctor Dowbiggin and denouncing
Saunderson as "fair dottle," in proof of which judgment
Kildrummie adduced the fact that the Rabbi had allowed a very happily situated pigsty to sink into ruin.
Kildrummie, still in search of agreeable themes to pass
the time, mentioned a pleasant tale he had gathered at
the seed shop.

"Yir neebur upbye, the General's dochter, is cairryin'
on an awfu' rig the noo at the Castle " — Kildrummie
fell into dialect in private life, often with much richness
— "an' the sough o' her ongaeins hes come the length
o' Muirtown. The place is foo' o' men — tae say
naethin' o' weemin; but it's little she hes tae dae wi'
them or them wi' her — officers frae Edinburgh an'
writin' men frae London, as weel as half a dozen coonty
birkies."

"Well?" said Carmichael, despising himself for his
curiosity.

"She hes a wy, there's nae doot o' that, an' gin the
trimmie hesna turned the heads o' half the men in the
Castle, till they say she hes the pick of twa lords, five
honourables, and a poet. But the lassie kens what's
what; it's Lord Hay she's settin' her cap for, an' as
sure as ye're sittin' there, Drum, she'll hae him.

"Ma word" — and Kildrummie pursued his way —
"it'll be a match, the dochter o' a puir Hielant laird,
wi' naethin' but his half pay and a few pounds frae a
fairm or twa. She's a clever ane; French songs,
dancin', shootin', ridin', actin', there's nae deevilry
that's beyond her. They say upbye that she's been
a bonnie handfu' tae her father — General though he
be — an' a' peety her man."

"They say a lot of . . . lies, and I don't see what

call a minister has to slander . . . ," and then Carmichael saw the folly of quarrelling with a veteran gossip over a young woman that would have nothing to say to him. What two Free Kirk ministers or their people thought of her would never affect Miss Carnegie.

"Truth 's nae slander," and Kildrummie watched Carmichael with relish ; "a' thocht ye wud hae got a taste o' her in the Glen. Didna a' heer frae Piggie Walker that ye ca'd her Jezebel frae yir ain pulpit, an' that ma lady whuppit oot o' the kirk in the middle o' the sermon?"

"I did nothing of the kind, and Walker is a . . . ."

"Piggie 's no very particular at a time," admitted Kildrummie ; "maybe it 's a makup the story aboot Miss Carnegie an' yirsel'.

"Accordin' to the wratch," for Carmichael would deign no reply, "she wes threatenin' tae mak a fule o' the Free Kirk minister o' Drumtochty juist for practice, but a' said, 'Na, na, Piggie, Maister Carmichael is ower quiet and sensible a lad. He kens as weel as onybody that a Carnegie wud never dae for a minister's wife. Gin ye said a Bailie's dochter frae Muirtown 'at hes some money comin' tae her and kens the principles o' the Free Kirk.'

"Noo a' can speak frae experience, having been terrible fortunate wi' a' ma wives. . . . Ye 'll come up tae tea ; we killed a pig yesterday, and . . . Weel, weel, a wilfu' man maun hae his wy," and Carmichael, as he made his way up the hill, felt that the hand of Providence was heavy upon him, and that any highmindedness was being severely chastened.

Two days Carmichael tramped the moors, returning each evening wet, weary, hungry, to sleep ten hours without turning, and on the morning of the third day he came down in such heart that Sarah wondered whether he could have received a letter by special messenger; and he congratulated himself, as he walked round his garden, that he had overcome by sheer will-power the first real infatuation of his life. He was so lifted above all sentiment as to review his temporary folly from the bare, serene heights of common-sense. Miss Carnegie was certainly not an heiress, and she was a young woman of very decided character, but her blood was better than the Hays', and she was . . . attractive — yes, attractive. Most likely she was engaged to Lord Hay, or if he did not please her — she was . . . whimsical and . . . self-willed — there was Lord Invermay's son. Fancy Kate . . . Miss Carnegie in a Free Kirk manse — Kildrummie was a very . . . homely old man, but he touched the point there — receiving Doctor Dowbiggin with becom-ing ceremony and hearing him on the payment of probationers, or taking tea at Kildrummie Manse — where he had, however, feasted royally many a time after the Presbytery, but. . . . This daughter of a Jacobite house, and brought up amid the romance of war, settling down in the narrowest circle of Scottish life — as soon imagine an eagle domesticated among barn-door poultry. This image amused Carmichael so much that he could have laughed aloud, but . . . the village might have heard him. He only stretched himself like one awaking, and felt so strong that he resolved to drop in on Janet to see how it fared with the old woman and . . . to have Miss Carnegie's engagement confirmed. The Carnegies might return any day from the South, and it would be well that he should know how to meet them.

"You will be hearing that they hef come back to the

Lodge yesterday morning, and it iss myself that will be glad to see Miss Kate again; and very pretty iss she looking, with peautiful dresses and bonnets, for I hef seen them all, maybe twelve or ten.

"Oh yes, my dear, Donald will be talking about her marriage to Lord Kilspindie's son, who iss a very handsome young man and good at the shooting; and he will be blowing that they will live at the Lodge in great state, with many gillies and a piper.

"No, it iss not Janet Macpherson, my dear, that will be believing Donald Cameron, or any Cameron — although I am not saying that the Camerons are not men of their hands — for Donald will be always making great stories and telling me wonderful things. He wass a brave man in the battle, and iss very clever at the doctrine too, and will be strong against human himes (hymns), but he iss a most awful liar iss Donald Cameron, and you must not be believing a word that comes out of his mouth.

" She will be asking many questions in her room as soon as Donald had brought up her boxes and the door was shut. Some will be about the Glen, and some about the garden, and some will be about people — whether you ever will be visiting me, and whether you asked for her after the day she left the kirk. But I will say, ' No; Mr. Carmichael does not speak about anything but the religion when he comes to my cottage.'

"That iss nothing. I will be saying more, that I am hearing that the minister iss to be married to a fery rich young lady in Muirtown who hass been courting him for two years, and that her father will be giving the minister twenty thousand pounds the day they are married. And I will say she iss very beautiful, with blue eyes and gold hair, and that her temper iss so sweet they are calling her the Angel of Muirtown.

"Toot, toot, my dear, you are not to be speaking about lies, for that iss not a pretty word among friends, and you will not be meddling with me, for you will be better at the preaching and the singing than dealing with women. It iss not good to be making yourself too common, and Miss Kate will be thinking the more of you if you be holding your head high and letting her see that you are not a poor lowland body, but a Farquharson by your mother's side, and maybe of the chief's blood, though twenty or fifteen times removed.

"She will be very pleased to hear such good news of you, and be saying that it iss a mercy you are getting somebody to dress you properly. But her temper will not be at all good, and I did not ask her about Lord Hay, and she said nothing to me, nor about any other lord. It iss not often I hef seen as great a liar as Donald Cameron.

" Last evening Miss Kate will come down before dinner and talk about many things, and then she will say at the door, ' Donald tells me that Mister Carmichael does not believe in the Bible, and that his minister, Doctor Saunderson, has cast him off, and that he has been punished by his Bishop or somebody at Muirtown.'

" ' Donald will be knowing more doctrine and telling more lies every month,' I said to her. ' Doctor Saunderson — who is a very fine preacher and can put the fear of God upon the people most wonderful — and our minister had a little feud, and they will fight it out before some chiefs at Muirtown like gentlemen, and now they are good friends again.'

" Miss Kate had gone off for a long walk, and I am

not saying that she will be calling at Kilbogie Manse before she comes back. She is very fond of Doctor Saunderson, and maybe he will be telling her of the feud. It iss more than an hour through the woods to Kilbogie," concluded Janet, " but you will be having a glass of milk first."

Kate reviewed her reasons for the expedition to Kilbogie, and settled they were the pleasures of a walk through Tochty woods when the spring flowers were in their glory, and a visit to one of the dearest curiosities she had ever seen. It was within the bounds of possibility that Doctor Saunderson might refer to his friend, but on her part she would certainly not refer to the Free Church minister of Drumtochty. Her reception by that conscientious professor Barbara could not be called encouraging.

" Ay, he 's in, but ye canna see him, for he 's in his bed, and gin he disna mend faster than he wes daein' the last time a' gied him a cry, he 's no like to be in the pulpit on Sabbath. A' wes juist thinkin' he wudna be the waur o' a doctor."

" Do you mean to say that Doctor Saunderson is lying ill and no one nursing him ? " and Kate eyed the housekeeper in a very unappreciative fashion.

"Gin he wants a nurse she 'll hae tae be brocht frae Muirtown Infirmary, for a 've eneuch withoot ony fyke (delicate work) o' that kind. For twal year hev a' been hoosekeeper in this manse, an' gin it hedna been for peety a' wad hae flung up the place.

" Ye never cud tell when he wud come in, or when he wud gae oot, or what he wud be wantin' next. A' the waufies in the countryside come 'here, and the best in the hoose is no gude eneuch for them. He 's been

"AY, HE'S IN, BUT YE CANNA SEE HIM."

an awfu' handfu' tae me, an' noo a' coont him clean
dottle. But we maun juist bear oor burdens," concluded
Barbara piously, and proposed to close the door.

"Your master will not want a nurse a minute longer;
show me his room at once," and Kate was so commanding that Barbara's courage began to fail.

"Who may ye be," raising her voice to rally her
heart, "'at wud take chairge o' a strainger in his ain
hoose an' no sae muckle as ask leave?"

"I am Miss Carnegie, of Tochty Lodge; will you
stand out of my way?" and Kate swept past Barbara
and went upstairs.

"Weel, a' declare," as soon as she had recovered,
"of a' the impudent hizzies," but Barbara did not follow
the intruder upstairs.

Kate had seen various curious hospitals in her day,
and had nursed many sick men, — like the brave girl
she was, — but the Rabbi's room was something quite
new. His favourite books had been gathering there for
years, and now lined two walls and overhung the bed
after a very perilous fashion, and had dispossessed the
looking-glass, — which had become a nomad and was at
present resting insecurely on John Owen, — and stood
in banks round the bed. During his few days of illness
the Rabbi had accumulated so many volumes round him
that he lay in a kind of tunnel, arched over, as it were,
with literature. He had been reading Calvin's *Commentary on the Psalms*, in Latin, and it still lay open at
the 88th, the saddest of all songs in the Psalter; but as
he grew weaker the heavy folio had slid forward, and he
seemed to be feeling for it. Although Kate spoke to
him by name, he did not know any one was in the
room. "Lord, why castest Thou off my soul? . . . I

suffer Thy terror, I am distracted . . . fierce wrath goeth over me . . . lover and friend hast Thou put far from me . . . friend far from me."

His head fell on his breast, his breath was short and rapid, and he coughed every few seconds.

"My friend far from me . . . "

At the sorrow in his voice, and the thing which he said, the tears came to Kate's eyes, and she went forward and spoke to him very gently. "Do you know me, Dr. Saunderson, Miss Carnegie?"

"Not Saunderson . . . Magor Missabib."

"Rabbi, Rabbi" — so much she knew; and now Kate stroked the bent white head. "Your friend, Mister Carmichael . . ."

"Yes, yes " — he now looked up, and spoke eagerly — "John Carmichael, of Drumtochty . . . my friend in my old age . . . and others . . . my boys . . . but John has left me . . . he would not speak to me . . . I am alone now . . . he did not understand . . . mine acquaintance into darkness . . . here we see in a glass darkly . . ." (he turned aside to expound the Greek word for darkly), "but some day . . . face to face." And twice he said it, with an indescribable sweetness, " face to face."

Kate hurriedly removed the books from the bed, and wrapt round his shoulders the old grey plaid that had eked out his covering at night, and then she went downstairs.

"Bring," she said to Barbara, "hot water, soap, towels, and a sponge to Doctor Saunderson's bedroom, immediately."

"And gin a' dinna?" inquired Barbara aggressively.

"I 'll shoot you where you stand."

Barbara shows to her cronies how Miss Carnegie drew a pistol from her pocket at this point and held it to her head, and how at every turn the pistol was again in evidence ; sometimes a dagger is thrown in, but that is only late in the evening when Barbara is under the influence of tonics. Kate herself admits that if she had had her little revolver with her she might have been tempted to outline the housekeeper's face on the wall, and she still thinks her threat an inspiration.

"Now," said Kate, when Barbara had brought her commands in with incredible celerity, "bring up some fresh milk and three glasses of whisky."

"Whisky !" Barbara could hardly compass the unfamiliar word. "The Doctor never hed sic a thing in the hoose, although mony a time, puir man . . ." Discipline was softening even that austere spirit.

"No, but you have, for you are blowing a full gale just now ; bring up your private bottle, or I 'll go down for it."

"There 's enough," holding the bottle to the light, "to do till evening ; go to the next farm and send a man on horseback to tell Mr. Carmichael of Drumtochty, that Doctor Saunderson is dying, and another for Dr. Manley of Muirtown."

Very tenderly did Kate sponge the Rabbi's face and hands, and then she dressed his hair, till at length he came to himself.

"This ministry is . . . grateful to me, Barbara . . . my strength has gone from me . . . but my eyes fail me. . . . Of a verity you are not . . ."

"I am Kate Carnegie, whom you were so kind to at Tochty. Will you let me be your nurse? I learned in India, and know what to do." It was only wounded soldiers who knew how soft her voice could be, and hands.

"It is I that . . . should be serving you . . . the first time you have come to the manse . . . no woman has ever done me . . . such kindness before. . . ." He followed her as she tried to bring some order out of chaos, and knew not that he spoke aloud. "A gracious maid . . . above rubies."

His breathing was growing worse, in spite of many wise things she did for him — Doctor Manley, who paid no compliments, but was a strength unto every country doctor in Perthshire, praises Kate unto this day — and the Rabbi did not care to speak. So she sat down by his side and read to him from the *Pilgrim's Progress* — holding his hand all the time — and the passage he desired was the story of Mr. Fearing.

"This I took very great notice of, that the valley of the shadow of Death was as quiet while he went through it as ever I knew it before or since. I suppose these enemies here had now a special check from our Lord and a command not to meddle until Mr. Fearing was passed over it. . . . Here also I took notice of what was very remarkable : the water of that river was lower at this time than ever I saw it in all my life. So he went over at last, not much above wet-shod. When he was going up to the gate. . . ."

The Rabbi listened for an instant.

"It is John's step . . . he hath a sound of his own . . . my only earthly desire is fulfilled."

"Rabbi," cried Carmichael, and half kneeling, he threw one arm round the old man, " say that you forgive me. I looked for you everywhere on Monday, but you could not be found."

"Did you think, John, that I . . . my will was to do you an injury or . . . vex your soul? Many trials in my life . . . all God's will . . . but this hardest . . . when I lost you . . . nothing left here . . . but you . . . — my breath is bad, a little chill — . . . understand. . . ."

"I always did, and I never respected you more; it was my foolish pride that made me call you Doctor Saunderson in the study; but my love was the same, and now you will let me stay and wait on you."

The old man smiled sadly, and laid his hand on his boy's head.

"I cannot let you. . . . Go, John, my son."

"Go and leave you, Rabbi!" Carmichael tried to laugh. "Not till you are ready to appear at the Presbytery again. We 'll send Barbara away for a holiday, and Sarah will take her place, — you remember that cream, — and we shall have a royal time, a meal every four hours, Rabbi, and the Fathers in between," and Carmichael, springing to his feet and turning round to hide his tears, came face to face with Miss Carnegie, who had been unable to escape from the room.

"I happened to call" — Kate was quite calm — "and found Doctor Saunderson in bed; so I stayed till some friend should come; you must have met the messenger I sent for you."

"Yes, a mile from the manse; I was on my way . . . Janet said . . . but I . . . did not remember anything when I saw the Rabbi."

"Will you take a little milk again . . . Rabbi?" and at her bidding and the name he made a brave effort to swallow, but he was plainly sinking.

"No more," he whispered; "thank you . . . for service . . . to a lonely man; may God bless you . . .

both. . . ." He signed for her hand, which he kept to the end.

"Satisfied . . . read, John . . . the woman from coasts of — of — "

"I know, Rabbi," and kneeling on the other side of the bed, he read the story slowly of a Tyrian woman's faith.

"It is not meet to take the children's meat and cast it to dogs."

"Dogs " — they heard the Rabbi appropriate his name — "outside . . . the covenant."

"And she said, Truth, Lord, yet the dogs eat of the crumbs which fall from their master's table."

"Lord, I believe . . . help Thou mine . . . unbelief."

He then fell into an agony of soul, during which Carmichael could hear: "Though . . . He slay . . . me . . . yet will I trust . . . trust . . . in Him." He drew two or three long breaths and was still. After a little he was heard again with a new note — "He that believeth . . . in Him . . . shall not be confounded," and again "A bruised reed . . . shall He not . . ." Then he opened his eyes and raised his head — but he saw neither Kate nor Carmichael, for the Rabbi had done with earthly friends and earthly trials — and he, who had walked in darkness and seen no light, said in a clear voice full of joy, "My Lord, and my God."

It was Kate that closed his eyes and laid the old scholar's head on the pillow, and then she left the room, casting one swift glance of pity at Carmichael, who was weeping bitterly and crying between the sobs, " Rabbi, Rabbi."

CHAPTER XXII.

DOCTOR DAVIDSON allowed himself, in later years, the pleasant luxury of an after luncheon nap, and then it was his habit — weather permitting — to go out and meet Posty, who adhered so closely to his time-table — notwithstanding certain wayside rests — that the Doctor's dog knew his hour of arrival, and saw that his master was on the road in time. It was a fine April morning when the news of the great disaster came, and the Doctor felt the stirring of spring in his blood. On the first hint from Skye he sprang from his chair, declaring it was a sin to be in the house on such a day, and went out in such haste that he had to return for his hat. As he went up the walk, the Doctor plucked some early lilies and placed them in his coat; he threw so many stones that Skye forgot his habit of body and ecclesiastical position; and he was altogether so youthful and frolicsome that John was seriously alarmed, and afterwards remarked to Rebecca that he was not unprepared for calamity.

" The best o's tempts Providence at a time, and when a man like the Doctor tries tae rin aifter his dog jidgment canna be far off. A 'm no sayin'," John concluded, with characteristic modesty, " that onybody cud tell what was coming, but a' jaloused there wud be tribble."

The Doctor met Posty in the avenue, the finest bit on our main road, where the road has wide margins of grass on either side, and the two rows of tall ancient trees arch their branches overhead. Some day in the past it had been part of the approach to the house of Tochty, and under this long green arch the Jacobite cavaliers rode away after black John Carnegie's burial. No one could stand beneath those stately trees without thinking of the former days, when men fought not for money and an easy life, but for loyalty and love, and in this place the minister of Drumtochty received his evil tidings like a brave gentleman who does not lose heart while honour is left. During his years in the Glen he had carried himself well, with dignity and charity, in peace and kindliness, so that now when he is dead and gone — the last of his family — he still remains to many of us a type of the country clergyman that is no longer found in Scotland, but is greatly missed. It seemed, however, to many of us — I have heard both Drumsheugh and Burnbrae say this, each in his own way — that it needed adversity to bring out the greatness of the Doctor, just as frost gives the last touch of ripeness to certain fruits.

" Fower letters the day, Doctor, ane frae Dunleith, ane frae Glasgie, another frae Edinburgh, and the fourth no clean stampit, so a' can say naethin' aboot it. Twa circulars an' the *Caledonian* maks up the hale hypothic."

Posty buckled and adjusted his bag, and made as

though he was going, but he loitered to give opportunity for any questions the Doctor might wish to ask on foreign affairs. For Posty was not merely the carrier of letters to the Glen, but a scout who was sent down to collect information regarding the affairs of the outer world. He was an introduction to and running commentary on the weekly paper. By-and-by, when the labour of the day was done, and the Glen was full of sweet, soft light from the sides of Ben Urtach, a farmer would make for his favourite seat beside the white rose-tree in the garden, and take his first dip into the *Muirtown Advertiser*. It was a full and satisfying paper, with its agricultural advertisements, its roups, reported with an accuracy of detail that condescended on a solitary stirk, its local intelligence, its facetious anecdotes. Through this familiar country the good man found his own way at a rate which allowed him to complete the survey in six days. Foreign telegrams, however, and political intelligence, as well as the turmoil of the great cities, were strange to him, and here he greatly valued Posty's laconic hints, who, visiting the frontier, was supposed to be in communication with those centres. " Posty says that the Afghans are no makin' muckle o' the war," and Hillocks would sally forth to enjoy Sir Frederick Roberts' great march, line by line, afterwards enlarging thereon with much unction, and laying up a store of allusion that would last for many days.

Persons raised to the height of a daily newspaper like the minister might be supposed independent of Posty's precis, but even Doctor Davidson, with that day's *Caledonian* in his hand, still availed himself of the spoken word.

" Well, Posty, any news this morning?"

"Naethin', Doctor, worth mentionin', except the failure o' a company Glasgie wy; it's been rotten, a' wes hearin', for a while, an' noo it's fair stramash. They say it'll no be lichtsome for weedows an' mony decent fouk in Scotland."

"That's bad news, Posty. There's too many of those swindling concerns in the country. People ought to take care where they place their savings, and keep to old-established institutions. We're pretty hard-headed up here, and I'll wager that nobody in the Glen has lost a penny in any of those new-fangled companies."

"The auld fouk in Drumtochty pit their siller in a pock and hode it ablow their beds, an', ma certes, that bank didna break;" and Posty went along the avenue, his very back suggestive of a past, cautious, unenterprising, safe and honest.

The Doctor glanced at the envelopes and thrust the letters into his pocket. His good nature was touched at the thought of another financial disaster, by which many hard-working people would lose their little savings, and all the more that he had some of his private means invested in a Glasgow bank — one of those tried and powerful institutions which was indifferent to every crisis in trade. Already he anticipated an appeal, and considered what he would give, for it did not matter whether it was a coalpit explosion in Lanarkshire or a loss of fishing-boats in the Moray Firth, if widows needed help the Doctor's guinea was on its way within four-and-twenty hours. Some forms of religious philanthropy had very little hold on the Doctor's sympathy — one of the religious prints mentioned him freely as a Unitarian, because he had spoken unkindly of the Jewish mission — but in the matter of widows and orphans he was a specialist.

"Widows, Posty said; poor things! and very likely bairns. Well, well, we 'll see what can be done out of Daisy's fund."

Very unlikely people have their whims, and it was his humour to assign one fourth of his income to his little sister, who was to have kept house for him, and "never to leave you, Sandie," and out of this fund the Doctor did his public charities. "In memory of a little maid," - appeared in various subscription lists; but the reference thereof was only known after the Doctor's death.

"The Western Counties Bank did not open its doors yesterday, and it was officially announced at the head-office, Glasgow, that the bank had stopped. It is impossible as yet to forecast the debts, but they are known to be enormous, and as the bank is not limited, it is feared that the consequences to the shareholders will be very serious. This failure was quite unexpected, the Western Counties Bank having been looked on as a prosperous and stable concern."

He read the paragraph twice word by word — it did not take long — he folded the paper carefully and put it in his pocket, and he stood in the spot for five minutes to take in the meaning in its length and breadth. A pleasant spring sun was shining upon him through a break in the leafy arch, a handful of primroses were blooming at his feet, a lark was singing in the neighbouring field. Sometimes the Doctor used to speculate how he would have liked being a poor man, and he concluded that he would have disliked it very much. He had never been rich, and he was not given to extravagance, but he was accustomed to easy circumstances, and he pitied some of his old friends who had seen it their duty to secede at the Disruption, and had to practise many little economies, who travelled third class and had to walk from the station, and could not offer their friends a glass of wine. This was the way he must live now, and Daisy's fund would have to be closed, which seemed to him the sweetest pleasure of his life.

" And Jack ! Would to God I had never mentioned this wretched bank to him. Poor Jack, with the few hundreds he had saved for Kit ! "

For some five minutes more the Doctor stood in the place ; then he straightened himself as one who, come what may, would play the man, and when he passed Janet's cottage, on his way to the Lodge, that honest admirer of able-bodied, good-looking men came out and followed him with her eyes for the sight of his firm unbroken carriage.

" Miss Kate will be grieving very much about Doctor Saunderson's death," Donald explained at the Lodge, " and she went down this forenoon with the General to put flowers on his grave ; but they will be coming back every minute," and the Doctor met them at the Beeches.

" May I have as fair hands to decorate my grave, Miss Catherine Carnegie," and the Doctor bowed gallantly ; " but of one thing I am sure, I have done nothing to deserve it. Saunderson was a scholar of the ancient kind, and a very fine spirit."

" Don't you think," said Kate, " that he was . . . like À'Kempis, I mean, and George Herbert, a kind of . . . saint ? "

" Altogether one, I should say. I don't think he would have known port wine from sherry, or an *entrée* from a mutton chop ; beside a man like that what worldly fellows you and I are, Jack, and mine is the greater shame."

"TO PUT FLOWERS ON HIS GRAVE."

"I 'll have no comparisons, Padre " — Kate was a little puzzled by the tone in the Doctor's voice ; "he was so good that I loved him ; but there are some points in the General and you, quite nice points, and for the sake of them you shall have afternoon tea in my room," where the Doctor and the General fell on former days and were wonderful company.

"It 's not really about the road I wish to talk to you," and the Doctor closed the door of the General's den, "but about . . . a terrible calamity that has befallen you and me, Jack, and I am to blame."

"What is it? " and Carnegie sat erect ; "does it touch our name or . . . Kate? "

"Neither, thank God," said Davidson.

"Then it cannot be so very bad. Let us have it at once," and the General lighted a cheroot.

"Our bank has failed, and we shall have to give up everything to pay the debt, and . . . Jack, it was I advised you to buy the shares." The Doctor rose and went to the window.

"For God's sake don't do that, Sandie. Why, man, you gave me the best advice you knew, and there 's an end of it. It 's the fortune of war, and we must take it without whining. I know whom you are thinking about, and I am . . . a bit sorry for Kate, for she ought to have lots of things — more dresses and trinkets, you know. But Davidson, she 'll be the bravest of the three."

"You are right there, Jack. Kate is of the true grit, but . . . Tochty Lodge."

"Yes, it will hit us pretty hard to see the old place sold, if it comes to that, when I hoped to end my days here . . . but, man, it 's our fate. Bit by bit we 've lost

Drumtochty, till there were just the woods and the two farms left, and soon we 'll be out of the place — nothing left but our graves.

"Sandie, this is bad form, and . . . you 'll not hear this talk again; we 'll get a billet somewhere, and wherever it be, there 'll be a bed and a crust for you, old man;" and at the door the two held one another's hands for a second; that was all.

"So this was what you two conspirators were talking about downstairs, as if I could not be trusted. Did you think that I would faint, or perhaps weep? The padre deserves a good scolding, and as for you —" Then Kate went over and cast an arm round her father's neck, whose face was quivering.

"It is rather a disappointment to leave the Lodge when we were getting it to our mind; but we 'll have a jolly little home somewhere, and I 'll get a chance of earning something. Dancing now — I think that I might be able to teach some girls how to waltz. Then my French is really intelligible, and most colloquial; besides revolver shooting. Dad, we are on our way to a fortune, and at the worst you 'll have your curry and cheroots, and I 'll have a well-fitting dress. Voilà, mon père."

When the two Drumtochty men arrived next forenoon at the hall in Glasgow, where the shareholders had been summoned to receive particulars of their ruin, the dreary place was filled with a crowd representative of every class in the community except the highest, whose wealth is in land, and the lowest, whose possessions are on their backs. There were city merchants, who could not conceal their chagrin that they had been befooled; countrymen, who seemed utterly dazed, as if the course of the seasons had been reversed; prosperous tradesmen, who were aggressive in appearance and wanted to take it out of somebody ; widows, who could hardly restrain their tears, seeing before them nothing but starvation ; clergymen, who were thinking of their boys taken from school and college. For a while the victims were silent, and watched with hungry eyes the platform door, and there was an eager rustle when some clerk came out and laid a bundle of papers on the table. This incident seemed to excite the meeting and set tongues loose. People began to talk to their neighbours explaining how they came to be connected with the bank, as if this were now a crime. One had inherited the shares and had never had resolution to sell them ; another had been deceived by a friend and bought them ; a third had taken over two shares for a bad debt. A minister thought that he must have been summoned by mistake, for he was simply a trustee on an estate which had shares, but he was plainly nervous about his position. An Ayrshire Bailie had only had his shares for six months, and he put it, to his circle, with municipal elo-quence, whether he could be held responsible for frauds of years' standing. No one argued with him, and indeed you might say anything you pleased, for each was so much taken up with his own case that he only listened to you that he might establish a claim in turn on your at-tention. Here and there a noisy and confident person-age got a larger audience by professing to have private information. A second-rate stockbroker assured quite a congregation that the assets of the bank included an estate in Australia, which would more than pay the whole debt, and advised them to see that it was not flung away ; and a Government pensioner mentioned casually in his neighbourhood, on the authority of one of the

managers, that there was not that day a solvent bank in
Scotland. The different conversations rise to a babel,
various speakers enforce their views on the floor with
umbrellas, one enthusiast exhorts his brother unfortunates
from a chair, when suddenly there is a hush, and then
in a painful silence the shareholders hang on the lips of
the accountant, from whom they learn that things could
not be worse, that the richest shareholder may be
ruined, and that ordinary people will lose their last
penny.

Speech again breaks forth, but now it is despairing,
fierce, vindictive. One speaker storms against Government which allows public institutions to defraud the
public, and refers to himself as the widow and orphan,
and another assails the directorate with bitter invective
as liars and thieves, and insists on knowing whether they
are to be punished. The game having now been un-
earthed, the pack follow in full cry. The tradesman tells
with much gusto how one director asked the detectives
for leave to have family prayers before he was removed,
and then declares his conviction that when a man takes
to praying you had better look after your watch. Ayrshire wished to inform the accountant and the authorities
that the directors had conveyed to their wives and friends
enormous sums which ought to be seized without delay.
The air grew thick with upbraidings, complaints, cries for
vengeance, till the place reeked with sordid passions.
Through all this ignoble storm the Drumtochty men sat
silent, amazed, disgusted, till at last the Doctor rose, and
such authority was in his very appearance that with his
first words he obtained a hearing.

"Mr. Accountant," he said, "and gentlemen, it appears
to me as if under a natural provocation and suffering

we are in danger of forgetting our due dignity and self-respect. We have been, as is supposed, the subjects of fraud on the part of those whom we trusted ; that is a matter which the law will decide, and, if necessary, punish. If we have been betrayed, then the directors are in worse case than the shareholders, for we are not disgraced. The duty before us is plain, and must be discharged to our utmost ability. It is to go home and gather together our last penny for the payment of our debts, in order that at any rate those who have trusted us may not be disappointed. Gentlemen, it is evident that we have lost our means ; let us show to Scotland that there is something which cannot be taken from us by any fraud, and that we have retained our courage and our honour."

It was the General who led the applause so that the roof of the hall rang, but it is just to Ayrshire and the rest to say that they came to themselves — all men of the old Scottish breed — and followed close after with a mighty shout.

The sound of that speech went through Scotland and awoke the spirit of honest men in many places, so that the Doctor, travelling next day to Muirtown, third class, with the General, and wedged in among a set of cattle dealers, was so abashed by their remarks as they read the *Caledonian* that the General let out the secret.

"Yir hand, sir," said the chief among them, a mighty man at the Falkirk Tryst ; "gin it bena a leeberty, ilka ane o's hes a sair fecht tae keep straicht in oor wy o' business, but ye 've gien 's a lift the day," and so they must needs all have a grip of the Doctor's hand, who took snuff with prodigality, while the General complained of the smoke from the engine.

Nor were their trials over, for on Muirtown platform —
it being Friday — all kinds of Perthshire men were
gathered, and were so proud of our Doctor that before
he got shelter in the Dunleith train his hand was sore,
and the men that grasped it were of all kinds, from Lord
Kilspindie — who, having missed him at the Manse, had
come to catch him at the station — " Best sermon you
ever preached, Davidson," — to an Athole farmer — " I
am an elder in the Free Kirk, but it iss this man that
will be honouring you."

It was a fine instance of the unfailing tact of Peter
Bruce that, seeing the carriage out of which the two
came, and taking in the situation, he made no offer of
the first class, but straightway dusted out a third with his
handkerchief, and escorted them to it cap in hand.
Drumtochty restrained itself with an effort in foreign
parts — for Kildrummie was exceptionally strong at the
Junction — but it waited at the terminus till the outer
world had gone up the road. Then their own folk took
the two in hand, and these were the guard of honour
who escorted the Minister and the General to where our
Kate was waiting with the dog-cart, each carrying some
morsel of luggage — Drumsheugh, Burnbrae, Hillocks,
Netherton, Jamie Soutar, and Archie Moncur. Kate
drove gloriously through Kildrummie as if they had come
from a triumph, and let it be said to the credit of that
despised town, that, the news having come, every hat
was lifted, but that which lasted till they got home, and
till long afterwards, was the handshake of the Drumtochty
men.

CHAPTER XXIII.

HEN the General and Kate were loitering over breakfast the morning after the ovation, they heard the sound of a horse's feet on the gravel, and Donald came in with more than his usual importance.

"It iss a messenger from Muirtown Castle, and he iss waiting to know whether there will be any answer." And Donald put one letter before the father and another before the daughter, both showing the Hay crest. Kate's face whitened as she recognised the handwriting on her envelope, and she went over to the window seat of a turret in the corner of the room, while the General opened his letter, standing on a tiger-skin, with his back to the fireplace in the great hall. This is what he read:

MY DEAR CARNEGIE,—When men have fought together in the trenches before Sebastopol, as their ancestors have ridden side by side with Prince Charlie, I hope you will agree with me they need not stand on ceremony. If I seem guilty

of any indiscretion in what I am going to say, then you will
pardon me for "Auld Lang Syne."

You have one daughter and I have one son, and so I do
not need to tell you that he is very dear to me, and that I
have often thought of his marriage, on which not only his
own happiness so much depends, but also the future of our
house and name. Very likely you have had some such
thoughts about Kate, with this difference, that you would
rather keep so winsome a girl with you, while I want even
so good a son as Hay to be married whenever he can meet
with one whom he loves, and who is worthy of him.

Hay never gave me an hour's anxiety, and has no entan-
glements of any kind, but on the subject of marriage I could
make no impression. "Time enough," he would say, or
"The other person has not turned up," and I was getting
uneasy, for you and I are not so young as once we were.
You may fancy my satisfaction, therefore, when George
came down from Drumtochty last August and told me he
had found the "other person," and that she was my old
friend Jack Carnegie's daughter. Of course I urged him to
make sure of himself, but now he has had ample opportuni-
ties during your two visits, and he is quite determined that
his wife is to be Kate or nobody.

It goes without saying that the Countess and I heartily
approve Hay's choice and are charmed with Kate, who is as
bonnie as she is high-spirited. She sustains the old traditions of her family, who were ever strong and true, and she
has a clever tongue, which neither you nor I have, Jack, nor
Hay either, good fellow though he be, and that is not a bad
thing for a woman nowadays. They would make a handsome
pair, as they ought, with such good-looking fathers, eh?

Well, I am coming to my point, for in those circumstances
I want your help. What Miss Carnegie thinks of Hay we
don't know, and unless I'm much mistaken she will decide
for herself, but is it too much to ask you — if you can — to
say a word for him? You are quite right to think that no
man is worthy of Kate, but she is bound to marry some
day — I can't conceive how you have kept her so long —

and I am certain Hay will make a good husband, and he is
simply devoted to her. If she refuses him, I am afraid he
will not marry, and then — well, grant I 'm selfish, but it
would be a calamity to us.

Don't you think that it looks like an arrangement of
Providence to unite two families that have shared common
dangers and common faith in the past, and to establish a
Carnegie once more as lady of Drumtochty? Now that is
all, and it 's a long screed, but the matter lies near my heart,
and we shall wait the answers from you both with anxiety.

Yours faithfully,

KILSPINDIE.

Kate's letter was much shorter, and was written in big
schoolboy hand with great care.

DEAR MISS CARNEGIE, — They say that a woman always
knows when a man loves her, and if so you will not be astonished at this letter. From that day I saw you in Drumtochty
Kirk I have loved you, and every week I love you more.
My mother is the only other woman I have ever cared for,
and that is different. Will you be my wife? I often wanted
to ask you when you were with us in November and last
month, but my heart failed me. Can you love me a little,
enough to say yes? I am not clever, and I am afraid I
shall never do anything to make you proud of me, but you
will have all my heart, and I 'll do my best to make you
happy.

I am, yours very sincerely,

HAY.

Carnegie could see Kate's face from his place, who
was looking out of the window with a kindly expression,
and her father, who was of a simple mind, and knew little
of women, was encouraged by such visible friendliness.
He was about to go over, when her face changed. She
dropped the letter on the seat, and became very thought-

ful, knitting her brows and resting her chin on her hand. In a little, something stung her — like a person recalling an injury — and she flushed with anger, drumming with her fingers on the sill of the window. Then anger gave place to sadness, as if she had resolved to do something that was inevitable, but less than the best. Kate glanced in her father's direction, and read Lord Hay's letter again, then she seemed to have made up her mind.

"Father," as she joined him on the skin beneath those loyal Carnegies on the wall, "there is Lord Hay's letter, and he is a . . . worthy gentleman. Perhaps I did not give him so much encouragement as he took, but that does not matter. This is a . . . serious decision, and ought not to be made on the spur of the moment. Will you let the messenger go with a note to say that an answer will be sent on Monday? You might write to Lord Kilspindie."

She was still standing in the place when he returned, and had been studying the proud, determined face of Black John's mother, who had not spared her only son for the good cause.

"Did you ever hear of any Carnegie, dad, who married beneath her, or . . . loved one on the other side?"

"Never," said her father. "Our women all married into loyal families of their own rank, which is best for comfort; but why do you ask? Hay is a . . ."

"Yes, I know; it was only . . . curiosity made me ask, and I suppose some of our women must have made sacrifices for their . . . cause?"

"Far more than the men ever did, for, see you, a man is just shot, and all is over, and before he falls he's had some good fighting, but his wife suffers all her days, when he is living and when he is dead. Yet our women

were the first to send their men to the field.   Heavens !
what women do suffer — they ought to have their
reward."

"They have," said Kate, with emphasis, "if they help
those whom they love. . . . Father, would you be quite
satisfied with Lord Hay for a son-in-law, and . . . would
you let us live with you here as much as we could ? "

"Kate, if you are to marry — and I knew it must
come some day — I have not seen a more honest man ;
but you are forgetting that Tochty Lodge will soon be
out of our hands ; I 'll have to get a bungalow somewhere, not too far away from Muirtown, I hope."

"If I marry Lord Hay, Tochty Lodge will not be
sold, and you will never be disturbed, dad.   We shall
not be separated more than we can help," and Kate
caressed the General.

"Do you mean, lassie," said the General, with a
sudden suspicion, lifting her face till he saw her eyes,
"that you are going to accept Hay in order to keep the
old home?   You must not do this, for it would not . . .
don't you see that I . . . could not accept this at your
hands? "

"You cannot prevent your daughter marrying Lord
Hay if your daughter so decides, but as yet she is in
doubt, very great doubt, and so I am going for a long
walk on the big moor, and you . . . well, why not take
lunch with the Padre at the manse? "

"Hay is a straight young fellow, and Kate would
supply what he wants — a dash of go, you know " — so
the General was summing up the situation to his old
friend ; " but my girl is not to marry Hay or any other
man for my sake, and that is what she thinks of doing."

"Did it ever occur to you, Carnegie, that Kate had a
. . . well, kindly feeling for any other man? "

"Plenty of fellows tried their luck: first subalterns, then aides-de-camp, and at last commissioners; it was no easy affair to be her father," and Carnegie gave Davidson a comic look. "I used to scold her, but upon my word I don't know she was to blame, and I am certain she did not care for one of them; in fact, she laughed at them all till—well, in fact, I had to interfere."

"And since you came to the Lodge"—the Doctor spoke with meaning—"besides Lord Hay?"

"Why, there is just yourself"—the Doctor nodded with much appreciation—"and that Free Kirkman. . . . Davidson, do you mean that—oh, nonsense, man; she was quite angry one day when I suggested a parson. Kate has always said that was the last man she would marry."

"That is an evidence she will."

The General stared at the oracle, and went on:

"She has made his life miserable at the Lodge with her tongue; she delighted in teasing him. Your idea is quite absurd."

"Carnegie, did you ever hear the classical couplet—

> "Scarting and biting
> Mak Scots fouk's 'ooing;"

and although I admit the description applies in the first instance to milkmaids, yet there is a fair share of national character in the Carnegies."

"Do you really think that Kate is in . . . has, well, a, eh, tenderness to Carmichael? it would never have occurred to me."

"How would you look on Carmichael as a suitor?"

"Well, if Kate is to marry—and mind you I always

prepared myself for that — I would of course prefer Hay, not because he is a lord, or rich, or any snobbery of that kind — you know me better than that, Sandie — but because he 's . . . you know . . . belongs to our own set.

"Don't you think there is something in that? " and the General tried to explain his honest mind, in which lived no unworthy or uncharitable thought. "I have not one word to say against Carmichael; he 's good-looking, and monstrous clever, and he has always made himself very agreeable, very, and the people swear by him in the Glen; but . . . you must understand what I mean, Davidson," and the General was in despair.

"You mean that though he 's a first-rate young fellow for a clergyman, he does not belong to your world — has a different set of friends, has different habits of living, has a different way of thinking and speaking — is, in fact, an outsider."

"That 's it — just what I was 'ettling' after — lucky fellows we Scots with such words," and the General was immensely delighted to be delivered of his idea in an inoffensive form.

"It is my own belief, Carnegie — and you can laugh at me afterwards if I be wrong — that this will be the end of it, however. Yes, putting it plainly, that Kate is in love with Carmichael, as he is certainly with her; and you will have to make the best of the situation."

"You don't like the idea any more than I do, Davidson?"

"Speaking in perfect confidence and frankness, I do not. 1 look at the matter this way" — the Doctor stood on the hearth-rug in a judicial attitude, pulling down his waistcoat with his two hands, his legs apart, and his eye-glass on his nose — "Carmichael has been brought up among . . . plain, respectable people, and theological books, and church courts, and Free Kirk society, all of which is excellent, but . . . secluded" — the Doctor liked the word, which gave his mind without offence — "secluded. Kate is a Carnegie, was educated in France, has travelled in India, and has lived in the most exciting circumstances. She loves soldiers, war, gaiety, sport, besides many other . . . eh, good things, and is a . . . lovely girl. Love laughs at rules, but if you ask me my candid opinion, the marriage would not be . . . in fact, congruous. If it is to be, it must be, and God bless them both, say I, and so will everybody say; but it will be an experiment, a distinct and . . . interesting experiment."

"Kate is not to marry any one for my sake, to save Tochty, but I do wish she had fancied Lord Hay," said the General, ruefully.

"The Free Kirk folk in the depths of their hearts consider me a worldly old clergyman, and perhaps I am, for, Jack, I would dearly like to see our Kate Viscountess Hay, and to think that one day, when we three old fellows are gone, she would be Countess of Kilspindie." That was the first conference of the day on Kate's love affairs, and this is how it ended.

Meanwhile the young woman herself had gone up the road to the high Glen and made her way over dykes and through fields to Whinny Knowe, which she had often visited since the August Sacrament. Whinny came out from the kitchen door in corduroy trousers, much stained with soil, and grey shirt — wiping his mouth with the back of his hand after a hearty dinner — and went to the barn for his midday sleep before he went again

to the sowing. Marget met her at the garden gate,
dressed in her week-day clothes and fresh from a morning's churning, but ever refined and spiritual, as one
whose soul is shining through the veil of common
circumstances.

"It 's a benison tae see ye on this bricht day, Miss
Carnegie, an' ye 'll come tae the garden-seat, for the
spring flooers are bloomin' bonnie and sweet the noo,
an' fillin' 's a' wi' hope.

"Gin there be ony sun shinin'," as she spread a plaid,
"the heat fa's here, an' save when the snow is heavy
on the Glen, there 's aye some blossoms here tae mind
us o' oor Father's love an' the world that isna seen."

"Marget," began Kate, not with a blush, but rather
a richening of colour, "you have been awfully good to
me, and have helped me in lots of ways, far more than
you could dream of. Do you know you 've made me
almost good at times, with just enough badness to keep
me still myself, as when I flounced out from the Free
Kirk."

Marget only smiled deprecation and affection, for her
heart went out to this motherless, undisciplined girl,
whom she respected, like a true Scot, because, although
Kate had made her a friend, she was still a Carnegie;
whom she loved, because, although Kate might be very
provoking, she was honest to the core.

"To-day," Kate resumed, after a pause, and speaking with an unusual nervousness, "I want your advice on
a serious matter, which I must decide, and which . . .
concerns other people as well as myself. In fact, I
would like to ask a question," and she paused to frame
her case.

It was a just testimony to Marget Howe that Kate

"YOU HAVE BEEN AWFULLY GOOD TO ME."

never thought of pledging her to secrecy, for there are people whom to suspect of dishonour is a sin.

"Suppose that a man . . . loved a woman, and that he was honourable, brave, gentle, true, in fact . . . a gentleman, and made her a proposal of marriage."

Marget was looking before her with calm, attentive face, never once glancing at Kate to supplement what was told.

"If . . . the girl accepted him, she would have a high position, and be rich, so that she could . . . save her . . . family from ruin, and keep . . . them in the house they loved."

Marget listened with earnest intelligence.

"She respects this man, and is grateful to him. She is certain that he would be . . . kind to her, and give her everything she wanted. And she thinks that he . . . would be happy."

Marget waited for the end.

"But she does not love him — that is all."

As the tale was being told in brief, clear, slow sentences, Marget's eyes became luminous, and her lips opened as one ready to speak from an inner knowledge.

"Ye hev let me see a piece o' life, an' it is sacred, for naethin' on earth is sae near God as luve, an' a 'll no deny that ma woman's heart is wi' that honest gentleman, an' a' the mair gin he dinna win his prize.

"But a man often comes tae his heicht through disappointment, and a woman, she hes tae learn that there is that which she hes the richt tae give for gratitude or friendship's sake, and that which can only be bestowed by the hand o' luve.

"It will maybe help ye gin a' tell ye anither tale, an' though it be o' humble life, yet oor hearts are the same

in the castle and the cottar's hoose, wi' the same cup o'
sorrow tae drink an' the same croon o' joy tae wear, an'
the same dividin' o' roads for oor trial.

"There wes a man showed a wumman muckle kindness, and to her fouk also, an' he wes simple an' honest,
an' for what he hed done an' because there wes nae evil
in him she married him."

"And what has happened?" Kate, being half Highland, had less patience than Marget.

"He hes been a gude man tae her through the dark
an' through the licht, an' she hes tried tae repay him as
a puir imperfect wumman can, an' her hert is warm to
him, but there hes aye been ae thing wantin' — an' it
hes been that wife's cross a' her life — there wes nae
'ther man, but her husband wesna, isna, canna be her
ain a' thegither an' for ever — for the want o' luve —
that luve o' luve that maks marriage."

Her voice was laden with feeling, and it was plain
that she had given of her own and deepest for the guid-
ing of another.

"Marget, I can never be grateful enough to you for
what you have shown me this day." As she passed
Whinny with his bag of seed, he apologised for his wife.

"A 'm dootin', Miss Carnegie, the gude-wife hes
keepit ye ower lang in the gairden haiverin' awa' aboot
the flooers an' her ither trokes. But she 's michty prood
for a' that aboot yir comin' up tae veesit us."

Such was the second conference on Kate's affairs on
that day.

No place could be more thoroughly cleansed from
vulgar curiosity than our Glen, or have a finer contempt for "clatters," but the atmosphere was electrical
in the diffusion of information. What happened at Burn-

brae was known at the foot of Glen Urtach by evening, and the visit of spiritual consolation which Milton, in the days of his Pharisaism, paid to Jamie Soutar on his death-bed was the joy of every fireside in Drumtochty within twenty-four hours.   Perhaps it was not, therefore, re-markable that the arrival of Lord Kilspindie's groom at Tochty Lodge post haste with two letters on Saturday morning—one for the General from his Lordship, and one from his son for Miss Kate — should have been rightly interpreted, and the news spread with such rapidity that Hillocks — a man not distinguished above his fellows for tact — was able to inform Carmichael in the early afternoon that the marriage between the young lord and the " Miss " at Tochty was now practically arranged.

" It 's been aff and on a' winter, an' the second veesit tae the Castle settled it, but a 'm hearin' it wes the loss o' the Lodge brocht the fast offer this mornin'.   She 's an able wumman, an' cairried her gear tae the best mar-ket.   Ma certes," and Hillocks contemplated Kate's achievement with sympathetic admiration, " but she 'll set her place weel, an' haud her ain wi' the Duchess o' Athole."

Carmichael ought perhaps to have taken his beating like a man, and said nothing to any one, but instead thereof he betook himself for consolation to Marget, a better counsellor in a crisis than Janet, with all her Celtic wiles, and Marget set him in the very seat where Kate had put her case.

" It has, I suppose, been all a dream, and now I have awaked, but it was . . . a pleasant dream, and one finds the morning light a little chill.   One must just learn to forget, and be as if one had never . . . dreamed," but Carmichael looked at Marget wistfully.

"Ye canna be the same again, for a' coont, gin ony man loves a wumman wi' a leal hert, whether she answer or no, or whether she even kens, he 's been the gainer, an' the harvest will be his for ever.

"It hes seemed to me that nae luve is proved an' crooned for eternity onless the man hes forgotten himsel' an' is willin' tae live alane gin the wumman he luves sees prosperity. He only is the perfect lover, and for him God hes the best gifts.

"Yes, a 've seen it wi' ma ain eyes," — for indeed this seemed to Carmichael an impossible height of self-abnegation, — "a man who loved an' served a wumman wi' his best an' at a great cost, an' yet for whom there cud be no reward but his ain luve." Marget's face grew so beautiful as she told of the constancy of this unknown, unrewarded lover that Carmichael left without further speech, but with a purer vision of love than had ever before visited his soul. Marget watched him go down the same path by which Kate went, and she said to herself, "Whether or no he win is in the will of God, but already luve hes given his blessin' tae man and maid."

Kate did not go to kirk on Sunday, but lived all day in the woods, and in the evening she kissed her father and laid this answer in his hands : —

DEAR LORD HAY, — You have done me the greatest honour any woman can receive at your hands, and for two days I have thought of nothing else. If it were enough that your wife should like and respect you, then I would at once accept you as my betrothed, but as it is plain to me that no woman ought to marry any one unless she also loves him, I am obliged to refuse one of the truest men I have ever met, for whom I have a very kindly place in my heart, and whose happiness I shall always desire. — Believe me, yours sincerely,

KATE CARNEGIE.

"You could do nothing else, Kit, and you have done right to close the matter . . . but I 'm sorry for Hay."

CHAPTER XXIV.

LOVE IS LORD.

T could not be said with a steady face that the proceedings of the Free Kirk Presbytery of Muirtown increased the gaiety of nations, and there might be persons — far left to themselves, of course — who would describe its members as wearisome ecclesiastics. Carmichael himself, in a mood of gay irresponsibility, had once sketched a meeting of this reverend court, in which the names were skilfully adapted, after the ancient fashion, to represent character, and the incidents, if not *vero*, were certainly *ben trovato*, and had the article ready for transmission to *Ferrier's Journal*. 'A Sederunt' did not, however, add to the miseries of a most courteous editor, for Jenkins, having come up for an all-night conference, and having heard the article with unfeigned delight, pointed out that, if it were accepted, which Carmichael's experience did not certify, the writer would be run down within fourteen days, and that, so unreasonable a thing is human nature, some of the Presbytery might be less than pleased with their own likenesses. "It's in the waste-paper basket," Carmichael said next morning, which, as the author was twenty-five years of age, and not conspicuously modest, is a conclusive testimonial to the goodness of one Presbytery, and its hold on the affection of its members.

Scots take their pleasures sadly, and no one can imagine from what arid soil they may not draw their nutriment, but it was not for motions of ponderous ambiguity and pragmatical points of order, that the minister of Kincairney rose before daybreak on a winter's morning, and worked his way to the nearest station, with the stars still overhead, and the snow below his feet, so that when the clerk made a sign to the Moderator punctually at one minute past eleven to " constitute the Presbytery," he might not be missing from his place. It was the longing of a lonely man, across whose front door no visitor had come for weeks, for friendly company ; of a weary minister, discouraged by narrow circumstances, monotonous routine, unexpected disappointments among his people, for a word of good cheer. A cynical stranger might discover various stupidities, peculiarities, provincialisms in the Presbytery — he knew himself who had a temper, and who was a trifle sensitive about his rights — but this middle-aged, hard-working, simple-living man saw twenty faithful brethren — the elders did not count in this connection, for they did not understand — who stood beside him on occasion at the Holy Table, and gave him advice in his perplexities, and would bury him with honest regret when he died, and fight like wild cats that his widow and children should have their due. His toilsome journey was forgotten when Doctor Dowbiggin, in an interstice of motions, came across the floor and sat down beside him, and whispered confidentially, " Well, how are things going on at Kincairney?" — Dowbiggin really deserved his leadership — or when the clerk, suddenly wheeling round in his seat, would pass his snuff-box across to him without a word, for the clerk had a way of handing his box, which, being interpreted, ran as follows : — " You suppose that I am lifted above all ordinary affairs in my clerkly isolation, and that I do not know what a solid work you are doing for God and man in the obscure parish of Kincairney, but you are wrong. You have a very warm corner in my memory, and in sign thereof accept my box." And the said minister, trudging home that evening, and being met at a certain turn of the road by his wife — sentimental at fifty, you see, after a quarter of a century's toiling and preaching — would enlarge on Doctor Dowbiggin's cordiality, and the marked courtesy of the clerk, and when they were alone in the manse, his wife would kiss him — incredible to our cynic — and say, " You see, Tom, more people than I know what a good work you are doing," and Tom would start his twenty-first lecture on the Ephesians next morning with new spirit. Such is the power of comradeship, such is the thirst for sympathy ; and indeed there is no dog either so big or so little that it does not appreciate a pat, and go down the street afterwards with better heart.

The Presbytery had always a tender regard for the Free Kirk of Drumtochty, and happened to treat Carmichael with much favour. When the " call " to him was signed at once by every member of the congregation, the clerk — who had been obliged to summon Donald Menzies from Gaelic by the intimation that Drumtochty was by the law of the Church " uni-lingual, and that all proceedings must be conducted in the English language " — arose and declared that " such unanimous attention to their ecclesiastical duties was unexampled in his experience ; " and when at Carmichael's ordination a certain certificate was wanting, the clerk, whose intervention was regarded with awe, proposed that the court should anticipate its arrival, dealing with the matter "proleptically," and the court saw in the very word another proof of the clerk's masterly official genius. It was he also — expressing the mind of the Presbytery — who proposed that the Court should send Carmichael as a commissioner to the General Assembly in the first year of his ministry, and took occasion to remark that Mr. Carmichael, according to " reliable information at his disposal," was rendering important service to the Free Church in his sphere at Drumtochty. Carmichael was very happy in those days, and was so petted by his ecclesiastical superiors that he never missed a meeting of court, where he either sat in a demure silence, which commended him greatly to the old men, or conversed with his friends on a back bench about general affairs.

It gave him, therefore, a shock to sit with his brethren in the month of June — when the walk through the woods had been a joy, and Muirtown lay at her fairest, and the sunshine filled the court-room, and every man had a summer air, and Doctor Dowbiggin actually wore a rose in his coat — and to discover that he himself was sick of his old friends, of his work, of his people, of himself. The reasons were obvious. Was it not a sin that thirty Christian men should be cooped up in a room passing schedules when the summer was young and fresh upon the land? Could any one of the Rabbi's boys sit in that room and see his accustomed place — a corner next the wall on a back seat — empty, and not be cast down? Besides, does not a minister's year begin in September and end in July, and before it closes is not the minister at his lowest, having given away himself for eleven months? "One begins to weary for a rest," he whispered to Kincairney, and that worthy man explained that he and his wife had been planning their triennial holiday, and hoped to have a fortnight in Carnoustie. Carmichael realised his hypocrisy in that instant, for he knew perfectly that he had lost touch with life because of a hopeless love, and a proud face he had not seen a year ago. He flung himself out of the court with such impatience that the clerk stayed his hand in the midst of the sacred words *pro re nata*, and Kincairney mentioned to his wife in the evening that Carmichael had never got over Doctor Saunderson's death.

Carmichael wandered up one of the meadows which are the glory of Muirtown, and sat down by the queen of Scottish rivers, which runs deep and swift, clean and bright, from Loch Tay to the sea, between wooded banks and overhanging trees, past cornfields and ancient castles ; a river for him who swims, or rows, or fishes, or dreams, in which, if such were to be his fate, a man might ask to be drowned. Opposite him began the woods of Muirtown Castle, and he tried to be glad that Kate . . . Miss Carnegie would one day be their mistress : the formal announcement of her engagement, he had heard, was to be made next week, on Lord Kilspindie's birthday. A distant whistle came on the clear air from Muirtown station, where . . . and all this turmoil of hope and fear, love and despair, had been packed into a few months. There is a bend in the river where he sits, and the salmon fishers have dropped their nets, and are now dragging them to the bank. With a thrill of sympathy Carmichael watched the fish struggling in the meshes, and his heart leapt when, through some mishandling, one escaped with a flash of silver and plunged into the river.   He had also been caught quite suddenly in the joyous current of his life and held in bonds.   Why should he not make a bold plunge for freedom, which he could never have with the Lodge at his doors, with the Castle only twelve miles away?   He had been asked in his student days to go to the north-west of Canada and take charge of a parish fifty miles square.   The idea had for a little fired his imagination, and then faded before other ambitions.   It revived with power on the banks of that joyful, forceful river, and he saw himself beginning life again on the open prairie lands — riding, camping, shooting, preach- ing — a free man and an apostle to the Scottish Dis- persion.

With this bracing resolution, that seemed a call of God to deliver him from bondage, came a longing to visit Kil- bogie Manse and the Rabbi's grave.   It was a journey of expiation, for Carmichael followed the road the Rabbi walked with the hand of death upon him after that lament- able Presbytery, and he marked the hills where the old man must have stood and fought for breath.   He could see Mains, where he had gone with Doctor Saunderson to the exposition, and he passed the spot where the Rabbi had taken farewell of George Pitillo in a figure.   What learning, and simplicity, and unselfishness, and honesty, and affec- tion were mingled in the character of the Rabbi !   What skill, and courage, and tenderness, and self-sacrifice, and humility there had been also in William MacLure, who had just died !   Carmichael dwelt on the likeness and unlikeness of the two men, who had each loved the highest he knew and served his generation according to the will of God, till he found himself again with the Drumtochty doctor on his heroic journeys, with the Rabbi in his long vigils. It was a singular means of grace to have known two such men in the flesh, when he was still young and impressionable. A spiritual emotion possessed Carmichael. He lifted his heart to the Eternal, and prayed that if on account of any hardship he shrank from duty he might remember MacLure, and if in any intellectual strait he was tempted to palter with truth he might see the Rabbi pursuing his solitary way. The district was full of the Rabbi, who could not have gone for ever, who might appear any moment — buried in a book and proceeding steadily in the wrong direction. The Rabbi surely was not dead, and Carmichael drifted into that dear world of romance where what we desire comes to pass, and facts count for nothing. This was how the Idyll went. From the moment of the reconciliation the Rabbi's disease began to abate in a quite unheard of fashion — love wrought a miracle — and with Kate's nursing and his he speedily recovered. Things came right between Kate and himself as they shared their task of love, and so . . . of course — it took place last month.— and now he was going to carry off the Rabbi, who somehow had not come to the Presbytery, to Drumtochty, where his bride would meet them both beneath the laburnum arch at the gate. He would be cunning as he approached the door of Kilbogie Manse, and walk on the grass border lest the Rabbi, poring over some Father, should hear the crunch of the gravel — he did know his footstep — and so he would take the old man by surprise. Alas! he need not take such care, for the walk was now as the border with grass, and the gate was lying open, and the dead house stared at him with open, unconscious eyes, and knew him not. The key was in the door, and he crossed the threshold once more — no need

to beware of parcels on the floor now — and turned
to the familiar room. The shelves had been taken down,
but he could trace their lines on the ancient discoloured
paper that was now revealed for the first time; there,
where a new shutter was resting against the wall, used to
stand the " seat of the fathers," and exactly in the midst
of that heap of straw the Rabbi had his chair. . . .

" Ye 've come tae see hoo we 're getting on wi' the
repairs " — it was the joiner of Kilbogie; " it 's no a
licht job, for there 's nae doot the hoose hes been awfu'
negleckit. The Doctor wes a terrible scholar, but he
wudna hae kent that the slates were aff the roof till the
drap cam intae his bed.

" Ou aye, the manse is tae be papered an' pented for
the new minister; a' cud show ye the papers; juist as
ye please; they 're verra tasty an' showy. He 's tae be
married at once, a 'm hearin', an' this is tae be the
drawin'-room ; he wes here ten days syne — the day after
he wes eleckit : they 're aye in a hurry when they 're engaged — an' seleckit a sma' room upstairs for his study;
he didna think he wud need as lairge a room for bukes,
an' he thocht the auld study wud dae fine for pairties.

" 'There 's juist ae room feenished, an' ye micht like
tae see the paper on 't; it 's a yellow rose on a licht
blue grund ; a 'm jidgin' it wes the Doctor's ain room.
Weel, it 's a gude lang wy tae Drumtochty, an' ye 'll no
be wantin' tae pit aff time, a' daresay."

It was a terrible douche of prose, and Carmichael was
still shivering when he reached the kindly shade of
Tochty woods. He had seen the successful candidate at
the Presbytery arranging about his " trial discourses "
with the clerk — who regarded him dubiously — and he
had heard some story about his being a " popular

hand," and bewitching the young people with a sermon on the " good fight," with four heads " the soldier," " the battle-field," " the battle," and " the crown " — each with an illustration, an anecdote, and a verse of poetry. Carmichael recognised the type, and already saw the new minister of Kilbogie, smug and self-satisfied, handing round cream and sugar in the Rabbi's old study, while his wife, a stout young woman in gay clothing, pours tea from a pot of florid design, and bearing a blazing marriage inscription. There would be a *soirée* in the kirk, where the Rabbi had opened the mysteries of God, and his successor would explain how unworthy he felt to follow Doctor Saunderson, and how he was going to reorganise the congregation, and there would be many jocose allusions to his coming marriage ; but Carmichael would by that time have left the district.

No one can walk a mile in Tochty woods, where there are little glades of mossy turf, and banks of violets and geraniums, and gentle creatures on ground and branch, and cool shade from the summer sun, and the sound of running water by your side, without being sweetened and comforted. Bitter thoughts and cynical criticisms, as well as vain regrets and peevish complaints, fell away from Carmichael's soul, and gave place to a gentle melancholy. He came to the heart of the wood, where was the lovers' grave, and the place seemed to invite his company. A sense of the tears of things came over him, and he sat down by the river-side to meditate. It was two hundred years and more since the lassies died, who were never wedded, and for him there was not even to be love. The ages were linked together by a long tragedy of disappointment and vanity, but the Tochty ran now as in the former days. What was any human life but a drop in

"HE SAT DOWN BY THE RIVER-SIDE TO MEDITATE."

23

the river that flowed without ceasing to the unknown sea? What could any one do but yield himself to necessity, and summon his courage to endure? Then at the singing of a bird his mood lightened and was changed, as if he had heard the Evangel. God was over all, and life was immortal, and he could not be wrong who did the will of God. After a day of conflict, peace came to his soul, and in the soft light of the setting sun he rose to go home.

"Miss Carnegie . . . I did not know you were here . . . I thought you were in London," and Carmichael stood before Kate in great confusion.

"Nor did I see you behind that tree " — Kate herself was startled. "Yes, the General and I have been visiting some old friends, and only came home an hour ago.

"Do you know " — Kate was herself again — "the first thing I do on arrival is to make a pilgrimage to this place. Half an hour here banishes the dust of a day's journey and of . . .

"Besides, I don't know whether you have heard" — Kate spoke hurriedly — "that it is now settled that I . . . we will be leaving the Lodge soon, and one wants to have as much as possible of the old place in the time remaining."

She gave him this opportunity in kindness, as it seemed, and he reproached himself because he did not offer his congratulations.

"You will, I . . . the people hope, come often here, Miss Carnegie, and not cast off Drumtochty, although the Lodge be not your home. You will always have a place in the hearts of the Glen. Marjorie will never be grateful enough for your readings," which was bravely said.

"Do you think that I can ever forget the Glen and my . . . friends here? Not while I live ; the Carne-- gies have their own faults, but ingratitude is not one. Nor the dear Rabbi's grave." Then there was silence, which Carmichael found very trying — they had been so near that day in Kilbogie Manse, with only the Rabbi, who loved them both, between ; but now, although they stood face to face, there was a gulf dividing them.

"It may not be easy for me to visit Drumtochty often, for you know there has been a change . . . in our circumstances, and one must suit oneself to it."

Carmichael flushed uneasily, and Kate supposed that he was sympathising with their losses.

"I hope to be a busy woman soon, with lots of work, and I shall use every one of my little scraps of knowl- edge. How do you think I shall acquit myself in my new rôle? "

It was a little hard on Carmichael, who was thinking of a countess, while Kate meant a governess.

"You need not ask me how I think you will do as . . . in any position, and I . . . wish you every success, and . . . (with a visible effort) happiness."

He spoke so stiffly that Kate sought about for reasons, and could only remember their quarrel and imagine he retained a grudge — which she thought was rather ungenerous.

"It occurs to me that one man ought to be thankful when we depart, for then he will be able to call Queen Mary names every Sunday without a misguided Jacobite girl dropping in to create a disturbance."

"Drumtochty will have to form its own opinion of poor Mary without my aid," and Carmichael smiled sadly in pardon of the past, "for it is likely, although no one knows this in the Glen, that I shall soon be far away."

"Leaving Drumtochty? What will Marjorie do without you, and Dr. Davidson, and . . . all the people?" Then, remembering Janet's gossip, and her voice freezing, "I suppose you have got a better or more convenient living. The Glen is certainly rather inaccessible."

"Have I done anything, Miss Carnegie, to justify you in thinking that I would leave the Glen, which has been so good to me, for . . . worldly reasons? There is enough to support an unmarried man, and I am not likely to . . . to marry," said Carmichael, bitterly; "but there are times when it is better for a man to change his whole surroundings and make a new life."

It was clear that the Bailie's daughter was a romance of Janet's Celtic imagination, and Kate's manner softened.

"The Rabbi's death and . . . your difference of opinion — something about doctrine, was n't it? we were from home — must have been a great trial, and, as there was no opportunity before, let me say how much we sympathised with you and . . . thought of you.

"Do you think, however, Mr. Carmichael " — she spoke with hesitation, but much kindness — " that you ought to fling up your work here on that account? Would not the Rabbi himself have wished you to stick to your post? . . . and all your friends would like to think you had been . . . brave."

"You are cruel, Miss Carnegie; you try me beyond what I can endure, although I shall be ashamed to-night for what I am to say. Do you not know or guess that it is your . . . on account of you, I mean, that I must leave Drumtochty?"

"On account of me?" Kate looked at him in unaffected amazement.

"Are you blind, or is it that you could not suspect me of such presumption? Had you no idea that night in Dr. Davidson's drawing-room? Have you never seen that I . . . Kate—I will say it once to your face as I say it every hour to myself—you won my heart in an instant on Muirtown Station, and will hold it till I die.

"Do not speak till I be done, and then order me from your presence as I deserve. I know that it is unworthy of a gentleman, and . . . a minister of Christ to say such things to the betrothed of another man ; only one minute more"—for Kate had started as if in anger—"I know also that if I were stronger I could go on living as before, and meet you from time to time when you came from the Castle with your husband, and never allow myself to think of Lady Hay as I felt to Miss Carnegie. But I am afraid of myself, and . . . this is the last time we shall meet, Miss Carnegie. Forgive me for my love, and believe that one man will ever remember and . . . pray for you."

Carmichael bowed low, the last sunshine of the evening playing on his fair hair, and turned to go.

"One word, if you please," said Kate, and they looked into one another's eyes, the blue and brown, seeing many things that cannot be written. "You may be forgiven for . . . loving me, because you could not help that "—this with a very roguish look, our Kate all over—"and I suppose you must be forgiven for listening to foolish gossip, since people will tell lies "—this with a stamp of the foot, our Kate again—"but I shall never forgive you if you leave me, never "—this was a new Kate, like to the opening of a flower.

"Why? Tell me plainly," and in the silence Carmichael heard a trout leap in the river.

"Because I love you."

The Tochty water sang a pleasant song, and the sun set gloriously behind Ben Urtach.

THE END.